THE TWISTED TRAIL

A NOVEL

LEGACY ROAD
BOOK THREE

M. DANIEL SMITH

BAY LEDGES PRESS

Copyright © 2022 M. Daniel Smith

ISBN: 978-1-7377843-6-4 (paperback)
ISBN: 978-1-7377843-7-1 (ebook)

All rights reserved. No part of this publication may be reproduced, stored in a retrieval system, or transmitted in any form or by any means, electronic, mechanical, recording or otherwise, without the prior written permission of the author.

Published by: Bay Ledges Press (bayledgespress.com), Inc., Phippsburg, Maine.

The characters and events in this book are fictitious. Any similarity to real persons, living or dead, is coincidental and not intended by the author.

I would like to dedicate this novel to all the people who participated in providing 'grist to my mill', helping to enrich my life experience by providing valuable lessons I needed to learn. I would especially like to thank my favorite editor, my mother, Melva Smith, who's been an inspiration to me throughout my life. I've been fortunate to be able to spend time with her these past few years, sharing my writing while listening to her thoughts, insights, and emotional reactions, echoing throughout every story I've ever written — and all those still to come.

CHAPTER ONE
SCOTTISH LOWLANDS
SCOTTISH LOWLANDS

Bargrennan, a village located in the southwest corner of Scotland, huddled at rest beneath a full moon. The sky was clear, the hour early, stretched halfway between midnight and dawn. A handful of stray dogs with heads lowered and tails tucked, skulked away as a group of men on horseback rode by, their faces shadowed by hooded cloaks. A tall, broad-chested man on an immense stallion led the way, with two men in trail aboard stocky highland horses, each with a hand near the butt of loaded and half-cocked pistols secured in their belts. They'd made their furtive approach throughout the night, moving along secret clan paths, avoiding dozens of small crofts. The first leg of their journey was behind them, the second one about to begin.

Shaun, laird of clan Scott, rode second in line, his lean, weathered face locked in a dark scowl. He was looking forward to making the acquaintance of an unknown man, said to be in residence at a large inn just ahead, described by a dying man as a *'fookin sodding fop'* with a preference for white attire. The other men were in as sullen a mood as their leader, having noted his brooding demeanor during the long ride down from the highland reaches.

Duncan, riding in front, frowned as he tried to work out his laird's intentions, the jovial natured man silent throughout the night, without offering his usual jests and jibes. The large man knew it to be a deadly combination, having stood by his kinsman's side throughout the years, helping him do the devil's own work. He shrugged, ready for whatever his laird required of him, swinging his head from side to side, searching every shadow, aware a storm of violence was about to break over the town.

The three riders came to a stop alongside a stable tucked in behind a large inn. The men slid from their saddles without a word, leading their horses into a paddock before moving inside, rousing a stable boy wrapped in a thin cloak, found sleeping on a pile of sweet hay.

Shaun tossed the sleepy-eyed youngster a silver coin, the lad trapping in on his chest, his eyes widening in shock when he noted its value. He leapt to his feet, opening his mouth to respond, stopped by Duncan who leaned down, pressing a finger against the boy's trembling lips. With no words exchanged, the three men dissolved into the shadows of the barn, moving toward the back door of the inn.

⚘⚘⚘

Lord Sandersen was in a deep sleep, dreaming of himself in a heroic pose on a white stallion, displaying courage while under fire. The thump of cannons, felt as much as heard, preceded the whimpering of shells in arcing fall, exploding in the air and on the ground around him. He held a sword his hand, sitting tall in the saddle as he urged his men onward. One of them reached up and grabbed his arm, whispering something to him, bringing him fully awake.

"Hate to disturb a man at his slumber, especially one enjoying what looks to be a —*pleasurable* dream."

Sandersen tried to swallow the bubble of fear rising from his chest as a wave of nausea touched the back of his throat. He closed then opened his eyes, hoping the image of a gray-haired man staring down at him would have faded away. It was still there, his face wearing a gentle expression beneath eyes reflecting a glow of candlelight. A pair of weather-beaten hands reached out, holding his clothes, white, made of the finest fabrics.

"You will need to dress, then come with us. There has been a change in plans."

Sandersen sat up, voice quivering, his small hands pressed against the mattress. "*What* change?"

"We've *done* the deed, ordered. So final payment is due, our hands bloodied by the task assigned. All of them, including women and children, slain."

"All?" Sandersen's close set eyes widened as far as possible. "It was *never* the plan. Only *him*. The others—of *no* consequence."

"Musket balls fired from the manor—shattering my comrades' bodies, leaving us little choice. Your named man is *dead*. The deed *done*." Shaun tossed the fancy clothes on top of the sheets. "Dress. Now."

The pasty-faced nobleman slowly complied. Once fully adorned, he faced the leader of the small group. "The monies are stored in a safe place." Sandersen sniffed. "I will, of course, require *proof* of his death. Along with the papers you recovered."

Shaun leaned in, smiling as he saw fear blossom in the man's eyes. "A payment of what's *owed* is to be first on the agenda. Then we will adjourn to a more secluded location, providing what you've earned—and come so far to receive."

"Of course." Sandersen stepped aside, going to stand in front of a mirror, placing a wig on his narrow head. "The funds distributed. Then a detailed accounting made of the results, so I may inform those-"

"Not *now*. And not *here*. I prefer holding my cards tight to my chest, for the time being." Shaun held out his hand, palm up.

"Your final payment. Of course. It is *here*, secreted beneath the mattress in *full*. Every coin owed you, upon my *satisfaction* of the assigned task's completion." Sandersen held out his hand. "I presume you've evidence *of* it?"

"I do. Outside with our horses. His scalp, as well as the others. Proof in hand, same as in the colonies where you once trod the soil—though not clad in such as those." Shaun looked down at the pair of white leather boots, then gave a nod to Duncan, who lifted the mattress with a meaty hand, exposing a brace of pistols, and four leather bags.

Shaun leaned over, handing the two pistols to Sandersen, who tucked one in his belt, holding the other in his hand while Duncan gathered the bags. "We shall be off as soon as you dress your feet."

Sandersen bent to the task, handing his pistol to the larger man, wincing, removing the second pistol from his belt and placing it on the bed. He slipped into the pair of tall riding boots, polished to a reflective sheen, then stood up, "I will need a drink of warm tea—" He saw a frown form on the leader's face. "Cold, if warm is not available. The night was—*vigorous*, with a young maid delivered to my room. Fresh— or she *was* before I—well, *you* know." The three men gave Sandersen hard stares in return, with Duncan going to over to the bed and pulling back the top sheets, revealing a bloodstain. Sandersen grinned. "*Prima Noche*, as it were. A tip of my hat to—*old* traditions."

Shaun shook his head, recalling the words of the dying man in the Pinch, realizing the other had been much too kind in express of a final opinion, chosen over a prayer to whatever god had been lying in wait to claim his damned soul.

"We *too* have our traditions." Duncan's voice was a deep rumble of thunder, his eyes blazing with anger, eager for its release. "A bit more ancient—though *equally* revered." He smiled, his finger on the hilt of a large knife. "Our time is wasting, and we've work to attend to."

Sandersen got to his feet, taking a moment to adjust his white shirt and pants, using the mirror to check their lines. Then he reached back with his arms, waiting as the gray-haired man helped him into his jacket, before handing him a white hat and small sword, encased in a white sheath. He smiled in satisfaction, admiring his image in the large mirror, then made his way through the door with a jaunty gait, forgetting the two pistols, collected by Duncan, a frown locked in place on the tall man's swarthy face.

⁂

The stable boy looked up; the three men returning with a man dressed all in white. The boy flinched, knowing it was the one who'd been demanding special services while staying at the inn, with little coin offered in return by someone of such self-proclaimed high status.

Services that had included the use of his younger sister during the previous night, just turned ten years of age. When he'd tried to stop them, the owner of the inn had threatened to feed him to the pigs if he dared interfere. His younger sister stepped forward, bowing her head to their demand, a small purse of coins tossed at her brother's feet.

"Watered your horses, sirs. All *three*. Fed *and* wiped down. Left them with their saddles on, not knowing of your plans." The boy pointed, then stepped back, staying clear of the man in white, his eyes aimed down at the floor of the stable.

Shaun reached into his pocket and pulled out a small bag of silver coins, one of many plucked from the muck and mire of the men's crushed remains back in the Pinch. Enough between them all to fund food and education for a score of deserving young men and women of the clan. He whistled, then tossed it to the youth, who caught it with dirt-stained hands, looking back at Shaun, tears in his eyes.

"My sister, sir. She was with him." He nodded at the man in white, Sandersen's head turned away, gazing through the open door, one hand on his hip. "In *his* room, sir—this past night. Have not seen her since."

Sandersen missed the exchange, working the tip of a finger in one corner of his thin-lipped mouth, a well-buffed fingernail used to remove a sliver of meat from between his teeth as he waited for the men to saddle his mount. Shaun considered for a moment, then nodded at Duncan. "She must still be inside." He went over and clasped the young boy on his thin shoulder. "I'll have my two friends go and rouse the inn keep." Shaun handed him a second pouch of coins, the boy's eyes widening as he felt the weight. "You keep these for your *good* service this night—and *silence* on what you've seen."

The boy nodded, swallowing his fear, realizing who it was standing before him. Stories told up and down the valleys and glens about the highland laird in constant watch over all members of clan Scott. Great or small. Young or old.

Shaun sighed. "Take your pick of one of the other horses, then you and your sister hie to the third croft farm in the *second* valley along the way we came in." Shaun pointed to the narrow track leading into the hills. "Let the old man and his wife living there know to take you in as if their own, with *five* of the coins given them. The rest buried where no one else but you or your sister will ever find them. Tell 'em who it was that sent you there, then forget you were ever *here*. Forget you ever saw this place." He turned his head. "Which has now been set afire."

They watched as the two men returned with a young girl curled up in one of Duncan's thick arms. He gave Shaun a quick nod as he sat her down beside her brother. The boy gave her a hug, then opened one of the stalls, releasing a sturdy mare. He tossed a blanket and saddle across its back, grabbed a small gunny sack holding their meager possessions, adding the two bags of coins to it.

Shaun lifted the small girl onto the mare, then stood back as the boy led it outside, careful to avoid the man in white. Once clear of the stables, he climbed into the saddle behind his sister, riding away without looking back.

The odor of smoke began to fill the air, flames starting to billow from the upper windows of the inn, opened to help the fire spread. The owner stood outside, his wife beside him, their eyes lowered, careful to avoid looking at the men standing in the door of the stable.

Duncan and the other man led their three horses into the yard, along with a large stallion, having released the other animals from their stalls into the paddock, with Shaun opening the gate to let them out in case the flames spread to the barn.

Stevensen, having finished with his oral hygiene, finally took notice of the goings on, his jaw dropping as he saw the leader of the men pass by on the back of his own mount, a beautiful Arabian with white coat, matching his clothes.

"My *steed!*" He swung his head, eyes glaring in anger at Shaun. "Climb *down!* This *instant!*"

Shaun shook his head, amazed at the man's lack of awareness, watching as Duncan went over to him.

"Hands."

"*Excuse* me? What is the *meaning* of—"

The slap to Sandersen's face was lightning quick, rocking him back, causing him to lose his balance. He stumbled to one side, hand raised to his cheek, tears in his eyes, gleaming from the light of the flames as they began to build in intensity, consuming the inn.

Sandersen opened his mouth to protest, the large man stepping forward, another slap following the first.

Duncan stared at him. "We can do this *all* day." He held up a thin piece of braided rope. "Hands."

Sandersen held them out, uncertain as to the sudden change in the other men's demeanor. His fear began to build, hands trembling as the large man bound them together, leaving a length of rope he tied to the saddle ring of an imposing black steed.

Shaun nudged his mount over to where the white-clad man was standing with a shocked expression on his pale face. "We are to ride in visit to a friend of mine. One with a large croft. A long walk for *you*. Or drag. Your call of which it is to be. Once there, I will require your story, told true. *All* you know of the plans of your group, shared with me." He watched as the doomed man's eyes widened in fear. "I will have the names, codes, means of communication, and *descriptions* of the men you've associated with. Along with all those you've employed, including detailed descriptions of deadly men—without names. *All* of it, no matter how long it takes. Or how *messy* it becomes. I have this day through into the next, if needed. While you have but a few hours to decide the length of time my large friend with a honed blade will spend—whittling the truth from you."

🌱🌱🌱

The sun was just past the top of its arc, falling off toward afternoon. Shaun watched as Duncan finished washing a layer of congealed blood from his wrists and hands, using a thin sliver of wood to clean beneath his fingernails. The huge man turned, looking up, a smile splitting his wide face, his thick beard framing a decent set of teeth.

"Poor Johnny. Hands cramping from all the writing he done. Glad *I* was on the *pointed* side of the exchange. Easier by far." Duncan held up his hands, opening and closing them several times. "There. Good as ever." He worked his head in a slow circle, loosening his neck. "What are we to do with the body? Should I dig a hole?"

Shaun drew in a deep breath, glad to be outside in clear air. Unlike the small barn where the interrogation had taken place. Urine, shit, and copious amounts of tears and snot made to flow. And blood. Enough to help lubricate the tortured man's flow of words, the information gathered as true as the priggish man had knowledge of. Valuable, Shaun knew, when added to what Harold's uncle had been able to gather, to hold in trust until he could reason out what to do with it. He gave Duncan a measured look. "The owner of this croft—has a *sizable* number of swine on hand."

Duncan lowered his eyes, staring at the ground and sighing; the only outward sign of any emotion shown since they'd arrived at the croft, earlier in the day. When he looked up, he gave Shaun a long stare, slowly shaking his head.

Shaun turned and spat on the ground, then wiped his lips, giving Duncan a sharp glare. "The *bastard's* dead. Not like I'm asking ya to toss him in *alive*."

Duncan shrugged, staring at the pigs moving about in their enclosure. "It's not that."

"Then *what* is your issue?" Shaun angled his head, confused by the other man's reluctance to feed the tortured body to the animals, removing all traces of the man who'd sent others in his place to kill members of the clan. Members of his own kin.

Duncan looked over, a sorrowful tone in his deep voice. "Just thinking, is all. I mean, is it fair to the *piggies*—feeding the likes of *him* to *them?*"

CHAPTER TWO

SCOTTISH HIGHLANDS

SPRING, 1775

Charles set three legs of an easel in place, spreading them apart on the coarse grass of a highland field, two days ride by horse from Bargrennan. He placed a small, wood framed canvas on the cross-piece, making a slight adjustment, angling the wash of light across its smooth surface.

"What are ya on aboot?" A youthful voice from behind pulled Charle's head around, a small brush in his hand, a warm smile on his lips.

"Painting. A landscape."

A boy on the cusp of adulthood stood several paces away in the middle of a narrow path, with a large sage hen cradled in one arm. "A *what?*"

"It's a type of painting." Charles angled his head, eyeing the boy. "A painting of the land, as opposed to a portrait. I could make it a portrayal of some *other* item of interest if you want."

The boy and bird came closer, the two of them eyeing the canvas with outstretched necks. "Why?"

Charles nodded. "Good question." He gave the hen a considered look. "Would you prefer I paint the chicken?"

The boy ignored the offer as he leaned in, watching as the man prepared his pigments. Watercolors, in a mix of green and blue."

"Ya come all the way up here—just ta paint a picture?"

Charles dipped the end of a fan brush into the combined hues, using it to create a base color on the primed expanse of white textured cloth. "As a matter of fact—I have."

The boy tossed the wild sage hen into the air, watching as it flew in a tight circle, coming to a stop a short distance away, lowering its head, probing the grass for insects or seeds. "Are ya heading up—or down?"

"Depends." Charles placed the brush to the canvas and spun it in a circle with his fingers, creating a swirl of color, matching that of the rippling blue-green hues of grass in the distance.

"On what?" The lad stepped back slightly, one hand in his pocket, the tone of his voice tightening.

Charles turned his head. "On how long you're to stand here, a knife in your fingers, trying to decide whether to go and bring back the others—or do for me yourself, here and now."

"There *are* no others."

"Then I'll be heading up, once I've finished capturing *this* fair view."

The boy frowned, hand still in his pocket, the hen feeding her way back to him. "Better for your health—if heading *down*."

"Definitely." Charles nodded, adding a few more strokes to the canvas, noting the boy had moved close to his side, wondering if his kidney would meet the working end of the knife, secreted in the small lad's hand. He used a small-tipped brush to describe a series of curved lines in dark blue, forming the outlines of the body of the sage grouse.

"Too large. The bird." The boy pointed with a narrow chin.

"It depends on the *viewpoint* of the observer."

The hen fluttered into the air, landing at the boy's feet. He reached down and picked it up, then stared at the painting. "You should make whoever is do 'in the looking to see it from further away. If they stand too close, they're liable to get a *serious* scratch."

Charles knew he was under observation, the lad sent down on a scout. The clan leader would be waiting above, deciding whether to see his throat slit now, or if a meeting of minds might be the wiser choice.

The amateur artist aware of who it would be, questioning the reason for his intrusion onto clan lands. The journey from England to the highland pass, though cautiously done, had exposed him to the watchful eyes of dangerous men, lurking everywhere. Nameless men, carefully avoided at every turn while moving from one out of the way spot to the next, despite unequivocal proof of his untimely death, one he'd arranged in advance, using a purchased cadaver to assist him in his fatal disappearance, making it appear that he'd drowned at sea.

Charles used a container of water to rinse his brushes clean, then began putting away his canvas and easel, hearing horses in the distance, coming down from on high.

※※※

A soft breeze wicked through the interior of the wee croft house, a small window left open, letting in a wide shaft of light. Harold sat at a table, across from Charles, giving him a quizzical look. "You're supposed to be dead—and long buried." He leaned back in one of the sturdy chairs. "A drowning, from what I was able to find out. Or rather, what my Uncle Shaun was able to find out, through the ears and eyes of men in every port of Scotland, and beyond."

Charles raised a glass of whiskey, one eye closed, gazing at Harold through the amber liquid. "As too are *you*. From a mix of brimstone and fire. Rumors in circulation having to do with your efforts overseas. The shattered remains of your body found alongside a well, badly mangled. Your face blown half-away, with left shoulder and arm torn off."

"A *risk* to my family—if a *new* rumor were to get out. Why I abide in *this* abode." Harold waved a hand, taking in the house. "With eyes and ears aplenty in watch over every approach known to the clan."

Both men took a sip of their drinks, their thoughts weighted by the roles each had once played in the shadows of a manipulated world, trying their best to shine a light on those behind the darkest deeds done.

Harold sighed, aware his uncle had paid the highest price, murdered along with his wife for having uncovered information about the secretive group of men standing behind the throne, fomenting unrest on both sides of the Atlantic, now at a fever pitch in the northern colony of Massachusetts, centered in the city of Boston and dozens of outlying towns.

"We are left observers of a world we both helped to create." Harold sighed. "Myself, the means of the destruction of a small piece of it. All for naught, with the feeble gesture having a negligible effect, despite the loss of so many lives—by *my* hand."

Charles leaned forward. "You managed a great blow, my dour friend. *Literally.* One shaking the foundations beneath thrones in several countries. Timetables thrown off, allowing those of my acquaintance to insinuate themselves deeper into the kitchens, hallways, bedrooms, and offices of those wielding the power."

He took a sip of the smooth whiskey, holding it on his tongue for a moment before swallowing. "With myself playing the *same* game. Our lowly group responsible for having placed spies in positions of servitude to those we are trying to forestall. Vainglorious men, their *egos* so large they cannot see the ground beneath their own feet."

Harold sighed. "There are none so blind as those who cannot —*fathom* that others might be as intelligent. And equally as *devious*."

Charles gave him a nod. "A twist in the saying, and true—myself having done the same to Nathan. And to *you*, working on both sides. Along with hundreds of other men like me, insinuating ourselves deep into the ranks of nobility, many of them men with *ignoble* souls. On every side of each ocean, and across every country's border. Our servile ranks widespread, seeking to maintain a measure of balance in the world's affairs. Failing, at times, though able to minimize the worst of damage done to the common man, who ends up suffering the most." He paused, looking down at the glass held in his hand, his voice soft. "When and *where* we can."

Harold sighed. "I was a *fool*, thinking I had a chance to change —*anything*. Willing to throw away my life, endanger my family—for what? To try and stop the world from slowly turning about its axis?"

Charles looked up, hooves in a slow approach, a weary voice calling out. The two of them went outside, the valley floor lined in shadows now the sun had fallen over the western side of the ridgeline.

Shaun slipped from his mount, a short-legged, sturdy mare. He held onto the saddle until his hip could bear the strain of walking, then handed the reins to Harold, who came over and gathered the animal in, leading it toward the stable, knowing his uncle would be staying the night.

※※※

"There was *no* one down below showing any interest in you *or* your horse. I had the lad you met ride down to Bargrennan and back. A two-day ride, made in one, using paths goats would turn away from in fear." Shaun smiled. "He was *not* much impressed with your attempt at —artistry."

Charles shrugged. "To each their own interpretation of the word." He paused, eyeing the clan leader closely. "The hen he carries about with him—your idea, or his?"

Shaun sighed, then scratched his head, the hair on his broad forehead receding, going over to a dark, thickly salted gray. "*His*. Helps put people off guard, in thinking him a bit *thick* in the head."

"I imagine he's good with a knife."

"Knife. Musket. Fists, and *bow*, having learned that skill from Harold's son. With myself teaching him the others, as taught me by my Da, with near a hundred kills to his name." Shaun paused. "Of men wearing red coats, or those posing a threat to the clan."

Charles ignored the other man's hard stare, glancing at a longbow, shorter than most found in the corners of farmhouses and hovels scattered throughout the English countryside. Used by people to defend their property from raids by wild animals, or thieves. Those without coin enough to buy pistols, powder, and lead.

Shaun noted his interest. "It belongs to my gran niece, Meghan. Given by me to her brother Aaron, who outgrew it."

The door to the wee croft house swung open, Harold back from tending to his uncle's mount. He came inside and pulled another glass from a small cupboard, setting it down in front of Shaun on the solid, rough-hewn table, pouring him a drink, then topping off the other two.

Charles watched as the amber colored liquor flowed, the scent of it hanging in the air, along with a host of impending questions from the two men sitting at the able, seeking answers. He looked at Harold. "Your son, Aaron. He is well?"

A smile blossomed on the other man's lined face. "Away at school. At Marischal—down in Aberdeen."

"Where *you* matriculated, if memory serves."

Harold nodded, sitting across from Charles, noting Shaun's frown at his having shared his son's whereabouts. "The *same*. Earning part of his keep by working in the stables, same as I did. A *fine* rider, as skilled as his great uncle Thomas ever was."

Charles lifted his glass, holding it up, waiting for the other two to join him. "To both your uncle *and* father. Two of the finest men I ever had the pleasure of knowing. As if members of my own family." He looked at Harold. "I understand your *son*—" He nodded at Shaun over the rim of his glass as he took a sip. "And *your* great nephew—has become close friends with two other students. One a Brit. The other a Scot, whose family is known to have one foot on each side of the Atlantic, between the port cities of Glasgow and Philadelphia."

Harold raised an eyebrow, considering the news. "And how is it you know of my son's situation?"

Charles smiled. "I received a report from one of the staff who works there. One of several placed within its walls, keeping an eye on any students deemed capable of securing positions in government. Or commerce."

"My son, as far as *I've* been given to understand, has little interest in *either* of those vocations."

"The group I belong to has eyes in every university, identifying the strengths and weaknesses of each student who might one day lead us into the future. To the good or detriment *of* it." Charles fixed Shaun with a firm gaze. "*All* those with the promise of being able to influence the direction of other men's lives, no matter the color of their skin, clothing, or choice of vocation. A man's decisions in life capable of leading him from hovel to manor. Some men, born to their lofty titles, ending up led by tethered hands, ending up at a croft—swelling the bellies of hungry swine."

Shaun smiled. "A man should *know* where he belongs. At *all* times."

He bottomed his glass, holding it out, waiting for his nephew to refill it. "And *my* place has and will always be *here*—in the highlands, doing what needs be done in order to protect the clan."

Harold tilted the bottle, aware something significant had just taken place, left standing in the shadows, watching as his uncle stretched out one leg, rubbing at his hip, a sour expression on his ruddy face. He gave Charles a searching look. "And where would *your* place be?"

Charles leaned back, the chair he was in squeaking, protesting the shift of balance. "A man *should* know the answer to that—along with his *limitations*." He took another sip of the smooth bodied liquor, then placed the half-empty glass on the table and stretched his arms above his head, eyes closed, allowing the tension carried in his thin neck and shoulders to slip away. When he opened them, both Shaun and Harold were staring at him. "*My* next destination lies over the sea, where I intend to apply leverage of right against wrong, using common sense to push back against the injustices of greedy men."

Harold shrugged, then crossed his arms on his chest, considering for a moment before speaking, his voice soft. "Where a man might lose himself in wilderness shadows."

Shaun chuckled, then slapped his hand on the table, drawing the other men's eyes. "You speak as if there might be an answer found capable of reversing the river of power that flows from the minds and hands of the few, as it *always* has, with little regard to small weirs put in place by common folk, trying to thwart its momentum." He hardened his tone. "Most men are just *that*. Common. Found everywhere you look, with a handful of men of destiny sprinkled in amongst them. Men not born into wealth and position, having to claw their way up, seeking a place of prominence. Be it within the church, commerce—or politics. Men demanding fair and equal representation for all."

Harold gawked, never once having heard his uncle speak so openly, and eloquently. Charles nodded, slapping his palm on the table alongside Shaun's.

"*Well* said, my friend. And I propose to *support* such efforts, with a desire to see it made so *this* time. A unique opportunity awaits in the colonies, rife with the scent of potential failure, going up against incredible odds. But one that has a *glimmer* of promise, because of men such as your nephew—" Charles gave a nod to Harold. "With the experience and *courage* required to help wrest control of it away from the few, claiming it for the many, and not for themselves." He paused, taking a moment to collect his thoughts. "With help from those like me, *multiply* the effort by providing information to them of events to come, long before they take place."

"You mean to *spy* on behalf of the colonists." Harold leaned forward, his elbows resting on the table. "To set up a network, using people in positions within the houses of power brokers on *both* sides of the conflict, passing along information vital to support or to prevent revolution."

Shaun grunted, holding onto his thoughts as he stood up. He took a moment to steady himself while he looked down at the others. "And you will no doubt *succeed*, at first. Then fail in the end, just as we did at Culloden." He grabbed the bottle, taking a long pull, then wiping his lips, his eyes bright with memories of the ill-fated battle. "But oh, how *grand* was the making of that *glorious* charge—in typical Scot fashion. Doomed from the start. The do 'in of it, turned into a legend. One that will live on forever in the hearts and souls of every one of us. Retold by countless generations to follow."

Shaun kept the bottle in hand as he opened the door. He paused, looking back, giving each a short nod. "I'll leave you to it, taking my leave to the stable, bedding myself down with the horses this night." Then he was gone, the silence settling in around Harold and Charles, both left staring at the glasses in their hands.

"He's not wrong." Harold gave Charles a quiet look. "Is he?"

Charles shrugged. "Not to malign the effort your uncle and men like him made back then, but it was an army of stiff-necked, *prideful* men, unable to back away from a fight. Even one stacked against them, with *terrible* odds."

Harold angled his head. "And the men over there—those I fought with? Bled with?"

"In need of a gifted strategist to help level the playing field." Charles smiled. "But early days yet, my friend. Time enough and more to bide awhile *here*, while I go and prepare the ground *there*."

CHAPTER THREE

SCOTTISH LOWLANDS, FALL, 1776

Marischal University was a bedlam of activity, students moving at rapid pace between buildings, seeking friends from the previous term, or left to wander aimlessly. Lost souls, looking around at those doing the same. Friendships arranged by happenstance, to blossom or wither away, depending on variables of personalities, family ties, or destiny's capricious whim.

Aaron found his assigned room, the same size as one shared with two other students during his first term. There were only two beds, one of his former mates already there, with claim made to the one closest the window.

"*Rory!* You survived the summer, wedged in the hold of a ship."

A dark-haired boy, of similar height and frame to Aaron, returned a wide smile beneath broad cheeks with a lighter complexion. He stood up and came over, taking Aaron's hand, grasping it firmly, squeezing as hard as he could, grimacing as he tried to pull away from the vise like grip of his highland friend, his fingers left feeling crushed. "You've gotten *stronger!* And here I was ready to prove *I* was the better man, working on the hoisting of sails, loading in and out of goods, and scrubbing away at pots and pans for hours on end."

Aaron grinned. "Your father putting you to *honest* labor. With you hoping to man the helm, binnacle in hands, helping him navigate treacherous waters." Aaron reached out and tousled Rory's hair. "Have you seen Allen?"

Rory nodded. "Got in yesterday—one day early." He frowned. "Bit priggish, that."

"The privilege of being English, and not Scots—like *us*."

"Like *me*, with your family straddling the border. Your wonderful mother, English. And your heroic father, God rest his soul, a mix of bloodlines from *both* sides."

Aaron held his tongue, unwilling to share his mother's true lineage, even with someone as close to him as the Scottish boy, one full year older, from a family in maritime service between ports in the colonies and the new one in Glasgow, at the mouth of River Clyde.

"I consider myself a true *son* of Scotland, having spent most of my life in the highlands."

"*Worse*, by far!" Rory grinned. "With your head tucked in the clouds." He paused, then gave his friend a mischievous smile. "Wishing it were under the fair Skye's skirts, instead." He ducked Aaron's blow to his shoulder, grabbing his wrist, trying to pull him off balance, failing to do so due to the highlander's muscular lower body.

"Would have thought you'd left such actions behind, being second termers now." A thin boy stood in the doorway with crossed arms, his light blue eyes, wide set, above narrow cheeks, and a thin nose, staring at the two of them. Then he smiled, his teeth a mismatch of angles and lengths. "Good to see you, *hunter* of stags."

Aaron came over and grasped Allen by the shoulder, careful not to hurt him, his bones thin beneath the fine shirt and coat he had on. "*You're* one to talk, with a dozen demerits posted against your name. Surprised they allowed you through the gates."

"His father's doing, no doubt." Rory held up one hand, mimicking the rubbing of a coin between his fingers. He ducked away as Allen picked up a pillow from one of the beds and tossed it at his head.

A sober voice resonated from the hall, a tall man with a thick beard, broad chest, and dark eyes standing in the door, cane in hand, helping to support his overweight frame. "I assume you to be having a *physical* demonstration of the kinetic energy of an object in motion, coming up against an unmovable force. A calculation of same to be on my desk by the ringing of first bell."

Aaron straightened, joined by the other two, their hands at their sides as the pillow slowly fell from the far end of the bed, landing with a muffled thump. "Yes, sir." He answered for all of them, the others nodding their heads.

The man was rector of the university. Stanton Addison, a veteran of the war against the Spanish, victim of a lingering wound. He returned their nods with one of his own, then winced in pain as he turned about and walked away, the tip of his cane thudding against the wooden floor of the hallway.

Aaron closed the door, then shoved an open hand into Allen's chest, causing him to stumble backward, having to catch his balance. His friend smiled. "You'll do the math for us—won't you?"

Aaron nodded. "Of course. As usual. With *you* buying the first round, when we get an opportunity to make our way to the local pub."

The three of them began to regale each other with tales of the past few months spent away at their respective homes. No one bringing up young Skye Addison, the beautiful daughter of the rector, or her voluminous skirts.

※※※

"You're looking quite hale. With good color." Skye fanned herself, the weather warm, a southerly front passing through, teasing a balmy breeze, causing it to flow across the marshlands, stirring the ends of her long, auburn hair. She angled her hazel eyes, looking at Aaron's body, an inch taller since the last time she'd seen him at the end of his first year of studies. Her hand trembled slightly, aware of his scent, bare-chested, his shirt hanging from the side of a large wagon as he toiled in the fields outside the university grounds, gathering hay he'd scythed a few days ago, having left it to dry.

"Sun will do that to a person. Chores out of door a requirement if you own horses, or cows." Aaron thrust a pitchfork into the ground, then straightened up, wiping the sweat from his face with the back of one arm. "You look—*perfect*. As always."

Skye hid her smile behind the fan, knowing her blush would have darkened her fair skin. "Too kind, sir." She twisted in the seat of the wagon, gazing at a mound of cut grass piled in back, the smell of it filling her nose, considering how it would feel against her bare skin, with Aaron's strong hands on her body. Then she shook her head, driving the thought away, for now.

A rider on horseback came up the narrow road, Allen in the saddle, a large-brimmed hat pulled low on his head, shading his fair skin. He nodded at Aaron, then removed his hat and bowed to Skye. "The headmaster would know of your whereabouts, Mistress Addison. He is quite *wroth*—your absence noted, sending me to find, then escort you back."

Skye pouted, her full lips drawn up, fan lowered as she gave Aaron a searching look. "I'll ride back on the wagon with Aaron—if he can be convinced to leave off his tireless chores."

Aaron heaved another forkful of dry grass into the bed of the wagon. "You should go with Allen, his steed being the speedier choice. I'll be a while longer, needing to get this in before the rain arrives. Due to start during the night." He gave them both a short nod, then turned back to his work.

The chores he performed around the stable helped pay for his room and board, though money wasn't an issue, his mother having more than enough funds to cover his expenses. A codicil added to his contract for admission, intended to help keep him focused, as his 'deceased' father, living up at the croft house had told him with a grin, before sending him off. Aaron didn't mind the labor involved in working in the stables, caring for the stock, being a gifted horseman in his own right, unlike Allen who was sitting his mount as if afraid it might turn and bite him. Again.

Allen slid from his horse, then extended his hand, helping Skye step down from the seat of the wagon, assisting her to mount the animal, where she sat side saddle while he gathered the reins, ready to lead it back to the university buildings.

Skye called out. "I'll see you later, Aaron—at the third termer's banquet?"

"Of course. I'm looking forward to it." Aaron nodded again, then returned to his work. Skye narrowed her eyes, a small frown pulling down the corners of her lips as Allen called to the horse, leading them away.

※※※

Soft music wafted throughout a small hall, slipping between tables surrounded by circles of people, mingling with others, everyone's eyes scanning the room to see who might be speaking to whom. Alliances between undergraduates formed, seeking future employment opportunities. Balanced against the possibility of arranging furtive liaisons with female members of the service staff, busy delivering drinks and food to those in attendance. Most of the students kept one eye focused on the rector, hoping for the honor of first dance with his beautiful daughter, currently centered amidst a throng of older students vying for her attention, receiving thin smiles and non-committal nods of her head in return.

Aaron slipped into the hall, dressed in a suit his mother had insisted he bring with him, selected from a closet in the highland manor. There had been no need to alter its lines, his frame a match to that of his father, the clothing fitting as if tailored for him.

He smiled at one of the wait staff, a pleasant looking girl, several years older, who bypassed several boys with outstretched hands, coming over and offered him a glass of wine, along with a searching gaze, her bodice swelled by her ample breasts, eyes fastened on his. Leaving with his thanks, and nothing more.

Aaron searched the room, finding his two friends, going over, and joining them alongside a fireplace, listening as Allen pontificated on the latest political events occurring outside the hallowed halls of Marischal.

"The thought of it—*rebellion* against the King, a *ridiculous* proposition. The colonies, though prosperous in population due to their wanton ways, are *penny* poor in the wealth needed for any hope of success. Their efforts doomed to fail, in trying to shrug off the Empire's righteous claim to fair taxes *owed*."

Rory shook his head, a glass of port in his hand, a smile on his round face. "You are *enabled*, allowed by heritage to opine without experience in having the *yoke* placed about *your* thin neck, my English born and bred brother, in academic studies." He reached out, touching his glass to Aaron's, then to Allen's, removing any tinge of offense.

"He's *right*." Aaron gave Allen a gentle poke with his finger, feeling the bones in the older boy's thin arm. "With *you* raised with the inherent belief that it is an *English* world. All the rest of us allowed to lay claim to the *edges* of it. The center of the world located in London, from whence all knowledge and commerce flows."

Allen replied, a tight grin on his lips, his eyes in a solemn stare. "Sayeth the *highlander*, with his lips on the breast of English monies in abundance. Along with the political heritage of a man who, while proposing a—"

"Careful." Aaron squared up, his wide shoulders forming an imposing figure, giving Allen a moment of pause. Rory leaned in, taking his friends firm hand, gently easing him around.

"He's not *wrong*, Aaron. Ill mannered, for some reason—in how he put it. But you *are* a man with feet on both sides of the line dividing Scotland from England. With England divided from the *rest* of the world, *including* the colonies. Loyal citizens, not in opposition to a level of taxation deemed fair, *if* allowed an opportunity of *self-representation* in Parliament. No longer willing to bow their heads, accepting a heavy hand yanking at reins attached to the yoke placed around their prideful necks."

Aaron shrugged away from Rory's grasp, about to respond, when a gentle voice from behind caused him to look around.

"Is the discussion of draft animals in yon stables such an enticement to you three, that you have forgotten to greet my father, begging for the favor of first dance? With myself reduced to *seeking* you out, as if no more to you than a half-sister, or distant cousin."

Allen brushed the other two aside with a sweep of one arm, stepping forward and bowing his head. "My apologies, Miss Addison. It was I, who initiated an exchange of poorly chosen words, in churlish tone, distracting my good friends." He straightened up, giving Aaron a rueful look, then stepped aside, grabbing Rory by the arm, pulling him away. The other two, left to themselves, though surrounded by a crowd of faculty, students, and staff.

Aaron gave Skye a slight nod of his head, his long hair queued with a silver clasp, pinned through, a thick ponytail falling down the back of his black suitcoat. "You look resplendent, Miss Addison." He paused. "Skye."

She returned a regal look, holding it for a moment before breaking into a wide smile, a stream of laughter coloring the moment. "As too, do you, Aaron Knutt. Master of the stables. The fields, and—all you see.'

"Including *you?*" Aaron grinned, then reached out, taking her by the elbow, escorting her to where her father was standing, surrounded by alumni, professors, and fawning students. He waited for the large man to notice them, then bowed.

"I would request the honor, sir, of first dance with your daughter. The lovely Miss Addison."

Stanton studied the young man's face. "If the lady agrees—"

Skye stepped forward. "I do, father."

"Then so it shall be." Stanton turned to the head valet holding station a few feet away and nodded. The other man's voice called out, letting people know to seek the seats assigned them. The orchestra, a blend of violins, harps, and a cello, fell silent, preparing to play once everyone had found their seats, all eyes on the young couple. A moment of silence followed as Aaron escorted Skye to the center of the floor where they stood, staring into each other's eyes, waiting for the first notes of a waltz to guide their steps.

Aaron could feel Skye's hand trembling in his. He leaned forward slightly, his words a whisper in her ear, barely stirring a thin curl of hair, cupping it in a silky embrace. "You're *scared.*"

"I *am.* Of your *big* feet. Afraid you're about to break out in a highlander reel and kick me in my delicate shins!"

The music began, Aaron moving with Skye as if one, his feet firmly pressed to the polished wooden floor, her own, in dainty steps, matching his every movement as they forgot about where they were, dancing with warm smiles on their faces.

"The stars are dimming. I'd rather hoped they would stay out." Skye leaned back into Aaron's firm embrace, the heat of his body helping to ward off the chill from the night air.

"The rains arriving. As predicted earlier this afternoon by a lowly worker, with fork in hand." Aaron sipped the scent of her hair, pressed beneath his chin, savoring its delicate flavor. He felt her pull away and opened his arms, reluctantly, allowing her to twist around, looking up at him. He stared back, aware their playful, teasing relationship, with easy exchange of verbal wits over the past year, was on the verge of becoming a much deeper connection.

Skye sighed. "I forget, at times—how *complete* a person you are." She reached up with her hand, touching his lips, stopping him before he could make some innocuous reply. "How unlike all the other students—all the other *men* you are. Born to a noblewoman, doing noble work. Your father—a decorated veteran and man of reason, gifted with an articulate manner. Lost, before his time."

Skye stepped away, turning to lean against a railing fronting the hall, overlooking the gardens below, swathed in a huddle of shadows beneath a lowering sky. She raised her hands, grasping her shoulders, feeling a chill. "And you, raised in the highlands alongside two sisters. The two of them as different as an ocean is from a lake. Yourself, a hunter of great stags since barely more than a child, using only a bow. Become a wise man, with a mind for numbers *and* letters."

Aaron removed his suitcoat, placing it about Skye's shoulders. He held onto her upper arms, looking at her as if for the first time. "You have sought out information. The source—of an interest to me."

She returned his gaze, a slight chill felt through the layer of his coat. "From Allen. This very day. Forcing him to share *some* of what he was willing to tell me regarding your family." She paused, swallowing, her eyes wide as she continued. "He seemed caught off guard by my questions. Reluctant to answer me, as if—"

Aaron released her and stepped back. "He swore a vow to never speak of what I've shared." He noted Skye's nervousness. "Although I cannot fault him for revealing a *wee* bit of my background, especially to an *innocent* query—from such a beautiful lass."

Skye blushed, a shiver of warmth rising from within, stirring her emotions. She turned away, staring out into the night, wishing to be back in the hayfield, alone with him. Separated from out of her life, able to fully express how she felt. To have what she'd wanted from the very first sight of the handsome and mysterious highlander boy. "I beg your forgiveness for my trespass. I did not intend to cause—"

Aaron reached out, his fingers touching her face, gently easing her around. "I cannot *give* it—as there is nothing to forgive. You are not at fault, but I. In having ignored your interest, while hiding mine."

Skye covered his hand with her own. "I had wondered if you saw me as more than just the rector's daughter. Had in fact wondered, at times, if you even saw me as a—lass." She hesitated, lowering her eyes along with the tone of her voice. "I had supposed some *other* girl to have caught your eye, capturing a piece, if not *all* your heart."

Aaron grinned. "Outside my sisters, mother, and grandmother—no." He waited until Skye looked up, a soft smile on his lips. "My Gran Uncle *did* bring a bonny lass back with him after a journey made throughout clan lands, checking on his people's needs."

"And did you—" Skye looked away again, her hands clenched.

"Nae. I did *not*."

"Not even a kiss—to test the waters?" Her voice was a whisper, barely heard in a slight breeze building, heralding the approach of the rain, carrying a hint of heather from the direction of a nearby moor.

Aaron cupped her chin, gently angling it up, his lips inches away from her own. "Nae. Not even a kiss. Saving it for someone who did not look as if a *twin* to my own dear *mother*." He smiled. "Which you, Skye Addison—do *not*."

Then he kissed her, feeling her arms around his neck, pulling him in, losing himself in the moment of intimate connection, eyes closed, heart swelling in his chest, as happy as he'd ever been in his entire life.

"The rector—" Allen's voice from behind broke the spell, causing Aaron to pull away. He twisted his head. "*Yes*—my friend?"

"He requests his daughter's presence in order to introduce her to a group of dignitaries who've *just* arrived."

Aaron released Skye, a look of exasperation on both their faces as she shrugged off his coat and walked away. Allen cleared his throat.

"My deepest and most *profound* apologies, my brother. I held off for as long as I dared, until—"

Aaron clapped him on his back, a bit more forcibly then intended, then laughed. "The story of my life, to date. Constantly interrupted by forces from outside my ken—or control."

Allen followed Aaron as he reentered the hall, remembering the story told him in strict confidence of events that had transpired in the highland hills. He knew his friend still carried the guilt of what he'd done in defending his family, seeing it haunting the corners of his eyes whenever he stared into the interior of Scotland as if searching for memories of happier days, spent in the highland glens.

CHAPTER FOUR
SCOTTISH HIGHLANDS
FALL, 1776

The arrow flew to one side of the hare, startling it into a rapid darting away, chased across the sun-bleached grass by a high-pitched curse, in Scottish accent. Marion stood up and tossed the ghillie suit from her shoulders, then slammed the bow onto the ground, followed by a quiver of arrows.

Harold shook his head, ignoring both the outburst and the poor treatment of the weapon, having been the one to insist his youngest daughter join him up at the croft house. He'd hoped to teach her a lesson in patience, helping to off-set her short fuse and icy temperament.

Sinclair had raised one eyebrow at his suggestion, shaking her head and walking away, the sound of her laughter trailing behind, stoking Harold's determination to prove his point. Failing, faced with an angry lassie in a stern pose, as if blaming him for the missed shot. The foul weather, and failed hunt having taken her away from her usual routine of pouring through books, back at the manor library.

"You'll have to look *elsewhere* to replace my *sister*. She's away another week or more, and you'll need *abide* it 'til then." Marion came up, her cheeks rubbed red by the cold breeze. She was shivering as she gave her father a toss of her head, then turned away, stomping through the wet coarse grass, back toward the croft stables.

"You'll wait on *me* to take you down to the final turn." Harold went into the field and retrieved the bow and quiver, along with the spent arrow and ghillie suit. When he got to the stable, Marion had already saddled her mount, a small bay. She was standing alongside it, stroking its neck, her lips pressed in a firm line.

Harold walked up. "I apologize—for having wanted to get you out into the fresh air, resting your eyes from your incessant reading."

"Not an *apology* I'm hearing. More an *explanation* from a lonely man. One with *too* much time on his hands—and not enough to *do*."

Harold kept a smile from his face, admiring his daughter for her willful nature. More self-centered than was her sister's, though as firmly bound within her fully formed body. Scottish lads were in constant hover around the manor grounds, invisible to her, her mind locked on an internalized view of the world, with minor concessions made to immediate family. Her Gran Uncle Shaun an exception, willing to engage with her for hours on end in discussions about all sorts of things, providing real-world observations to her questions about politics and commerce, along with management of the clan, thrown in for good measure.

"You're right. The idea of the hunt had more to do with her absence. With Meghan's. Along with that of your mother."

Marion pouted. "It was *I* the one she should 'ha took with her to attend to matters in London. Not *Megs*, with no head for figures, other than those of the boys hanging around her all the time, with foolish smiles on their fat, sweaty faces."

"You've been down the mountain with your mother and back a dozen times or more, these past two years. It's good for your sister to meet those who've fallen on challenging times, due to bad decisions in who they settled for."

Marion shrugged, then turned her eyes down, scuffing the floorboards with one toe of her highland boots. "I miss my brother."

Harold came over and took her hand, squeezing it slightly. "As do we all, daughter-mine. As do we all." He let go, then prepared his mount for the ride down to the manor. Once outside, he watched as

Marion, an excellent rider, leapt into the saddle. With a heavy sigh he closed the stable door, the two of them slowly riding away.

※※※

Marion smirked. Her sister was in full pout, having returned from an unsettled bout of travel with their mother. The two of them were in their shared bedroom, sitting on the edge of the one large bed, their feet reaching the floor now they'd come into full bloom, both of an age.

"They were all so—" Meghan paused, hands clenched, her voice tight with frustration. "So *abused* by their circumstances. The children, their little faces drawn and shadowed—it near broke my heart in seeing them so helpless."

"The world provides harsh lessons, for *most* people. The strong-minded ones, able to turn them to their advantage." Marion sniffed, lifting one hand, admiring the play of candlelight on her smooth skin. Then she frowned, seeing the thickened patches on the outside of forefinger and ring finger, caused by the hours of forced practice with the bow, over the past month. "Is why I intentionally missed *hitting* the hare during my hunt with our father, making it look like a lack of talent, hoping to avoid any repeat of the event. Ever again."

"Father took you on a *hunt?*" Meghan took in a breath, ready to scold her for having used her bow.

Marion placed her hand on her sister's. "Father was *beyond* lonely, dear one. Missing you and our mother." She paused for effect, playing each of her older sister's heartstrings as she'd learned to do from having observed how her great uncle would bind men to him with a jovial nature, before bending them to his indomitable will with a glare. "And our *dear* brother, too. Away from us for so long."

Meghan reached over and took her sister's hand, squeezing it. "Of course. I certainly understand his wanting to seek you out, knowing how *difficult* it must have been for you. The highland meadows—no place for someone as *studious* as yourself."

Marion gave Meghan a warm smile, aware of the hidden meaning in her sister's words. "As too the lowlands, especially south of the border. A far different place for you there than here, with people in such distress, living in horrible situations. A tug to your emotions, sweet as you are."

Sinclair opened the door, sticking her head in. "When you two have finished regaling one another with mutual tales of woe, there are dishes to be cleared, cleaned, and put away." She grinned. "I'm off to the croft, so mind you get your chores done and tend to your grand ma's every need while I'm away."

※※※

Harod cupped his hand around the curve of Sinclair's breast, light from a half-moon streaming through the small window of the croft house. She sighed, covering it with her own, pressing it against her flesh.

"It seems but a blink of my eye since we were lying here, a wee babe in my womb. Before the world spun us around in its grasp, then tossed us down." Sinclair turned her head to the side, finding Harold's profile, seeing his eyes directed outside an open window into the night sky. "You seem troubled, my love."

Harold was silent, his breathing having slowed as he kept his thoughts to himself. He finally rolled over, facing her, then reached out and touched the side of her beautiful face, looking into eyes reflecting the silvered light of a near full moon. "I was with a vision, just now. Starting after we finished making our *reintroduction*." He tried and failed to hold a smile on his lips. "One I am not wanting to share."

"But will—if it has to do with our children." Sinclair narrowed her eyes, her head angled as she looked at Harold. "Am I right?"

Harold nodded, then slipped his arm from under her shoulders, sitting up, his feet finding the floor. "Tea?" He gave Sinclair a look that spoke volumes, then stood up and moved toward the slate stove, reaching for the kettle, left to steep.

"No. I'm more in a mood for some of your Gran Da's whiskey, if any is left."

Harold nodded. "One bottle, then no more. Shaun gifting it to me during his last visit here."

"With Charles." Sinclair sat up, pulling the sheet around her shoulders, her body thickened about the waist, though still a vision, surrounded by the fall of light from outside.

Harold nodded. "Yes. His visit the probable cause for what I've just seen." He pulled a brown bottle from the rafters, along with two chipped glasses from the cupboard, placing them on the table, staring at them for a moment before uncorking and pouring each half-full.

Sinclair took the one handed her and held it to her pert nose, sniffing it before taking a sip, feeling the warmth as she swallowed. "Our son—the one in your vision."

Harold nodded, staring at the glass, then setting it on the table, untouched. "A man full grown. Broader than me in the chest, with thicker legs, raised on high." He sat down on the edge of the small bed, feeling Sinclair's hand on his thigh, warm against his bare skin. The scent of her filled him with a longing to hold her, and never let go. To stay here, with her, as if able to step outside of time itself, the rest of the world left to drift away, only themselves remaining. Then he took in a deep breath and let it out, accepting his lot in life. Accepting his destiny, and that of his children. Starting tonight, with the vision of his son.

"He was in the new world, in great pain. The weight of deeds he'd done or *witnessed* done—burdening his soul. His body left torn, life balanced on a razor's honed edge—crying out for his—" He stopped, unable to continue.

"For me." Sinclair placed the glass of whiskey on a small bedside table then wrapped the sheet around her and leaned in, her head pressed against Harold's chest, feeling his arm slip around her shoulder.

"Yes. I could see your face, as if in a mirror, or pool of dark water. He was calling out to you." He turned and looked down, finding her eyes. "But it wasn't *you*. It wasn't you there—wherever he was. It was *someone* else. A young woman, holding him while he was shaking. Whether from fear or fever—I cannot say, with the vision fading away."

Sinclair released one edge of the sheet and wiped her eyes. She shook her head, her voice tight with anger. "Will it *never* end? Will it never be peace for my *men?* Without violence, or injury? Without pain?" She wept, silently, her shoulder's shaking as Harold pulled her into his embrace, his own tears joining hers as he leaned down and kissed her cheek.

"I will need to leave. Again."

She pulled back, her eyes wide, mouth open in shock. "You *can't*. You *mustn't!* You're a man believed *dead!*" She sat up, the sheet falling away from her body, puddling around her waist. She took his hands, holding onto them. "You're *safe* here! Only *here!* Only while you're protected by hundreds of eyes in watch. With your uncle having your back. If you leave—if you step from this mountain, then you'll never see it *again!*"

Harold leaned back slightly. "Is that *your* vision?"

"No, you *daft* fool of a man. It's the *truth!* The same one you *know* it to be." She paused, her face square to his, eyes looking straight into his. "If you leave me—if you choose to leave *us* again—there will be *no* coming back this time."

Harold nodded. "Then come with me. Our son—will *need* us. Or only *you*. The reflection of your face in his thoughts, driving this vision of where he will end up—shown me this night."

Sinclair stared at the man she'd seen walk away before, driven by his destiny to walk the shadowed path where nothing was clear, with doubt as to the decision he should made, with dire consequences faced, either way. She'd sent him away in a storm of angry, hurtful words, watching as he rode off, swallowed up by darkness. She knew she could not do so again.

"Alright, husband mine. When the time comes, and you *know* it to be so—I'll go. But not while our boy is standing on Scottish soil. Not while he's still tied to Scotland's sod."

CHAPTER FIVE
SCOTTISH LOWLANDS
FALL, 1776

A full moon hung high in a cloudless sky, perched above a lowland marsh covered in a layer of misty gray. The hour was late, two men on horseback coming out of the shadows of a thick grove of trees, easing their way toward a light in the distance. A hound began to bay an alarm, silenced with a fist, whimpering as it lay down, its head between its large paws as it watched the two figures approach the small farm.

Shaun tugged the reins of his horse, a small mare, easier to climb onto and down from. His feet found the ground, his aching hip offering a sharp stab of burning pain. He hid his wince beneath a warm smile as he reached down and rubbed the ears of the hound, its long tongue licking his hand, tail wagging in greeting.

"The night air is known to be bad for the lungs. A bit of whiskey to make you feel whole again?" A short, reed thin man with long, gray stringy hair leaned against a railing, a pipe in one hand, bottle in the other.

Shaun glanced at Duncan, who remained silent, his eyes searching every shadow looking for danger, before holding out two thick fingers. Shaun stepped forward into the light, his craggy face lined with age and the burden of constant pain in his body. Every ache deserved, earned throughout the years, and now come home to rest.

"A half-glass, for me. Two fingers, for my friend."

The old man grinned. "You'll have to measure by swallows. I've no glasses near to hand. But the drink is sound—and well-aged." Duncan came forward, taking the bottle, handing it to Shaun, giving him the honor of first taste. When handed back the bottle, the tall, broad chested and silent man wiped the neck with his hand, then tipping it up, the moon gleaming off the dark glass.

"You have what I asked for?" Shaun stepped forward, Duncan at his side with one large hand in his coat pocket, not trusting the farmer, a lowlander with tenuous ties to the clan. The dog stood up, hackles raised, a low growl in its throat. The old farmer gave it a look, then shushed it with a wave of his hand, pointing at the huddled shape of a broken-backed barn half a hundred paces away.

※※※

"This is a shit hole of a place, ripe for ambush. No true man of the clan, this one." Duncan stood beside Shaun, watching as the farmer made his way to the back of the barn, a lantern in his hand, rummaging through a wooden crate, the dog lying at Shaun's feet, looking up.

"I trust this man with my life. He's been there, where you are now, alongside me when the tide turned against us. Had my back then. Has it now. So—not to worry on my account."

Duncan shrugged, his shoulders tense, his mood dour. He turned and spit on the floor, barely missing the dog who growled, the hair on its back raised. The large man mimed pointing a gun at its head, pulling the trigger, making the sound of a shot, chuckling as the dog backed down.

"I've found them. Still like new. Oiled, and ready to go." The old man came back, lantern in hand with halting steps, casting shadows on the weather-beaten boards of the wall, the sound of pigs muttering at rest joined by the cooing of doves in the eaves. He held out a pair of pistols, placing them on top of an overturned barrel, having pulled them from a sack in his hand. He handed one to Shaun.

"Just as I remember them to be. Fine pieces. Fit for the job at hand." Shaun turned, thumbing the hammer to full cock, and pointing it at Duncan, pulling the trigger, the flash of light highlighting the shocked expression on the big man's bearded face as the lead ball punched into his stomach, knocking him back two paces, folding him in half, barely able to stay on his feet. "You *sold* them out. The *lot* of them. My *kin*. Members of your *own* clan. For a bag of *silver*."

Duncan stumbled to one side, almost falling to his knees, the dog on its feet, teeth bared, ready to lunge forward to protect its owner and guest, known to him from previous visits. Made alone, without the presence of the dying man. Duncan held out his hand, a pistol clenched in his fist, eyes gleaming as he swung it toward Shaun.

Another shot rang out, the second pistol in the other man's hand fired, a hole appearing in Duncan's forehead, a mist of red gore and white fragments of brain and bone painting the wall behind him. The big man stood for a moment, then fell onto one side, the weapon still in his hand, eyes open, a look of surprise on his face.

Smoke from the discharge of the weapons filled the interior, teased away by a thin breeze starting to build as the moon angled over, on its way to the horizon, the hour late. The farmer came over and nudged the dead man's cheek with the toe of a worn boot.

"You'll be having to help me drag him to the pens. Either that or I'll need to get a saw." The man gazed down at the mound of dead flesh and bone. "And an axe."

"I've strength enow to get him there in one piece." Shaun set the pistol down on the barrel, waiting as the farmer gathered a thick rope. Then the two of them bent to the grisly task at hand, bringing the turncoat's body to where the pigs had gathered, their squeals filling the air as birds, roused from their roosts once more, flew out from the interior of the barn. The dog looking up, watching as they flowed away into the moon-lit sky.

※※※

"Hard to believe it of him." Harold lowered his eyes, staring into the flames of the manor fireplace, invited by Shaun to join him there, with no danger of anyone from outside the manor seeing a dead man, walking. "How did you find out?"

"I didn't. Wasn't until I had the pistol fully cocked, with his hand starting to come out of his pocket with a pistol that I knew for certain. The look in his eyes telling me he was guilty—the bullet already on its way."

"Hard, hearing it. Knowing he—that he could *do* such a thing." Harold shook his head, then glanced at the door of the salon. "Does Sinclair know?"

"And why do ya think I'd burden the lass with any of that?" Shaun pursed his lips, staring at his nephew. "She's *your* wife, still and *always*. If anyone's to tell her, it'll be you."

"Of course. I spoke without thinking. The thought of it, someone who ate with us, bled with and for you on many an occasion—who *played* with my children, trading our lives for money."

"Was never about the money. Not certain they paid the bastard for having let them know the lay of the land. But there were no one else could ha' done it. Himself the only one with an absence unexplained. Seen on his way down in the lower valley, heading into Bargrennan. By one of my own. A sharp-eyed laddie named Allyn."

Sinclair came into the room, her eyes on Harold, uneasy seeing him there, his presence a painful reminder of the past, when they were still husband and wife. Shaun stood up, needing a moment to gather himself, then moved past her, heading to the kitchen where Eira was doing a bit of cleaning up.

Sinclair shook her head. "He's moving with more difficulty, every turn of season made. I worry for his health, bound as he is to remain in constant movement throughout clan lands."

"No worries on *that* account. His destiny told him by my Gran Da, when he first became clan leader." Harold looked at the doorway, listening to the sound of laughter from the kitchen as brother teased sister, Shaun and Eira always close. "He'll find an ending in his bed. Or chair. It's to be an easy death for him, without blood on his lips."

"Blood." Sinclair paused. "No doubt what's brought him here so late this day, sending Meghan to bring you down from your highland aerie." Sinclair came over and touched him on his shoulder. "Will you be spending the night?"

Harold looked up at her, his eyes holding a measure of pain. Sinclair left wondering if it was from what he'd lost in leaving her, or news placed there by the conversation with his uncle. "I'll stay—but out in the barn. Honoring our agreement as best I can." He paused. "Then leave first thing in the morning."

Sinclair lowered her eyes and walked away. She headed to the bedroom, shared with no one else, and gently closed the door behind her with a palm muffled sigh.

☙☙☙

Harold could feel the touch of a hand through the heavy veil of his dream. Meghan's, his Irish love, her deep laughter ringing in his ears as they lay in the shadows of a thick wood, watching the playful antics of three fox kits in a glade of sun-kissed, green grass. Robert, coming on the run, musket in hand, face covered in sweat, telling him to come. Aidyn needed him. George needed him. A'neewa needed him. The spell broken by a throaty whisper in his ear, drawing him back to the scent of hay, and the soft murmuring from horses in their stalls below.

A finger traced a line along his cheek, causing him to open his eyes. A shadow knelt beside him, one with a familiar scent. His raven-haired woman, with small cleft chin. Her lips finding his. Her body forming against him. One dream exchanged for another. Able to forget, for a moment, of all he'd lost. Everything he'd given up along the way. Knowing, as he twisted his hips and shoulders, looking down at her face, barely visible in the filtered light from an open hayloft door, that destiny would soon force him into a return to a world lying an ocean away. The blood he'd spilled there calling out for him to return. To begin anew. His path, painted red, still before him.

CHAPTER SIX
ABERDEEN
EARLY-SPRING, 1777

The weather was clear, clouds driven inland by a bank of air warmed by the North Atlantic Drift, running just off the coastline. Aaron rode beside Skye, the two of them on horseback, making their way up Brimmond Hill lying just outside the city limits. Their relationship had evolved from friends to something slightly less than lovers, with passionate embraces and kisses exchanged in moments of privacy. Reduced to lingering looks when others were about.

Skye's father, rector of the university and responsible for the behavior of every student, allowed his daughter a free rein, aware she was spending her free time with the young highlander. Stanton, familiar with Aaron's family, trusted the grandson of a man he'd fought and nearly died with during the siege of Gibraltar by the Spanish. Sergeant Major Richard Knutt, a fellow soldier and good friend, left with a deep puncture wound delivered from a Spanish officer's sword in his lower abdomen, still able to carry him to safety during a frenzied ambush, a pistol shot to the Spaniard's chest helping them break through. A debt he still owed, with a down-payment now made, trusting the moral fiber of the young man, full grown in build and temperament.

"The view—is *resplendent!*" Skye turned and looked at Aaron, who stared back with a quiet expression on his face.

"It certainly is. As beautiful as there is in Scotland—nae, the *entire* world. The pleasure mine—in looking at *you*."

Skye blushed, her long lashes framing the tops of her cheeks, shadowed by a large hat protecting her from the glare of a mid-day sun. "You have such a—*honeyed* way with words. How were you able to avoid finding yourself in a lassie's arms, while living amongst the clouds?"

"From my being surround by sisters with daggers worn 'neath their skirts. Along with a sharp-eyed mother and grandmother to boot." Aaron nudged his mount closer to Skye's, the two animals greeting each other with a touch of their long noses.

"You *jest*. Your *'lassies'* of more genteel comport, being from such noble lineage. Lord Haversham known for his concern for the common people. The thriving communities stretched alongside his vast estate, proof of his generous nature."

Aaron grinned, his teeth white against the sun-bronzed color of his skin, blue eyes gleaming in the bright light. "Was my *own* dear mother, as his adopted daughter, who encouraged the change in him. Her the one making improvements to the lives of those serving the needs of his vast estate. Modern tools, healthy animals supplied them, along with basic medicines and education, helping improve their lot in life. Benefiting all, the people healthy and prosperous, increasing the value of the estate and surrounding villages."

"I should *love* to meet her. Your mother, Lady Sinclair. Her reputation and support for such a worthy cause is something I should like to emulate, when given the chance."

Aaron leaned over, lips close to Skye's ear, his breath warm against the side of her neck. "Then we need but turn around and go down to the east end of town. There are plenty of people there in need of succor and second chances given them."

Skye pulled back, facing him. "You *know* this to be true?"

"Aye. Been visiting them this year and last, bringing what I can from the kitchens and stockrooms, with the approval of the head of household services. Doing work where and when able to manage it, helping the locals to improve their water supply by putting in a new well. And a small mill built next to a stream nearby with dry storage for produce from their gardens. Grain from the fields, and the like."

Skye lowered her eyes again, her hands clenched on the reins of her mount, the mare sensing her distress, moving ahead several paces. Aaron's steed, raising its head and looking back, waiting for a nudge of his knees.

Aaron complied, coming back alongside, noticing tears in Skye's eyes. "Have I upset you?"

She shook her head. "Is not your doing—but my own, in speaking of my ambitions with no *substance* behind the words. My life one of education and strict adherence to society's requirements of my position *in* it, with no—" Skye glanced at Aaron, noting the scars on his fingers and back of his hands. "With no *dirt* under *my* nails. No *calluses* on my fingers. No—*sweat* on my forehead from long days of *honorable* toil."

Aaron took her hand, bringing it to his lips, kissing each knuckle. "Not for want of your *consideration* of it. Only a lack of *opportunity* to do so."

Skye reached out and covered his hand. "Would you take me there? Take me with you on your next visit?"

Aaron shrugged, looking back toward Marischal, the granite edifice glowing in the angled rays of light as mid-day began to fall away, the single note of a church bell echoing in the distance. "It would not be possible—without approval sought from and *given* by your father."

"We could ask it of him. Together!" Skye gave him a smile, her eyes bright with excitement. "You'll do that, won't you? Support me in asking it of him?"

Aaron nodded, his eyes focused on hers, a tremor passing through him, knowing he would never deny her anything, once asked. "Of course. Then pack my bags and hie to the hills, my *buttocks* left bruised and in a sling."

Skye laughed, her heart opening to the idea of helping others. "Then I shall *visit* you there, in midnight's hour, covering each wound with healing kisses. The two of us soothing each other's bruises."

Aaron nodded without further response, turning his horse around, starting downhill. Skye angled her head, calling out as he headed away. "Are we not having our picnic?"

Aaron's voice floated over his shoulder, finding her ear. "There's no father *here* telling us *which* direction to take, in making our return to the stables."

※※※

A small child slid from Skye's lap, her unshod feet leaving a smudge of dirt on the pale fabric of her skirt. The girl, clad in rough spun clothing stopped and turned around, giving her a dimpled smile, her wide eyes white circles centered by blue irises, showing through the dirt-stains on her pinched face. "Ye fod yn un da, a'm diolch i ye, colli."

Skye turned to Aaron, who watched with a bemused smile. He translated. "Ye be a good one, and my thanks to ye, miss." Skye blushed, waving to the waif who rushed away, a sack of food in one hand, her bare feet flashing as she dashed between several men with small sacks of wheat kernels on their shoulders.

Aaron straightened up, finished with his repair of the drivetrain of the mill, having installed a new gear, fashioned in the workshop back at the university stables. He eased a crick in his lower back, Skye coming over and putting her hands on top of his, helping to massage the stiffness away.

It was her third visit to the small huddle of homes on the outskirts of Aberdeen, delivering food collected from the college stores, placed in a wagon with her at the reins, stopping to toss small bags to mothers lining the narrow street, the hooves of the draft horse splashing through a layer of muck as it moved along, caking its lower legs a light brown.

Her father, when approached about aiding the downtrodden community had hesitated for a moment, eyeing Aaron first, then her, before nodding his head and turning away without comment, his cane tapping the floor as he headed toward his office.

Rory and Allen had come running up, clapping Aaron on the back, while bowing to Skye, congratulating them on their having won the day. Then the four of them had headed off to celebrate, with a lively argument ensuing based on the latest news from the colonies. The colonial general Washington having made a strategic maneuver, turning certain defeat at the hands of Cornwallis into victory against a smaller force at Princeton. The result had left the colonials emboldened, with the British forced to cede New Jersey, making their winter retreat to New York.

Rory had done his best not to sound too excited by the news, received four weeks after the battle, which had occurred in early January. The Scottish broadsheets had trumpeted the victory with hushed enthusiasm, the spirit of nationalism strong, still seeing the English as an occupying force. Allen, in a gloomy mood, had complained about the losses suffered on both sides, feeling each one as if a member of his own family having gone into the ground, with several of his relatives serving in the upper ranks of the British army.

Aaron and Skye had listened as the other two regaled them with the reasons for and against the uprising, one barely supported by most citizens, choosing to remain loyal to the crown. With slight nods of their heads, they'd ordered several rounds of drinks, paid for with Allen's coins earned by Aaron's diligent mathematical efforts made on his behalf.

The two other young men, firmly affixed on opposite sides of the border between Scotland and England finally agreed to disagree, shaking hands, and wishing it would end quickly with no further bloodshed. Each left with their own idea as to what victory would mean to the colonists.

🌿🌿🌿

The day faded with the sun, well down in the western sky, the view from the top of the university, stunning. Aaron held Skye's hand, her head against his shoulder as she hummed a soft melody. He pulled away, looking at her, the slanted angles of the wondrous sunset coloring her hazel eyes with flecks of yellow and gold.

"That's—different. Not one I've heard before."

"Because its *mine*. One I've been working on for a few weeks now."

Skye lowered her eyes. "Lacking the words—though I've worked out all the notes."

Aaron leaned down slightly, looking into her eyes. "The image, in your mind as you sing it?"

She blushed, the rose-red sunlight a match to her smooth skin, gone a shade darker from all the hours spent assisting him in the small village. "Of two lovers—star-crossed, due to their disparate backgrounds. Hearts yearning for something they can see, taste, and touch—but lies beyond their ability to *grasp*. Forced to seize the moment, leaping over the divide between."

Aaron looked at the crenulated design running along the top of the granite wall of the large building. He lifted Skye into one of the square edged openings, then joined her there, holding her hand as they looked down at the ground below. Then he leaned over, touching his head to hers. "Do we dare the leap—into what lies beyond? Facing the consequences of it together? Avoiding the certainty of pain to come, shared—our hearts tattered and torn when reality rears its head, assigning each to their proper station in life."

Skye looked up and nodded, tears in her eyes. "I would willingly go where you would take me—no matter the cost to my position or reputation. I *would*. I *will!*"

Aaron kissed her, his eyes closed, aware of how much he'd come to love her. Need her. Want her. Aware of how difficult it was going to be in letting her go, untouched. Unwilling to be the cloud on her horizon, following behind as she made her way through the life her father had planned for her. "And that is why, my love—I must say *no* to you. To *us*. My own death, one I'd face with open eyes. But to see you made to pay the price for *my* needs—would prove an impossible burden to carry."

Skye shook her head, twisting away as if to leap. Aaron pulled her back into his embrace, surrounding her slim waist with his arms, holding her, kissing her tears away, his voice soft. "You know—you *knew*—before our first dance together, that your future would never be that of a highlander's wife. Knew I could not abide a life lived below."

"I could—"

"No. It would only be a promise broken, made up of loving words, but never a story told true. Time would have its way with us, leading to silent, wayward glances to high places or low, each wishing to be where their families and friends are."

Skye stared at Aaron, her lips trembling. Aching for him, needing to feel him. To hold him inside her. She parted her lips, her eyes half-open, leaning into him. He returned her kiss, knowing it would be their last one, her father letting him know his only daughter would be in a coach bound to London in the morning, with himself home to the highlands for the mid-term break.

☙ ☙ ☙

"She has benefited greatly—from spending time with you." Stanton found him in the stables, the walk a difficult one for the heavy-set man with a bad leg. "You've given her a view of the world that will serve her well as she moves on with her life."

Aaron nodded, putting away an oiled harness then going to wash his hands and arms before donning a linen shirt, held out to him by Skye's father. "I have kept my vow, sworn to you. She is *still* a maid."

Stanton stared at him, shaking his head slightly, a strange look in his dark eyes. "You are so much like him—your grandfather, Richard. As I *remember* him to have been. A bit older than you when we served together—but blessed with the *same* vision. Able to see outside himself, like you." He paused, taking a moment to consider his words. "Your father, much the same, from everything I've read of him. His efforts in Parliament to stop the—" The old soldier lowered his eyes. "I apologize, my words uttered without consideration of your feelings." He waited, watching as the young man shrugged, his fingers fastening the top buttons of his shirt.

Aaron gave Stanton a quiet look. "He died. Whether in opposition to, or a member of the group of men killed that night. His body shattered, made unrecognizable from what my gran uncle was able to learn." Aaron pointed to a seat, waiting until the other man sat down. "I love your daughter and made clear to you from the beginning my intention was to make her my wife. To live in Bristol. At my parent's manor."

"And you would have left her devastated, lad, in leaving her." Stanton smiled, taking the sting out of his words. "Not with forethought, and through no fault of your own." He paused, tapping the end of his cane on the wooden floor. "It is your destiny, same as with your father. And grandfather, Richard—a courageous soldier and good friend who fought—"

"I *know* his story. Told me by my grand uncle Thomas."

Stanton leaned forward, using the cane to help support his weight. "Then you *know* the generational curse placed on your head, and shoulders." He looked away, his expression dark. "A long, horrible war is in build across the way. With no easy *end* to it, not for years to come. Not until thousands of good men and boys lie buried in the ground, whether from disease, or wounds suffered in battle. No way around it, with nothing you or *anyone* can do. Your father unable—" Stanton stopped, looking down.

"My father was a *fool*, thinking he could effect a change as grand as the one he proposed. I'd like to think he died making an—*ineffective* gesture, delaying but not able to prevent the conflict currently at hand." Aaron paused, giving Stanton a hard look. "But I am *not* my father. I might—*might* be my grandfather, in the best of ways. But this war will *never* be mine."

"Then your plan is *not* to return to the highlands, managing a property covered in sheep and cows? To instead use your education, your *abilities* with numbers—to enter commerce, your highlander soul left to dwindle away while you count coins with one hand, wiping tears of frustration away with the other." Stanton sighed. "I feel I'm speaking with *him* again. Your grandfather. Hearing the *same* words exchanged between the two of us before we signed the forms—then again *after* we were there. In uniform, with blood in the air. Our own blood, spilled on the ground."

"You genuinely believe me *capable* of such a thing? Of leaving a wife and going off to fight in a lost cause, no matter which side I would make my sworn vow to support?"

"She's to be married—this fall. To another."

Aaron slowly straightened, his eyes dark in the shadowed interior of the stable. "You—you *can't* be serious." He moved closer to the other man, his face set in stone as he stared at him. Skye's father met it without blinking. "She loves *me*."

Stanton smiled. "Of *course*. As if she ever had a choice, with your life experiences far beyond those of her own, due to harsh lessons learned, if the rumors I've managed to uncover are but *half*-true."

Aaron was silent, his face a mask to his emotions. "You could not know of—"

"Your *eyes*, lad. It's written there, plain enough for an old veteran like me to see. Enough to let me know you've crossed to a place you can *never* return from."

"Then why? Why agree to my having—"

"Because I *also* understand *women*. Particularly *this* one, young as she is." Stanton sighed. "To have denied her your company would have resulted in one of two scenarios. The two of you in a hastened marriage. Or doing something even more foolhardy, running back to your highland home or heading overseas. Either result bound to end in heartache for you both."

"It seems I am caught in the jaws of your *prediction* of what my *path* is to be." Aaron looked up, staring into the shadows, his jaw clenched, hands formed into fists. "*Damned*—no matter *which* way I am to turn."

"*Blessed*, lad, truly, to have known such a wonderful thing as first love, unblemished by time without recriminations and anger. Her destiny to wed a man with a less—*compelling* future. Someone willing to allow her to follow her passion of helping those less fortunate. A passion *you've* helped to initiate—among others."

"She has the wind in her sails, with every moment spent comparing herself to my mother. Wanting to do the same."

"A saint, to be certain, Lady Sinclair. With a son worthy of her in having done *excellent work* here, earning my respect. Which is why—"

"Why you allowed me the honor of first dance. Trusting me to do the right thing. Or rather—to not do the *wrong* thing."

"You see it clearly." Stanton struggled to his feet, Aaron taking his hand, helping him rise. He grasped the young man's shoulder, squeezing it slightly. "A difficult mission assigned you, soldier. One I would not wish to go through again, myself. Once enough for this old heart." He started to walk away, stopping when Aaron called out.

"Who was she—the one *you* let go of?"

Stanton turned around. "The daughter of a nobleman. Above my parent's station, thus above my own. Which is why I'm the rector here and not chancellor." He walked away, the sound of his cane tapping the ground swallowed by a late afternoon breeze, slipping in from the coast.

CHAPTER SEVEN
SCOTTISH HIGHLANDS
SPRING, 1777

Meghan knelt, touching the imprint of the stag's large hoof. It was a young bull, three years old, and fat, moving at a sedate pace along the side of a steep ridge. She eyed the terrain ahead, spotting a dark red shadow beneath a small island of stunted trees, nodding as she slid back. Her ghillie suit softly rustled, covered in gray strips of cloth, brushed by a slight wind coming from her right, helping guide her scent away from the animal's track.

Harold watched with pride, having noted the furtive movements below. Stationed well above his daughter, he'd been watching as she made the first moves of a solo hunt. Asked to stay back and observe, only needed to help haul the kill down off the hill, if his daughter was successful. Or to commiserate with the long-faced huntress, if not. He smiled, his wager placed on his feisty, determined daughter, admiring how patient she was being this day as she made her way toward the trees.

A memory from the past found him, blurring his vision. His son in a similar pose. Icy rain that day, he said to himself, with biting wind. The stag, an animal of impressive size. Its rack mounted on the manor wall, with Aaron's name on a plaque below it. Harold shook his head, feeling his son's energy as if he were sitting beside him, then slid back from the top of the rise, making his way along the opposite side of the valley wall, finding a position across from where Meghan was heading to. Once there he reclaimed a position at the top and hunkered down, avoiding the worst of the wind.

※※※

"It stepped ahead on my release. Why I needed the second shaft." Meghan frowned, wiping a line of sweat from her forehead with an elbow, her hands bloody from dressing out the large-bodied beast. "It should 'na have been needed."

Harold shrugged, his hands holding the stag's rear legs apart, while his daughter bent to the task of removing the animal's heart and liver. "Your first shaft would have done for him. His lung hit fair. No more than a hundred paces or so would have seen him on the ground."

"Still—Aaron only needed *one* arrow to make his first kill." Meghan. "And he would 'na have needed any help—though I don't mind your company."

Harold gazed at his daughter, recalling her namesake, kneeling in the same position, binding the wounds of an injured soldier. A stain of red on her cheek, strands of sun-kissed hair falling across her face, hands covered in the gore of a man, dying despite her best efforts. "It's been my pleasure, allowed in on the humane ending of *this* one's life."

Meghan glanced up, one arm up to the elbow in the chest cavity of the stag, a grimace on her face as she yanked the last of the viscera away. Then she wedged a hardwood stick in place, holding the chest cavity open to cool in the late afternoon air, with the sun arcing over the ridge, the valley beginning to collect a host of shadows. "Do we quarter it now and take the first load down, or should I run and get the horses? Or are we to return in the morning, the night cold enough to keep the meat sweet?"

Harold shrugged, waiting to see what his oldest daughter would decide. She didn't disappoint him. "We'll haul to the horses, load one, leaving it tethered. Then come back for the rest with your mount. Get the meat down to the croft house just after dark." She eyed the sky. It was clear, with a half-moon to come. "It will be light enough to avoid any small stones, the horses not made to pay with an injury for the work asked of them."

Harold's heart swelled with pride, seeing his girl as a woman, full grown. Radiant in spirit and raw health, with unobstructed vision of the world about her in their highland perch, though woefully unaware of the dangers of the world below, despite having attended her mother on several trips to Bath, Bristol, and London.

"A fine plan." He stood up, helping her roll the animal over to begin the process of separating the beast into loads small enough to strap to the wooden frames of their two packs. When they were ready, he followed his daughter, the two of them making their heavily burdened way down to the valley floor.

※※※

Aaron rode up to the highland manor. He stopped at the stable, opening and closing the large door, taking care of his horse before heading toward the house. There were lights glowing through the kitchen window, raising a smile on his lips, his stomach grumbling in anticipation of a warm meal. Left unfilled since the previous afternoon, with only a handful of dried meat, an apple, and generous swallows of water pulled from his canteen to tide him over. His mount had been satisfied with oats pulled from a feedbag, along with water from a small spring-fed pool tucked beside an unmarked clan trail.

A voice called out, masculine, deep in tone. Allyn stepped out of the shadows, pistol in one hand, hanging at his side, having recognized both horse and rider as they'd come up the road. "You're even *bigger* than when you left."

The boy, near an age to Aaron, smiled, the light from the kitchen window revealing a line of perfect teeth in a square cut jaw, with dark eyes beneath bushy eyebrows poised above a broad forehead. He shook his head, tucking the weapon in his belt. "No doubt from too much food, and not enough work. In chase of an education instead of highland stags."

"And yourself, lurking about the place, when the others are away, moving stock through the Pinch." Aaron clapped the young man on his wide shoulder, unable to move him from his stance. "I imagine one of my sisters is to blame for that. Presuming it to be Meghan, the lucky lass who's caught your eye."

"Only choice left to me. T'other always away, going off to England with your mother." Allyn shrugged. "Besides, your older sister is—*difficult* to avoid, with a host of duties for me to perform. Always asking me to help her out with one thing or another."

Aaron grinned, moving toward the kitchen door, his hunger rising within, stirred by the scent of venison stew filling the air, along with the aroma of fresh baked bread. When he entered the heated room, his grandmother looked up, a smile slowly blossoming on her lined face.

"You're back. And you've only just left." She started to stand up, then sagged, needing another push of her thin arms to make the move. Aaron went over and gave her a cautious hug. He kept a look of surprise off his face, seeing the woman he loved more than any other, outside his broken-hearted Skye, looking so frail.

"It's good to see you again, Gran Ma."

Eira pulled back, a confused look on her still mostly unwrinkled face. "Aaron? I thought you were your father. You've grown *again*, since last you were home." She paused. "Have you finished your term?"

"Only halfway through it, Gran Ma. With a return in two weeks." Aaron glanced into the salon. "Is mother here? And Marion?"

"You're to sit and let me feed you. I have a bit of stew left on the stove. And fresh bread baked for tomorrow. There's a small loaf, mostly crust, for your father. Though he won't mind it going to you."

Aaron helped her fill the bowl and gather a plate for the bread. He looked around, Allyn having slipped away, hearing his voice down the hallway, calling out to the others. Marion came on the run, followed by his mother.

"You're early by *two* days!" Marion tossed herself into his arms, followed closely by Sinclair, the two of them dancing him around, their voices filled with laughter, and questions, berating him for his early return, a party planned, the surprise ruined.

"I'll leave once I've eaten. Then come back on the morrow—if you'll only let go of my arms."

Sinclair reached up, cupping his cheek, staring at him for a moment then letting a sly smile slip across her full lips. "You've met a lass. Down below." Marion stood back, eyes fixed on her brother, a curious look on her face.

Aaron nodded. "I have. And no, she's not *my* lass—promised to another. Though she *is* a friend—and an incredible woman." He looked at his mother. "Looking to follow in *your* footsteps."

Sinclair exchanged a glance with Eira, both women nodding as they placed food on the large, work-scarred surface of the wooden island. Marion came over and took her brother's hand. "Father and Meghan are at the croft. Meghan is seeking to take a stag, all on her own."

"With *what* bow?" Aaron saw Allyn's eyebrows rise. "With *mine?*" He shook his head. "She doesn't have strength enow to draw it full."

Allyn shook his head. "You're not the only one who's grown. Meg's strong enough to get it done—and deadly accurate. As good as you." He paused, considering for a moment, noting Marion's narrowed-eye look. "*Almost* as good."

Aaron opened his mouth to reply, closing it as his mother pulled him to the table to eat. She poured him a glass of ale, then opened a small loaf of bread with a knife, steam rising as a slice of butter dropped inside began to melt into its center.

"Eat, son. Your days of chasing stags are at an end, with the university and education where you're to aim your arrow now." She kissed his cheek, brushing an unruly lock of black hair back from his face.

⚜⚜⚜

Aaron sighed, holding a glass with an inch of whiskey in it between his hands. He looked at his father, sitting across from him at the table in the croft house, joining him in a drink after a day spent replacing slate tiles on the roof, several having cracked from the weight of moss grown too thick.

"It still hurts. An ache in my chest, finding me at times with my breath coming short. Left wondering when it will pass." Aaron took a sip of the strong drink, enjoying the heat of the fire from the stove, his eyes heavy with emotional and physical fatigue.

"I wish I could tell you that it will. How one day you'll awake, picturing her face, and not feel the pain of knowing she's not coming back into your life." Harold leaned forward, studying his son's face, seeing a reflection of himself in the bruised look in Aaron's eyes. "But it hasn't happened for me, despite having found your mother's love, which is as bright as the sun."

"You're referring to the woman in your journal. The one my sister's named after. The mirror image of her, based on the drawing you did."

"The same."

Aaron shrugged. "No hope for a cure, then."

Harold shook his head. "You don't *cure* the loss of people you love. You hold on to the memories. Cherish the moments spent with them, good and bad, added to all those still ahead of you. With another to hand, soon enow. The world's a wide stage, filled with people in your path, men, and women, made friends or enemies—or more. As happened with me."

"Then I made the right choice?"

"You tell me."

Aaron lowered his eyes. "A father asked me to do what he thought best for his daughter. Saw the pain in his eyes, when telling me he'd had to do the same." He glanced up, noting the same look of in his father's eyes. "Yours—a more difficult loss, I think. One I cannot imagine being able to survive. Which you would not have done, if not for your native friend." He paused, waiting until his father gave him a slight nod. "A'neewa. You were in love with her, too."

"I was. And still am. *Different* then what I share with—"

"I do not question what you share with my mother. Obvious enough to all how the two of you feel." Aaron clenched his fingers around the glass he held. "And do not wish to pry into your past, not destined to walk the same path as you, despite what Stanton—what the rector said to me."

Harold angled his head slightly, waiting while his son took a sip from the glass. "He told you—"

"That I was destined, or doomed, to repeat the past. To follow in your footsteps. And those of *your* father. Called it a generational curse, passed down the line. War, or conflict of one kind or another, finding men coming of age, compelling them to enlist. To hie to the sound of bugles and drums, eager to join themselves to a righteous cause. Or a fool's game, according to speeches made in Parliament. By *you*."

Harold nodded. "I would not fault a man, or men from following the path they choose, as long as they choose it for *themselves*, knowing the consequence to body and soul." He reached out and placed a hand on his son's broad shoulders. "And you've been made to bear the cost to the latter one, in service to the highest calling of all—that of protecting your loved ones from harm."

Then he stood up and stepped outside, looking up at the mountain, the stars limning its night-black silhouette, knowing that when morning arrived, he'd invite his son to make the trek to the top, putting their backs to the cold stone crypt, sharing stories of women loved, then let go of.

CHAPTER EIGHT
NEW JERSEY
MORRISTOWN, SPRING, 1777

Charles entered a command tent and gave a nod to General Green, another offered to the taller man posed beside him, who glanced up from a study of a large map. Charles held a non-descript hat in his hand, waiting until Washington turned around and greeted him with a thin smile, then beckoned him over.

"My good man, of mysterious background—allow me to express my heartfelt appreciation for the information provided us. Your efforts helped me to achieve a *great* victory."

Charles stepped forward, noting two sentries stiffen as he did so. They eyed him closely, protective of their leader, as were all the soldiers seen while moving throughout the encampment, with an abundance of positive energy and good will in evidence. Too soon, Charles thought, knowing the odds stacked against them, despite their recent success against an element of the English army. One led by Cornwallis, a gifted officer, who would not make the same mistake again.

"I am, as ever—in service to *you*, along with members of my group —" Charles paused, eyeing the sentries. Greene noted the look and motioned the two soldiers outside, Washington oblivious to the exchange, staring at the map, one hand cupping his chin, the other pointing at the enemy positions as if he could move them with his will.

"Along with those of my *own* group. Mobilized throughout the colonies, gathering information where they find it. Risking their lives."

Greene nodded. "As are we *all*, sir—swimming in the same dark waters. Your information providing a glimmer of light, toward which we have aimed our latest efforts. A fruitful partnership having blossomed these past few weeks since our victory at Princeton."

"Yes." Washington turned, gracing the two men with another weak smile. "Partnership. The very word to describe our *mutual* efforts, indeed. Which leads me to ask—have you heard news of what General Cornwallis is planning to do next?"

Charles shrugged, repressing an urge to yawn, worn to his core by fatigue, though his posture remained ramrod straight. "No news of any major movements, relayed from my sources. However—a reasonable guess would be to expect a series of armed forays made by the English throughout the countryside to supplement their supplies. Which will provide opportunity for colonial militia groups, familiar with the ground, to gnaw at their flanks, inflicting a death of a thousand cuts, as it were. Attacks based on intelligence gathered from eyes in every town. At every crossing. Collated, then provided you forthwith."

Greene studied Charles, a man whose identity was unknown to him, with a heavy responsibility assigned him by the General. The English were not bound by the civility of war when dealing with such men as these. Their fate, if caught out though carelessness, or revealed by the greed of turncoats within their shadowy group, would be to dangle from the end of tight rope. "You risk *much*. And yet seek no reward." Washington's second in command hardened his voice. "Why?"

Charles leaned back slightly, his posture relaxed, enjoying the heat from a nearby brazier. "A man acts *where* and *when* he chooses, against the few on behalf of the many. And, while the risk to myself and my companions is, as you point out, *dire*—it's worth the price we're sometimes made to pay."

"A dangerous game." Greene looked at Washington, noting the tall man was standing up, his attention turned away from the map. "What are *your* thoughts, General?"

"Few among us are born to lead. Most are meant to follow." Washington eyed both men individually. "Some men, led by their *own* view of the world about them, willingly search through the shadows, looking for a single blade of truth hidden in fields of lies. Or perhaps—trying to seek out the lie—in a forest of truths." He paused, glancing down at the map. "It would seem to depend on the man, and those he chooses to—associate with."

"Well said." Charles gave the General who was risking everything he had to lead the nascent nation, a solemn nod of his head. "Sir." Then he handed Greene a thick envelope, containing detailed maps showing potential English resupply routes, along with proposed lines of march throughout the countryside, raiding farms, communities, and storage silos, commandeering supplies in the name of the King.

"Copies of locations where our people will guide the militia to, working with their leadership groups. Liaison made with your own forces, based on anticipated numbers to be engaged."

Greene opened the trove of information, noting several pages stained with dried blood. He offered them to Washington, who shook his head, refusing to take them. Greene looked at Charles, his voice low, respectful in tone. "I would have a dozen more like you. My own advisors and scouts, forced to act under my direct orders, unable to move as freely about the countryside as are *your* independent agents."

"It is a commendable group you lead, General Green. One I am willing to work *with*—but not for." Charles stepped back, looking at Washington, who chose to ignore him. A nod from Greene released him, the warmth of the tent left behind as he stepped outside, stopping to look up at the stars, seeking out the constellations, marking them where they hovered in the chill air.

Greene followed him out and touched his shoulder, moving him further away from the sentries. Once they were out of earshot, he leaned in. "He—the General, is wont to wrap his hands around every element under his command. The idea of men like *you* is—counter to his *sensibilities*."

"Leaving him *exposed* to risk of losing his army one day, due to a lack of trust in the visibility he receives from men *and* women, willing to put their lives at risk—without *any* protection." Charles spit the words out without hesitation, having felt the disdain of Washington's false praise for having provided information vital to his continued success.

Greene kept his tone even, his eyes on the secretive man's face, seeing something there that caused a chill to run along his spine. "I can and *do* appreciate your position, assuming the ways in which your people gather your data to be—"

"*Immoral*, in nature." Charles saw Greene nod. "I am part of a group whose roots extend back *hundreds* of years, bringing a measure of balance against those seeking personal gratification at the expense of the rights and needs of the many, as was stated inside."

"I sense you speak of men standing on the *outside* of military or political circles."

Charles sighed. "I find myself in a quandary. Unable to speak clearly to a man I sense has the vision—that another lacks." He eyed Greene. "Please forgive my blunt assessment."

"Indeed. Though I realize the value the General brings to the field. A leader his soldiers will follow, no matter how difficult the road that lies ahead. A man capturing their—" Greene hesitated, shaking his head.

Charles gave him a quiet look. "Their minds. And hearts."

Greene nodded. "Yes. Willing to give him their *lives*—without hesitation." He sighed. "I am the better man at moving the army, protecting it using strategic ploys, avoiding *unnecessary* losses. But it is the *General* who holds them in his hands, as if a father with countless sons."

Charles looked back at the tent, seeing the shadow within, standing, no doubt, with chin in hand, staring at the map, trying to work out how best to wrest a new country away from the desperate grasp of those unwilling to let it go. Determined to lead his forces to victory. Then he gave Green a short nod and walked away.

※※※

A large man dressed in a gray cloak slipped from behind a stand of trees, his breath fogging the air as he watched Charles come to him. He gave the smaller, thin-framed man a cold-stiffened smile, seeing the anger in his eyes.

"Is ya belly warm with the thanks of them nobs—filling it near to bursting with their heartfelt appreciation?"

Charles raised one hand, holding an imagined knife to his throat, drawing it across. "One of them would prefer to give me a red-lipped smile. His words of gratitude for our ongoing efforts, as hollow as a porcupine's quill."

The big man turned away, leading Charles into the woods, two horses there, swinging their heads as the men approached, neither one making a noise, trained to silence while engaged in subversive movements, made through dangerous lands.

Charles mounted, turning toward a nearby marsh where several other unknown men were waiting. He grimaced, considering the difference between what he and his people were doing and those used by the secretive cabal, their real enemy. Other men without names, sent forth by those tugging the strings, sending them out to leverage the deaths of those standing between them and vast storerooms of gold, earned by replacing vital goods needed for support of a royal cause.

An owl called out, asking for their names. Charles let a wry grin find his lips, tempted to shout back, 'a damned fool, that's who', knowing it was a thankless task, risking his life to help change the tide of war. One destined to turn against the colonial forces once the summer season began.

CHAPTER NINE
MARISCHAL
SUMMER, 1777

Rory chucked Aaron on the shoulder. "Drink up, my friend—and *lose* your dour look. There are plenty of *other* fine ladies about." He noted Allen's look of caution. "What? Am I not allowed to point out that our woeful comrade has garnered the attention of every comely lass in Aberdeen proper, their eyes turning his way wherever he goes?"

"You've had too much drink, you besotted Scot, loosening your tongue. Best to gather it in, lest you're fed your *teeth* for dinner." Allen chased his comment with a wide smile. "Aaron has the right to mourn his way through life. No doubt destined to end up alone, living in the hills, without—" His words came to a stop, seeing a hard look in his friend's blue eyes.

"*You're* one to talk. Looking for a way out of your *own* engagement to a lady of nobility. A comely enough and *virtuous* woman, with gentle manners." He paused. "And *sound* teeth! A rarity in English folk."

Allen blushed, then looked away, studying a buxom woman parting a sea of young men and old, serving drinks at the tavern, just down the road from Marischal. "Virtue is—*overrated* at times." One of the serving girls caught his eye, noticing his stare as she passed by, smiling, a light floral scent left in her wake.

"Your intended is indeed a *fine* lady." Rory tapped his stein against Allen's. "But she's not *here*. Nor are you *formally* pledged."

Aaron watched his English friend's face, pleased when Allen shook his head, his honor beyond reproach. "My father's made *his* pledge, and I have promised to abide by it." Allen considered for a moment, taking a small swallow of the ale. "And Lady Grayson is a *good* match, with *flawless* reputation."

"As is your *own*." Aaron tapped Allen on the shoulder. "Different rules here, in Scotland. With life grasped by its throat and shaken a bit, sharing of a drink or two, then starting again the next day." He gave Rory a grin, the Scot downing his third drink, eyes bright, a bleary look on his face. "As our brother here is proof of."

The young server returned with the total owed, her hand out, waiting. Allen reached for his purse, Rory stopping him. "My treat, brother. I've ridden on your—on your wagon, long enough. Time to stand on my own—" He hesitated, covering his mouth, the server pulling an empty tankard from the tray she carried, handing it to him as he started toward the door.

Aaron followed, waiting as Rory reached an alleyway and spilled the ale he'd only just imbibed, handing him a rag grabbed from the bar. "A high price paid for the *borrowing* of refreshment." He shook his head. "Not like a Scot to squander hard-earned coin, with nothing to show for it, other than a stain on the ground."

Rory raised one hand, waving it slightly. "Enough. I am in a mix of emotions this day—with a decision made that will alter my future."

Aaron narrowed his eyes, looking at his friend with a concerned look. "Have *you* also gone and pledged your troth to some sweet damsel?"

Rory shook his head, slowly, his stomach still unsettled. "Nae." He gave Aaron a steady look. "I've decided to go. To go over to help the colonials. Signed myself aboard a transport this very day. Departure in a fortnight. With plans to jump ship once in the colonies, then join them, doing all I can to help throw off the yoke of British rule." He paused, covering a wet burp with his hand. "A better chance of it happening *there*, than here. Our leaders' wills weakened by the false titles given them, overlooking the squalor of those forced from their highland homes."

"You cannot be *serious*." Aaron stepped ahead and lowered his voice. "A *fool's* game, being played by men led by *inept* leaders."

"A *victory*, recently won." Rory stiffened his posture. "The broadsheets are full of news of enlistments by colonials eager to show the — the *bloody* redcoats what men can do when fighting for the right of self-governance."

"Rory—you *must* reconsider. The risk to you—"

"The decision's made and no words of yours will move me from it. I'll join men willing to revolt against tyranny, unlike those here—" He paused again, looking about, as if hunting for snakes lying coiled in the trampled patch of muddy earth. "Who've made *no* move to join me and several of my hometown friends."

Aaron stepped back, giving Rory a hard look. "There is little pride earned from chasing a *fool's* dream, trying to find it in the deaths of men led to their slaughter by those whose feet ride high in the stirrups, and not down in the bloody muck."

"As if *you've* any knowledge of such things, living your life away— nae, *above* it all in your little kingdom in the clouds." Rory swayed, his face red from anger, his words tossed as if embers from a glowing circle of flames. "One of a handful of holdings that never felt the press of boots to their necks. Your family—"

"*Careful*, my brother. I'm more than willing to offer forbearance due to your inebriated state, though the bond, once torn *apart*—will not easily be re-mended."

Allen's voice slid through the heated air, having paid their tab before coming outside, joining his two friends. "We've come too far, too closely bound, to falter this close to the end of our efforts to make something of our *own* selves, stepping out from behind the shadows of our fathers." He glanced at Aaron. "Including your mother's *excellent* work, done these past twenty years and more."

The mention of his parents helped cool Aaron's temper. He stepped back a pace, hands crossed, aware of the dangerous game his family had played, with consummate skill, during the highland clearances. His father's service records and marital ties to the daughter of Lord

Habersham used by the laird of clan Scott as a shield, protecting the clan's interests during the forced migration of highlanders from their ancestral lands. Great Uncle Shaun forced to bend a knee to English rule, while holding a dagger behind his back. Willing to play the long game in trying to win a political battle, fought with words and coins, not muskets and swords.

Rory blinked, a chill wind swirling through a section of pens and feedlots, bunched herds of Scottish cows and pockets of rooting swine turning their backs to it, their heads lowered, teasing bits of food from the dark soil, churned by their hooves. "I spoke *rashly*, without care. My apologies, Aaron. I never meant—"

"Was but a passing breeze, with my feathers left unruffled." Aaron went over and touched Rory on his shoulder. "We will discuss your plans on the morrow. For now, let us seek *less* ale here and more substantial fare—back at Marischal."

※※※

The morning broke beneath a steady downpour, the air heavy with moisture and low-lying clouds, painting the horizon dull gray. Aaron stood in an oiled cloak, on the top of the university roof, one foot resting in the same squared opening where he'd stood and broken the heart of the woman he'd loved, then let go of. The wind tugged at his clothes, his head uncovered, hair wet, clinging to his cheeks.

The pealing of church bells announced the hour. It was early, dawn only just recently arrived. The city, spread out below, seemed to be biding its time, slow to awaken, the streets empty of foot traffic with heavily laden wagons winding their way through the muddy streets, bringing in food and goods to feed the needs of the thousands of people living there.

"You are standing at the precipice again, my lad." Stanton came over, clad in the same dark garb, his head covered, eyes shadowed by a hood on his head. "Regretting your decision made—no doubt."

Aaron nodded. "More than one of them, sir. Though not that of letting her go—your dear daughter." He turned and nodded; his tears mixed with the rain on his cheeks. "It was, as you suggested, the right path for her. Your words prescient as to my, as you named it —destiny."

"You are planning to join the colonist's cause—alongside your intrepid Scottish classmate."

Aaron lowered his head, a smile on his lips, water dripping from his firm chin. "You are, again, without peer when it comes to seeing over the horizon."

"Without benefit of the 'sight' your lot are known to hold claim to." Stanton stepped closer to the edge of the roof, looking down. "I respect the strength it took, in releasing my daughter. To see beyond your own desires, bowing to a father's wishes. The mark of a man worthy of the last name you were born to." He faced Aaron. "I wish you well, knowing you're going off to fight against everything I stood for, while serving alongside your grandfather. What we *both* bled for, so many years ago."

"My father, as well. Paying as heavy a price on behalf of the British Empire. His story known to me in detail." Aaron paused. "Written in his journals."

"With your *own* tales soon to be penned, no doubt."

Aaron angled his head, a considering look in his eyes. "You believe me a man destined to conflict. I would suggest it to be a *lesser* role. That of helping guide a good friend along a—more *sensible* course."

Stanton held out his hand, waiting as the young man he'd come to admire shook it with a firm grip. "There will be an opening here for you—when you return. You have my promise."

"I will hold you to it, sir." Aaron turned away, heading to a doorway, leading down a spiraled stairwell. As he slipped from sight, Stanton sighed, aware in his heart the lad would never return. That his future, his path through life, lay over the tumultuous motion of a wide, windswept gray-green sea.

CHAPTER TEN
COOCH'S BRIDGE
LATE SUMMER, 1777

Rory clenched his fingers on the musket he was holding, his breathing loud as he stood alongside the edge of a field, a dozen men to his right, with twice as many to his left. Aaron leaned over and reached out, nudging his friend on the shoulder. "Relax. *Ease* your mind. It's only wearing you out, anticipating what's to come."

"Easy for *you* to say, having been through it before." Rory gave Aaron a quick glance, licking his dry lips, trying to take a deep breath, failing, left panting like an overheated dog. Several men of the militia force smirked, then noted Aaron's cold stare and looked away, their smiles gone, remembering their first time facing the possibility of injury or death.

"Not the same *now* as then. Forced to protect my family, with my focus aimed out, not in. With no regard for my *own* safety, only theirs."

"Then would you be so kind as to go stand on the approach to the bridge, musket raised, so I can shift my attention to saving your skinny *Scotch-English* ass?" Rory chased the question with a smile, tight at the corners, his eyes filled with awareness of what was heading their way. Rumors of Hessian mercenaries in support of a column of English troops, escorting supply wagons. Their own force, recently formed, made up of veterans from the previous war and young volunteers scrounged from the docks as they slipped away from transport ships in Perth Amboy. Givin a handful of hours training in the use of musket and bayonet before marching out to meet the enemy at a small bridge.

Aaron chuckled. "I'd only end up frightening them away, leaving us without the chance to prove ourselves." He glanced to his right, watching as two scouts returned from their forward position, coming to alert them the moment of truth would soon be upon them.

※※※

Smoke drifted back from the first line of men, ramrods clicking as new rounds were prepared, using their teeth to tear the ends from reloads of powder and ball, shoved down musket barrels, their hands stained black with the residue of burnt powder. Another volley sounded out from a second line of men who rose and stepped forward between the first line, putting down a score of men in green coats beneath black hats.

Aaron pulled Rory back with him, the other boy trembling, his trousers stained with urine, musket unfired. They slipped behind the second line, joining the others who were pulling back, finishing their reloading, ready to stop, stand and fire again.

"Your *musket!*" Aaron reached out and tried to pry it from Rory's hands, intending to use it once he'd fired his own, again, aware his friend was in shock. Unable to force its release, he turned around and took aim, waiting for the line of men in front to pull back. Once they'd cleared his line of sight, he raised the weapon, centering the barrel on a thick chested man doing the same, fifty paces away.

They fired at the same moment, a fog of smoke hiding the result, a whisper of lead bees sighing past his ear, with grunts of pain coming from each side, the return fire striking home in the bodies of men left falling away, their rifles dropping to the ground as they struggled to move back.

Rory called out, his voice a high-pitched gasp, words pinched off from pain. Aaron spun, watching as his friend stepped back several paces, hands on his abdomen, a dark stain spreading beneath his fingers, other men in militia colors stumbling away with wounds to their bodies, or assisting comrades unable to retreat on their own.

Shouts from behind pulled his head around, the men on the roadway making their advance, bayonets leveled, held in the hands of men with serious expressions. Professionals, Aaron told himself, grabbing Rory around his waist before he could crumple to the ground, seeing the rest of the line folding in two, the center holding for a moment before breaking, disintegrating into knots of men running away or stopping to provide cover for friends lying on the ground, dead or dying.

Rory clung to Aaron, his eyes wide, whites showing, face pale, his breath coming in short gasps. Aaron knelt, folding him over his shoulder, standing up and heading into a thicket of small trees and brush, moving at an angle to the line of men in approach. A shout in a foreign language called out an order, causing him to force his way forward, his thighs trembling as he climbed a small rise, aiming for an opening in a tumbled fall of rocks at the base of a fractured granite wall. He let Rory slip to the ground, then grabbed him by his shoulders, pulling him into the shadowed opening, hiding him from sight. Then he exited, seeing the flicker of light reflecting from polished steel as faceless men pushed through the thick woods, calling out as they stopped and thrust honed points of steel into the protesting bodies of wounded men.

Aaron shouted, drawing their attention, then darted into the woods, hoping to draw them away.

※※※

It was dusk. Heavy clouds, pregnant with rain, filtered the light, blending shadows and rocks into a dull canvas of gray. He finally found the opening in the rock fall, crawling in, reaching out to touch Rory, afraid he'd find his friends body stiff, cold to the touch. A hand reached out, taking his wrist in a talon grip, refusing to let go.

"Aaron?" The sound of Rory's voice was a thin whisper, though his grasp was strong as he clung to Aaron's lower arm, afraid of his leaving again.

"I'm here. The Hessians are gone. The militia scattered. Survivors headed to the barn where we formed up, earlier." Aaron slid alongside his wounded friend, touching his midriff gingerly, his fingers coming away bloody.

"Aaron? Is that you?"

"I'm here." Aaron clenched his friend's other hand, hearing the weakness in Rory's voice. "I'm—here."

"It's so dark out. With no stars."

"Yes." Aaron swallowed his fear. "It's late. Heavy clouds overhead, hiding them from view." Aaron waited, silence stretching into a long minute, beginning to fear the worst.

"I'm cold. My back—it aches." Rory rolled his head to one side, a groan slipping from between his clenched teeth. "I'm sorry. I couldn't do it. Couldn't aim—couldn't pull—failed—"

"Rory?" Aaron touched his face, then his throat, feeling for a pulse, finding none. He lowered his head, pressing an ear against Rory's chest, his friend's heart stilled. He reached out, closing Rory's eyes, then leaned back, sadness welling up within him, his hands shaking, hating the moment, but not the men involved. Aware everyone had been where their destinies had brought them to, including himself. Then he stiffened his resolve, knowing what he had to do. Wait for full night to fall, then take his friend to where the others had regrouped, laying him to rest with words spoken over him. Then he'd rejoin the militia, who would be licking their wounds, and begin again. But not with musket and bayonet. Next time he faced the enemy, Aaron swore it would be with a bow, and arrows tipped with honed heads. And a small sword, near to hand.

※※※

Charles studied the paper, going through the list of names gathered by an unknown man working alongside one of the militia groups. His eyes found, then stared at one name, a shiver running through him at the thought of a friend's son falling in some meaningless action on behalf of an unwinnable cause.

"He was unharmed?"

An old man with a crutch under one arm, missing his leg below the left knee, nodded. "The only blood was on his clothing, that of a close friend, carried in on his shoulder. Another newcomer, like himself." The veteran gave Charles a hard stare. "I thought I recognized him, before learning of his name. Like I was seeing a ghost, that of his father—come back to life. A man I served with until I lost this." He looked down at the stump below his knee, then back up. "A lad like him, if he's anything like his father in mind, body, and spirit—*wasted* in the militia. Or the army. Better if he's kept close to hand."

"Used for raids." Charles pursed his lips, looking out at the encampment, a mix of both militia and colonial soldiers, some of them laughing as they prepared for the next engagement, while others milled about in restless knots of somber faced soldiers, their spirits broken by the forced retreat at the hands of professional soldiers in green coats. "Thank you—for this."

Charles held out his hand, the old man taking it, then turning away. He stopped, looking back over his shoulder, leaning on the padded crosspiece of his crutch. "He's *different*. Watched as he sat there, crafting himself a bow. One near as long as himself. Worked up a few dozen arrows, too. Using scraps of metal, heated, hammered, formed into heads with the help of a local smithy, lending him use of anvil and forge."

"He's gifted with the use of one. A longbow—having learned as a child." Charles gave the other man another nod then walked away, heading toward the throng of disheartened soldiers. He smiled, knowing he'd just found the first member of a new force, one he'd form from experienced, battle-hardened men, and the son of a gifted strategist. A group of insurgents capable of operating independently, interdicting the supply lines of the British army.

⁂

A column of wagons, protected in front and rear by a split platoon of soldiers in red and white uniforms, neared a narrowed section of a road they'd been following for the better part of three days. Their pace was slow, the wagons weighed down with materials seized from warehouses, local farms, and homes along the route. Houses and barns left burnt to the ground if their occupants dared to resist the demand for half of their holdings. Stubborn farmers and shopkeepers losing everything if they resisted, including their lives and those of their families, left tied up inside the buildings, then set afire.

Two soldiers marched alongside an officer on horseback, their purses heavy with coins found beneath the floorboards of the last house they'd searched through then burnt. Each one eyed the other, sworn to secrecy. A year's pay gained for little enough risk, other than the scratches on one man's cheek from the fingernails of a young girl, forced onto the dirt floor of a stable, her maidenhead plucked before slitting her throat.

A hissing sound, followed by a thud and low moan of pain from above, caused the two of them to look up, noting a surprised expression on their officer's face as he stared at an object jutting from his chest. A short length of dark wood, with three brown and black feathers fastened to it. He touched it with his fingers, his mouth dropping open, blood gushing over his teeth. Then his eyes folded back, his body slumping to one side as he fell out of saddle, landing on the ground with a muffled thump.

One of the soldiers spun around and started to yell a warning, a second shaft entering the front of his throat, ending his effort as it slipped through his neck, embedding itself in the side of one of the heavy wagons. Another shaft caught the other man as he turned to run, punching him beneath one arm, burrowing into his chest, his musket falling into the muddy road alongside the other's. His knees folded, leaving him stretched out face first on the ground, hands grasping the wet soil, trying to pull himself away.

A flurry of shots rang out, bracketing the escorts with a hail of lead balls, smacking into exposed flesh, tearing their way through red cloth, men dying by the handfuls as several more arrows came hissing in, quickly pinning the cloth on the backs of three men who were almost clear of the killing zone. Their bodies twisted as they fell, their cries of pain absorbed by a spattering of raindrops, starting to fall.

Not a single man in a red uniform remained standing as a group of men in drab clothing moved in. They carefully prodded the bodies with the ends of their bayonets, looking for wounded among the dead, the honed tips used to silence pleas for mercy, wielded by hard-eyed men who'd witnessed the carnage left in the British column's wake.

Their leader came up and watched as a young man went about the grisly task of removing arrows from the bodies of men pinioned by his deadly shafts. "Six of them down by your actions. In less time than it takes for a man to empty his bladder."

Aaron nodded, inspecting the shafts and heads carefully, snapping a few honed points off, tucking them away in his pocket, the shafts splintered as the soldiers, their lungs penetrated, had thrashed about in agony, left to drown in their own blood. "If you would heed my advice and let me train up some of the other men, *all* could have been put down, without the firing of a single shot."

The older man, dressed in leather leggings and an old militia coat having seen service in the previous war, smiled, then shook his head. "I've told you no—*twice*. Won't have the same argument again." He turned his head and spit. "Besides, we both know it would take *too* long, getting any of 'em caught up to where *you* are."

"Twenty men in a doubled line. Twelve arrows to the minute, released into a compressed line of infantry in steady advance from a hundred paces away. Four volleys before they close within musket range. Near a thousand shafts dropping in amongst them. Tell me— how would that *not* be an advantage in fighting this war?"

"You'll not be confusing me with numbers like those. I know what I *know*—and that's final. I've given you the right to tag along. So, finish collecting your prickers—and make ready to depart. I've an itch in my back that tells me there's trouble heading our way. We need haul these wagons away, and soon. Our side desperate for what's in 'em, almost as much as the damned English."

Aaron watched the decorated veteran slouch away, biding his time, knowing someone would eventually be willing to listen, releasing him to form a band of men to harry the enemy forces as they left their city redoubts. Soldiers sent out to gather supplies, or replace losses to their armies in the field, seeking to engage with then destroy Washington's army, once they could pin it in place.

❦❦❦

Charles approached the shelter, a rectangle of stained cloth, angled from a ridgepole to the ground, a figure poised inside, squatting with legs crossed, working on retipping a thick bundle of shafts. A longbow, crafted from elm, leaned nearby, unstrung, allowing the wood to maintain its strength. He stopped, watching for a moment until the young man looked up, his eyes widening in recognition as he set the shafts down and stood up.

"Charles? Is that *you?*" Aaron came over, head angled slightly. "You've shorn your curly locks and *roughened* your genteel demeanor."

"I've adjusted to the local environment." Charles took Aaron's hand, squeezing it, feeling the strength in his fingers. The boy was known to him by frequent visits made to his childhood home in Bristol, and in the cities of Bath and London during his father's political service. "While I see *you* are still on familiar ground, if somewhat lower in altitude." He paused, placing his hand on Aaron's thick shoulder. "I heard about the loss of your friend. It must have been difficult, happening so soon, and under such *terrible* circumstances."

Aaron lowered his eyes. "Time—makes no difference. Nor the means of it." He raised his head. "I've managed to balance the books on his account—with more work yet to do."

"I'm surprised, your parents allowing you to join the effort over here, considering what your father went through and barely managed to survive."

"I didn't solicit their permission. The decision made in haste to try and keep the friend you mentioned—to stop him from doing something foolish." Aaron lowered his voice, subdued. "Failed in that." He sighed. "And not likely to be my *last.*" Then he forced a grin, his lips tight at the corners. "No one here able to be convinced to a change of tactics. Or weaponry used."

Charles nodded. "Why I'm here, to move you from the militia group to one with a more—*open-minded* approach, created to interdict the enemy's movements throughout the countryside over the next few months." He waited to see the young man's reaction.

Aaron nodded, his eyes without expression. "Why?"

Charles shrugged. "In order to curtail, cut off, and constrain—"

"Why are *you* here, Charles? Not exactly the cup of tea I'm used to seeing you drink from. Yet here you stand, as if it is completely normal, with you showing up without an explanation for your presence—far from where I last saw you."

"You have your father's eye for things." Charles nodded. "I'm part of a subversive group doing what it can to interfere with the operations of another equally subversive group that is trying to interfere with the direction this world is heading in." Aaron didn't respond, looking straight into Charles's eyes, causing the older man to blush. "I'm trying to hold back the tide, with little more than a teacup. Along with a small army of like-minded people, dedicating their lives to the same cause. And we require an armed group designed to perform missions that will cripple the efforts of the British army *here*. Causing disruption to the plans of people in power over *there*."

"I *read* my father's journals. Spoke at length with him as to the proposals made by him in Commons. Before he disappeared, with his death reported in rumors brought to our door."

"I spoke with him—a few months ago. With your father and his uncle, both." Charles hesitated a moment, seeing Aaron's hooded gaze widen slightly. "Your great uncle is a *dangerous* man—with cunning mind. We shared a bottle of your great grandfather's whiskey, up at the small stone house in the hills."

Aaron nodded, then took a deep breath, exhaling slowly. "No secrets, then—between us."

"No." Charles hesitated, giving the serious faced lad a quiet look. "Another thing for you to consider before agreeing to the assignment. If you join—you're all but guaranteed to end up dead."

Aaron looked away, watching as several men, hard-edged with loose gaits passed by. "Will I be able to make a difference—like my father did in the previous war?"

"Yes. You will." Charles felt a chill worm along his spine. "Though your tale will never be told."

Aaron nodded. "Then I better prepare more arrows." He turned around and went back to his shelter, returning to his labors while Charles watched him, remembering the young boy, tottering on wobbly legs, growing into a child with a discerning expression, absorbing everything he could find in books, or in the world outside his door. A gift to his parents. To his family and clan in the highland hills. A deadly tool, now, honed to a specific purpose. One he would use, then let go of, his destiny hidden in the shadows of a dark and unforgiving world.

CHAPTER ELEVEN
HIGHLAND MANOR
LATE SUMMER, 1777

"This is—*not* possible." Sinclair gave Shaun a stare freezing him in place. "You *cannot* be telling me this." She turned around and faced the wall, her hands clenched, knuckles white as she trembled with fear.

"I'll go—go there and find him. Bring him back. Bring *both* lads back." Shaun stepped closer, starting to reach out to her, then lowered his hand. "He won't be hard to find. A man like him—"

Sinclair spun around, her light-colored eyes gleaming with tears and anger. "A *boy*, Shaun! Only a *boy*, wrapped in the body of a man. But *still* a child—*my* child. Somewhere—*out* there, God knows where, at the beck and call of men. Desperate men. Dangerous men—willing to lead innocents like him to the—"

"He *does* know, Sinclair." Shaun moved closer. "*God*. Holding your son, now fully a man, in *his* hands. Your fears, warranted, as other men will see greatness in him, bending his abilities to their *own* ends." He stepped closer. "But Aaron's formed of the same steel as his Da. And you." He paused, daring to reach out and touch her clenched hands. "He will be *bent*, yes—but *not* broken."

"Men like *you!*" Sinclair stepped back. "Leading people by their noses, using them to *your* own purpose. Watching them die, at times, on your whim, brought to their—"

"On the *clan's* behalf, *woman!*" Shaun fought against loss of emotional control, knowing Sinclair would meet him with fury and fire, loving her for the woman she was, yet in fear of her wrath, in equal measure. He stepped away, going to the fire glowing in the hearth, one hand pressed against the mantle as he stared into the coals.

He felt a light touch on his shoulder, soft words in his ear. "He is part of *you*, too. With a depth to him—to his *soul* not unlike your own. Tied to you by blood. Bonded to a man he has looked up to, ever since he was old enough to run and greet you, with a smile on his face."

Shaun nodded, afraid to turn around, knowing he would take her in his arms, holding her close, unable to let go. He fought back the urge, settling for a draw. Aware he hadn't the strength to ever defeat it.

"Our boy—" Sinclair swallowed her fear. "My *son*, a man of the highlands—is on his path. As his father predicted. *Foresaw*. With me not wanting to believe it possible, seeing only the child."

Shaun twisted to one side, glancing out the salon window, looking toward the snow-topped peaks in the distance. "I'll go. Go to the mountain, letting him know."

A voice rumbled its way across the room. "I already *do*." Harold stepped in, coming over and taking Sinclair in his arms, her will breaking, her body trembling as he held onto her, supporting her, his eyes on Shaun. "I'll *find* him. I've contacts there who'll help me do so."

"Charles?" Shaun uttered the name, seeing Sinclair react on hearing it.

She looked up, tears in her eyes, seeing Harold's nod. "He's *dead*— these past two years."

Harold leaned in, his forehead on hers. "Charles is alive, and over there. Has been for months." He cut Sinclair off before she could ask the question, one he could see blossoming in her eyes. "He came *here*, before leaving. Came to let me know where he was bound and *why*. Revealing secrets, ones I *cannot* share, not even with you, no matter the cost to me in feeling your anger."

"The *hell* with my feelings, *husband!*" Sinclair pulled back, enough to be able to look at him fully, her hands grasping his upper arms. "Can he *truly* help you to find him?" She gave Harold a firm look, still trembling, though back in control. "Can he help you to find, then bring our son back home?" When Harold nodded, she pressed her hands against his chest. "Go then. This hour. Do what you must to bring him back to me."

Harold slipped away, heading back to the croft house to gather his things. Shaun joining him when he returned, a fresh horse in hand, the two of them heading to Glasgow to arrange his nephew's passage on a ship bound for the colonies, climbing aboard during the night, remaining below deck, unseen.

⚘⚘⚘

Meghan waited until the everyone had cleared the room, her mother heading to the kitchen where her grandmother was at her usual routine of preparing food for the day. Her father, off to his aerie. Gran Uncle Shaun in the stables, preparing the horses. She slid along the hall, entering the salon, the vibrations of energy still reverberating around the room. She went over and looked through the window, seeing her father riding off, understanding little of what she'd overheard, but aware her brother was in peril. Somewhere over the sea. Over the horizon, out of her reach.

The knowledge was beyond her capacity to bear, causing her to sink into a large leather chair, bringing her knees up, circling them with her arms, trying to find a place for the pain in her heart, the worry in her mind. For the hole felt in her soul. A hand touched her head, fingers softly rubbing her scalp beneath the thick fall of her sun-kissed hair.

Marion leaned down, her lips near to her sister's ear. "Everyone is so—*emotional* this day." She curled up alongside Meghan. "Our brother is where he *should* be. As are *we*. And you *will* see him again. I promise you. Everyone will—except our grandmother and gran uncle." She paused. "And me."

Meghan twisted around, facing her. "But—*why?*"

Marion smiled. "Because grandmother will soon pass on. And our gran uncle and I will be staying *here*. While the three of you go off on a *grand* adventure. Like characters in a story, finding love, pain, joy, and all the other things waiting for you—over there." Then she gathered her sister in her arms, the two of them sharing the warmth of each other's body. As if babes again, in their mother's womb.

※※※

Harold tossed in his hammock, the roll of the ship swinging him to and fro, roused from sleep by images of his son in distress. His arms reaching out, calling to him. Unable to let him know he was a week away at most. The winds favorable since leaving the dock in Port of Clyde, after making a furtive visit to the university before embarking. Frowned upon by Shaun, his thoughts made clear in a terse exchange.

"You've *no* idea of the mettle of this man. *None!*" Shaun's words, clipped at each end, revealed his ire, having managed to secure his nephew an anonymous passage on board a cargo ship. Harold now risking all to contact the rector at Marischal. A man he'd already met with himself, when told of the wayward youth's sudden disappearance and reasons behind it. Having come to investigate when Aaron had been a day late getting home after the end of his second term.

"I've already had from him *all* there is to tell. Nothing gained in revealing yourself to him, the man and the rest of the world thinking you *dead*, years ago." Shaun paused, knowing his argument had fallen on deaf ears, Harold staring back with a patient expression on his lined face.

"He will see *me*, and know me not as a man of reputation, but as a *father*, wanting to learn about a son's motives."

"I told you already it was a broken heart led him to it. And no more than—"

I would hear if from *him*, direct. Father to father." Harold shrugged. "You've done all and more to help see this through. I appreciate it, Uncle, I do. But there are things in play here that are beyond your ken. So—your *trust* and a *message* delivered is what I'm asking from you this day."

Shaun arranged a meeting in the university stables, deemed acceptable by Harold, facing Stanton there, amidst the mixed odors of horses, leather, and manure.

"You are—familiar to my eye." Stanton proffered a bottle, dark bodied, with stoppered opening. Harold shook his head, watching as the large man took a few shuffling steps, going over and sitting down on a bale of hay. "I can blink my eyes and see him there, beside you. Your *father*. When he was still hale. Before suffering his injuries. Before he saved my life, risking his own. Left paying dearly for the deed." Stanton worked the cork from the neck of the bottle, tipping it to his mouth and swallowing. He lowered it, wiping his lips, staring at Harold.

Harold leaned back against a wooden support; his arms crossed. "My son—he did not make his decision based on a relationship gone sour. He would have hied to the hills. To the high places, bow in hand, a stag made to pay with its life for his sorrow—if such was the case."

"True. It was not." Stanton fixed Harold with a firm gaze. "Your son, a man beyond reproach, broke two hearts, before—" He paused, glancing toward the opening of the stable. "He heard the words of a father, asking him on behalf of a vision seen—to do what was needed to prevent a greater hurt, later on."

"That would have broken your daughter's heart, along with his own."

Stanton nodded, not surprised by how quickly the man standing opposite him had worked it out. "Your son's honor was before him, everywhere he went. Whether in classroom, stables, or helping those in need on the outskirts of Aberdeen, lending his time, sweat and—occasionally—his blood, providing them clean water and a reliable source of income."

"He went in support of another."

Stanton looked down, nodding. "You have the truth of it, based on what another student told me. In support of a young Scot, as close to him as a brother." He paused. "The news related to me by a student named Allen. An Englishman from a fine family. Not unlike the one I arranged betrothal of my daughter to. Which I now question—"

"Do *not*. As a father, you should not have to explain, or question your instincts regarding what's best for your child."

Stanton nodded. "I thank you for that. Whether it's true in this case or not."

"The one he went in support of. His name?"

"Rory, as he called himself. Ruairidh, on his forms. Thomson. A fine lad and close friend to your son and the other boy, Allen. The three of them, a perfect match of disparate skills. Often finding me with a grin hidden behind a stern look, admonishing them for one mild infraction or another."

"As any parent often does, when raising willful children."

"Yes." Stanton looked up, holding out the bottle. Aaron took it, taking a drink, handing it back, watching as the heavy-set man did the same. "To our *children*, may they ever be so. Living their *own* lives, as destiny dictates. Following their own path. Hopeful it will coincide with ours, at times."

"Is there anything else to tell me in relate to his destination—now that his motivation has been made clear?"

"They shipped out aboard a ship bound to Perth Amboy. Where the trail to find them will begin." Stanton struggled to his feet, eschewing use of the cane. He stretched out his hand, Harold taking it. "Good fortunes to you, my unknown friend, father to a lad I'd happily have laid claim to as my own."

"Along with others who know him. My son a man with a good sense of who he is." Harold paused. "The same offered regarding your daughter. No doubt a lass equal in spirit and spit to my lad. Able to have caught his eye and heart—surely a woman of beauty, in both soul and substance." He shook the other man's hand, then walked away, stopping as the other man called out.

"God speed, sir. May your father watch over you—helping to guide you safely home."

Harold felt the roll of the ship, the bow finding an angle more suited to the wind and northerly current of the great sea, adjusting itself to a slight change of course. Close, Harold whispered to himself, alone in a cramped space below deck, assigned to galley stores again. His presence enough to keep most of the rats at bay.

He closed his eyes, aware they were nearing shore, about to nose into the mouth of a wide river, fresh water mixing with salt. Another day slipping into night needed to reach his point of debarkation, slipping over the side with a well-oiled pack, sealed against moisture, swimming to shore then disappearing into the woods, following his nose, trusting his instincts to lead him to his son.

※※※

Charles looked up, one of his unknown men at the flap of his shelter, looking in, eyebrows raised. He stepped back, holding it open, allowing a tall man to step through. Charles set down a map he'd been preparing, then motioned to a stump of wood, watching as Harold sat down. "Was expecting you to show up—at *some* point."

"And I am now *here*." Harold gave the small man a solemn nod, noting his curly hair had filled back in, framing his narrow face in a cluster of tightly braided twists of black hair. He followed it with a stiff question. "Where's my *son?*"

Charles leaned back, staring at Harold. "Out—and about. Where? I cannot say. And wouldn't tell you if I *knew*." He paused, raising one hand. "Which I *do* not, I can assure you. Helping keep him safe if I fall into the hands of those searching him out." Charles let a thin smile slip across his full lips. "He is a *large* thorn, pricking the English in sensitive areas, then slipping away to sting them again." He gave a slight shake of his head. "Masterful, how he's taken control of his destiny. A far better student of how to manipulate events to his every advantage than you were able to do, despite your broad acclaim to fame."

"A tool for you, then. And nothing more." Harold leaned forward, hands clenched. "As *I* have been, since our first meeting, so many years ago." He gave the man he'd once counted as a close friend a cold stare. "You're little different from those you profess to resist. Using people to your own view of the world as you see it to be. Of how you think it should be, ignoring the truth that it is *exactly* as it *is*, and will never be anything more. Like the weather, with regular periods of seasonal change."

"Or—like the tide." Charles returned a steady gaze. "Sitting in the shadows alongside a dozen thrones, lining the shore, my partners and I trying to hold it back with our wills. As *you* once tried to do."

"To no *beneficial* effect." Harold stared down at the ground. "Nothing changed by my having killed so—"

Charles laughter stopped Harold. "You've *no* idea of what you accomplished. Unlike your *son*, who's doing his best to slow down the *entire* English army." He shook his head, giving Harold a look of sincere appreciation. "You *forestalled* a force prepared to raise an insurrection, delaying it by a full half-year and more, tearing their plans to tatters. With others having to reassemble the entire network. More damage done by your lighting of a single fuse than all the cannons and muskets fired since the *beginning* of this revolution." He paused again. "With your son's arrows now added to the mix."

Harold looked up. "My son—my boy—is hunting *men?*"

"He's hunting *answers* to tough questions, each one testing his innate knowledge of how to seek out and then place himself precisely where he and those men assigned him can lie in ambush. Striking with deadly precision, then fading away into the shadows, to strike again. Causing havoc, along with sleepless nights for men lying in their beds. Officers and enlisted men alike. Sentries, firing at shadows in the night, afraid of a knife to their throat should they dare close their eyes to yawn."

Harold looked down. "I've created a darker version of the man I was. Of the son I raised. As if leading him to a bow would have kept him away from pistol or musket, preventing him engaging in the shedding of other men's blood."

"You allowed him to take his rightful place in this time of *profound* change. A bastion of freedom, built on the bodies of those on *both* sides, helping create something where—where the *lantern* of democracy might light the way for others to see, and follow the *same* path."

"A *dream*. One doomed to failure. With people believing they can outrun the failures of past societies. No republic left un-shattered by the incessant *greed* of a handful of men, seeking power over others. No words, inscribed on mud, stone, or parchment, ever enough to halt the fall of civilizations once those made victims of it come and batter down the gates."

"A *drink*, my friend." Charles held out a glass. "To toast the divide of faith between us. One I have straddled the line of for many years, believing in the possibility of seeing a democratic society rise once again, from a seed planted *here* on the edge of a *vast* continent, with countless acres of rich soil helping it to spread."

Harold shook his head, holding out his hand, waiting as Charles filled his glass with watered wine. "At the expense of those people already here and willing to fight for it as well. Either with or against us, when the *opposite* should be the aim of those who would rule this phantasmal vision, you propose."

"To the *dream* of it made real, then. On the shoulders of those with the will and capability to see it through." Charles held out his glass, touching it to Harold's, both men drinking while staring at each other, a small fire in a brazier casting their shadows on the fluttering wall of the fabric enclosure.

※※※

Forty men in red uniforms marched with their muskets shouldered alongside four wagons loaded down with supplies. Two officers, mounted on horseback, rode together at the front. They watched as a handful of men in leather clothing scouted ahead, making regular darts into the woods, seeking signs of ambush from the group of irregulars who'd been attacking them from out of dense cover with arrows and accurate musket fire.

"It was foolish, the major having ignored the use of natives to clear the way. His death—a hard one. Earned by his disregard to my suggestion of more flexible tactics to be employed." The officer, a captain in his late twenties, reached up and tucked a stray curl of hair back in place, his wig jostled as his mount stepped into a hollow in the rutted surface of the road.

"As too, that of his men." The other officer, younger, a second lieutenant, tossed the remark over his shoulder, his head swiveling about, as if trying to see in all directions at once, heeding advice overheard from a grizzled sergeant major, a veteran of the French and Indian wars, cautioning his men to so the same.

"The men will *follow* orders. Good ones *or* poor. It is incumbent on those with authority to set the tone. Theirs to obey—or feel the lash."

"Of course." The younger officer hesitated. "Sir."

The captain, leader of the supply train and tasked with getting it safely to the encampment a dozen miles ahead, yawned, then coughed. He coughed again, his hand going to his chest, touching the pointed end of an arrow protruding from his chest, just below his throat, a white wrap of linen darkening with blood as started to choke. The other officer stared, watching as the eyes of his superior rolled back in his head, his body falling away to one side, head lending on the ground below his mount with a sickening crack, his long legs trembling as he lay there.

"We are—" Another arrow ended his attempt to call out, punching through the left side of his chest, unable to shout as blood filled his lungs, his hand waving to signal the others to circle up, as had been pre-arranged should an attack happen. To no avail, most of the soldiers turning to face the woods, muskets raised, several firing without waiting for orders, clouds of thick smoke drifting back in their faces.

Aaron lowered his bow, giving a nod to the thick-armed man at his side. "We go." The two of them slipped back into the woods, running to the rear of the line of wagons, away from the native scouts who would be searching for them. He smiled, knowing the tribesmen would soon filter away, leaving the column behind when the rest of his men rose from their hiding positions and decimated the stunned soldiers with well-placed shots, each of his men armed with two muskets each, and a brace of pistols tucked into their belts. Skilled marksmen, selected for their experience at close in warfare.

The man running with him chuckled. "My aim is improving." Aaron nodded. "Your *boasting* of it, as well. Better than the curses endured when you were first learning how. My tender ears *singed* from your crude invective."

"*Fook* you and your snobbish remarks." The large man stumbled, Aaron reaching out, helping him stay on his feet. Both men looked back, no one behind them.

"Let's try and get back to the group without suffering a broken bone, so you might survive long enough to improve your aim."

The woods thinned, the two men well around the end of the column, its length gnawed into pieces by a deadly barrage of lead balls, with a handful of arrows from the bows of a group of strong-armed young men, sprinkled into the mix.

※※※

There were no survivors, purposely so, the wounded dispatched with little regard by those willing to attend to the grisly task. Others, unable to stomach the sight, knelt alongside the bloodied column, eying the woods for any sign of the native scouts, none daring show their faces, dissolving away into the forest, unwilling to confront the deadly force.

"Your change in tactics worked out. Three men with minor wounds. No losses—again. Another stone added to our side of the scale." The veteran, the same man who'd led the militia during the ill-fated battle at the bridge two months ago, turned and spit. "Though there *will* be an accounting to come, the world always wanting to bring things back into a balance."

"Your optimistic input, as always, is welcome. Though I've had the same thought myself, held in one hand, with a view of our efforts as seen by the enemy in t'other. Trying to keep both as far apart as possible, that they might never meet." Aaron swallowed his bile, seeing several men walking by, fresh scalps strung over their shoulders, allowed the brutal acts based on promises made to them by Charles. Monies taken from purses and other keepsakes also allowed as war prizes, removed from the dead.

The veteran noted the look on the young leader's face, having to remind himself he was speaking with a man new to the game, one played with fatal results on both sides of the board. He shook his head. "The small man has given you the lead—and you've earned my *trust* these past few months. And though I've not asked about your particulars, I've a sense of who you remind me of. Spoke of it with him who's been busy stirring the pot, his knife to my throat, telling me to swallow any thoughts on the subject." He spat again. "Which I have managed to do—though it does cause me to wonder, at times."

"You fought in the war against the French." Aaron fixed the older man with a firm look. "What actions were you in?"

The man stared, silently considering before providing a name.

"Bloody Rock, for one." He paused, sensing a shift in their relationship, leader to former leader. "Might have made the broadsheets over in—wherever it is you come from. The tone of your words—sliding from England 'cross the border to Scotland and back, depending on your mood."

"I will admit to having read of the battle, named, and having a deep appreciation of what happened there. And of the men involved, actions taken." He paused. "Sacrifices made, with terrible losses suffered on *both* sides of the lines."

"Too *damn* familiar—your words and how you say them. It irritates me to no end. Causing me fits in trying to place them."

"I have the advantage of you, sir. In knowing more of you then you may know of me. Suffice it to say that I am deeply indebted to you and others in helping me arrive to this moment, my being here the direct result of deeds you and others did that day." Aaron walked away, smiling widely when the older man yelling out.

"I've not the patience *or* wits to untwist the meaning in your *words!*" He muttered beneath his breath, the words muffled by ears abused by years of musket fire, at close range. "Youth is *wasted* on the young."

※※※

The howling call of a wolf broke the silence of the night, a rare occurrence in the hills bordering a valley where the movement of men and materials funneled between heights running along both sides. Watchful eyes were on guard, reporting what they saw back to a central hub where Charles used the information to weave timely responses by militia and continental forces. Along with insurgent groups like the one Aaron was leading, guided with advice from the wily veteran who would often stare at him, shaking his head, spitting on the ground as he walked by, cursing beneath his breath.

Aaron stepped outside his shelter, the same one used when first meeting Charles over a dozen engagements ago. He slipped into the nearest shadow, passing between two small fires burning down to embers, four men huddled between them, pulling spits of roasted meat into their fingers, taking cautious bites to prevent burning their lips.

He found a private spot and relieved himself, then returned to the shelter, coming to a sudden stop when he saw someone standing there, a faceless shadow in the moonless night. He reached for his knife, given him by his second in command, hand forged, honed to razor's edge.

"You're a long way from Marischal." Harold's voice was hard-edged, formed around a softer tone hovering just beneath the surface. Aaron felt his heart lurch, tearing free from where he'd carefully secured it, hoping to avoid the long-lasting damage done to his father's during the previous conflict, having read every one of the words in his journals. "Father—"

Their embrace was wordless, a coming together of child to parent, pressing their mixed emotions between arms wrapped around one another. The space between them, no wider than their ages, crossed on a bridge of mutual experiences, shared.

The men at the fire looked away, maintaining the strict protocol they'd all agreed to. To never ask and never tell their personal stories. Adhering to a phrase binding all to the task at hand; 'that what isn't known can never be told', protecting all against risk of any of their group ending up captured by native scouts or enemy forces, tortured to reveal secrets. Death, preferred to disclosure, their vows made in blood to a small man with dark skin and curly hair before joining the irregular and deadly force.

※※※

The delicate scent of clover filled the late morning air, accompanied by the steady drone of bees lining their way across a field, carrying pollen to a hollow tree somewhere in the woods, then making their return.

Harold glanced up, watching one pass by, close enough to snatch with a cupped hand. "Your grandfather—he showed me how to line bees. To follow them back—"

"To their hive." Aaron cut him off. "You've told me the story, more than a dozen times since I was a child."

Harold nodded, looking down, studying the scar on his left hand, where he'd lost the outside finger to a British ball fired by a young sentry on his side of the sorry affair between two nations. "Strange, the contrast between father to son, with one generation making way for the next."

"You've found me, having located and spoken with Charlie." Aaron gave his father a quick glance, wishing to avoid direct eye contact, trying to settle into their altered relationship, based on where he was and what he'd been doing. "After learning where I had gone off to—from Stanton, no doubt."

"It's good to see your education being put to effective use, able to have worked out all the machinations—used to foster strategic success *here*." Harold leaned back, using the base of an oak to rest against. He studied the side of his son's face, no longer able to see the child, only the man. One he barely recognized. "My premonition was correct, to date—though not yet fully realized."

Aaron stared back; his eyes shadowed by the overhanging limbs. "Meaning?"

"You need not worry—though you *will* suffer a loss."

"An attempt to bend me from my course?"

Harold clenched his lips, then relaxed. "There's no hope of that, not from *my* end. My own decision, made long ago, was much the same, refusing to heed *my* father's words." He straightened out his legs, easing a cramp before it could take hold. "Your mother, sweet woman though she is—" He paused, seeing the corners of his son's lips curl up at the edge. "Would no doubt use the knife on her thigh to remove my heart, hearing what I've come to say."

Aaron sighed. "Then *do* speak plainly. I've a mission to prepare for. Orders to assign to the men."

"You're on the path you were born to, without effort on my part to divert you from it—not even if it means your death. Your life will come to an end, no matter the number of days, seasons, or years left to you."

"Again—the *point* you would make, requested."

"I'm leaving. Today. Making my return to your mother. To your two sisters—intending to bring them back *here*, to the colony of Pennsylvania. Somewhere on the outskirts of Philadelphia, where they'll wait to hear from you."

Aaron stared at his father, unable to form an image to the words.

That of his family living in a country torn apart by war, with death all around. Countless families caught in the middle. "You're *not* serious! Only trying to—"

"I *am*." Harold leaned forward. "*You're* the one blind to reality. Immersed in a pot of blood brought to a boil, then left to simmer in seeking revenge, along with these men. Unable to see that this country, formed from diverse colonies, holds hundreds of thousands of people untouched by violence meted out by a *handful* of men, here and there. Easily avoided if one keeps their head down."

"I'm here, in the *middle* of it—and have been unable to find any such place to *exist*."

Harold reached out, his hand rejected by his son, his own pulled back into his lap. Silent, he watched as another bee slid past, the sound of its wings loud, quickly absorbed by the rustling of leaves overhead, along with the vibration of his son's heated emotions.

Aaron finally spoke, sounding more the child than the man. "Why would you—why *do* that? Bringing them all here?"

"I made the pledge to your mother. Or rather—*she* made the pledge to me."

"Before you came?"

"*Well* before that." Harold waited, wondering how much of his vision he could share without interfering with his son's destiny. The moment passed without further inquiry made.

"Then it appears *everyone* is on their *own* path." Aaron turned and gave his father a look that let Harold know the bond of son to father was no longer there.

Harold nodded, feeling another piece of himself sliced away. Aware the boy he'd spent so much of his life being a hero to, was no more. Gone over to a place where such emotions must be set aside.

CHAPTER TWELVE
HIGHLAND MANOR
FALL, 1777

Shaun stood beside Marion, one arm wrapped around her shoulders. The two of them listened as Harold explained to Sinclair the reality of where her son was, leaving out the more gruesome details, shared with him during their ride from Port of Clyde into the highlands.

Meghan, sitting on the floor in front of the fireplace, her back to its heat, shook with cold anger at her brother for having abandoned her, resisted an urge to scream at her father, telling him to go and bring him home. To take her brother by the shoulders and shake him until he came back into himself. She lowered her eyes, unwilling to believe Aaron would have deserted her without returning home to tell her himself, disbelieving the story offered on his behalf. Convinced in the depths of her soul it was not due to the girl who'd broken his heart, sending him away in sorrowful despair.

Sinclair listened as Harold explained the circumstances her son was involved in, and why he'd failed to bring him home. She nodded, then turning about and left the room without a word.

Marion looked up at Shaun, a quizzical look on her face. "Not what I was expecting." He returned her gaze, seeing too much of himself in the expression on her face, and the discerning look in her sky-blue eyes.

"Nor I."

Harold went over and knelt, touching Meghan on her shoulder, his head at a level with hers. "I did what I felt best. For Aaron, and us. An impossible situation for him. Your brother—unable to leave."

Meghan looked at her father. When she replied, it was with a voice as sweet as honey, though laced with arsenic. "You are a wise and *venerated* speaker. A *hero* of war. Capable of *so* many wonderful things as a man of the people." She paused. "And a *miserable* failure as both *father* and *husband!*"

She stood up, giving Shaun and Marion a look of dismissal. "And *you* two are *no* better. Neither of you owning a soul large enough to hold the love he gave us. My *brother*, already as if dead and buried by your acceptance of this—this *travesty* of a decision." She pointed at her father. "By a man who '*died*' while off to some unnamed place doing some unknown thing, leading to the deaths of those men who were marching here to kill *us*." She left the room, following in her mother's footsteps, the sound of a bedroom door slamming shut behind her, echoing along the hallway.

Marion lifted her arms and crossed them on her chest. "So emotional, *that* one." She saw her father look up at her, still on his knees by the fireplace. "*What?* Am I the only one, other than my dear gran Uncle who can *see* that?" She looked at Shaun, who shrugged without offering a response. With a shake of her head and loud sigh, Marion left the room, heading toward the kitchen.

Harold stood up and went over to the window. He looked out at the overcast sky, heavy with the promise of snow by evening. "You *know* what happens next." He turned and gave his uncle a moment to reply, getting nothing back. "We'll be leaving, Sinclair and I, along with Meghan, who will already be making plans to go there on her own."

Shaun cleared his throat. "You have omitted one member of your family. Or rather—*two*. Although my sister is too fragile to leave the manor."

Harold nodded. "Eira and Marion will stay here, with you. All of this—" He swept his arm in a half-circle. "To become Marion's, as it should be—her feet wedded to the sod, bleeding red *and* green, as you well know." He paused. "I trust you'll continue to *guide* her—or rather, help to curb some of her more untenable notions of how the world works, outside these walls."

Shaun gave him a slow nod. "She has the backbone for it, along with the will." He paused. "As to the temperament—"

Harold shrugged. "I understand, and trust you'll use as *light* a touch as is needed on her reins."

Shaun nodded, a thin grin creasing the edges of his lips. "Aye nephew, indeed." He came over and placed his hand on Harold's broad shoulders. "She has exactly what's needed to run this holding, as well as the others, from on high down into the lowlands. To take on the responsibilities of becoming the head of clan Scott once I've climbed the mountain a final time."

"There's no man born, wearing clan tartan that will—"

"A *husband* will need be in attach, nephew. In *name*, only. The decisions hers to make. With the working edge of a knife pressed to his throat should he step on her toes. Like the one you supplied her, whether she kens the need of it now, or no."

Harold stared at his uncle, trying to form the vision of his daughter as head of clan Scott, unable to hold it in his mind. "I wish you luck, with no idea how it's to be managed."

"In the same way I was handed it by your Gran Da', holding the title before me. With use of cunning, conniving, while honoring our name. With the ability to do what needs doing to protect our people, whatever it takes. *All* our people, whether they be here—or over the *damnable* sea."

⁂

Meghan released the arrow, hitting the center of the practice butt dead center, the shaft slapping against several others, already there. She'd taken over full ownership of her brother's bow, angry at him for leaving her behind. Her questions to her father met with a wall of silence, enhanced the tart flavor of her emotions, causing her aim to waver slightly, the next shaft an inch from where her eye had bidden it to go.

Her brother's voice whispered in her ear. "Look your arrow into the target. Don't aim. See where you want it to land, picking one hair on a stag's side. A single point to focus on, then release the string without further thought." She'd looked up at him, Aaron's face returning a patient look. "Why is it so *easy* for you, drawing and releasing without hesitation, and never missing?"

"Thousands of arrows, sister-mine," his reply. "Over hundreds of days. Thousands of paces to and from the target butt, or hours spent on hands and knees, searching for wayward shafts, learning from failure. The *best* way."

"Then I'll *easily* surpass you, my failures becoming *monumental* in number and scope."

He'd smiled, then nodded, bidding her make another attempt, then another, until her fingers were raw. Calluses had evolved over the weeks. Her aching muscles, strengthened, no longer feeling the pull. Her mind no longer judging the release. Eyes fixed on where the arrows ended up. Over thousands of moments spent seeing it happen, her mind one with the effort, until she'd caught up to him. Until the first time in the mountains with a stag in approach, hands trembling, her arrow hitting too far back, leaving the animal gravely wounded. Aaron sending a shaft through its heart, bringing it down. Tears in her eyes, watching as the beast died before her. Swearing to never again take a life. Then a week later taking the next animal with a perfectly placed arrow. And then another, on their next hunt together, as the need arose for fresh meat. Until she was near an equal to her brother, with a rack of her own placed alongside his in the manor hall. No celebration with the men of the clan in attendance for her. Enough to have had her brother there at her side, arm around her shoulder, leaning down, calling her Artemis, goddess of the hunt.

She could no longer see the target, her eyesight blurred by her tears, her knees folding, the bow left lying on the ground. Hands pressed in the grass with her heart broken in two.

"You'll see him again. I *promise* you." Harold touched his daughter on her neck, his fingers moving aside her thick braid.

"Liar." Meghan's voice was a whisper in the wind, starting to build.

"You'll see him again. With someone standing at your side. And another one—from your womb."

She twisted her head around, tears streaming down her cheeks. "How can you *say* such a thing—and expect me to believe it *true?*"

"Same as it's *always* been with me, and other members of our line. Back through—for as long as *any* can recall. The curse of it passed along from one generation to the next."

"Then why did you not see Aaron's *leaving?*" She wiped her eyes, standing up, her father's hand offered her, and accepted. "Why not have seen and prevented *that?*"

"I did. A vision shown me, while there." He pointed to the croft house. "In a dark moment—shared with your mother. Our son, your brother, in need of succor, calling out to someone, with the same look of your mother." He paused. "The vision growing cloudy—then gone."

"My mother—she knew of this and did *nothing?*"

Harold turned his daughter around, taking her face in his hands, his heart squeezed by how much she looked like another. "A vision is never clear in *detail*, only in what's felt. The before and after—unknown. How it's been since well before you were born. Before I met your dear mother. Same as the one shared with me by your great Gran Da. Right *here*, where we're standing now. Coming true some years later."

"Do I—have I the *same* thing in me as you?"

"Nae, not that I know of. But it *is* in your bloodline, when and if it comes to you." He leaned down and touched his forehead to hers. "Not a gift you'll be thanking the gods for, believe me. No control over what's seen, good or bad. Leaving you wishing you didn't know, or to be able to fully *ken* the things seen."

"Then *tell* me. Tell me what you *saw*. Tell me *true*. All of it. And I'll be searching your eyes to see if you're holding anything back." Meghan reached up, cupping her father's face while he held hers. Harold sighed, then took a deep breath, releasing it slowly, letting her know everything he'd seen.

Sinclair stopped brushing her hair, seeing the look on Harold's face in her bedroom mirror. "Meghan?"

"Here. Gone off to bed. Worn from the walk up and ride back down. But hale enow in body *and* spirit." Harold waited a moment, his eyes on Sinclair's face, his breath short as he lost his focus for a moment, drinking in the image of her, more beautiful to his eyes than ever. "Marion?"

"*She's* a lark, landing on the smallest twig, perfectly in balance. Nothing knocking her from her perch in the world. Insists she'll be staying here with Shaun—and Eira." Sinclair spun around. "What are you going to do to break her of *that* notion?"

"Nothing. She has the right of it. Here is *where* she belongs. Here is where she'll *stay*." Sinclair stared at him, the silence building as storm clouds crept over the horizon. Harold went over and took her hand, holding it, her skin cool to his touch. "You know it to be the right decision. *Her* decision, supported by Shaun." He paused. "And Eira, who I spoke with about it."

"This is part of the price I'm to pay—in going to look for my son?" Sinclair turned to the side, staring in the mirror, seeing an older woman returning her dour gaze, hair going over to gray along her temple and the sides. "How did it come to this?" She turned toward Harold. "How did it come to my being made to choose between living here, or there? Torn between one child and the other?"

Harold pulled her into his embrace, burying his face in her hair, as if for the first time. Breathing in her scent, his fingers grasping her shoulders. "I regret *nothing* I've done since the vision shared with me by the father to my mother. The pain he described—my own to bear at the time, trying to avoid any danger caused to my family—to you and our children—all of it. Without any regrets."

He pulled back and looked at her, seeing the young woman in the doorway of a house in Bath. Of the young girl pictured in a thumb-worn cameo, in a silver locket with broken clasp. "For it could 'na have happened without my meeting you. Without seeing you, standing before me, a vision of a *different* kind—come to life."

Sinclair leaned forward, her shoulders shaking, feeling the tug of her womb. "Okay. We'll *go*, the three of us. Find a place there, making a home where he can find *us*. Or where we can go in search of him. To be wherever our son needs us—to be able to bring him safely home."

CHAPTER THIRTEEN
PRIVATE HOUSE
SPRING, 1778

A short, thin-framed young woman pushed her way through a throng of hard-eyed men, derisive calls left in her wake as she moved toward a table where several men were sitting, tankards of ale in front of them. She slammed a leather bag on its ring-stained surface, staring at the youngest man sitting on the opposite side, his eyes fastened to hers.

"My *dues*—paid in *advance*. More than enough proof in there to allow me to join your little *club*." Her voice was a blend of French patois with hint of a drawl, her clothing drab, no flash of metal on wrists, fingers, or dangling from her slender neck. She wore a simple shift, tied at the waist with a leather strap, foul with the scent of dried blood, wood smoke, and lack of a recent scrubbing.

Two of the men slid back in their chairs and stood up, hands drifting toward their belts, stopping when she turned and spit a stream of sharp-edged words in their faces. "*Touch* your weapons—and I'll add your *zozos* to the bag!" They raised their hands and moved back, leaving their leader alone with the wild woman, her light-colored hair falling in a seaweed tangle over the shoulders of her mud and blood-splattered dress.

Aaron measured her with a discerning look, ignoring the

disheveled clothing and lack of basic hygiene. He focused on her eyes, a hazel-green in the light streaming in through a large, open window at his back. "Your entry fee is accepted, in theory, though no *dues* are required for admission to this *club* you speak of."

"I wanted your *attention*." She leaned forward, sliding the bag across the table, her narrow shoulders pocketing the top of her dress, revealing small breasts with thin scratches on her skin, along with a sprinkle of freckles dusting her arms and high cheekbones. Or dirt, Aaron thought as he reached out and touched the damp surface of the leather pouch, moving it to one side.

"You *have* it, fair lady."

"Nothing is *fair* about me, or the life handed me at the end of British bayonets." She pulled a chair over with the tip of one foot, then sat down. "Painted red—with my father and two brother's blood."

"This being a—*recent* occurrence?" Aaron raised a hand, signaling for a server.

"No. When I was a child. My family and all Acadiana people brutally cleared from our ancestral lands. Sent to every part of the blood-soaked English empire. My own fate to end up in the swamplands outside New Orleans."

"You have my sympathies." Aaron glanced at the bag, beginning to understand what it might contain. "And interest—" He circled a finger, taking in the crowded interior of the pub. "Along with that of my companions, based on what's in *there*." He glanced at the bag, a clear liquid with reddish tint leaking from the opening, secured with a twist of leather.

"I had the *right* to take them—the ears of men in redcoats who would not *listen* when I asked them for what they *owed* me. Their *lives*." She shrugged. "So, I *took* both, with what's in there—proof of my abilities."

"You wish to join us?"

She leaned forward, one hand slipping below the top of the table. "I had hoped *you*, as leader of these *others*, might be able to *hear* my words." Her light-colored eyes gleamed in the flickering light of a lantern. "I may have been wrong."

"You *may* want to rethink use of the knife in your hand, with a leap planned through yon window, making your escape." Aaron raised a finger, keeping the others back. "I welcome an opportunity to discuss terms with such a—*sweetly* scented rose, albeit one with a *sharp* thorn."

※※※

"She's a *risk*. One we *cannot* afford." The older veteran, going by the name of 'Falcon', protecting against a forced reveal of his family name if caught, gave Aaron a cold stare.

It had been a fortnight since the odd woman had joined the group. The experienced killer unsettled by her presence and closeness with the young man assigned to lead them, wishing her gone. Held back from insisting on it, with General Greene himself having made it clear to him that he was to continue to provide the young strategist guidance as required, without questioning his orders. A situation chafing at him, convinced the thick-shouldered young man standing before him was making a serious mistake.

Aaron, given the name 'Wolf' by the men of his command, based on his reputation for deadly strikes made from close range, shrugged. "She has a role to play, bloody as it is. And the results so far have disrupted the morale *and* effectiveness of the British response. Slowing down their forays for goods, with the redcoats forced to increase the number of men used to protect the wagons, pulled from other duties, sent against us."

"With *additional* risk, making us a target of their wrath, due to the —to the *atrocities* done to their officers, when captured alive."

Aaron nodded. "Agreed. Creating even *more* disruption to their side, leading to more losses on their side, while increasing the odds in *our* favor. Officers looking over their shoulders, focused on personal survival and not clear-minded strategy." He reached out and touched his second's arm. "She is a *tool*. Sharp edged, with a flexible mind. One we will *continue* to use." Aaron hardened his voice. "Was there anything else?"

Falcon shook his head, unhappy with the decision, leaving without a word. Aaron knew the older man would follow his lead, their own casualties since the interdiction campaign had started, minimal. The enemy made to pay with hundreds of men lost. Along with dozens of officers, helping to drain the ranks of the British army.

Once he was back in the large shelter provided him as leader, the woman whose insurgent name was Chatte slipped in through a slit in the back wall, placed there to provide a quick exit in case of attack. Aaron had tried to prevent the damage done, explaining how unlikely an event that would be. Her reaction had been a glowering pout of defiance, eliciting a stern look from him, expecting her to comply. The standoff had ended with a slash of a knife pulled from beneath her skirt, reminding Aaron of the ones carried by his mother and two sisters back in Scotland.

"He would see me *gone*. Prefer to see me *dead*." Chatte, French for cat, came over and put her hand on Aaron's neck, rubbing it gently. She'd recently bathed, her hair washed, hanging down, drying in the heat from a brazier confiscated from an English supply wagon. Packed along with their meager belongings, strapped to carrying poles whenever they moved camp. No horses allowed them, on Aaron's orders, leaving tracks behind a blind man could follow. Everything they needed, carried with them, with resupply of goods gathered from English supplies captured along the way. The rest of the goods made available for locals to reclaim, or remaining behind, burnt along with the wagons and draft animals they killed in place, their brands precluding use as plow horses by farmers. A hanging offense if found in possession of any of the King's horses.

Aaron shrugged. "He's afraid of what might happen to his *soul*, due to the work you do. Your knife providing intelligence from men pleading for their lives, then left begging for a *quick* ending to them."

"I will not see heaven. I have accepted the price to *my* soul." Chatte paused, slipping her hand down the front of his shirt. "I seek my reward *here*, while in *this* life." She took Aaron's hand, leading him over to their bedrolls, sinking to her knees, pulling him down. Each of them taking full advantage of the what the other had to offer, asking nothing in return.

Charles glanced across the encampment, noting the strict adherence to cleanliness and order, with everything secured in packs, ready for a quick retreat. The smoke from dozens of fires, circled by knots of leather-clad men, was all but invisible, the secretive force restricted to using dead wood for fuel.

He gave the young strategist leading them a quiet look. "You've produced *remarkable* results, with few losses. Our side of this sorry affair would already have won if Washington could be convinced to emulate your methods."

Aaron shrugged. "You're exaggerating, knowing our main forces are as rigidly bound to the same regulations and codes of conduct as are the British." Aaron nodded at two young members of his force passing by, carrying in a load of firewood. "We are a group of individuals, *loosely* assembled. Each man capable of taking the lead. Each segment of our force able to operate independently for days at a time. Supplies cached by individuals in remote places, left untouched until needed. With only themselves knowing where they're secreted, unable to tell tales if captured alive. The goods, abandoned in place."

"Preventing the British or their native allies from discovering your *main* group." Charles motioned toward a small command tent; the sole affectation of leadership allowed by the young man leading the effort against the British supply lines. Once they were inside, he pulled out a letter, along with several maps.

"This is a commendation from Washington, which you will no doubt burn without reading. These—" He waved the maps. "Are to be memorized, *then* burnt."

Aaron smiled. "Is there *another* way to do it?"

Charles mirrored his expression. "Touché." He took a moment to study the other's face, trying to find the young boy who'd come into his father's office in London, reading everything he could find, with endless questions asked. Followed closely by reasoned opinions offered. He shrugged, no longer able to see him. "There is an issue to discuss. One that has recently come to my attention. How—I cannot say."

"You *will* not say. But *could*—if pressed." Aaron held up one hand.

"But I won't. It's enough to know *someone* has brought it to your attention." He paused, stiffening his posture. "She is under *my* protection."

Charles nodded, having expected Aaron to read his thoughts. He sighed. "And *you*—are *still* under *my* command. Correct?"

Aaron hesitated a moment, then nodded. "Of course. I owe my position to you. My *life*, as well. A soldier in either army faces long odds against surviving more than a few battles—according to news gathered from the locals, with scores of relatives left lying in graves. Or from officers in *red* coats, eager to reveal their innermost secrets."

"Which brings us to the *secondary* purpose for this visit." Charles turned, watching as a young woman carried several pine knots into a half-shelter, her hair gleaming in the sunlight, a slight smile on her lips, humming a song he did not recognize. "That of her—*behavior*, toward wounded men."

"*Officers* only. And just the handful. Thus far." Aaron crossed his arms, jaw set in a stern expression.

Charles displayed a tight-lipped smile. "I'm not here to question the lady's methods, or why she has such hatred for those she places under her knife." He faced Aaron. "I'm here, reluctantly—to encourage *more* of it to be done." He saw a grimace of disappointment on Aaron's face. "You presumed I would order you to put a stop to it?"

Aaron softened his demeanor, looking down. "I'd rather hoped you *would*." He turned away, staring at men moving about, stringing sacks of supplies on long shelter poles they would carry when breaking camp. The small force changed its location every few days, leaving little sign behind. Men, long used to living in the wilderness, biding their time until the next ambush, haunting the nightmares of English troops circulating fireside rumors of ghosts in the woods.

"*Morale* is as much a part of men's will to fight as is *revenge*. The British soldiers are not here to inflict death due to the *latter*. Which leaves us to do what we can to weaken the *former*." Charles considered the young man's profile, noting his clenched hands. "You are torn between the delicate petals of the flower—and the hate lying *within* its twisted roots. The cause of it, unknown to you."

"For the most part. Though she *has* made mention of some of it.

Enough to let me know she's justified in her feelings—" Aaron looked over. "Though her methods are those of the devil himself."

"And that's why she is *valuable* to our cause. And must *continue* her efforts, while Washington gains men enough to cover recent losses. His ranks depleted, due to mistakes made, along with constant attrition from sickness, disease, and lethargy of spirit for those who have served with him the longest."

"We are to *move* on then, nibbling at the foundation of the machine of war, placing grains of sand in its gears."

Charles reached out and touched the heavily callused tip of Aaron's forefinger, hardened by the slip of a bowstring, countless times throughout his life. "Were we to have a hundred more like you, with equal skill, Franklin's suggestion of how we might be able to reduce the enemy with flights of several thousand arrows delivered into the concentrated ranks of men in slow advance could be achieved."

He nodded to the young woman as she slipped by, heading off with two buckets in her slim hands to gather water. "And we could use a dozen more like *her*."

※※※

Aaron slid a scented bar of soft soap down Chatte's shoulders, using a circular motion, leaving a film of suds on the smooth surface of her skin. The soap was a portion of goods confiscated from an officer's belongings. The owner no longer requiring them, having died beneath the practiced strokes of her thin blade.

His hand quivered, the soap almost slipping from his fingers. He was torn between pulling away, denying himself the pleasure of her body, or pulling her around to kiss her. To touch her. To lay with her again. And again. Each time delivering him to a place he'd never known to exist. The first time, for him, having been a moment of release bringing him to a new world, with his flag firmly planted in the richness of her body. The immediate effect, leaving him fumbling his way to an apology while she looked up at him, her perfect face giving him a quiet look.

☘☘☘

"It is *always* this way, when new to the sharing of oneself with another." Chatte's voice was a murmur. "You will see, young as you are, how quickly you will be ready to—rise to the moment, anew." She reached up and touched his face, turning it until she could see into his eyes. Gazing at him until he found hers, a look of exasperation on his sun-bronzed skin. "Lie down beside me. Hold me, as I hold you. Listen to the rain. How it finds a rhythm all its own. The fabric above our heads like skin, trembling from its touch."

Aaron stared at the woman, still a stranger to him, yet more compelling than anyone he'd ever met, a flush of blood darkening the color of his skin in the light from a small candle. Skye's face flashed through his mind's eyes, the door quickly closed as he leaned forward, drinking in the heated scent of Chatte's body. Her tawny skin, a rich canvas for his lips, with a myriad of small scars scattered across her arms and legs.

"This—" He reached out and touched one, a thin line an inch long, just above her elbow. "What story does it tell?"

Chatte twisted onto her side, her head resting on the palm of one hand, elbow pressed into the tarp covering the ground. She smiled, her light-colored eyes gleaming with pleasure. "The tale of a man who would not take no for an answer. Paying for his deafness to my pleas with his ear. Taken from him by this." She reached out, taking his hand, moving it to a leather sheath tied in place between her waist and upper thigh, holding a small, bone handled knife. One she was never without. Even now, lying with him.

He touched the handle, then moved his fingers over, touching her, slowly easing into the warmth of her body, her moan of pleasure encouraging him, his lips finding hers, pressing her back until she was lying beneath him, again. Moving slower this time, entering her, a gasp from them both filling the night air, becoming words in his ear, urging him on, her hands pulling him in, his breathing hoarse as he thrust with a lower body strengthened by years of highland mountain climbs. Ending with a shuddering release that threatened to snap his spine, his head lying on her shoulder, her hair in his eyes and mouth as he whispered breathless words, letting her know how much he needed her.

He never asked her given name, letting her know to never reveal it to anyone. To choose another, like all the men scattered in shelters throughout a section of thick woods behind the farm of a man who asked no questions, accepting whatever they felt fair to pay him for the goods he supplied.

She told him to call her Chatte, then gently touched his lips, asking if he knew what it meant.

"It is French for cat. A *female* cat."

"Yes. It suits me, does it not?" She grinned, baring her teeth, white and gleaming, the tip of her tongue, pink between them. Daring his kiss, her breath flavored with a sprig of mint.

He readily complied, then leaned back. "We never ask or speak of personal details. Part of our code, sworn to before joining the 'club', as you call it."

"Even with those you are lying with?"

He blushed. "You tease." He hesitated, taking her in in full. "It is to protect one another in case —"

She tightened her smile. "I *know* the reason. I too am careful with what I share, and with whom. My name *and* body. Neither one available to any but those I have come to trust." She lowered her eyes. "And lost."

"Then we shall leave it there." Aaron angled his head to one side, listening to the rain. "It will clear by morning." He took one last look at her in the light of the candle, then put it out, lying down beside her, pulling a blanket over them. "I normally sleep fully clothed, ready to move if needed."

"Me too."

They lay in the darkness, their naked bodies touching. Chatte rolled into the crook of his arm, head on his chest, her breath a warm flutter on his skin. The rain increased, the sound of it filling the shelter, shielding them from the world outside.

⁂

"You are having a *serious* thought. The washing of my back—at a standstill." Chatte looked back over her shoulder, her eyes finding his. "Are you troubled?"

"Yes." Aaron continued moving the soap, then reached down and wet it again from a bucket of warm water heated by the sun, brought inside a temporary enclosure formed outside their shelter. Made of sheets of heavy cloth tied off to the limbs of a pine tree, the ground covered with a thick layer of needles, cushioning their feet. "I have spoken with the one who brings orders of our next mission, escorted here by Falcon—who has talked out of turn."

Chatte turned and faced him, her breasts touching his chest as she leaned in. "The small man, who you were speaking with?" When Aaron nodded, she angled her head to one side, water dripping from the ends, hitting the top of his foot. "Is it not a violation of an oath, of this one named Falcon—his doing that?"

"It is a violation of a *rule*, not an oath sworn. Troubling, but not a punishable offense. A warning in his ear will be enough, for now." Aaron lifted the bar of soap and started in again, two pert targets presenting themselves for his attention, a wide smile on his face as he focused on the task at hand.

Chatte leaned back, one of his arms cradling her as she closed her eyes, enjoying his attention, her mind working out how best to remedy the potential for damage to their relationship should she decide to take the matter of punishment into her own hands.

CHAPTER FOURTEEN
HIGHLAND MANOR
SUMMER, 1778

Shaun finished supervising two lads loading a large wagon with chests and containers carried from the manor house. They contained clothing and assorted items for shipment to the colony of Philadelphia from the port of Glasgow. Taken from there inland to a small farmstead near a busy crossroads. A place of commerce, purchased in advance by Sinclair, providing for their personal needs and the potential for business transactions. A location ensuring a seamless transition into a new life for herself and Meghan.

Harold had already left, choosing to travel alone, seeking out a fishing boat with a familiar name, intending to make his way to the farm by a circuitous route, avoiding encounters with anyone other than the men whose names were on a list given him by Charles before he left. A request made and agreed to without any questions asked. Code names provided, along with information vital to a man wishing to go about the colonies unnoticed. The information memorized, then destroyed by flame.

"You have done an excellent job of getting this done." Sinclair stepped forward, touching Shaun on his arm. "Will you be traveling with us—your lower back and hip improving enough to allow it?"

"Nae. I'll be staying here, with young Allyn having the pleasure of seeing you there and safely aboard. With the other lad helping him with return of the wagon, and to lend a hand around the manor."

"Then I'll bid you goodbye, but *not* farewell, as I intend to return within the year, with my son in hand. Brought to his senses, then back to his rightful home."

Shaun nodded, keeping his thoughts to himself, having shared them with Harold two weeks ago, just before he'd slipped away, needing additional time to reach the colonies to rendezvous with his family once they arrived.

⚘⚘⚘

"She's not in her *right* mind. Making *no* sense. The lad's no child and has the *right* to choose for himself." Shaun gave Harold a firm nod of his head.

"She is who she's *always* been. And I've seen Aaron at the end of a dark path. One leading him to a place far beyond anything I went through."

Shaun eyed his nephew. "You and your *damned* sight. Passed down to you by my own *sister*. Herself *cursed* with it, same as our Da." He turned and spit, making the sign of the Cross. "I have 'na doubt as to your vision coming true — only to your *surviving* to see it through. You'll be in harm's way — every *step* you take in that foreign land."

"Agreed. But it's *my* journey to make, tying to right as many wrongs as I can. To atone for my sins. Most of them in not having been here when needed. Having brought danger to my kith. To my kin." Harold gave his uncle a shadowed look. "To you."

Shaun shrugged, reaching up to scratch his head, the hair thinning on top, his eyes rheumy with the onset of age. "And we *handled* it, then buried the tale. With you managing to get back where you needed to be — in time."

"My son, daughter, and wife made to pay a heavy price."

"Aye, lad, they *did*." Shaun gave Harold a solemn look. "Due to your reputation, hard earned. Sinclair, the same. *Named* people — made targets by those living in the world below. Why I prefer staying high, above all the nonsense, keeping the clan isolated from the misery coming from those seeking power, determined to improve their station in life, standing on the backs of others."

He spit again, rubbing the ground with the tip of a boot. "I *know* my place. My days of seeking glory, gold and—" He smiled, his eyes glowing with memories of younger days. "And *women*—behind me now."

"Marion will be in good hands, then. With enough of her own mettle to stand the tests you're to put in front of her." Harold hesitated. "Do you still ken she's the one—to guide the clan?"

"She's more than a match in wits to me. Our 'discussions' as she calls them, chasing me in circles, leaving me chewing my own tail, with her watching me with a smile on her face." Shaun grinned. "But no longer daring to mock me. Not since the lashing given her when a child, teaching her a valuable and well-deserved lesson in showing of proper respect to her elders."

Harold reached out, giving his uncle a firm grip on his shoulder, getting one in return. "I'll not be seeing you again."

Shaun sighed, holding on, looking his nephew straight in the eye. "No. Don't imagine you're ever to set foot on these highland paths again."

Harold pulled away without looking back, taking the back trails and hidden paths, leading down to the lowlands.

☘☘☘

With the wagon loaded to Sinclair's satisfaction, Allyn backed a team of draft animals into place. He attached their harnesses, smiling as they whinnied, the large beasts eager to leave. He knew they would have an easy time of it, due to the mostly downhill slant of the hills, running all the way to Aberdeen and the port in Glasgow. Then he leapt into the seat, Meghan sitting beside him, their shoulders touching despite ample room to either side Their close posture drew Sinclair's eye, a small frown tugging down the corners of her lips.

Shaun noticed as well, clapping one hand on the lad's forearm, squeezing until the young man's eyes widened slightly, his body sliding a bit further away. "You're to get them there in *one* piece, with nothing touched or put out of sorts. Do ya take my meaning, lad?"

Allyn nodded, then snapped his hands, signaling the team. Sinclair followed behind on horseback, intending to bring her favorite horse with her, at extravagant cost.

Shaun had tried to dissuade her, pointing out there would be opportunities to buy another mount equally as good, once there. His words met with a tight-lipped smile as Sinclair placed a saddle on her mount. He waited until she climbed aboard the stallion, then stepped forward, handing his wife in name only a piece of parchment.

Sinclair opened it, her eyes filling with tears as she read it. Then she nodded her head, nudging the mare with her heels, moving ahead without comment.

⁂

It was their third full day at sea, the ocean with a moderate swell, the winds fair, the ship with a bone in her teeth as the crew moved about the deck with smiles and loose-limbed gaits. Sinclair watched them, her stomach calm, having lost her queasiness during a previous voyage made from London to Philadelphia, when Harold had taken her to visit her father's grave.

"You've been at sea before." A voice from behind pulled Sinclair around. A man, who'd been aboard when she and Meghan had made their way up the gangway, stood near the rail, hat in hand. He made a small bow. "I did not mean to disturb your—study of shipboard duties. An excellent crew and captain." He paused, touching his firm stomach, his body trim, with long legs and an inviting smile. "The cuisine—not bad, though the cook's sparing use of spices lends a certain *blandness* to his dishes."

Sinclair measured him carefully, her instincts kicking her with pointed shoes. "I do not recall the captain, or anyone else, having made an introduction—sir." She saw him recoil slightly, then recover, sweeping his arm while making an exaggerated bow, his fingers almost brushing the deck.

"My *sincerest* apologies, Madam. I am your humble servant, Arthur

Lee. A minor player of little note, acting on behalf of a handful of prominent people interested in forming a close embrace with acquaintances of a—*Francophile* affiliation."

"You are working on behalf of the recently formed Continental Congress, hoping to engage the support of the French government."

The man blinked, several times, a smile frozen on his full lips. "You are—extremely well *informed*." He paused. "Madame."

Sinclair grinned. "I am no spy, sir. Only an avid reader of publications, pouring through them with fervor, seeking to remain tied to the —to the tides of politics, commerce—and *war*."

"A martial interest." He held a hand to his chin. "Unusual in someone so—" He reconsidered, seeing Sinclair's eyes narrow slightly. "So *open* to the ways of the world, without. Knowledge helping to expand the mind. A *rich* dish indeed, for those with the taste for such things, willing to get ink stains on their fingers."

"Far better than the blood being spilled by young men on *both* sides of the divide between Crown and colonies."

"I concur, Madame—?"

"Haversham." She saw the man's eyebrows rise. "Knutt."

Arthur was unable to hold back his smile, allowing it to blossom on his face, taking a step closer, bowing again. "It is my *extreme* pleasure to make your acquaintance, Lady Sinclair Haversham-*Knutt*."

He straightened up, his eyes dancing with excitement. "I had the pleasure of hearing your husband speak—" Arthur pulled back, his face red from embarrassment. "I—I spoke in haste, Lady Sinclair. My apologies, again, in having broached such a painful subject."

"My late husband had *two* sides. Optimistic *and* pragmatic, with his feelings made clear. Though his thoughts were often troubled, from his sense of morality pulling him in different directions."

"I was one who found his—*troubled* thoughts—to be excellent in concept, when first hearing them proposed. We would not now be where we are, if more had the wisdom—and fortitude, to have heeded his excellent advice."

"Or lacked excessive *greed*." Sinclair had decided to like this man, though she held no illusions as to where he stood. For today it was enough he held position on the deck of the same ship she and her daughter were on. Along with a young stowaway, spending his time below, fed half-rations by his red-haired accomplice.

"I bow to your wisdom, Lady Sinclair Haversham, in journey to the colony of Pennsylvania. No doubt fully *aware* of the current circumstances."

"I have friends ready to take myself and family in, upon our arrival."

Arthur nodded. "Then I will take my leave, a letter waiting below deck requiring a response. Good day, Lady Sinclair."

Arthur strolled away, heading to the lower deck where several staterooms were located. Sinclair followed him with her eyes, feeling unsettled, as if he'd seen her plans written on her face. She shook her head, letting go of her worry, shifting her focus on what to do about young Allyn, wondering what Shaun must be thinking, with the lad not having returned from Glasgow.

※※※

Meghan moved the plate of food closer to Allyn, encouraging him to finish it, her own stomach cramping from hunger, though her mood was light. "You'll need your strength, once we are in port."

"I'll be in chains before then, most likely. The captain not looking favorably on my having snuck aboard." He eyed the young woman he'd been smitten with since first seeing her, years earlier, riding a small mare across a gorse covered field, hair streaming behind her as if on fire, glowing in the sun. "Not that I'm complaining—our time alone these past few days, worth any number of stripes on my back."

"There'll be *no* such abuse aimed in your direction. I've coins saved, *more* than enough to compensate for your passage, with no diminishment of ship stores. The food and drink already paid for in full, by my mother."

Allyn gave Meghan a hard look. "It will be by *her* firm hand—the lashes delivered me when found out. Lady Sinclair not someone to trifle with."

"She would *never* hurt you. Not after what happened that day in the Pinch." Meghan took his hands, holding them, leaning in, her eyes on his. "My mother loves you *dearly*. As does my gran uncle. Both will understand how impossible it would have been for you, watching me sail away." She fluttered her eyelids, hating herself for doing so, having ridiculed the same behavior in her cousins during their visits, doing their best to draw Allyn's attention their way. "I'm right, aren't I?"

He returned a soft edged smile, reaching to touch her face, his fingers brushing back a stray curl of red hair. "It would have been more than I could have borne." Then they kissed, again, the heat of their passion building until a noise from outside the storeroom door pulled them apart, their hearts beating as much out of fear of discovery, as from their deep affection for one another.

The moment stretched, the sound of footsteps moving on, the two accomplices daring to release deep breaths. Meghan stood up, then looked at an earthen pot in the corner of the small space between bundles of sailcloth, its opening covered with a piece of thick cloth. "I'll take care of *that* and be back before the next bell." She grinned, reaching out and tousling Allyn's thick black hair. "Don't run off." Then she was gone, honeypot containing his waste in her hands as she opened the door, peering out, before flowing away like the wind, heading above deck.

※※※

A rider perched in a wagon approached the manor, Shaun busy at the front door, making an adjustment to the lower hinge. He straightened up, easing the pain in his hip with a rub of his hand, squinting to see who it was, having expected Allyn back a day ago.

The rider was familiar, a close friend of the lad, one year older and with similar build. Someone Shaun considered to be level-headed, capable enough in chores assigned, with an easy hand when aboard a horse helping move the stock from highland pastures to low.

"You're back with news of a wayward lad gone missing, I assume." Shaun stepped away from the manor steps, reaching out and setting the brake of the wheel while the tall boy leapt down beside him, causing a wince on the older man's weathered face, his free hand finding his hip again, rubbing away at a sympathetic pain. "He's boarded a ship to Pennsylvania colony, no doubt."

The young man, named Logan, of clan Scott blood, lowered his eyes, staring at the ground, the horses sensing his disquiet, whinnying, and jerking their heads.

Shaun frowned. "You knew of his plan."

Logan looked up. "I tried to tell him—to let him know to come to you first."

"I'd ha' stopped him. No other choice to make, with the lady of the manor putting her knife to my throat, otherwise." Shaun beckoned the lad over, handing him the reins. "Take care of the team. They're to be in *your* hands now, if'n you've a mind to stay on and fill the scoundrels' footprints." He shook his head. "This place needs young hands with an able mind to help keep it fit. And mine have held too many weapons, glasses of whiskey, and the hands of too many fine ladies to do all that's needing doing."

"I've *some* say in who stays—and who *goes*." Marion was in the doorway, her hair bound atop her head in a thick black knot, blue eyes glowing in the sunlight as late afternoon changed over to early evening. "Being as *I* am now the lady of the manor."

Shaun made a slight bow, as far as the tightness in his lower back would allow, then nodded in agreement. "You have the right of it, Lady Marion." He stepped to one side, bidding the lad move forward.

Logan stepped ahead and looked Marion straight in the eye, then grinned. "Are ye open to my staying on?" He paused. "Or *no?*"

Marion waited, determined to count to ten heartbeats as her mother had taught her to do when dealing with moments of importance, especially with the men in her life. She reached eight before nodding, slightly. "It is of little concern to me who works here. One—no different than the next." Spinning around, she went back inside, closing the door behind her with a muffled thud, the hang of it in the frame, perfectly balanced.

CHAPTER FIFTEEN
PENNSYLVANIA FARMSTEAD
SUMMER, 1778

Harold folded over the top of a large sack, then ran a large needle with twine attached through the gathered material, sealing a four-stone load of kernels of grain inside. He slung it across his shoulder, then went over to a wagon, adding it to a dozen others.

The air was sultry, the bags of grain warm against the side of Harold's bearded face as he stacked them. Collected from local suppliers, they were meant to support Washington's army once inserted into an underground network, with operatives moving goods and arms through hundreds of back country paths and dozens of secluded waterways. Carried on the backs of horses and men when no other means were available. Added to a trickle of desperately needed supplies, becoming a flow, then a torrent, helping keep men and muskets in the field, able to resist the English armies that were constantly seeking them out.

When the 'Neewa had finished its voyage from a small harbor north of Glasgow to a secluded bay up the coast from Philadelphia, Harold had disembarked, thanking the two sons of a man who'd helped him to destroy one tentacle of the beast wrapped round the thrones of multiple countries. Wounding it, though not able to seriously impact its ability to continue squeezing the lifeblood from the emerging group of colonial men banding together to form the framework of a free and democratic society.

Once ashore, he'd put some of the money secured from sale of his estate in Bristol, its ownership having gone to Sinclair upon news of his untimely death, to effective use. Used to purchase a farmhouse attached to a small warehouse sitting at a crossroad twenty miles outside Philadelphia. Along with two hundred acres of fields and woods, tied to the ends of a network of roads built along old native paths. A few of the oldest ones still used, weaving inland through dense woods and marshlands, providing for furtive movement to a small, run-down cabin located in the foothills, a day's ride to the west.

When finished with the loading of the wagon, Harold gathered a team of horses from the small stable behind the main house, tying them into the traces. Then he climbed aboard, with a nod of his head to the older of three men he'd hired, helping to bring the repair of buildings and fallow fields along. With a soft command to the horses, he guided them and the wagon along the road leading into the western hills.

As he made his way on the narrow lane, Harold shook his head, frustrated that his plan to evade discovery by elements of the secretive cabal had failed, with a message from Charles reaching him one month after he'd settled into the back-breaking work of rebuilding the barn and tables, repairing a well, and planting of winter crops. He'd believed himself safely hidden until a woman with infant in arm stopped him as he passed through one of the outer settlements, handing him a coded note. One he'd quickly deciphered, revealing a date and location to meet at a familiar locale, over a day's ride from the farmhouse.

🌲🌲🌲

"Well met, my friend!" Charles extended his hand, his face beaming, his hair grown back in since the last time they'd met at the croft house. The dapper man led Harold into a familiar cabin, where he'd once shared a jug with a veteran and his two sons. The door was missing, the roof sagging, the floor soft with rot.

"The first of what I have to share—is to let you know your son is still hale, as of a week ago." Charles eyed a chair, seeing the stain of mold and bird droppings covering the seat, deciding to remain standing. "Aaron and a group of veterans continue to make raids against the stream of supplies and reinforcements intended to support the English army, in pursuit of colonial forces." He gave Harold a solemn look. "His strategic ploys are helping to keep the enemy off balance, never the same one used twice. Men in red coats on their heels, looking over their shoulders every step of the way."

Harold leaned back against a wall, with his eyes focused on Charles. "There's more you're *not* saying."

Charles lowered his gaze and tone. "You are, as always—able to see to the core of the apple, not distracted by its polished surface." He sighed, then went over and looked through an empty window frame. "The addition of another—*strategist* to his force has helped *enhance* his string of successes. Someone with a *cutting* way of, shall we say—peeling the apple, revealing seeds of truth, hidden inside."

"*We* are not saying *anything*. Speak plainly, Charlie. Then point me to him so I may ascertain for myself how sound he is."

"That I *cannot*, nay, *will* not do. It would be a violation of our strict protocol for contact. Not allowed, on pain of death."

Harold angled his head, his eyes wearing a cold expression. "You would *threaten* me with—"

"Not *my* protocol—but *his*. Your son is no longer the boy you remember, or the person you met on your last visit here, He's become someone who's able to—" Charles paused, swallowing, looking at Harold with a strange look in his eyes. "To cause *immeasurable* harm to any who go against him. English troops, led by skilled officers with their wits about them, hunting for him in every corner of this vast countryside, filled with colonists eager to aid him in his efforts to dissolve into the shadows, untouched."

"How?" Harold firmed up his posture, leaning forward, bringing a father's concern to the fore. "And do say it *clearly*."

"He has gone beyond *personal* choice of a longbow used as a weapon, reintroducing its use on a larger scale. Forming a small group of—youthful bowmen, though none are close to his equal in accuracy or rate of release. Though more than capable of delivering devastating blows to men standing in close formation, from well over a hundred paces away, releasing concentrated volleys into their ranks, then fading away as if clouds of smoke from muskets."

Harold closed, then opened his eyes. "It makes sense, though difficult to train up men, new to the game. Take years of practice, and the hardening of arm, shoulder, and fingers to pull a proper longbow to full draw, trying to kill men from more than a handful of paces away."

"It *is* possible, demonstrably so. Your son selecting those used to hard labor with saw and axe." Charles paused. "I've seen it for myself, allowed to accompany him on a raid. Going along as observer to it." He raised a hand, stopping Harold's reply, needing a moment to collect himself, then continuing. "It was a—a *masterpiece* of manipulation and lethality. As if a play, the actors in perfect lockstep, moving of one mind—"

"Lose the flowery description of it—telling it *straight*."

"Your son laid a trap that allowed not a single man of fifty to escape with their lives. Eliminating them without loss to his own side. Two British officers captured. One seriously wounded, dying before the *questioning* could begin. The other—" He tightened his lips, ignoring Harold's glare. "The other—" Charles swallowed, his eyes glancing to one side. "He died as *horrible* a death as one could imagine, in their *worst* moments. In—in the depths of a *horrific* nightmare. Something I shall carry with me to my grave, wishing to be set free of it. The memory—" He shook his head, then pulled a flask from his pocket, removing the stopper, taking a drink.

"My son—*Aaron*—the one who—"

"*No!* Not *him*." Charles gave Harold a pained look. "*Her*. A woman of the southern swamps. Her beauty matched by the hatred she harbors toward the redcoats, especially their officers, whom she treats most cruelly. A thirst for revenge inside her, one left unquenched, no matter the amount of blood released from their bodies by the edge of her blade."

"And Aaron—*allows* this?"

"He does. Ordered to do so. By me."

"Why?" Harold's face held the first sign of despair, his eyes narrowed in confusion, hands clenched as he shook his head.

"It has proven to be *extremely* disruptive to the English efforts in the field. Thus, it's not only *countenanced* but *encouraged* by those benefiting from the results, knowing it cannot last long. The British are sending out their own irregulars to hunt them—to hunt down your son and his men. A high price offered those managing to bring back his head, once found. The price doubled—for *hers*."

Harold reached for the bottle, taking a long swallow, handing it back. "He is near to where we are—my son?"

Charles gave him a look promising nothing in return. "You must *not* try and find him, Harold. It would place excessive burden on him, seeing the look in your face. The same one I'm seeing now." He came over. "Your son's caught up in an uneven struggle, emotionally *and* mentally. It's nothing short of a miracle he's been able to hold himself and the men he's leading together." Charles paused, giving Harold a soft look. "Or perhaps—he's where he's *destined* to be—like his father, before him. Doing what he feels is right to bring about change. To help birth a nation. One the world may never have an opportunity to see again."

He stepped outside, his eyes following several men as they swept along the edge of woods, providing protection to their leader. "We have the ability, today—to tear continents apart with massed armies and modern weapons. Along with improved means of communication due to thousands of fast ships crossing every ocean using navigational tools we could not have imagined, a hundred years ago."

Harold scoffed. "He'll change *nothing* by what he's doing—or a *thousand* others like him. The forces at work behind the scenes determined to keep hold of what they've built. Same over here, now, as it is everywhere around the globe. No different outcome—at the end of this fiasco, with countless bodies left buried 'neath the same sod as in *my* war."

"This is *different*, Harold. There is a *real* chance to see it through to a successful conclusion, led by men willing to sign their names to the bottom of an *incredible* document. One that—"

"Based on *native* philosophies, using *their* laws. The same words of agreements made between themselves, co-opted as if our *own*. Or rather, *their* own, the leaders you speak of. Franklin, Hamilton, Jefferson, and the rest." Harold muttered a curse beneath his breath, his shoulders hunched, eyes narrowed in anger. "We are leaning on the wisdom of people we've spent generations *fighting* against. Shoving them back from lands, rightfully theirs, pushing them into those belonging to people further west."

He let out a long sigh, trying to release the tension he could feel swirling inside. "They are *only* words, Charlie—those of the natives, along with the Magna Carta, and the democratic principles of the Greeks. All of it slanted by the few, to benefit those willing to subscribe to the same doctrines, adhere to rules from the same belief systems that have led us to *where* we are today. Forcing a way of life on people we deem to be *lesser* beings. The same form of tyrannical behavior we're fighting against *now*. The same faceless enemy *I* fought against for all those years—losing in the end. The same group my son is fighting against today."

"You helped open the door, Harry, then wedged your foot in it, until those following in your footstep were ready to build on *your* efforts. Men like your son, doing what he can to help Washington, a man I personally despise for his dismissive personality, but respect for the *love* his men have for him. The backbone holding this fragile package together, with men of decent morals helping form the *strategies* needed. Your son—*one* of them."

Harold gave Charles a quiet look. "My vision, a curse. Passed down to him."

"No." Charles shook his head. "Not a curse. Your vision, your will and—*stubbornness*—are *gifts*. Your ability to see the field from your opponent's side of the board—stronger in Aaron. As it should be, with a son starting out standing on—"

"On a *parent's* shoulders." Harold stared at Charles. "So, tell me, my friend—tell me there is a chance he will *survive* it. That my son will not lose himself to the madness you've been loath to describe in full. That the damage done to him will *heal*."

"Aaron—" Charles hesitated, then reached out and placed his hand on the taller man's shoulders. "Your son—will be the man he is *meant* to be. The man you've *raised* him to become. That is all I know—*all* I can promise you." He shook his head. "Along with this. I will do everything I can to guide him toward the light, where and whenever possible."

Harold lowered his head, knowing when Sinclair and Meghan arrived, he would have to let her know their son was beyond reach. Unable to answer questions as to where he was, or what he was doing.

CHAPTER SIXTEEN
HIGHLAND MANOR
SUMMER, 1778

Logan forked another helping of hay onto the floor of the stall, one of a half-dozen running down the side of the manor stables. He set the pitchfork down, then raised one arm, wiping his forehead, shirt left hanging on a hook nearby, sweat beading his skin. A whisper of air stirred the dust, irritating his nostrils, eliciting a sneeze covered with the back of his hand.

"Bless you." A feminine voice spun him around, Marion standing with arms crossed, backlit by the light streaming in through a large set of doors, opened to let the heat out. Logan looked away, having seen the shape of her body through the thin fabric of her dress.

"Thank you. For your blessing." He grabbed the fork and bent to his labor, aware she'd closed the distance, the scent of her floral perfume pushing back against the humid reek of animals and their leavings.

"Hot, for such work. One would assume an outdoor chore to have been the wiser choice."

Logan shrugged, his eyes on the tines of the fork, careful to avoid an injury, with infection a certainty, leading to risk of losing a foot, or leg. "*One* is welcome to grab a shovel and *join* in. If one has the *knowledge* of how to *do* so. Without soiling their clothes.

A long silence followed, followed by Marion, dress rolled to her upper thighs, pinned in place with a silver brooch, her bare feet with perfectly formed toenails standing alongside his own. Logan grinned as the two of them finished the mucking out and strewing of fresh hay in each of the stalls.

Once they'd completed the chore, they washed their feet and lower legs with water from a large well, the bucket hoisted and poured, ice cold on skin warmed by the press of a bright sun, the two of them standing on a granite slab, watching a pool of water soaking into the ground.

"You should be wearing a hat, my lady of the stables—to protect your fair skin against burn from the sun." Logan handed Marion a towel. She refused to take it, leaning back against the top of the rock-walled well, raising one leg, waiting for him to dry it, a thin smile on her face, cheeks red from the heat of the stables.

Logan complied, taking his time, enjoying the feel of her toned flesh beneath the pressure of his fingers, her legs firm. The other one dried as well, with him looking down, afraid to meet her gaze, knowing he would not be able to deny himself the pleasure of a kiss, risking a slap, or worse, her gran uncle's wrath should she carry a complaint to his ears.

Marion sat up. "You must be hungry. All this work with little fare, your breakfast meal at dawn, and not much of it, according to my grandmother. You are ever a worry to her, in not eating a proper amount."

"I do not wish to be a burden. I've meat of my own, from a red grouse taken by a sling, yesterday morn."

"You are a huntsman, then." Marion knew as much about him as he did her. Strangers to one another, still, though it had been several weeks and more since he'd made a return of the wagon and team. "Do you know how to shoot a bow?" She paused. "Or the use of a snare?"

Logan placed the bucket back in the opening of the well, then turned and faced her. "I've no need of them. My aim with a sling stone, adequate to knock one down."

"Then the taking of a stag is beyond your ability." Marion sniffed.

"Too bad. A man able to provide venison on a regular basis would be quite useful."

"As was your brother, a *skilled* hunter." Logan stared at her. "But I'm not *him*. Not interested in being a *brother* to ya."

Marion tried to mirror the look in his eyes, chiding herself for playing at silly games. Not like her sister, who'd delighted in running poor Allyn in circles, testing her ability to hold, then dismiss his intentions toward her. "I'm *done* here, with more important things to attend to." She turned and started to walk away.

"*You* know how. To use a bow. You and your sister, *both*." Logan paused for a moment. "A *longbow*."

Marion nodded, refusing to turn around. "I do. Not as capable as my sister, who, while not able to bring Aaron's bow to full draw, is as deadly in aim. One of the larger racks in the hall, belonging to her."

"Is she also as skilled in use of the *snare*, mentioned?"

Marion spun and gave him a crooked smile. "Now *that* I'm the master of, knowing all the tricks—and the best places to put one."

Logan buttoned up his shirt, taking his time, nodding his head as he did so. "Then you could show me, some morning when the mist layers the heath in gossamer drift, birds in red dress probing the soil for seed and insects, both."

Marion returned a thoughtful gaze, eyes wide. "*Well* said." She swallowed, untying a warm smile, aiming it his way. "Tomorrow, then. At *dawn*." Then she was gone, leaving the light fragrance of her perfume, sweat, and residual odor of the stable in her wake.

Logan returned to his work, aware he'd made a move that could provide him an opportunity to secure his future or lead to his dismissal. It would depend on how his clan leader would react once made aware of the feelings he had toward the nominal lady of the manor. An interest that included the vast, sweeping reach of grounds attached. All of it with potential to become his, now he'd opened his hand, tossing the weighted dice from his hand.

☥☥☥

Eira held out her cup, her hand trembling as Shaun poured it half-full of tea. He added a small drip of honey, smiling at his sister as she stirred it in, watching as she leaned forward, breathing in its aromatic scent. Her voice was soft, barely more than a whisper, matching the sound of the breeze outside the window.

"He seems a *decent* sort. This new boy."

Shaun raised his eyebrows as he went to the window and looked toward the barn, his back to the kitchen where his sister spent most of her waking hours in, no longer with an interest in tending the gardens, or going to the croft. The trip there and back sapping her dwindling reserves of energy. "He—*is*. Though I have my concerns about his background. His people, known to me. With rumors their hands have been known to dip into places where they should not be."

"You mustn't hold him responsible for *their* stains, if true. Only those of his own." Eira sipped her tea, her voice sounding stronger. "Has there been any issues *here?*"

"None. His efforts, tireless. A hard worker, with an eye for what needs doing. Always one step ahead of my suggestions, which means he's quick—or I'm slowing down." Shaun looked at Eira, still seeing the beauty in her face, beneath the wrinkles and faded color of her eyes and hair. "Life has a way of moving on, whether we wish it to or not."

"Harold—is he soon to come down from the croft? I don't recall his last time here. Must be off hunting again, with Aaron." A slight hiss of water boiling on the large stove caught Shaun's ear as he bowed his head, aware his sister's lapses in memory often caused her to stare at objects, or people, uncertain of what or who they were. Other times, Eira's mind as sharp as a needle, with cutting wit and humorous asides, everyone in attendance needing a half-moment to realize they'd been artfully skewered.

"The father and son are where they *need* to be, sister-o-mine. As too Sinclair and Meghan." Shaun paused, a frown in his face. "And young Allyn, though I suspect *his* hide's been well tanned by now."

"He's been *flogged?*" Eira stirred, her hand trembling, tea nearly spilling over the rim. "For what *crime?*"

"Not flogged but *scolded*. For the crime of *love*, which it often is, for all the trouble it brings those grasping for it, wherever and whenever they can."

≢≢≢

"I have no intentions. At all. Was only a hunt for grouse, lying in the wet grass, waiting for them to feed themselves into the snares." Logan shook his head, pulling handfuls of feathers from two plump birds, several of them circling in the late morning breeze, landing in his thick hair.

Shaun pursed his lips, considering the tone of the young man's words, nothing ringing false. He shrugged. "Does *she* have intentions toward *you?*"

Logan looked up, confused. "Am I a *seer*, able to read a woman's mind?" He grinned, his hands working away. "Have *you* had any success, in all your visits made to croft farms throughout clan lands, in being able to decipher the truth hidden within a woman's innermost thoughts?"

"No. Most of the time learning what they wanted from me, and failed to get, with a door slammed in my face, or slap *across* it." He hesitated. "Or a wee bairn—thrust into my arms."

Logan let the smile drop from his face, focused on the job at hand, not acknowledging the comment to avoid his laird embarrassment. "I'll get these cleaned, then up to the manor." He looked at Shaun. "Unless you'd rather I didn't visit there again. Your decision on what I'm to do next."

Shaun let go of his previous concerns, seeing the look of fealty in Logan's eyes. "Is *your* decision to make, lad. The hill you're wanting to climb, a steep one—with twists in the trail and known for sudden bouts of changeable weather." He held out his hand, shaking the younger man's, feeling the strength in his grip. "I wish you luck, son. I fear you'll need it before you're through."

≢≢≢

"In a great church. In London, I think." Marion hesitated. "No. Bath. There are many beautiful ones there. Not like here."

"Aberdeen—is *not* London, nor Bath. But it *is* nearer to hand. On Scottish land. And far less expensive to—" Logan saw Marion's jaw tighten. He backed away; hands raised in surrender. "Whatever you decide is *fine* with me. It's to be *your* wedding. I'm happy enough to stand alongside the priest, ready to make my vows. Whether in a fine church, a heather-sweet moor, or atop a snow-capped mountain."

"It's to be a *church*. In *Bath*." Marion nodded. "Or London." She turned and gave Logan a stern look. "But *not* Aberdeen."

※※※

"You'll not be convinced to wait for your mother to return? It's only a matter of a message sent and a month and a week for her and your sister to arrive. Two months, at the most. Surely you can wait that—" Shaun stopped, his voice lowered, eyes focused on Marion's face. "You're not—"

"Don't *fash* yourself, Gran Uncle. I've not been so foolish as to risk *that*." Marion put her hands on her hips and leaned in. "And if I *had* walked that path, I've knowledge of the timing of a woman's flow, and when the time is ripe—" She grinned as Shaun covered his ears and moved away, unwilling to hear such things, especially from one so young.

Eira came into the salon, a measuring string with knots strung along it, her eyes smiling. "Masterfully done, child. A man with the blood of dozens of men on his hands, undone by such a small thing as that."

The two women laughed, the joyful noise chasing Shaun out of the kitchen, into the clear air outside.

※※※

The vision of his bride standing at the end of the aisle caused Logan to swallow, his future assured once Shaun delivered Marion into his hands. A vast fortune available, easing his path through life, and that of his extended family. The thought of inheriting the title of clan leader, of becoming laird of all Scott lands, brought tears to his eyes, brushed away with the back of his hand as he reached for Marion's.

The wedding was perfect. Everything planned out to perfection. From the arrangement of flowers, selection of songs, all the way through to the weather itself, managed by Marion's exacting eye. The guest list, prepared to include those she favored while excluding those who'd crossed her during her life to date, brought a smile to her lips as she imagined people's distress at not having received an invitation.

Eira had acquiesced to standing in for Sinclair, dissatisfied in not having her adopted daughter there but understanding Marion's desire to not let anything stand in the way of her detailed plans, explained to her a dozen times over, with multiple contingencies prepared for. And additional options waiting in the wings, if needed. Eira left with a dizzying headache, unable to keep up with her granddaughter's razor sharp and over-active mind.

Later that night, when Logan consummated the marriage, long delayed at Marion's request, he became frustrated when she forbade his finishing, her time near to hand, a child not in her immediate plans. The shunning had sent him through the bedroom door in a huff of anger, left unvoiced until he was clear of earshot, his muttered curses filling the gardens, disturbed a flock of doves from their roosts as the bells of the church rang in the end of the day with twelve solemn notes.

※※※

"You're my *wife*. By *all* meanings of the word. Legally and *religiously* bound. There *must* and *will* be an accounting made of monies accrued, with access provided *me*." Logan set his glass down with a thud, a remnant of whiskey slipping over the edge, dripping onto the polished wood of a table in the salon.

"And I'll tell you a *final* time—the money you seek is locked up in various places, invested in over a *hundred* directions, hither and yon, earning enough to cover the ongoing expenses of my mother's establishments, throughout England and beyond."

"There has to be some measure of liquids—of—"

Marion smirked. "Liquidity?"

Logan snarled. "*Yes*. Of *money*. Where a man—nae a *husband* can hold it in his *hands*. Count it out. Provide for—"

"His family?"

"Yes!"

Marion sniffed. "*I'm* your family now. Or rather, you are part of *mine*. And without recourse in this matter, the papers already signed. The law, *clear*."

"I did not understand what I was *signing!* And will hire barristers, to fight for what is rightfully mine by *established* law."

"Hired with *what* coin?"

"I will find one *willing* to do the work, with payment made once my rights are recognized!"

"Which *one?*" Marion smiled. "I have them *all* in my hand, along with the justices." She came over, placing her hand on his cheek. "These are *my* people, Logan. They live in *my* world. Friendships cultivated since I first attended my mother on our frequent trips throughout the realm, ever since childhood." She tilted her head, eyes gleaming. "*All* of them, cherishing me as if their *own* daughter, niece, or sister. All their children—*my* friends, soon to step into positions of power."

"Then why *marry* me?" Logan took her hands, squeezing them, his eyes dark. "Why—"

"I *didn't*. It was *you* who married *me*. And are now *my* husband, with everyone throughout clan lands knowing it. Their eyes on you *everywhere* you go, with people watching your every move. Why you are *here* now, no longer free to do as you please. A man of clan Scott, with the title in hand once Shaun passes it to *me*. Yours to wear—*mine* to use."

His hands found her throat, his anger before him, unchecked. Then his eyes widened as he felt a sharp pain in his lower body. Logan looked down, blood seeping from his fly. A knife in his wife's hand. The blade touching his manhood, hard enough to draw blood.

"I *will* need a child, someday. You, to provide the *seed*. But only to me—and *none* other. For if you do—if you try and emulate my dear gran uncle and lie with a woman of the clan—then your *life* will be one of *misery* beyond your *ken*." Marion paused, her hand on the hilt of the thin-bladed knife, twisting it slightly. "Do you *hear* me, husband dearest? You are to be nothing more than a *figurehead*. *My* antlered rack, placed upon the wall of the manor, alongside that of my brother's and sister's."

She reached up and shoved him away, the knife still in her hand, the tip of it red with his blood, a single drop falling to the surface of a polished wooden floor.

CHAPTER SEVENTEEN
PHILADELPHIA MANOR
SUMMER, 1778

The bedroom in the manor, now belonging to George's mother, was the same. Unchanged since the last time Sinclair had been in it. She put her clothes away in the closet, eyes blurred by tears, wishing the past to have been but a bad dream. That her husband and his large friend were out on a ride through the countryside, with a dinner party planned.

"Everything is to your satisfaction, my dear?" The words from George's mother stirred the still air of the room, left untouched since her son's death in a mysterious explosion, several years ago.

"We're fine. Your concern for my daughter and I, appreciated." Sinclair came over and took the elderly woman's hand, frail with age spots and cool to the touch. "The news of the loss of your son caused me *unfathomable* grief. A great man—as close to me as if a brother."

"As too the unexplained loss of your husband. A wife or mother ever in worry for those she loves. The pain, unbearable, our loved ones taken from us—though we manage to survive it. Somehow." She moved away from the embrace Sinclair started to give her, crossing to the door, leaving without a word, her steps slipping along the hallway, lightly scuffing the wooden floor as she walked away.

Meghan passed by outside the bedroom window, smiling, Allyn

beside her, holding her hand. The two of them were sharing an intense conversation, laughing, heading toward the stables where a few horses were located, far less in quantity and quality then before.

Sinclair sighed, feeling a tug as she watched them, remembering the walks and words shared with Harold. Then she smiled, remembering her confrontation with the stowaway and his accomplice, resulting in threat of a severe flogging by the captain of the ship. Held in abeyance should the lad agree to work off his debt as part of the crew, sent below to scrub the bilge, scour the deck, and help replace worn rigging, climbing high on swaying masts in gusting winds. Allyn had readily agreed, taking to the tasks assigned with a wide grin and winning smile. The captain and crew left begging him to stay on at voyage end.

Megan, expecting a private administration with paddle or belt, had been surprised when her mother pulled her aside, asking a series of probing questions concerning activities below deck. Assurances offered that nothing like that had happened, yet, though both were eager to wed as soon as possible.

Sinclair returned to putting her clothes away, planning to stay at the estate, the grounds much smaller in acreage with a sizeable portion sold off, along with another headstone added to the family plot. She would wait there until her husband sent a coded message, letting her know the property she'd selected before he left for Scotland was ready for occupancy. A farmhouse sitting at a crossroad, with a crew of men building a store and warehouse. Then she'd join Harold, asking him where her son was, and how soon she could recover him.

※※※

Harold stepped out from behind a large oak, his hand half-raised in greeting to his wife as she approached on horseback, her hair in a tight braid draped over the back of a black riding coat. He moved into the lane, taking the bridle in his fingers as she pulled up, waiting for her to dismount.

Sinclair slid down, her hand clinging to the road-dusted leather of the stirrup, gathering her balance as the blood rushed into her cramped legs, her mouth dry, the ride over dusty roads leeching the moisture from her body and skin. "Husband." Her voice, cracked with weariness and tension, was husky.

Harold offered her a canteen, gratefully accepted. As she took a mouthful and swirled it in her mouth, Sinclair tried to stay her nervousness, the coded note slipped into her hand by a young boy three days earlier, while visiting a small shop in Philadelphia, naming a place and day to meet.

Sinclair leaned over and spit, then straightened up and took a longer drink, eyes closed, preparing herself. When she lowered the canteen, she gave her husband a searching look, noting the pinched corners of his eyes, fearing the worst, her hand going to her mouth.

"Our son—is alive."

Sinclair felt her knees buckle, a feeling of relief washing through her, tears springing from her eyes, overflowing, drawing dust-brown streaks down her narrow cheeks, her lips quivering as she shook her head, staring at the man she'd loved, lost, then loved again, and now felt separated from.

Harold reached out, touching Sinclair's shoulder, inviting her into a one-armed embrace, leaning his head into the angle of her neck, taking in her scent, along with that of the horse, road-dust, and blanket of leaves beneath the sheltering limbs of an ancient oak tree.

"He is—hale?" Sinclair looked up, touching Harold's face. "He is whole—in *body?*"

"Yes. As of two weeks ago."

Sinclair wiped her eyes on the linen shirt her husband had on, leaving a smear of dirt behind. "I've been unable to sleep these past few days. Worried out of my mind." She stepped back. "How did he look? Was he in good spirits? Where is—"

"I did not *see* him." Harold led the horse into the shadow, Sinclair left standing on the edge of the pool of slightly cooler air, hands at her sides.

"Then how are you able to—"

"Charles." Harold tied off the reins to a low hanging branch, the horse tugging it toward the ground as it swept its large nose above the leaf littered earth, looking for grass. Finding none, it snorted in displeasure. Harold poured some water into his hand, using it to wash the dust from its flared nostrils. Then he cupped a small amount in his palm, watching as the animal wet its tongue, then shoved its nose against his chest, looking for more. "He was with him. Charles. With Aaron. Unable to reveal his location to me, or to anyone else."

Harold turned and fixed Sinclair with a firm look. "Our son is leading an insurgent force of hardened men in raids made against the English supply lines. And moving ahead of their army, burning bridges, forcing them to find alternate paths or stop and build new crossings."

"Our son, Aaron—is their *leader?* A boy—with men willing to follow *his* orders?" Sinclair stared, then stepped forward, the shadows unable to hide the gleam of frustration in her light-colored eyes. "You could not make him—*force* Charles to lead you to our son?"

"He does not know *where* he is. His eyes covered when guided there during the night, meeting inside a temporary shelter, leaving with his eyes bound once more."

Sinclair shook her head, the braid slipping over her shoulder. "This is *beyond* belief—that our son is *here*. Out there—" She swept her arm in a half-circle. "*Somewhere.* Beyond my reach, and yours, if what you say is the truth and not some tale told to spare my feelings. Or a lie told you by Charles." She hesitated, her voice breaking. "Charlie—*here* as well. Acting as *what?* An intermediary between Aaron and you?"

She sank to the ground, unable to hold the improbable news in her mind, feeling the world shift under her riding boots, one hand raised, denying Harold's approach, needing time to accommodate to the knowledge she would not soon be able to hold her boy.

Harold knelt two paces away, remembering the day Sinclair had visited the grave of her father, lying a horizon to the west away in the wilderness. He recalled the strength of the woman he'd pledged himself to, in full. Returning her love with his betrayal, abandoning her and his family to try and stem the tide leading to war. Unable to do more than delay it a while, based on what Charles had told him. Now back again. Back to the beginning of a new path, this time with Sinclair. The next twist in the road starting from beneath the shadows of a large, sheltering tree.

CHAPTER EIGHTEEN
RANGING AFIELD
LATE SUMMER, 1778

A short man with close-set eyes held up a length of rope, a series of knots tied into it at irregular spots. He grumbled beneath his breath, watching as another man finished digging a two-foot wide by six-foot-long hole, removing one foot of soil, scattering it among tall blades of grass. Then he slung the rope across his neck and leaned over, picking up and tossing square cut clumps of grassy sod as far away as he could. "It dinna make *any* sense, the digging of shallow holes 'cross this end of the field. To what end?"

The other man, on his knees, was busy scooping out the blade-loosened soil. He looked up. "Orders are orders. Been good ones from our young captain so far. Now hand me the free end of the damn rope and run out the string toward the stakes, just there." He reached out and pointed, indicating wooden sticks jutting from the far end of open grassland. A dozen more groups of men were working to either side, bent to the same task. Told to dig pits at every knot, then fill them in with thick armfuls of fresh cut grass, brought over by other men working fifty paces away.

The shorter man frowned, wiping sweat from his eyes as he backed away, rope in hand. "It's fookin' *bollocks!*"

"It's *fookin'* orders!"

A quiet voice from one side swiveled both their heads around. "It's the *length* of a horse's stride, when in full gallop, staggered enough in measure to cause them to land in one or more holes during a charge. Inducing a stumble, spilling their riders to the ground."

The man on his knees remained in place, not standing to salute, orders issued and strictly adhered to against showing any sign of respect to higher authority. The other man shrugged, his shoulders rising then falling as he stared at the rope in is hands, then down at the hole in the sod.

"Then why not dig them *deeper*—to cause more damage?"

Aaron knelt, his hand in the hole, measuring the depth, giving the man with the spade a nod of satisfaction. Then he looked up, a smile on his face. "We are about the business of killing *men*, not innocent beasties. The holes will suffice as is, with the riders left on the ground where our arrows and bullets will find them."

The man on his knees alongside Aaron laughed. "I *told* him you had a plan. Like you've *always* done, since taking over from Falcon. Only a handful of us lost since then, mostly due to their own stupidity, not listening to what you told them to do." He glanced up, giving his partner a hard look, the other man nodding, pulling on the end of the rope, walking toward the far-off stake. He stopped at the second knot this time, waiting for the other man to join him. One of the grass collectors came along behind, spreading armfuls of fresh cut grass, filling in the depression, then going to harvest more.

Aaron stood back, watching as his men put one phase of his plan in place. Then he turned his head to see the next one in progress, with several other groups of men digging small pits with the same dimensions, placed alongside the length of the field. Enough, he thought to himself, to allow forty men with two muskets and a brace of pistols each to lie down in, wearing ghillie suits adorned with twists of grass, springing up and releasing volleys from their weapons, then running away to prepared positions at the far end of the field, while an element of British lancers followed close behind, charging to their doom.

Falcon, second in nominal command, the same man who'd once scoffed at the idea of using 'prickers' against musket toting soldiers, came over, rubbing his chin, a tight look on his lined face. "A risk, this.

You and your group of young archers at the far end, exposed to sword and pistol fire from the damned lancers. If you end up having gotten it wrong." He paused, turned his head to one side, spitting a stream of tobacco juice on the ground. "*This* time."

Aaron gave him a sideways glance. "It's always nice to have your positive shade on things, especially on such a sunny, bright day."

"It's my *nature*, I reckon—from seeing *other* plans go to hell in a barrow, once the shite hits the cow's tail."

"Speaking of which—mention was recently made to me concerning rumors having reached the ears of those we are in *support* of." Aaron squared up, facing the taller man, who returned his stare. "Brought to me by a man I have the *utmost* respect for."

"It is no secret to any how I feel about the methods being used to extract information—through some senseless need for revenge—just to salve your slip of a girl's hurt feelings." He leaned forward and spit again, aiming at a spot halfway between them. "All of us carry things causing our blood to boil, in seeing what's been done to innocents—killed in their own homes."

"Still—a violation to speak of tactics used here, by *me*." Aaron leaned forward. "I shall prefer charges once this day's action is behind us, recommending your dismissal from this force. You will be free to join with the militia, or the army. But you will no longer serve with *us*."

"*If* we survive such nonsense as this plan promises to be." The man kept his voice low, his eyes fastened on Aaron's, unblinking.

"See to your *own* skin, then. As will I." Aaron watched as the man turned and walked away with a long, loose gait, slipping into the shadows of the woods running along all four sides of the long, narrow stretch of grass. He turned about, heading to where his most accurate men with muskets were preparing their ghillie suits and seeing to their weapons of war.

Neither man noticed as a slightly darker shadow peered at them from between a thick clump of trees, watching without moving until they walked away, then slipping back into the depths of the forest.

᭥᭥᭥

The British scouts returned, a handful of natives moving with a loping pace. They'd ranged ahead to search out the group of men the English were searching for, the officer in charge aching to bring them to bay before they could elude his force of lancers and column of soldiers on foot. Traveling at speed, without use of wagons, enhancing their rapid movement through the countryside. A change in tactics designed to improve their chances of success.

The leader was a Captain in the King's Light Dragoons, with experience in routing enemy forces with lightning quick charges, breaking their lines, their morale, draining their will to stand and fight, sending them fleeing in disarray. "Go—and see what they have to report."

His second went forward, listening as an interpreter translated from French to English, returning with a pinched expression, saluting. "They found recent sign of the ones we're after. In woods to the right side of a clearing, just ahead. Evidence of them having moved on only an hour or so ago." He hesitated, drawing a sharp look from the captain. "The scouts said there were no tracks leading away from where they'd camped. Said it was like they were—*their* words, sir— said it was like the men had turned into *spirits*. Sir." The officer, a First Lieutenant with a solid reputation and ten years in service, looked back over his shoulder, watching as the natives headed to one side of the column, keeping to themselves, waiting for a decision from the captain.

"The usual nonsense—from *ignorant* people, First Lieutenant. We shall push on at pace, hoping to catch them up before they reach the next bridge, where they are no doubt already hard at work, trying to destroy it before we can cross."

"Sir." The second in command saluted, then reclaimed his saddle, waving his hand and pointing forward, the column of lancers and foot soldiers resuming the chase, based on plans recovered from a pack lost by one of those they were seeking. Their orders clear. To find, fix, and destroy the insurgent group, returning with the heads of their leader, called the Hood by soldiers wearing redcoats, along with that of his lover, said to be an evil witch. Their bodies burnt, along with those of the rest of their force. Whether men lying dead, mortally wounded, or captured alive. Their hands and feet tied, then tossed into the flames with the rest.

※※※

"The fat—is in the *pan*." A thin, wiry man named Smoke, with a fire-scarred face, and of indeterminate age, cracked a smile that creased his dirt-stained face, revealing a line of white teeth, several gone missing. He chuckled, then turned away, heading back into the woods, climbing into the lowest limbs of one of dozens of leaf-heavy oak trees, where he and several dozen others had been hiding for the better part of the morning. They'd held their breath, listening as the native scouts passed underneath, scouring the thick wood line for signs of an ambush.

The English, leery of having the same tactic employed against them again, with the insurgents making their attacks from concealment, had taken to using their scouts to scour every tree line they came to. Wolf, meeting the new tactic with one of his own, had ordered his men into hiding, clinging to the topmost limbs of the trees, uneasy due to their precarious position. Sighs of relief offered once the natives finished their hurried scout and headed back to their main force. The men, with their worries now behind them, had dropped to the ground, their attention focused on sliding into position behind rocks, or tree trunks, weapons readied. Once there, they listened for the sound of hooves on dry ground, approaching along a narrow path that opened into the long field, heavily seeded with men in grass suits, and a hundred shallow, grass covered holes.

Aaron took a deep breath, holding it for a moment, then releasing it. He stood at the far end of the prepared field, his eyes narrowed in thought as he watched Smoke run back to his perch in the trees. He had his longbow and two quivers of arrows with him, a dozen trained archers taking up position twenty paces behind him in the edge of woods, well beyond the last of the grass covered holes.

He turned and gave them a smile, waving his bow at the group of fleet footed men, most as young as himself. They returned the gesture, looking at him with confident, unlined faces, free of the least sign of fear, having never known failure since joining his force. Their sturdy backs and strong legs had been vital in helping to carry supplies from campsite to campsite. Their time in between spent learning how to draw back stiff-limbed longbows, Aaron showing them the ins and outs of hitting targets with iron-tipped arrows, carried in quivers slung at their sides.

"They will be here soon. With lancers to the fore, eager to charge forward to rout us, thinking we're the rear element." He gave each man a long look, watching as they lost their smiles, several swallowing with difficulty as his serious mood washed over them. "We *will* lose friends this day, their force too large by half. Unable to defeat them with the number we have on hand. But General Washington is counting on us to turn them away, allowing him time to seek a stronger position."

"We'll *win* though—right?" The youngest among them, a boy with hair the color of sun-dried grass gave Aaron a look that tugged at his heart. He tried to remember the last time such innocence had found its way to his own face, picturing a hunt with his sister in the highlands, a rabbit made to pay with its life for Meghan's success.

"Of *course*. We have *right* on our side, and the trust of Washington himself in our ability to overcome the odds, great or small." It was all he could do to keep from going over and tousling the young man's hair. "See to the stringing of your bows and remember to match my angle of aim—releasing on *my* command."

❦❦❦

"*There*, sir! Ahead and to the left. In the tree line at the far end of the field." The first lieutenant pointed. The captain squinted, barely able to make out a dozen or more men, oblivious to the danger heading their way.

"Form the line, Lieutenant."

The other officer saluted, then waved one arm, his voice kept low, signaling the mounted lancers behind to spread out in line abreast, swords loosened in their scabbards, pistols brought to half-cock, readied to fire once they'd closed the distance to their targets, more soldiers starting to emerge from the trail behind, moving forward, into the bright sunlight.

A series of commands echoed throughout the column of men on foot, trailing the lancers by half a hundred paces, their own officers having them well in hand, arranging them into two broad lines, the men eager to move ahead at pace, staying as close to the lancers as they could, until the charge would begin.

⁂

"They are lining themselves up as if turkeys on a limb, our lead balls will tear through them. Impossible to miss." The short stocky man, who'd been the one to stare at the knotted rope in confusion, turned his head, looking at his partner. *"Fookin'* idiots—with *no* sense of tactics."

"You don't say." The other man shook his head slightly, causing the grass of his covering to rustle, looking to see if any of the men on foot half-a-hundred paces away had noticed. He whisper-shouted to his friend. "Close your maw, and see to your first piece, coming to half-cock only."

A hand muffled click answered him, joined by dozens of others in the hands of men lying close enough to have heard it, with the signal passed along to the rest of the men lying crosswise to the line of march of the lancers, with the British infantry lined up, close behind.

⁂

Men, tucked into the edges of the woods, done with their imitation of squirrels, moved forward, kneeling, readying their weapons. Each man had two muskets and two pistols near to hand. They watched the lancers advance, their responsibility to fire into the stacked ranks of the infantry then retreat, moving through the woods, toward the far end of the field, coming out and picking off any surviving riders left struggling to their feet once their mounts stumbled, spilling them to the ground.

The man called Smoke knelt beside Falcon. "It promises to be another bloodbath—for *them*."

The wiry, stern-faced man gave him a cold look. "There will be enough pieces of lead flung back and forth today to give *everyone* cause to duck." He turned his head to the side and spat. "*No* one without risk of catching a ball, if'n their luck runs out." Then he focused his attention on the end of the field where the group of men calling themselves the 'bait' were milling around, acting confused by the sudden appearance of men on horseback.

※※※

The captain waved his sword, eschewing use of a pistol, anticipating the sweep of his honed blade against the upraised arm of a man, eyes wide in fear, slicing through his neck, blood lust hazing his vision as his horse leapt ahead, the thunder of its hooves joined by dozens of others, creating a cascading rumble in the air.

His second rode at his side, pistol brought to half-cock, prepared to use it when opportunity presented, charged with preventing the enemy from pulling his senior officer from his mount, should their attack falter. He spurred his own mount, a sense of unease creeping along his spine. His eyes swiveled to the woods passing by to his left, aware the scouts had already cleared them, but feeling a cold ball of fear burying itself in his scrotum. Then he leaned forward, lowering himself in the saddle, his pistol held out, alongside the outstretched neck of his steed.

※※※

Aaron calmly notched an arrow, taking a moment to inspect the honed blade of the head, provided in the hundreds by a smithy, fashioned to his exact specifications, delivered in the bottoms of kegs filled with thin wooden shafts. Turkeys, taken for food, had provided feathers for vanes, fastened in place using native techniques, as had the arrow points.

He watched from the corners of his eyes as the young men on either side copied every one of his deliberate motions, their trust in him complete, bringing his emotions to the surface. He dampened them down by performing a quick calculation of twenty men times twenty-four arrows, minimum. With another twenty-four shafts at hand, ready for each archer in sheaths packed full, lying to one side. Almost a thousand arrows released from bows only the strongest men could pull to full draw. Now in the hands of young men who'd been practicing for hours each day, in between their campfire chores.

Enough, Aaron whispered, as he watched the line of horses coming to full gallop, nearing the prepared ground. Enough he hoped, as he came to full draw, mirrored in angle by the others, releasing a first volley at the foot soldiers over a hundred paces away, ignoring the officer in the lead of the lancers, waving his sword, the sun glinting from the polished surface of fine English steel.

※※※

The horse seemed to drop out from beneath the first lieutenant, his body rising from the saddle, trying to cling to his mount with his legs as the heavy-bodied animal slipped to one side, stumbling, almost able to catch its balance, then going down in a blurring motion as the earth and sky traded places. He felt his shoulder snap on contact with the ground, his vision going dark, the sound of horses in panic filling the air, then silence as his senses left him, preventing his being able to feel the waves of pain sleeting through his damaged body.

The captain urged his mount ahead, hearing the screams of his men as they urged their own mounts on. His vision filled with the image of a man centered amidst a group of wide-eyed youths with raised bows. He leaned forward, the tip of his sword outstretched as if a finger, poised to strike the man through, knowing, with utmost certainty this was the Wolf. The man they were looking for.

A smile creased his lips as he rode directly at him, a flight of arrows slipping over his head, impacting somewhere far behind. Of no real bother, his destiny lying straight ahead. Then his world turned upside down, his arms akimbo as he flew from the saddle, landing flat on his back, the wind knocked from his lungs. He stared up into the face of the enemy leader, who looked down, a look of pity in his bright blue eyes.

※※※

A rush of boots pounded along the sunbaked ground, creating as great a vibration as the lancers, the soldiers in two lines breaking into a fast pace just as a wall of lead from one side of the thick woods decimated their ranks with raking fire, bullets worming their way through several men's bodies at a time, blood spraying through the air creating a mist of fine droplets of red rain. Men fell to the ground with shocked cries, missing vital pieces, crawling on the earth, seeking to try and rebuild themselves, dying with outstretched hands clinging to tufts of grass, or to the legs or arms of comrades doing the same. All of them wanting to escape the endless wall of lead coming from out of a cloud of thick smoke. Arrows, falling from the sky at an angle, sighed into the dry ground, dozens nosing into the bodies of men. Luck of the draw determining which form of lethality struck first. The bunched formation of men, churned into a sea of writhing forms, struggled to escape the deadly storm sweeping through them.

Those having escaped the initial onslaught moved on, their eyes focused to the woods on the right, unaware until too late that the grass field to their left had risen, a barrage of musket balls tearing into their ranks, helping finish the slaughter, men spinning in place then dropping to the grass.

※※※

Aaron picked his way between knots of men turned into huddled piles of blood, urine, and bowel-stained clothing, a loose arrangement of bodies with shattered limbs, staring eyes, and clenched hands. A few survivors lay among them, on their backs, their shocked eyes unable to focus. Hands trembling, mouths working in wavering screams, trying to clear their ears, their mouths, their minds of the gore covering their faces.

Horses, some with broken legs from careless tumbles and the

hooves of those coming along behind, shrieked in a chorus of misery, ended as quickly as possible by men moving throughout the field, knives used to end the suffering of the beasts. The soldier's gift, given to enemy soldiers mortally wounded, including three of their own. Hands, clasped over nose and mouth, ending pain-filled moans from dying men, fingers covering their horrific wounds, trying to keep vital fluids from leaking out as the glimmer of life slowly dimmed in their questioning eyes.

Aaron came to one of his own men, Falcon, lying to one side of the mayhem, staring up at the sky with open eyes, a large crater in his forehead, exposing his final thought to any who cared to look. He stopped, waiting to feel something as he rubbed the sticks of his humanity together, trying to ignite an emotion of sadness, loss, or concern for the man's family. Unable to do so.

"It was a stray shot—most likely from one of our own, done him in." Smoke, who'd been the one to make report of the forces coming their way, stepped over. "He was drawing down on you. Could see his intent, standing right alongside him, seeing his finger on the trigger." The man shrugged. "Reached out to try and stop him—just as he fell, mortally wounded." He leaned over, spitting in the dead man's face. "Would ha' done it myself—the *bastard*!"

"He was a *good* fighter. One of our best." Aaron looked across the bloody field, appreciating that the numbers killed here this day, when added to all the others, paled in comparison to those his father had written of. He sighed, staring across the field, littered with the dead, knowing each man's death was a tragedy, measured the same by those who'd fallen, and the loved ones left to mourn. His own journals overflowing with the same thoughts and observations made in those of his father, without added description of places or names, lest it provide the enemy vital information. A moot point, he knew, for these men, having greeted their final day.

"Help the archers to refocus their thoughts, gathering up any spent arrows worth saving. Then assemble the men. *You're* my second, now." Aaron walked away, going far enough into the woods to where he could find a place to sit and let the emotions buried deep within come to the surface. To release as much of the horror as possible, aware from conversations with his father it would poison his soul if left to fester.

Chatte found him, as she always did, telling him she was able to sense where he was by following the sound of his generous heart. Her own kept locked away, warmed by coals of hatred for the men in red uniforms, flaring up when using her knife. Revenge found in the scent of their blood, in their mewling cries, begging her to stop. Like her two young brothers had done, shuddering in agony on a sand beach painted red with their blood. Decades ago, unable to recall the details of their murder, left with faded images of thin arms reaching out, trying to push aside the tips of bayonets, failing, unable to prevent them from piecing their bodies. Left alongside a father with a deep slash across his throat from an officer's sword. Made to watch, holding the tied hands of her mother. Then watching again, kneeling in the lower deck of a transport ship at sea while the same officer stood to one side, directing his men in the repeated rape of her mother.

She shook her head, the words of her grandmother in her ears, telling how she'd saved her. Pulled with a raptor's grip from the arms of a mindless victim with nothing left to live for, climbing over the railing of a ship, child in grasp. The broken woman left falling into the heaving sea below. Her young daughter spoon-fed the memories of it throughout her life, constantly reminded of the deeds done to them both. Her thirst for revenge well stoked, helping to form the blade of her desire, sharp edged, honed by English blood.

"You have won your battle, *again*."

The sound of her voice stirred a reaction from Aaron. He was sitting stone-faced, in the middle of a thick bed of moss, having managed to slip across the sea to the highlands. He released the image, getting to his feet, knowing it was time to return to being the man his men expected him to be.

"I have done *nothing*—except engineer the slaughter of men, led by a fool." Aaron gave Chatte a quiet look, reading the question in her eyes. "Their leader lives. Under guard. In a state of shock at how quickly his life has turned upside down." He noted the slight upturn of the corners of his woman's full lips, a cold shiver spreading along his spine as he considered what the night would bring.

"His second—and the officers leading those on foot?" Chatte came a step closer, unable to hide her thirst for what was to come.

"The first is—*also* alive." He paused, questioning how he could care for a person with two such opposing sides. Able to lie with her between engagements, while aware the darkness was always there, lurking in the shadows with feral energy, waiting to be fed. "They're dead. Along with the men they led. Two of them—mortally injured." He paused. "I gave them the gift. By my own hand."

She narrowed her eyes, hands clenched in anger. "You promised to stop *doing* that! To allow them to linger, dying in *pain* while crying out for their *mothers*! The same way *my* brothers cried out for *theirs*."

"I made you *no* such promise."

"You did. Your silence, an agreement *made* to me." Chatte spun around, turning her back to him. "You cannot know—you have *no* understanding of what they *took* from me. What I saw *done*. To *all* of them, seeing them killed. With my *own* eyes."

"Not by *these* men, most of them not born when the clearance of your people in Nova Scotia occurred. Most of the others, only children, like yourself at the time." Aaron came over and touched her shoulder. "You see the *uniform*—and I understand what it *does* to you. How it makes you feel."

Chatte's voice was a low-toned moan of pain. "You—see *nothing*. Understand *nothing*." She turned into him, placing her head against his chest, fingers clutching his shirt, pulling at the hair on his chest.

Aaron absorbed the pain, holding her, drinking in the scent of her hair. Inhaling the ripe sweat of her body, the odor of burnt gunpowder on her slim hands. He took in a long, sighing breath, letting it out, failing to erase the odors lurking in the air. Of wood smoke, and blood, soaking into the field from unstrung men and horses. Along with the gore he knew would soon be dripping from the edge of her heated blade. The two officers left pleading for their lives as their torture began. Left begging for their deaths, once Chatte began to release their secrets with deft strokes of her delicate fingers, knife in hand.

He struggled with the love felt for the damaged child in his arms. Wrestled with his desperate need for her, helping him to escape, if only for brief moments found here and there, to a place where nothing else mattered except the joining of their bodies. Each finding something within the other, gone missing in their own lives. Her need to lie in the sheltering arms of someone she could trust, helping to keep her demons at bay. His need to lie in the sanctuary of her body, seeking forgiveness for his sins.

CHAPTER NINETEEN
A HIGHLAND DRAW
SPRING, 1779

Dusk was a faint hint of red in a lowering sky, clouds gathering for a solid night of rain to come. It was cold, the air heavy with moisture, a light wind sweeping from low to high, stirring the mane of the small mare Shaun was riding.

He was alone, Logan having turned down his invitation to tag along with a slight shake of his head, eyes downcast, his mood sour. Shaun left thinking the lad must have lost another battle of wills to the woman who ruled the roost. Marion firmly in control of the manor, and soon, the entire clan.

Shaun had spread the word to any with a say in the matter as to his choice of replacement. Most had nodded their heads to his suggestion, trusting his judgement. Others, a handful of middle-aged men, had scoffed at the idea, with understanding made clear to them that Logan would have the title, but not the power. Most bowing in agreement, while the youngest among them shrugged, their displeasure hidden behind false smiles and claps of hands on their lairds back.

"The weather—" A voice called out from behind where a man stood at the end of a thin footpath, traced into the slanted face of a hill, feeding down into the narrow draw. "Promises to be a *wild* evening—bad for your *health*."

Shaun pulled at the reins, bringing the weary mare to a grateful stop. "Douglas—cousin to Duncan, my former friend and confidant—gone missing this past year, and more."

"And you—laird to a clan I would see left in the hands of a *man*. One I consider a *close* friend to me. With title only, for the moment, led around by a ring in his nose. One *you* helped put there, tugged by your gran niece, who considers herself *equal* to any man of the clan."

"You'd not dare speak so openly, unless you had others at your back." Shaun looked around, raising his voice. "Will ya not make yourselves known? I've a bottle, with enough Aquae Vitea left in it to share—should ya dare show yourselves." He reached into a pack at his side, the man standing behind him pulling out a pistol, bringing it to half-cock.

"You'll be sliding from your horse, hands kept clear of the sack." Douglas slid closer, though careful to stay far enough away to avoid potential of a knife slash from the ancient warrior, known for sudden and savage acts with his back pushed against a wall. Two other men stepped out from the mouth of the draw. The one in front, a large brute of a man, carried a claymore in his thick fingered hand. The other, slim in build, stayed back, holding a short sword.

Douglas sighed, shaking his head as he stared at the bigger man. "*Really*, Conor? You came armed with a *long* sword? We're not to engage in a duel, you *daft* fool."

"I find it a decent enough weapon, to do what needs be done." The man with the claymore walked up, a bear of a man with broad shoulders and wide hips. A match to his brother gone missing, his face covered in a thick, bushy beard with a deep scowl on his face.

Shaun nodded at the imposing figure. "I see you've got your *growth*, almost as big as your brother Duncan was—'fore I cut him to pieces, feeding him to half a hundred hungry *hogs*."

Conor glowered, his face chiseled from dark stone, eyes locked to Shaun's as he moved to one side, the other man with him sliding away, staying clear of the large sword hanging alongside Conor's thick leg, the tip touching the soil.

Shaun worked his arms, loosening his shoulders, ignoring the sharp pain in his hip and lower back. His breathing came easy, a smile on his face as he heard the rasp of coarse breathing from Conor and Douglas, knowing their emotions would stiffen their limbs with anger, and fear.

He didn't bother with any more banter, setting to work, a knife slipped into one hand from his sleeve, while his other snatched a purse from his belt, heavy with coins, tossing it to the man with the pistol. He waited for him to reach out to catch or deflect it, then lunged forward, driving his blade up and under the startled man's jaw, burying it to the hilt, pulling it out, sliding to one side, a hiss from the tip of the claymore missing his shoulder. He reversed his turn, driving the knife into Conor's side, the blade penetrating halfway in, locked in place by the thick bones of the big man's ribs. The hilt was torn from his fingers as the struck man pulled away, leaving him facing the third man, who slid to a stop, sword held at a slight angle, hands rock steady, looking to see if the battle-seasoned laird was holding a second knife.

Shaun stepped back, keeping his eyes locked on the unknown man as he listened to the wet coughing from Coner, his punctured lung started to fill with blood. "You're the best and only *good* decision these two idiots made. Hiring a man with experience. A soldier, no doubt — or highwayman."

"Both." The man looked to one side, Shaun stepping back, the claymore missing him by a foot, with Conor struggling to lift it to strike again. Shaun stepped in, driving his fist against the hilt of his knife, forcing it in all the way, the point reaching the wounded man's heart, finishing the job. "You seek *all* the money, beyond that of the purse paid you for this day's work." Shaun eyed the sky. "Or rather, this *night's* work."

The remaining man nodded, reaching out with the tip of his sword, indicating the one still clung to by Conor, who'd fallen to his knees, his eyes wide as his heart wound down to a fluttering stop. "An opportunity given you, to die with steel in your hand, out of respect for the small army of Englishmen you've killed over the years."

"It would be the lad, Logan, I imagine, putting the others on my trail. Bitter, the taste of his lot in life, married to money he cannae touch. And to a woman holding his manhood in her hand, with the will and ability to remove it with her *own* honed blade."

"Wouldn't know as to any of that. You'll need ask these two — when you see them again. Soon, I wager, with myself having miles to go before dawn." The man peered at the mare. "Your horse looks to be a sweet lass. I'll be taking her with me—once I finish you."

"To the *living* go the spoils." Shaun reached out and kicked the claymore from Conor's hand, picking it up, hefting it, the weight familiar, though a bit wieldy in his weakened grasp. No longer able to hold it properly. He gave the other man a nod, then set himself for the dance to come.

⚜ ⚜ ⚜

Shaun had added the slain men's purses to his own, creating a heavy burden on a body taxed by a sore hip and aching back. The mare whinnied as she approached the manor stable, eager to be home, anxious to enter her stall, with fresh hay and water provided after a long, uphill ride.

Shaun slid from the saddle, painting the side of it red, a gash in his lower ribs oozing blood. Enough, he knew, that it might end him. Determined to reach the manor before it did. He made his way out of the stable, leaving the main door open, the mare left behind to fend for herself.

Shaun forced himself toward the house, reaching the kitchen door, stumbling inside, looking for his sister. He shook his head as he reached the table, remembering she was gone, buried up at the wee croft house alongside her mother. Buried with his mother, he added, his thoughts swirling from loss of blood.

He lost his balance, falling back, his elbow knocking a large cannister of flour from the counter, sending it to the floor with a heavy thud, spilling a wash of yellow-white meal across the floor, followed by the sound of someone coming on the run.

Marion came to a stop, her eyes taking in the scene, a small towel grabbed from a hook by a large slate sink, used to staunch the blood seeping through her gran uncle's shirt. She tore apart the cloth, pressing the wadded-up towel over a deep cut, holding it in place while she listened as Shaun whispered in her ear.

Marion nodded, using her free hand to wipe away her tears,

helping her mentor slide to the floor, cradling him in her arms, stroking his face, her own locked in a silent stare, her mind at work on what to do next.

※※※

Logan opened the stable door, back from another jaunt to a croft farm half a mountain away, having left the day before, visiting with a daughter of a distant relative. Far enough removed in bloodline to allow for several opportunities for more than a kiss. His pent-up desires released inside her willing body, promises given to everything she asked of him, knowing them for the lies they were.

He stopped, seeing the Shaun's mare standing by her stall, head down nosing the rails, staring at a pile of hay. She whinnied, wanting him to let her in. Logan removed the saddle from her back, missing the stain of blood as he placed it aside with a confused look, having paid for the killing with coins saved up from his meager allowance, the deed left undone.

When he finished caring for both mounts, he went up to the manor and found Marion there, her hands stained with blood, holding a large bag of coins.

"You will *not* speak." She glanced at the table beside her, a pistol lying there, fully cocked. "You will *take* this money and leave—never again to step foot on Scottish soil. On pain of *death*. Your *whore* and her entire family, sent away, forced on a ship bound for the colonies. *You*— with a choice of where you will *go*, making certain it is *far* away from *here*. From lands high *and* low. All of Scotland—no longer your home."

Logan started to open his mouth, stopping as Marion tossed the leather bag at his feet, watching as she reached out and picked up the pistol. "*Blood* money. The return of the coins paid for the death of our laird. Your death now, with a price placed on your head *three* times as great. Paid to any who finds you still in Scotland—*two* days from now. The time allowed to make your way clear. Is that understood?"

Marion raised the pistol, the end of the barrel pointed at Logan's face, his eyes widening as she placed the tip of her finger on the trigger. "We've pigs enow here to do the job of removing all traces of you from this earth. *Tonight*—if you're foolish and say but a *single* word." She motioned with the pistol, indicating the door he'd just come in through.

Logan bent over and collected the bag, his eyes locked on the end of the pistol, taking the coins with him as he left, returning to the stable and recovering his steed, resaddling it, ignoring its snort of displeasure as he yanked on the reins, guiding it downhill toward the port of Glasgow.

※※※

Marion returned from the highland croft, having gone to lay flowers on two graves, her heart heavy, missing one of them most of all. Her mare noted her mood, moving with a measured pace as it eased down the trail to the manor, standing patiently as Marion dismounted and led her into the stable.

The house was quiet, the walls bereft of voices in earnest discussion of current affairs, sprinkled between stories from the past. Some heard more than a thousand times. Others, new to her ear. The scent of fresh brewed tea from the kitchen caught her nose, leading her to the kitchen doorway where she stood with crossed arms, a smile on her lips as she watched Shaun, decked out in an apron, mixing up a bowl of flour, butter, eggs, and milk.

"You—*cooking?* Have I gone *mad*, with my eyes betraying me?"

Her gran uncle turned his head, shrugged, then spooned the mixture onto a floured board, forming scones to bake in the large oven heating the room. "I *miss* my sister. Hoped the scent of these would ease my pain. In body *and* spirit." He sidled around the butcher block table, coming over to give his gran niece a kiss on her cheek, her skin cold from her visit to lay flowers on her grandmother's and great grandmother's graves.

Marion shook her head, going to pour them two cups of tea, a splash of fresh cream added to hers, the other left as it was, her gran uncle preferring his dark.

"The croft house—is in good repair?" Shaun moved aside, taking the cup, settling himself into a large wooden chair with a grimace, needing a moment before he could fully open his eyes, the wound still bothering him, his voice weak with his color slow to return.

"Aye. The stables will need attending to—once this *new* lad arrives, along with the men needed to move what's left of the stock to the upper pasture." Marion finished forming the scones, adding dried fruit to the base layer of dough, along with a drizzle of honey to help moisten the filling. She folded in the three corners of each triangle, then slid the tray into the oven, tipping a glass jar of spring water to one side, a small hole in the cork stopper starting to drip, knowing when it stopped, the scones would be ready.

"I apologize *again*, for having agreed to let—" Shaun stopped himself, seeing a glare starting to blossom in his gran niece's eyes, having forbidden him from ever mentioning Logan's name again. "This *new* lad is from a *good* family. One with a *well-grounded* upbringing. He has a keen mind—with his eyes always looking up, eager to live on high."

Marion leaned against the counter. "And what of his *looks?*"

Shaun hesitated, looking over at the oven, the scent of the scones beginning to sift through the kitchen air. He glanced at the window, watching as Marion went over and cracked it, letting in a pulse of cool air, sweat beading the surface of his forehead, more of it visible each week of his slow recovery. She came over and felt his cheek, warm to the touch, a frown on her lips.

"You're heated—but not *hot*. With no sign of a fever."

He closed his eyes, sighing. "The air feels good, with the scent of the mountains. Enough to take me there, in mind, if not yet able to sit a horse."

"Soon enow, Gran Uncle, and then you'll be able visit her. Putting flowers on her grave with your *own* damn hands!" Marion softened her words with a wide smile, hands on her hips. "You were speaking of his *looks*—this lad you've gone and hired."

Shaun looked to one side, unwilling to face her. "He's not like the '*other*' was. More an image of *another*, with features you might find —familiar."

"To my—to those my *father?*" Marion leaned forward, fixing him with a penetrating gaze. "Tell me you didn't go and—"

"*Nae*, Lass. Not your *father*. Your brother, though not as tall. With narrower shoulders and lighter colored hair."

"Not *much* better, Gran Uncle!" She shook her head, then noted the water had emptied out, crossing to pull the pan from the oven, the scones a golden brown, the aroma stirring a rumble in her stomach. "The question remains—will he be someone I can work with, to the advantage of the clan?"

"He'll bear the title more ably then t'other." Shaun paused, taking the plate she handed him, closing his eyes, drinking in the rich aroma of the pastry, tears on his cheeks when he opened them again. "He's a capable enough young man, Marion. More than capable of providing what you might require of him." He lowered the plate and wiped his eyes, his voice tightening as he gave her a firm look. "But you will need *bend* your tone a bit—and your *stubborn* Scott's pride, asking what you will from him *first*, giving the lad the respect deserved."

Marion pulled back slightly, considering for a moment, then went and grabbed the tea kettle, refilling Shaun's cup, her lips pressed tight, aware his energy was flagging.

Shaun took a bite of the scone, savoring the flavor of fruit and honey, using a mouthful of tea to wash it down. Then he grinned, easing Marion's mood. "Until he proves *otherwise*. Then it's down the hill and *away* with him. With another one found, and then another. With myself willing to search the *whole* of Scotland, if need be, in finding you a *worthy* match!"

CHAPTER TWENTY
CROSSROAD FARMHOUSE
SPRING, 1779

Allyn came out from the barn, set fifty paces away from a small farmhouse. He crossed the yard and stopped by a large wagon, picking up a heavy chest, one of several dozen filled with Sinclair and Meghan's belongings. The move to the new location, a few hours travel away by horse from the ever-expanding city limits of Philadelphia, completed.

Two draft horses, purchased for the eventual hauling of trade goods between the farm and Philadelphia, were in the paddock. Thick-bodied animals, used by Harold to tug stumps from a piece of newly cleared land, followed by the pulling of a plow. The move from manor to farmhouse having had to wait while Sinclair finished selecting furnishings needed to outfit the farmhouse, taking her time, choosing quality over quantity.

"You've been of immense help, Allyn. To us all, Meghan and myself." Sinclair waited for Allyn to set the chest down on the front porch, then handed him a glass of cool water, pulled from a well near the back of the small house. The dwelling was a squared box with two floors, the topmost one holding three bedrooms and a small study. "A real gentleman, from all I've witnessed—and been told to me by my daughter."

Allyn drained the glass, wiping his lips, giving Sinclair a short nod. "I thank you, Lady Sinclair." He glanced over her shoulder, seeing Meghan peering through a window, her hand pointing to the rear of the house. "I'll go and place this inside, then look at what's needed for repair of the well house. The rope's badly frayed and will need replacing, with a new bucket fashioned."

Sinclair stepped back, watching as Allyn picked up the chest and moved inside, about to follow him when she spied Harold in the opening of the barn, his hand in a slow wave, bidding her join him there.

※※※

"They have become — close." Harold glanced at Allyn and his daughter as they walked toward a small structure, three wooden walls and an angled roof surrounding the sides of a stone-faced well. The two of them, their shoulders touching, were holding hands. "Interesting — you're having agreed to the lad coming along."

Sinclair shrugged, taken aback by the close-cropped hair, thick beard and glasses Harold was wearing. Intended to prevent recognition by any veterans of the previous war he might run into. "There was *little* choice given me. The young man unable to swim the distance back to Glasgow — once I discovered him to be aboard."

Harold narrowed his eyes, angling his head as he gave Sinclair a questioning look. "With the two of you having *no* knowledge of his having stowed away?" He paused, shaking his head. "That seems — unlikely."

Sinclair lowered her voice. "*One* of us knew."

Harold nodded, then pursed his lips, looking back toward the young couple. "How much of an *issue* will it be, in my sending him *back?*"

"The price paid — will be your daughter's love." Sinclair reached out and touched his arm. "They have abstained from any behavior that would create — *complications*. Allyn's comported himself as a *true* gentleman." She leaned in, finding Harold's eyes. "They are to wed — with *our* blessing." She paused. "They already have mine."

"She's still a child. Barely of age for any such—"

"She is *sixteen*, husband. And mature enough to know her mind, raised to an understanding of the realities of life—and death."

Harold took a deep breath, remembering the scene of his daughter and wife, their bodies draped over Aaron's shoulders, his own arms wrapped around them all. Two dead men lying on the ground, brought to the end of their lives by arrows. He released a soft, resigned sigh. "You've been a witness to the path they've walked, to get here. Your view of things is—clearer than mine."

Harold removed Sinclair's hand from his arm, taking it in his, looking into her eyes, dark in the shadow of the barn's interior, the sunlight slipping away as afternoon eased over toward dusk. "And where are *we*, in all the miles and days between *our* last time together—in the *wee* croft house?"

Sinclair lowered her eyes, staring at the packed earth of the barn floor. "Back to our *original* arrangement. You, in your remote cabin in the woods, or in the barn when staying *here*. With me coming to you when and as I'm able to." She looked up, refusing to let the tears in her eyes fall. "The divide is *still* there—in my lying with you as wife again." She released his hand and stepped away. When she reached the sunlight outside, Sinclair turned around. "Where once there was an ocean between us, with you leaving me and your children to come *here*, in doing what you *did*— there is as great a distance *still*. One equally as wide. And *deep*."

⚘⚘⚘

Meghan joined Allyn, sitting beside him on a moss-covered log lying on the ground beneath a thick layer of limbs, the green buds starting to turn into new leaves. She touched his hand, gingerly probing the edges of a deep cut on its back. It was well on its way to healing, the balm her mother had daubed in place keeping sign of an infection away.

"It looks—better, than it did yesterday." She gave him a tentative smile, hoping to break him loose of his dour mood.

"I'm lucky not to have weakened it, your father checking it for damage, having me squeeze his hand as hard as I could." Allyn nodded, then took her fingers, raising them to his lips, kissing them gently. "I'm sorry—for my distance these past few days. It was difficult, having to rely on your father's help to get things put right, helping me with tasks at the farm. As if I were but a child." He blushed. "Which he no doubt sees me as, my mewling about a bit of blood spilled—"

"It was *more* than a bit, Allyn. The blade of the axe opening a cut one could poke a finger—" Meghan stopped, seeing the blood run out of his face, his cheeks pale. "It is enough you are better *now*. Able to place your focus ahead. On *us*."

"So strong—your father." Allyn shook his head. "I was amazed, thinking I might be near enow to his own strength. Left with the realization I'm not the man I need to be to strike out on my own." Allyn heard Meghan's sudden intake of breath. "I meant to say *our* own." He squeezed her hand. "Please tell me you know my meaning, my love."

"Of course. Where *you* go, I go too. Standing beside you, not behind. Same as my parents do." She hesitated. "Or how they once did, and will do so again—once everyone has had a chance to settle in."

Allyn shook his head. "Don't you see that's the *issue*? With us living with your mother and father, when its safe for him to do so. The two of us remaining as children in their eyes." He stood up, staring across the newly planted field to the barn where Harold was working on repair of a heavy harness. "He's doing what *I* should ha' been taking care of. If not for this." He lifted his damaged left hand, the bloodstained bandage starting to come loose. Meghan got to her feet, reaching to put it right.

Allyn pulled away, his jaw tense, eyes narrowed in frustration. The accident with the axe had been a set-back to his plan to speak with Harold about his daughter. Left all but an invalid now, for the better part of another two weeks or more, according to her mother. Having to wait until the gash to the back and side of his hand could heal enough for him to return to carrying his full share of the load.

"You'll *not* be looking at me with *anger* in your eyes, husband to be." Meghan grabbed his wrist, pulling it close, placing his hand on the swell of her breasts while she retied the bandage. She buried her smile as she felt his fingers close slightly, rubbing her flesh beneath the light linen shirt she had on, sensing his mood improve as he watched her at work, tending to his needs.

"You have my apologies, sweet one. With not enough hours in the day to make my amends."

"Roses—scattered in manure. All you highlander boys the same. With a poet's soul buried deep inside ya, struggling to squeeze its way past the stubborn Scot pride that makes us hate ya a *wee* bit less than *love* ya." Meghan looked up and kissed him, feeling him begin to respond, wondering how many more nights she'd have to wait until the feel of his body, fully joined with hers.

⸙⸙⸙

Sinclair slid the document across a kitchen table, watching the expressions on the young couple's faces as they read it. "The land and new house will be yours, providing you opportunity to earn a decent living. Repayment made with a portion of what you harvest, sold through the store. Which both of you will help run. Allyn seeing to the hauling in and out of produce and other products, while you, daughter dearest, will manage the selling of merchandise and restocking of shelves, putting up orders for delivery, and other such things."

Allyn pulled the sheet closer, reading it through again before sliding it towards Meghan who did the same. He could sense her enthusiasm, her leg pressed against his beneath the table, trembling in excitement, finding his hand, squeezing it gently, careful not to cause him any pain. His wound had healed, though the tendons beneath the skin were still finding their way back to where they'd once been.

"We will consider your offer and give you an answer on the morrow. If that is agreeable, Lady Sinclair." Allyn, aware Meghan was cutting him a glare hot enough to start a fire in wet grass, continued. "Both my intended and I—appreciative of the opportunity to be part of your plans."

Sinclair nodded. "Of course, Allyn. As is your right. This agreement will bind you to staying *here*, close by, while so many others are looking west where land is far less expensive—and *further* away."

Allyn nodded, a frown on his sun-bronzed face. "Lands that will end up under *who's* rule, Lady Sinclair? English or Colonial?"

She stared at him, knowing his thoughts, expressed freely while at dinner, the three of them bandying opinions for and against either side winning out at some point in the future. Current military activities at a stalemate, outside of a few minor skirmishes here and there, of no real consequence to most people going about their business, leading the same lives as before. "*God's* rule. The only one that matters."

"Or they will seek *self-determination*, with a nod made in God's divine direction each Sunday. Their *own* choices made throughout the week." Harold stepped inside the small sitting room, located on the first floor of the farmhouse. "I will be needing your help, Allyn, with the loading up of goods, if your hand is deemed strong enough by these two lovely ladies."

Allyn stood up and nodded to Sinclair, then leaned down, kissing the top of Meghan's head. Their wedding was a week away, with a host of people from the local church eager to help celebrate their union.

"I'm right as rain, Harold." He hesitated. "Sir." His face reddened as he followed the man who would soon to be his father-in-law out of the house, leaving the sound of feminine laughter behind.

Once they'd loaded the wagon and hitched the team, the two of them began the long journey to a warehouse outside the city, where Allyn would sell or trade the goods and produce gathered through their own and local farmer's efforts, swapped for essentials needed in return. Brought back and placed in storeroom shelves for reissue, making a small profit from those coming to the crossroad store, looking to trade.

Harold noticed the team's ears perk up, followed by the sound of hooves in approach. He tugged the reins, halting them in place as he lowered the brim of a large hat shadowing his face, a frown on his lips. A small force of colonials on horseback made their approach, led by an officer in a white wig, dusted with a hint of road dust about the edges.

The officer pulled up, raising one hand, signaling a stop, clearing his throat. Forced to do so again, a cloud of dust drifting along the length of the column, enveloping him in a light brown swirl. "Good day to you, sir." The officer touched the tip of his hat, eyeing Allyn, noting his age and solemn-edged look on his face, deciding to ignore him for the moment, taking note of the load in the wagon before nodding. "You are *well* provisioned. No doubt heading to the warehouse in Greenway." Harold returned the nod, waiting for the young officer to make the next move. "I would ask from whence you are bound?"

"Stettel farmstead, by route of Robert's Mill."

"Your list of goods?" The officer leaned forward, easing the ache in his genitals, the hours spend in the saddle causing sores that never fully healed. A common malady amongst all riders, no matter the color of their uniform.

Harold pulled a note from his purse, stamped by the owner of the mill, detailing the bags of flour in number and type. He held it out, one of the soldiers dismounting, coming over in hunched approach, straightening up, easing the ache in his back as he took the paper from Harold.

"Twenty and five sacks of wheat, ground to flour. Ten of barley, and five of sorghum. Thirty of cornmeal. Sir." The soldier looked up at the officer, receiving a curt nod, handing the list back to Harold.

The officer leaned forward, his eyes narrowed. "Any other items?"

Harold shrugged. "Three cannons. A dozen kegs of gunpowder. And a *noose* you'd place around my neck were I foolish enough to haul contraband in the middle of the day—on such a well-traveled road. One known for patrols led by astute colonial officers—such as yourself."

The officer tried but failed to hide a smile, his thin lips cracking along their dust-stained corners. He started to respond, stopping as he watched Harold lift a jug from between his feet, holding it out to the soldier standing alongside the wagon. "Spring water, not corn liquor. Satisfying a parched throat, coated with what used to be the *King's* dust. General Washington's, *now*."

The officer nodded, the jug brought over and handed up, the stopper removed, taking a small sip, swishing it in his mouth, then spitting to one side, before taking a long swallow, handing the jug back down.

Harold waved at the rest of the men on horseback. "Keep it. Leave it at the mill, should you end up passing it. Or at the last house at the crossroad ahead, when you happen by again. There's a run of water in good flow three miles on for your horses, should they need it."

The officer sent the soldier around to the others, a few men taking a drink, the rest sitting in sullen silence, eyeing both Harold and Allyn with hard looks. Veterans, with tales in their ears of loyalist's having run amok while English troops held the city of Philadelphia, most having slunk back into the countryside, shedding their uniforms, looking no different than these two. Prepared to act as saboteurs, hoping the British might soon return.

"I thank you for the water. Your previous attempt at humor—*less* so." The officer grinned, removing any offense, then raised his hand, lowering it, nodding as he passed by the large wagon, his men following behind in single file. The last one leaned down, handing Allyn the jug, with Harold reaching to take it himself.

He called to the team, moving them ahead, waiting to answer Allyn's unspoken question until the soldiers were away. "Your bandaged hand, son. With a wound easily mistaken as result of a sword, or bayonet." He shook his head. "Their officer—not one to let it pass without notice, if called to it by those who were staring at us with hate filled eyes."

Allyn lowered his head, feeling his heartbeat in his ears, the sudden appearance of the mounted soldiers a reminder of the war still going on throughout the colonies. Violent skirmishes between men in uniform, along with deadly raids by native groups allied with the British. Armies on both sides jostling for the upper hand, with countless small battles waged in places without names. Tensions were running high, despite the strained smiles on people's faces, with most colonists in support of the King.

He listened to the steady clop of large hooves as the wagon moved along, feeling small in the seat beside the man he knew had once roamed these same lands, leaving his own blood spilled upon it, along with that of French soldiers. Men no different than those who'd just passed them by.

"I have—so *much* to learn. This place—no highland cradle, surrounded by my kin. By my clan."

"With luck you'll have the time to figure it out. As to kin—well that's on you and my daughter to provide once you're properly wed and able to bed her."

Harold could feel the heat from Allyn's red face, blood rushing to the lad's beardless cheeks. He smiled, trying to remember ever having been as young. Unable to do so without thinking of his brother Jackson. The thought of him a dark cloud, brushing the lightness of his mood away, the reins flicked, coaxing the team to pick up their pace.

CHAPTER TWENTY-ONE
SOUTHERN CAMPAIGN
SPRING, 1779

Aaron studied a handful of notes, handed him by Charles, his lips pursed as he compared the information they contained to a map of the local area. He carefully refolded them, handing them back without comment.

Charles cleared his throat, taking the papers, having noted Aaron's reaction, aware he was concerned by the lack of details. "Their leader, a loyalist colonel of unknown reputation, is rumored to have raised a —*sizable* number of men. He's planning to march south, to join up with *another* loyalist group. A move that will not bode well for our upcoming efforts made *here*, in the Carolinas—the English believing the southern colonies will join their side of the conflict."

Aaron nodded, his eyes on the map. "And what *exactly* is the number of men you consider to be *significant?*"

"Between eight—" Charles hesitated a moment, then cleared his throat, again. "And nine *hundred*—by my people's best estimate." He watched as the gifted strategist closed, then reopened his eyes, a frown on a face no longer youthful, deep lines having creased his face during the past year of deadly toil. Success in a war of constant attrition, while highly effective, had left its mark on him physically. His spirit aged as well, grown sober in tone.

Aaron turned, staring at Charles. "And you consider my force of one hundred and *four* men *significant* enough in number to turn them away?"

"I consider them the *only* option." Charles stepped over, placing his hand on the young man's shoulder. "General Greene is counting on you coming up with ways to *harry* their column as they move through the countryside, using your usual bag of tricks—along with any *new* ones you're of a mind to craft." He removed his hand. "They have no knowledge of your tactics to date. Which is why Green ordered you *here*, at *my* insistence, away from the environs of Pennsylvania. Your overexposure *there* increasing the possibility of your being killed. Or worse—captured alive, tortured, then hung. The British currently doling out dozens of heavy purses to anyone willing to take them, searching for you in every hollow, swamp, or dense growth of forest. Your efforts there brought to a sorry end—with an opportunity provided *here* for you to begin once more."

Aaron shrugged. "I'd already come to understand *that* side of the equation, having done the math." He faced Charles with crossed arms, his voice low. "But *this* request seems beyond the pale, with more to this sudden *redeploy* then you're able to reveal, leaving my people standing in the shadows."

"For *now*, yes." Charles watched a flash of irritation cross Aaron's lined face. "Due to my oath *sworn* to Greene not to reveal *more* than is necessary. To anyone. Not even to the son of someone I consider a friend."

"Really?" Aaron scoffed as Charles tossed the notes onto a brazier, both men watching as they burst into flames, casting their shadows onto the side of the cloth-walled shelter. "*That's* how you see the relationship with my father to have been?" He squared up, giving the diminutive man a long look. "I find it hard to believe you've ever *had* a friend. One you could be honest with, without having to measure every angle, protecting yourself. With no one seeing you for who you really are." He softened his tone. "Known as Charles, to me. Charlie, to my father. As to the man you see when you look in the mirror—well, that's between *you* and whatever god you follow, if any."

Charles pulled back, keeping a look of disappointment off his narrow face. "A fair enough assessment of the man I had to become—and must *continue* to be. But not *all* one's story is known by reading the title on its cover. Or learned from a few sentences perused, here and there."

"Then I look forward to someday reading *yours* in its entirety, once you've published it for all the world to see."

A slight scrape of a soft-soled boot from outside a thin layer of oiled cloth brought both of their heads around. Aaron pulled back the flap, allowing Chatte to enter. She had a bottle of wine in one hand, unopened, a recent acquisition from a small party of redcoats led by a Sergeant Major in a redcoat, a reed thin man who'd died a lingering death. His men given swift, merciful deaths, then left tied to trees alongside their leader. A calling card to any loyalists happening by, letting them know a dark cloud had arrived. One hovering in the skies in the southern end of the campaign against the English, with battles yet to come.

"I sense there is a great *thirst* in the air. One we might quench with whatever is inside *this*." Chatte held up the bottle, then reached through a slit in her skirt, pulling out her bone handled knife, using the narrow blade to penetrate the cork, working it free, careful not to cut her fingers on the honed steel. She took the first pull, the delicate line of her throat revealed as she swallowed, seeming out of place with her reputation for brutal lethality, both men looking on with a measure of awe.

"A fine suggestion, Lady Chatte." Charles reached for the bottle, following suit, consuming a quarter share of the heavy bodied red wine. He lowered it, offering it to Aaron, who shook his head.

"I've a plan to put together, based on what you've just provided for information. I'll leave you both to the task at hand, while taking my leave to go confer with my second."

After Aaron left, Chatte added a pine knot to the brazier, using it to scatter the ashes of burnt paper. Then she sat down, her knees folded with her chin resting in cupped hands. She stared up at Charles, then at the ground, waiting until he joined her, his legs angled to one side, looking uncomfortable as he returned her steady gaze.

"You consider me to be a *demon*." Chatte smiled, her eyes reflecting the glow of coals in the brazier. "One wearing a dress. A very worn and tattered one—in need of replacement." She leaned back slightly, head turned at an angle, studying the diminutive man. "My demeanor is *unsettling* to you, though the results I've provided have proven to be valuable. *Extremely* so, to those you are working for. And I am not speaking of the idiots on the colonial side. Or the British. Aware you and the people you work with have interests on *both* sides of this silly game."

Charles nodded. "I *do*. The group I belong to—not limited to support of one side against the other. Our interest in helping to maintain a *status quo* if you will. Attempting to try and keep the world—in *balance*." He paused. "More or less."

"*Less*, if you ask me. My efforts, intended to bring balance to my *own* world, more *cut*—and dried. Each death, atonement for the drops of blood my family spilled from their torn flesh. Or the trail of blood dripping down my mother's thighs as she balanced on the railing of a ship at sea."

"The clearances. In Nova Scotia. Your people swept up with a careless and unfeeling hand from the new world. Torn from homes lived in for many generations."

Chatte leaned back slightly. "And where were you and your group *then?*"

"Your people's plight, while one of great misery, with your family subjected to the *worst* of what men are capable of when released to their darker side—deemed *unworthy* of our interference. Your plight considered *insignificant* to our cause, at the time." Charles shrugged, his eyes on hers. "A sad situation for *you*. Your personal tragedy not large enough in scale to incur our intervention in the English efforts to erase your heritage, scattering it to the four winds."

Chatte's voice was a thin whisper, stirring the hair on Charles neck. "I could easily *slit* your throat for saying that. Your casual dismissal of my people's *forced* departure—leading to my family's *deaths*. My *tortured* life, spent hearing about it—*over* and again—from my grandmother's mouth, pressed to my ear."

Charles shook his head, crossing his arms on his narrow chest. "*Poisoning* you, with her words. You would have been a young child then, having only just learned to walk, or run. Your memories, your *thirst* for revenge, have never been yours—but *hers*. With you made to carry her torch. And, by doing so, helping to carry mine." He held out one arm, exposing his wrist. "Cut *me*—if it will alleviate your need to seek satisfaction of the debt owed by the prolonged death of others. If it will return you to an innocent child, no longer a weapon of vengeance. One your beloved grandmother helped create."

Chatte stared at him, her lips parted in a silent snarl, her hands shaking, fingers working as she touched her knife, the bone hilt felt beneath her skirt. Then she lowered her eyes, staring at the ground, silent, without moving, without looking up as Charles rolled to his feet and stepped outside, the sound of his weary footsteps slowly fading away.

※ ※ ※

A heavy growth of basket like oak trees, densely limbed, overhung a well-traveled path running between steep sided hills, forming a shadowed passage from north to south. A long column of men and supplies moved past in a slow procession, with a dense collection of laughing soldiers employed to either side, moving in a relaxed gait. They were on their home ground, with little regard for any risk in moving to meet up with another sizable group of loyalists, a few days march ahead.

A handful of men, tasked with scouting the woods on either side of the road, slipped in and out of the shadowed edges, waving each time they reappeared. A peaceful enough scene, with the well-armed group in high spirits, marching in support of their King and colonies. Unaware of the men watching them from the hills above.

Aaron rolled onto his side, eyeing Smoke, seeing the older man grin, his face lit up with anticipation of what was to come. He shook his head, frowning at the older man. "These are *not* redcoats—the men below are *colonists*. Your *own* people."

Smoke snarled, his eyes cold. "They are *traitors* to our cause. *Bootlickers*. Lower than the *shite* of pigs, and—"

"Save your breath for the chase ahead, once they're squeezed into the pass, unable to deploy." Aaron slid back, then started down the backside of the hill, Smoke following close behind, muttering a string of invectives under his breath, having no trouble in keeping up with the much younger man.

Once they were back with the others, Aaron used a stick to draw out the plan of attack. He used handfuls of small stones and sticks to detail how they would strike, then pull back, moving away to set up again, gnawing at the enemy each time the loyalist force reformed and began to move out. The first step would be to eliminate the scouts as they probed the edges of the killing ground, replacing them, wearing their hats and coats, then waving the column ahead, directly into withering fire and deadly clouds of arrows. The first ambush of more to follow, whittling their numbers, helping render them ineffective as a fighting force.

※※※

The loyalist column advanced without concern, unaware of the men lying in the edge of woods, with two muskets each at hand, and two pistols tucked in their belts to repel any who would dare charge their way. Younger men, with longbows in hand and two quivers filled with honed arrows, knelt a few paces behind, anxious to stand and release four volleys of arrows into the concentrated flank of the column, before fading away with the others, moving back into the forest to reorganize, before rushing ahead of the line of march, crossing to set up another ambush from the opposite side of the widening valley floor.

The loyalist scouts were the first to appear, Aaron's men cutting them down with arrows, knives to their throats to silence cries of warning. Coats and hats swapped out, allowing men of matching size to step into the open and wave, letting the loyalists know the way ahead was clear. A few minutes of peace followed, before a storm broke over the bunched column, leaving dozens of men and a handful of horses lying in twisted shapes, their bodies littering the ground.

Aaron watched as smoke filled one side of the wide roadway, loyalist men kneeling in the open, firing at ghosts, his men having pulled back after releasing two volleys of musket fire, along with hundreds of arrows sent in arched waves, decimating a fifty-pace long section of the column, leaving a hole the enemy was slow to fill, their eyes probing the undergrowth, firing indiscriminately at every shadow.

"We have *bloodied* them, but they are not *broken*." Aaron glanced at Smoke, standing alongside, with a wide grin creasing his heavily wrinkled face. "We'll not catch them out again. Not with the same results." The old veteran shrugged, his jaws working away at a plug of tobacco. "A decent enough start." He spit, careful to avoid splattering Aaron's feet. "With a long road ahead, with plenty of opportunities for you to come up with a few *new* surprises."

"Or fall flat on my face. The odds against us still stacked to the sky. I'm bound to make a misstep before we're finished here."

"Not a man among us will hold you accountable for it. We're with you, no matter what." Smoke paused, giving Aaron a confident look. "Sir."

Aaron swallowed, the rare words of respect from the aged warrior catching him off guard. He bowed his head and vowed to do all he could to continue seeing things from the other side of the board, working out how to avoid any false moves. Determined to keep his men from falling into a reverse trap.

※ ※ ※

A group of young archers, fleet of foot, had stayed behind, waiting until the cautious Loyalist column moved on, their dead left unburied, with wounded men loaded on top of the wagons, their torn bodies lying in the open on crates of supplies. The colonel had screamed at his officers, ordering his force to clear the narrow deathtrap as quickly as possible, his face white with rage as he watched his men trying to regroup from their losses, eager to reach open ground where they could maneuver.

Once the narrow pass was clear, the archers darted out, retrieving as many arrows as they could find, pulling them from the bodies of men, many with bullet holes torn through their stiffening flesh. Then they headed back into the hills, running in a ground-covering lope toward a rock-topped ridge where they would join up with their friends.

One of them stopped in a thicket of brush, letting the others pass by, having felt a shiver slip down his spine. He moved several paces to one side of the trail they were following, kneeling behind a large rock, searching the woods behind them for movement. None showed, leaving him to curse under his breath as he started to rise. Then he froze, a flicker catching his eye, as if the cautious flick of a deer's ear. He swallowed, watching as a man in leather clothing came forward in a wary crouch, eyes focused on the ground, searching for tracks.

The man passed by, then stopped, searching the lower limbs of the trees, sweeping his gaze to each side, the sound of his breathing loud as he nosed the air. Satisfied no threat existed, he stepped ahead, a look of surprise on his sun-weathered face when struck from behind, the bloody head of an arrow jutting from his chest, the fingers of his free hand rising to touch it as his musket fell to the ground, eyes rolling back in his head as he landed on his side.

The young archer came over and knelt, reaching out to close the dead man's eyes before pulling the arrow all the way through the wound, leaving the feathered vanes clotted with blood. He dragged them through a handful of leaves to clean them, then gathered the slain man's musket, powder horn, and pouch of supplies. With a satisfied look on his face, he stood up, heading to the rendezvous point with a story to tell his friends.

※※※

A herd of half-a-hundred cattle milled along a roadway passing through the center of a long, open field. Their heads were down, bunched in thick knots as they licked at a dozen blocks of salt, fastened to the packed earth. A large bull bellowed, shoving his way through the others, stopping to paw at one of the white blocks. Several cows protested the incursion, shouldering him to one side, vying for control of the country lane.

The column of loyalists, bloodied, no longer moving in a loose gait, eased ahead in hunched postures, waiting on the hiss of arrows or whine of lead balls, announcing the next ambush. They carried their muskets leveled to one side, pointing toward a thick wood, trying to look in all directions at once. The wounded, lying in the open beneath a hot sun, moaned in pain, begging the others to stop and erect shelters. With water provided, along with a more thorough examination of, and attention paid to their grievous wounds.

The colonel in charge of the snaking column of men walked beside his horse. He'd removed his officer's hat, the buzzing of lead balls passing close by his head during the first engagement having dissuaded him from sitting his mount. He glanced at the men positioned to all sides of him and his valuable steed, making certain he was well protected. When the lead element came to a halt, he shouted for an explanation. Getting none, he shouldered his way forward to find out for himself the reason for the delay.

"The beasts are sign of a *trap*, sir. I'm certain of it." His third in command, replacing his second, lost to service due to an arrow passing through his abdomen, turned, shouting at him from the head of the column, hands clasped to the sides of his face. "We must halt and form up, waiting for our scouts to reconnoiter—"

"They are but *animals*, doing what animals *do* when in a pasturage." The colonel's face turned red with anger. "You are to keep moving. The light is fading, and we've little time left to reach the next post."

"Sir, I *recognize* our position. As too does our *enemy*. No doubt in direct observance *of* it. I recommend we send a sortie ahead to check the woods for men lying in ambush. As well as a foray made in force to the opposite side of the field, preventing potential for attack on our exposed flank."

"A *capital* idea, Lieutenant. One I'm certain will work out in our favor, *delaying* us further. Left marching in the dark to reach safety, with arrows falling from the sky, unable to return fire."

"We are to be in the heated pan or the coals beneath it, either way." The lieutenant paused, then purposely saluted. "*Sir.*"

"Lead us forward, *Lieutenant*. At a quick march. The wagons and wounded will need to keep up. It is of *utmost* importance we reach our destination, forthwith."

The junior officer lowered his eyes, wondering if any of his command would survive the journey south. Then he raised his arm, waving his soldiers ahead with a heavy heart.

The forward element of the loyalist column edged into the frenzied cattle. The animals ignored them, their heads down, focused on the blocks of salt. They began to shove against each other, intent on an equal share of the salt. The men, preventing by the cattle from gaining way, skirted around the sides of the herd, eyeing the sloped ground of the narrow road to either side, wondering if the wagons would be able to make it past without tipping over. The column slowed, then came to a stop, bunching up as the wounded who could manage it raised their heads and cursed in frustration, before falling back.

The colonel opened his mouth, prepared to direct the soldiers to clear the road, his jaw left hanging as a loud bawling of bovine voices called out in panic when a dozen arrows fell in among them, scoring their sides and backs, causing them to stampede along the road. They scattered the column, oxen harnessed to the traces of the heavy wagons lunging to either side as they turned to follow them, joining in their panicked flight.

"My *horse!*" The colonel screamed, pounding several men on their shoulders and backs, urging them to recover his mount, the large horse lashing out with its hooves, pulling away from a soldier clinging to its reins. One hoof connected with the man's shoulder, snapping bones, the wild-eyed animal leaping away.

The ground to one side of the first third of the long column, already well into the field, rose in silent eruptions of thick grass, as if torn open by unheard cannon fire. Bursts of smoke from dozens of muskets blossomed into life, soon followed by another volley. Lead balls sighed through the air, slapping into flesh, cracking bones. Another eruption from dozens of other muskets rippled from the shadows of the woods on the near side, joined by volleys of the dreaded arrows, their razor-sharp blades penetrating bodies of men as they tried to run away, adding to the chaos of the frantic column, starting to come apart at the seams.

Handfuls of men dropped, stepped on or over by an assortment of beasts and retreating men, causing others to trip, their muskets dropped, then picked up, searching for targets. Their foe in the open field were already a hundred paces away, moving at a rapid pace. The others had disappeared, having slipped back into the shadowy shelter of the thick woods.

※※※

"They are not *ghosts!* We *saw* them. Men in the *open!*" The colonel gave his officers, less the lieutenant leading the first element, crushed beneath the hooves of a large bull, a fixed glare. "They are *men*, no different than *us!*"

He stomped his foot, grimacing in pain. His riding boots, worn during the horrific carnage of the day, had caused blisters to form on his feet. The elegantly styled footwear specifically designed for stirrups, and not walking on packed earth. He'd lost his personal effects, one of the panicked teams having carried his wagon away. Still missing, his men unable to recover it after having searched among the wreckage of the other wagons left behind, destroyed in the stampede.

"Where then, did they *come* from?" The man who spoke was a revered veteran of bloody encounters with native tribes. He stepped forward, shouldering the others aside. "No such tactics ever used *here*. No attacks of *any* kind happening—such as these. We're facing something new, and must—"

"*You*, sir, are facing a court martial and *noose*. A summary execution if I hear *one* more word from you!" The colonel spun about, giving his junior officers a warning nod, seeing them stand down, unwilling to test his authority, the results dire should he follow through on his threat. "We will *gather* the remaining wagons. *Tend* to our wounded. Then send *new* scouts with *woodland* experience ahead to search out these—these *irascible* rebels, arriving from out of nowhere to plague me this *day!*"

※※※

The night was a mix of rain and fog, the air warmed by a southernly front passing through. The noise of small frogs filled the vacuum, providing cover for the stealthy approach of a line of men dressed in dark clothing, their faces and hands blackened with soot. Their own scouts had spent the day luring those of the loyalist column away, leaving false trails, keeping them busy chasing their tails until they'd returned, their eyes left heavy with fatigue, yawning, their morale low.

Two of the loyalist scouts, posted as sentries, were peering into the dark, nervously watching drifts of mist in the edge of the light from their small fire, the entire encampment surrounded by torches and firepits, trying to hold back the terrors of the night. One leaned over, his voice a thin whisper.

"It ain't right, spirits rising from out of the ground. Ain't nothing natural in any of that."

The second man shook his head. "It was *men*, not spirits. With rifles, and pistols. Their backs shown to us while they ran away, backs covered in grass."

"With no *trail* left behind, when we went and looked for them, while the others were busy corralling the stock."

"No trails we *dared* follow, having lied to the colonel, afraid to probe further into the forest."

There was no answer, the other man silent, his head down, musket falling to one, the heavy barrel striking his friend in the thigh.

"For the love of *God*! Watch yourself—you *idiot!*" When there was no response, he leaned over and touched the other man. His friend slumped to the side, landing on his back, steam rising from a wash of blood coming from his slit throat.

The sentry opened his mouth to scream a warning, stopped by the cold slip of metal across his throat. He reached up, trying to close the wound, the backs of his hands warmed by the flow of his blood, dying without a sound. One of a handful of men dressed in black gently lowered him to the ground, then closed his eyes, before slipping away.

※ ※ ※

Charles had stayed clear of the night attack, just like the one made in the afternoon, and the one earlier in the day. The three lightning quick strikes had disrupted the column, halting its progress, with men beginning to desert, heading back to their homes along the main road. The soldiers sent to arrest them had joined in the exodus. The sight of their sentries, their throats cut, bodies hanging from nooses tied to tree limbs, enough of an incentive to convince them to head north, without looking back.

He lowered the glass he was using to observe the loyalist force, careful to avoid letting the sun touch the lens, not wanting a glare to signal his location, high on a hill, lying atop a bald knob of limestone. He handed the metal tube to Aaron, who lay alongside him, a warm smile on his face.

"Commendable. An *incredible* effort. Your finest work—to date."

Aaron shook his head, closing the glass and putting it away in a leather sheath. "A butcher learns his trade through frequent practice. Dismembering a beast, little different than that of a—" He looked at the column moving forward in a sinuous line below, wagons in concentrated groups, with bands of men to either side and in between, providing sharp-eyed escort, preventing another surprise attack. "*Snake.*"

"You've helped prevent a greater butchery to come, if these—" Charles nodded toward the disheartened army below. "If *none* are left to join with the others, leading to a groundswell of support for the British." He paused, noting the faces of Aaron's force, scattered in pockets of shade, looking well-rested from their late-night raid on the column in bivouac, with ten wagons set afire, the sentries watching over them cut down, eliminating those with skill in woodcraft, helping remove the ears and eyes of the loyalist army.

"Greene." Aaron looked at Charles. "He's being sent here by Washington." He watched as the slim man turned away, a muffled curse released, swept away by a gentle breeze, painting the sunlit day with a pleasant scent of woods and grasslands.

"You see—more than I can share *with* you. My word—"

"*Given*. Yes. I understand your situation. With Washington, and the other men you serve, hiding behind walls of secrecy. Shadows, within shadows. The whole damn thing a game, played by faceless men with little flesh in the game. Not like *these*." Aaron pointed at his men. "Standing in the line of fire, without any idea of who they've swore their loyalty *to*."

Charles eyed Aaron. "And what does that say about their *leader?* Who's reasoned out the lay of the land, yet keeps it *from* them?"

Aaron nodded, a thin smile on his lips, his eyes reflecting the blue of the sky. "I will weaken *these* men, first. Then turn my sights on the English army. After that?" He shrugged, hearing the call of a raven sawing away in the distance. "Perhaps I'll go after the ones *you're* fighting against. Or turn my attention *toward* your group—once we've forced a treaty with England." He offered a smile, softening the edge of his remark.

Charles gave him a weak grin in response, a cold shiver creasing his spine as he considered the possibility of the younger man turning from an asset into an enemy. "The future is full of twists and turns. As you well know. Your own father, proof of that."

Aaron nodded his head, studying the man he respected, but could not bring himself to trust. Then he rolled away and went to see to the mood of his men.

CHAPTER TWENTY-TWO
HIGHLAND MANOR
SUMMER, 1779

Marion closed a leather valise stuffed full of pamphlets and broadsheets covering the ongoing strife in the colonies. The papers, with detailed descriptions of recent actions taken, touted each success of the English armies in large typeface. The setbacks, named by the authors as strategic repositioning of troops, carefully hidden away on inner pages printed in a compressive typeface, difficult to read.

She sighed, considering her latest plan, knowing that, as signatory to her mother's estate, she had control of a vast sum of monies in bullion, available due to shrewd investments starting over two decades ago.

"Is there anything further you need, my Lady—" A young man named Declan, of an age to her own and rangy in build with a square jaw and blue eyes beneath sandy-brown hair, blushed red as he saw her eyebrow raise, indicating her displeasure. "I mean—Marion."

He looked away, needing a moment to recover his wits, taken back whenever he came into a room, seeing Marion as an angel come to life. Embarrassed by his clumsiness when speaking with her, encouraged to do so by the former leader of the clan, spending his time in the manor, sitting in front of a fire while staring out a window.

The past month and more had been a blur, Declan arriving at the highland manor in a rush, summoned by the former laird and put to work in the barn, stables, and paddocks. Then told he was to be married, with his family arriving the next day, joined by the former laird's confidants and friends, witnesses to his being handfasted to Marion. Declan's head was still spinning from the sudden elevation in his position. His strong hands left in a nervous twist, long used to hard toil. Unsettled by his removal from tending to the countless chores. Others hired in his place. His responsibility clearly spelled out: to attend meetings throughout clan lands, representing the one with the power behind the title, leading the way. His wife, as of a week ago.

"Is there anything further you need me to gather?" Declan glanced at a large chest lying on the floor of a tall safe, the top open, revealing bags of what had to be coins stacked inside. He swallowed, wondering if his bride expected him to be able to lift the metal banded chest, not wanting to disappoint her. The same way he'd felt when approaching their wedding bed, hands in front of him, unsure what to do. Given little advice from the former laird on the subject, the gray-haired man having laughed as he'd walked away when asked, wishing him luck.

"A means by which to gather *this*—" Marion touched the chest with the tip of a gray shoe. "And get it secured to the carriage, just *there*." She pointed outside a window of her mother's inherited estate, located on the outskirts of London, indicating a matched team of geldings, the highland raised horses shaking their heads, eager to be away from the constant noise and noxious odors of the city, filled to overflowing with people.

Declan went over and stared at a dozen leather bags inside. He touched one with a finger, feeling the shape of the coins inside. "Can we nae *remove* these first? With the chest made manageable enow to carry on my shoulder. The bags loaded—*after* it's in the carriage." Marion looked at him, then nodded, starting to agree when he interrupted. "Better still—if'n I gather a dozen clay pots from the kitchen, along with a bag of dried beans from the storeroom."

Marion gave her husband a puzzled look, then grinned, reaching out and touching his shoulder. "*I* should have thought of that. Less conspicuous than using the chest."

He pointed at the bags. "A moral upbringing preventing you from seeing the world the way those with bad intentions might." He paused. "Wife."

It was Marion's turn to blush, her new husband's voice soft, his eyes open, looking at her without turning away. His honest nature having drawn her to him, watching as he'd toiled in the stables and paddock, speaking to the stock in a gentle tone, attending to their needs with a loving manner. She felt a stirring in her lower body, wanting the same from him, now.

Declan nodded. "I'll gather the pots. Then fetch the beans to pour over the bags."

"Reducing the risk of theft, while transporting the money." Marion nodded, appreciating Declan's awareness, startled when he stepped over and took her hands.

"*Nae*, lass. The money means *nothing* ta' me. Only the slightest chance of risk to *yourself*." Then he was gone, Marion locking the door behind him with a firm twist of the lock, leaning against it, frightened for the first time in her life. Afraid of something she could not properly identify, knowing that her heart would be in her throat until they had the gold safely stored away back at the manor. Until Declan was lying with her in their bed, holding her in his strong arms, again.

※※※

Two men clad in decent clothing, though daubed with stains gathered from nights spent in the open, stepped out from a thicket at the near end of a bridge, perched over a deep run of water. Their faces wore nervous expressions beneath desperate eyes, the two horses reacting to their sudden appearance with nervous shudders and tossing of their heads.

Marion opened her mouth to order the two men to step aside, clearing the lowland trail leading into the highlands. Declan stopped her with a light touch on her hand, then secured the reins, greeting the men with a wide smile.

"*Perfect* timing!" He reached into the back of the carriage, lifting the lid from one of the large clay pots. "If ya wouldn't mind lending a hand, taking the bridle of the horses in hand while I reset the load, a' fore I have beans scattered in every *nook* and *cranny!*" His fingers closed on the hilt of a knife, secured beneath the seat, his other hand holding the lid. "We have plenty, if ya fancy some for yourselves. You look to be needing a decent meal, times tough in these parts. Fortunate enow, my own self, to have this fine lady hiring me on to help her get back home."

One of the men approached, the other making a show of controlling the team, both men with a hand in their pockets, scowls on their faces.

"Drop the talk of *fookin'* beans, ya *daft* fool. We'll be taking it *all*! Carriage, team, and—" He turned his head, giving Marion, frozen in her seat, a leering stare. "And the pretty *lady*, too." He started to face Declan, the lid already in the air, aimed at his thin chin. It struck him square, driving him back, knocking him to the ground.

Declan leaped down, moving toward the first man, aware the second thief had slipped around the team, torn between running off or going for Marion. The man making his decision, climbing up, a knife in his hand. Another one driven into his stomach, the blade dragged up until it jammed against his ribcage, his abdomen opened, releasing ropes of intestines as he fell away, landing on his back, mouth open in shocked surprise, arms akimbo.

Declan stepped on the first man's throat, ending his struggle to catch his wits. Then he leapt into the carriage and called out to the horses to start up. He glanced at Marion, seeing the pale shade of her skin, her eyes wide, hands trembling, one of them covered in gore, her dress splashed with a bright red stain.

"There's a spring ahead where you can wash. Until then, find a spot on the far horizon and look at it. Follow the curve of the hills. The tops of snow-capped mountains, beyond. Hear the horses. The sound of the wheels. Feel the movement of the seat on its springs." He saw her lurch forward and to one side, spilling the lunch she'd eaten onto the side of the pathway, his hand bunched on the back of her dress, keeping her from falling out.

He continued to speak to her, his tone as smooth as honey. "You did what needed doing. He'd a knife in his hand and would have put it to ya throat—if you hadn't done for him." Declan felt Marion trembling through the material of her dress. He dropped the reins, pulling her into his arms with the animals moving ahead, knowing the road. He held onto her until they reached the spring, then jumped down and tied off the team. Taking her by hand, he helped her down, then carried her to the small pool of clear water where he began cleaning the blood from her hand, lower arm, and the front of her dress.

Declan gazed into her shock-kissed eyes. "I should have found another way. Not to ha' placed you at risk like that. I should 'na—"

Marion turned into him, clinging to him, her head buried against his chest, sobbing as she tried to release the image of the man's doe-brown eyes, staring back at her with a shocked expression, his mouth framing teeth stained by tobacco, with a thin beard on his skinny face. Every detail, frozen in her mind's eye.

The threat of violent death had never landed on her shoulders. Her grandmother slipping away in the middle of mixing up scones, the kneading of bread beyond her fading abilities. And now, her gran uncle, ever at death's door from his troublesome wound, a smile on his face, telling her both God and the Devil were fighting it out, with neither one willing to let him in. But never like this, with someone made to die by her own hand. Aware, peripherally, of some of what had happened at the grist mill that awful day. Aware, less so, of what her own father had been through, half-listening as Aaron shared stories with Meghan, her own nose buried in a book.

"I—I *killed* him! Took his *life* from him. Without thinking. Without hesitation, in seeing you outnumbered. Willing to *defend* you—" She pulled away, looking up at Declan, her eyes red, nose running, seeing her image reflected in his eyes. "While you were protecting—*me*."

"Of *course*." Declan leaned down, touching his nose to hers, his voice soft. "You're my *everything*. My *every* dream come true. Since seeing you the first time, same as now. Same as it will *ever* be. Long as you can abide me." Then he kissed her, feeling her open to him, fully, completely, with an intimacy between them far greater than before, their vows sealed anew with the press of his lips on hers.

Shaun studied his gran niece and her husband while the two of them shared the story of what had happened below. "*How* many?"

"There were *two* of them. Both young. No one—"

"The *gold*. How many bags?"

Declan stepped back, looking at Marion. She held her head up, giving Shaun an imperious look. "Enough."

"That's no *answer*, girl!" Shaun glowered as he struggled to stand, Declan coming to assist him, and waved away. When he failed to make it to his feet, Shaun reached up for the young man's hand, letting him help pull him to his feet. He started to admonish Marion, stopping when Declan leaned in, his voice low.

"She is *my* wife. No longer spoken to in that tone. A woman married in full, to the *laird* of this clan, which yourself approved of. So, best tread *lightly*, lest I'm forced to fight ya—*losing* no doubt, but willing to take my lumps."

Shaun closed his eyes, feeling faint, the blood rushing from his head, his heart skipping several beats, causing him to stumble to one side. Declan assisted him to a divan, his usual haunt during the day. Placed near the fireplace for him to use at night, after spending hours in restless pacing wondering where the time had flown to, with a hundred ghosts in steady visit, more real to him than people visiting the manor house. Old friends from below, and highland crofts, recalling stories of adventures throughout clan lands.

"You must *keep* it."

Marion came over, placing the back of her hand on her beloved gran uncle's forehead, finding it cold, looking at Declan, shaking her head. She leaned in. "The *gold?*"

Shaun shook his head, reaching out, clamping Marion's wrist in his fingers. "Your *promise*—sworn to see to the protection of the clan. All the clan—high or low—wherever they are. And you must keep *him* as close to ya—close as if your *own* soul. One of the rare ones—like your Da. With the hope he never has to—never has to make the same choice. But if he does—you must *forgive* him, lass. Forgive—him—"

Marion knelt, placing her head on her gran uncle's chest, her husband's hand on her neck, his other reaching out and closing the former laird's eyes.

The last of the gathering of clan members rode away, leaving Declan and Marion waving goodbye from the front steps of the manor. The fare-the-well ceremony for the venerated Laird, well attended, had included several dignitaries of note making the journey all the way from London to bid their condolences. Everyone had complemented Marion on having continued the work of Lady Sinclair, carrying on her mother's legacy while she was away in the Pennsylvania colony, doing the same over there while waiting for cooler heads to prevail, with Washington and his cohorts draped in chains, the colonies returned to the welcoming embrace of Mother England.

Marion gave Declan a look letting him know she was at the end of her tether. Her ability to make small talk with small-minded people, many of them men, having exhausted her. He gathered her in his arms, telling her how much he admired, adored, and loved her, having watched as she spun between numerous conversations with ease, leaving each person who'd come to pay their respects made to feel the center of her undivided attention. An act, he knew, serving to cement her reputation as the power behind the title, worn by him.

"Come, my love. A warm bath and glass of wine will help ease the burden made on your gran uncle's behalf."

Marion sighed, shaking her head. "There is too much left to do. Letters to write, sent by hired messengers to the hands of people I *do* not know, wondering whether they are trustworthy." She looked up at Declan, her rock, the one person she need never question as to his loyalty and love for her.

"Cannae they be set aside until tomorrow?" He rubbed her shoulders, trying to coax her from her path. She shrugged off his hand.

"No." Marion stepped away, then turned. "It's not to be *our* life, husband, held in *our* hands—but *theirs*." She swept her hand in a half circle, indicating the clan lands. "Every decision, every *thought* of what needs doing, *done*. Starting *now*. With a letter written, handed to a lad with a lock and key for a mouth, reaching out to someone I need have a conversation with." She started to turn away, then stopped, looking at Declan, one eyebrow cocked. "Well?"

He hesitated. "His name—the one to be found, then brought here?"

Marion sighed. "Nae, husband. You're right. It will wait until tomorrow, with the warm bath, wine, and your firm fingers on my shoulders, *first*." She hesitated, then gave him a heated look. "For we've a *bairn* to make—the time for it *ripe*."

CHAPTER TWENTY-THREE
CROSSROAD STORE
FALL, 1779

Meghan clutched a large hen to her chest, cradling it between her breasts. A pang of loneliness slipped through her heart, remembering the trio of red grouse snared on a misty morning in the highlands, far and away. Her sister, lying alongside her, waiting on their brother's signal.

Allyn crawled out from beneath the coop, his face beaded with sweat, rubbing his hands in a layer of dirt, cleaning them of droppings. His shirt was open, exposing his muscled chest, causing his wife to draw in her breath as she released the wayward chicken into the repaired enclosure.

Meghan went over and took her husband's wrist, turning it over, seeing a trace of blood on his palm. "What have ya gone and done?" She grinned, the sun reflecting from her blue eyes, her hair a glow of red and gold, as happy as she'd ever been. "I'll need to put a salve on that, the soil 'near a coop known to harbor bad spirits."

"You've no belief in such sayings." Allyn paused, then shrugged. "Though I ken the ancient wives' tales do seem to have *some* measure of truth behind them. My own dear mother with such phrases near to hand, reciting them like psalms sung in church."

Meghan pushed him toward the small farmhouse standing apart

from the store and warehouse, rebuilt to her mother's requirements. Proud of Allyn, kept busy making two trips each week to warehouses outside the port of Philadelphia. Aboard their large wagon, loaded down with produce and handmade products, returning late in the day with goods needed by local communities. A profit made each way, the money earned, used to help support women and their families, whose husbands and sons were off fighting for the loyalists or colonials.

When Allyn finished washing up at the well behind the house, he used the towel Meghan handed him to dry off, then followed her inside, surprised when she pulled him into the narrow stairway, leading up to their bedroom. "The kitchen and your *potions* are t'other way, wife."

Meghan gave Allyn a mischievous smile. "I've a *different* treatment in mind for you. One that will help take your mind off your pain." Then she tugged his hand, pulling him up the narrow stairs.

※※※

Harold stepped out from the shadows of a forest, the reins of his horse in hand as he scanned the ground of a small glade, searching for signs of another rider having passed through. He saw a line of tracks in the grass, freshly pressed by the shod hooves of a single horse. It was early morning, the sun hidden behind a thin layer of clouds scudding by overhead, with promise of rain before midday, clearing by late afternoon.

He took a moment to breathe in the scent of the sweet grass and musty oak leaves lying along the edge of a thick hardwood, having walked his horse through them, forgoing use of the narrow trail. His senses were on high alert, probing the opposite side of the opening while his horse tugged at the reins.

The mare lowered her head, seeking a mouthful of grass. She muttered her displeasure, roused from a warm stall while still dark. The steep climb from the farmhouse into the hills following a circuitous route between closely bunched trees, an additional strain on its patience. Harold eased the reluctant mare back under the trees, leaving her tied to a low hanging branch with a lead long enough to allow her to graze. Then he checked the priming of a pistol pulled from a stiff leather strap on his side, remembering the advice given him long ago by Robert, the image of the older man's face causing a moment of joyful sorrow, still missing him, especially now.

With a shrug of his shoulders, Harold lowered his head and pushed forward, staying to the shadows of the trees, heading toward a ramshackle cabin a half hour away on foot, where he was to meet up with the man who would fill him in or recent events concerning his son.

※※※

Charles glanced up as a figure filled the slanted opening of a small cabin, its walls struggling to keep the moss-laden roof suspended above the mold-spotted floor for as long as possible. He greeted Harold with a warm smile, pleased to see him again. Doubly pleased to be bringing him good news.

"Hail to you, my friend—and well met."

Harold glanced at the sagging rafters, barely higher than his head. "A sad epithet—chiseled on your stone. A man like yourself, brought to your end by collapse of a moss-thickened roof." He stepped inside, testing the floor, satisfied it would hold him. "An interesting way to get me a message. A bundle of parchments, tucked in a crate of goods— tied with a *bowstring*. Your note in the middle of the stack."

Charles nodded, a grin on his lips. "I expected you would get my meaning—and will get straight *to* it. Your son is in the south, at my suggest, with Greene soon to follow. Aaron is helping to prepare the ground, carrying on the same type of work performed hereabouts. With far *greater* success. His strategic brilliance witnessed with my own eyes."

"He is *hale*—in body *and* mind?"

The shorter man, with a wash of gray lightening the edges of his thick curls of jet-black hair, nodded, his eyes shadowed in the subdued light of the musty interior. "He has managed to strike a balance. One keeping him upright, able to see the world about him as it *is* and *should* be. Or, rather—as it *might* become, given half a chance."

"Easier on him, if his path hadn't been *twisted* by men like you." Harold held up one hand. "I realize you're acting against those on the opposite side of the scale, doing what you think best to try and keep the needle somewhere near the center, leaving it to future generations to sort out which side was right."

"Well said." Charles leaned forward; his small hands clasped between his knees. "Though I'm afraid that *your* situation, my friend requires an—*adjustment* to be made." He tightened his lips. "There are rumors afloat, on the tips of branches I've strung my web between. *Subtle*, thus far, though the vibrations have—*disturbed* my sleep."

Harold nodded. "Assume it to be the reason for inviting me *here*, where I once had a drink with a good and honorable man, along with his two sons." He paused, lowering his head, then looked back up. "The movements described—having to do with *me*."

"You've felt the same tug?" When Harold nodded, Charles sighed. "Then I am *doubly* troubled, knowing what I've long feared on your behalf may soon come to pass. *If* you choose to stay where you are, on the *familial* side of things." He gave Harold a sad look, one reaching to the very corners of his dark eyes. "You will need to leave. Today, if possible, extracting yourself from the loving arms of your wife and daughter."

Charles reached into his pocket, removing an envelope and purse of coins. "Enough in here to see you to wherever it is you might go. Along with two passes. One signed by Washington. The other by Cornwallis."

Harold reached over, taking the papers, ignoring the purse. "*Your* signatures, I presume, having watched you attach my name to bills passed on to Parliament. Ones I could not bring myself to sign off on."

"The one from Cornwallis, *yes*. Though I *could* have managed to acquire an authentic one, with a few of my best people near to him." He hesitated. "You will forget my having said that. It was—"

"I heard only the chirping of birds, roosting in the rafters of this fine building." Harold gave Charles a considered look. "Having once belonged to an old friend of mine. Now in the business of fishing for cod, last time I saw him. Along with his two sons, each at the helm of their own ship."

"He is land bound now. Head of a vital strand of my web. An anonymous and *deadly* man, more so than those *you* went up against." Charles returned Harold's look. "Asked me to inform you—*how* did he put it? Oh *yes*. To tell you that: *anytime, anywhere, anything*—yours."

"Bit wordy—for him."

"I got the feeling he knew more than he felt free to reveal, even to me. Though he did mention he would provide coverage for your—most *valuable* assets, living hereabout—should the need ever arise." Charles reached out, offering the purse, again.

Harold shook his head, then stood up, his hand out, feeling it might be the last time he would see the man who'd been with him, in one fashion or another, since his first steps into the shadows of political warfare. "Walk with caution, Charles. And give my son a father's regards—next time you see him."

Then he was gone, Charles feeling the loss of the only man he'd ever envied and grown to admire. His son, a close second. He stared out into the breaking dawn, watching as birds, roused from their night-time roosts, fluttered from a broken-backed barn before rising into the sky, leaving him with a heavy heart as he stepped outside, mounting his horse and slowly riding away.

☙❧☙

Sinclair stared, hearing the words, unable to process their meaning. She blinked as Harold ended his sentence, waiting for more. An explanation she could reason with, trying to bend his decision in another direction, one that would still include her in his life. The look in his eyes let her know it wasn't possible. The past always there, lurking behind his eyes, haunting his thoughts. Along with the image of him standing in the doorway of a house in Bath, his hand raised, cheeks red with embarrassment, staring at her as if seeing a goddess.

The memory fading away, knowing she was a no longer a goddess to him. Only a wife, twice abandoned. She turned around and walked away without looking back, knowing there would be no second mending of her heart, left torn in two. Again.

Harold remained in the shadows of the barn, wishing to be able to go back to the moment of his leaving Sinclair the first time, in what seemed to have been a lifetime ago. To choose instead to toss aside his concerns for the good of common and decent men. He watched as she slipped through the farmhouse door, then opened his mouth, his voice a whisper, making her one final promise. "Another time, my love—we *will* meet again. In this life—or the next." Then he folded himself into the woods, moving away with a measured pace.

CHAPTER TWENTY-FOUR
HIGHLAND MANOR
MID-WINTER, 1780

The wind was out of the lowlands. Cold, with a hint of sleet, promising snow before night. Marion watched as a small, oddly shaped boy of eleven years grasped the stirrup of a long-legged stallion and lifted himself off the ground, scrambling his way into the saddle, settling himself with a shrug of his thick hips. He turned and gave her a wave of an oversized hand, his short legs thrust out to the sides, his thick-set face set in a determined look as he nudged the reluctant steed ahead.

Declan stood alongside his wife, feeling the cold but refusing to allow himself to shiver. Marion wore a thick shawl pulled over her shoulders, a plain linen dress underneath, her belly swollen. He raised his voice against the wall of chill air, keeping his tone level. "I've made my feelings known to ya, lass. It's a *fool's* errand you're sending the young lad on, thought the *need* of it is righteous enough." He gave her a hard look. "But it should be *me*—the one *doing* it."

Marion looked away, measuring the lowering clouds racing by in a gray-faced churn, painting her cheeks red with ice-tipped brushstrokes. She watched as the boy, named Angus, disappeared into the distance, swallowed up by a curtain of gray mist. "He—he's wearing an *oiled* cloak. My gran uncle's—with wool enough in the sweater worn beneath to recoat half a dozen sheep. He'll—he'll be *fine* once he clears the Pinch. Then down to Glasgow by morning next, with shelter provided at any of a handful of croft farms along the way."

"Still, his journey is not to be only there and back. Sent over the sea to France, then inland to Lisieux. The lad without the language or social skills needed to pull this off." Declan spun his wife around, wanting to shelter her from the wind, their unborn bairn at risk. He saw tears on her cheeks, along with a worried look in her eyes.

Marion buried her head in his chest, rocking back and forth, her shoulders trembling from fear and the cold. Declan wrapped her with his arms, moving her back through the manor door.

She looked up at him. "I've little choice, needing the message sent directly to the one intended, requiring *someone* to deliver the papers. Someone *trustworthy*, with Angus the only one to go. No one will suspect him to be a courier. Yourself—too well known to avoid those at watch in every port. Gran uncle Shaun having told me of people paid to watch there, and in every public house, livery stable, inn, and such—marking down departures and arrivals of people of note."

Marion pulled back, reaching up and touching his face, her fingers cold. "I'll not have you put at risk. Our child born—without a father to help raise him." She paused, her eyes filling with tears, reflecting the fire burning in the salon fireplace. "Like Angus, with his parents dying of a flux."

"The church did right by the boy, placing him with a good family, then handing him on to us. Paid a good wage for the work he does." Declan took Marion's hands, the warmth starting to flow back into them. "Though I fear this task assigned him may prove to be *beyond* his capability."

"He's got clan *Scott* blood—somewhere in the mix. And is much too stubborn to *know* that!" Marion squeezed his hands. "The lad's convinced he can do *anything*, once his mind's been set to it."

Declan turned and looked out the nearest window, watching the sky darken, with the wind curling around the eaves of the manor in a shrill howl. "May God guide him, this night through all the rest. Until he's safely back to home and hearth."

※※※

The deck of the ship rose, then fell away, another large swell passing under its hull, with a strong wind quartering the bow, causing a heavy roll. Angus flexed his knees, adjusting to the change in the angle of the deck, resisting the force of damp sea air against his body. He leaned as far forward as possible, staring at the horizon as if willing the ship to reach France, lying somewhere ahead over a wave-whipped horizon.

"You're wasted in a life lived ashore. *Here's* where ya belong. Standing watch, your hand to the wheel." A deep, sea-spray roughened voice boomed out from behind. The helmsman, done with his watch, had come forward, standing just behind the small, thick bodied young man.

Angus turned his head slightly. "Your voice cuts through the wind. Loud enough to stir the gulls in La Havre from their dockside perch." Then he returned to staring straight ahead.

The helmsman chuckled. "How *old* did you say you were?"

"Didn't." The young Scot spun around, the stiff wind ruffling his short, reddish-brown hair. "I'm educated, is all. Taught my letters and such by my second parents. Taken in, then raised to be someone of account."

The seasoned sailor cracked a smile, his teeth, with a gap here and there, matching the gray shade of the late afternoon light. "Then I'll leave you to your solitary watch." The man paused. "Standing here, no doubt counting the leagues we've put behind us, and those ahead."

Angus returned to his study of the sea, measuring the speed of the ship, watching a patch of seaweed slip alongside the hull, aware the next day would see them outside the harbor, waiting to dock.

※※※

The city of Lisieux, threaded through with narrow streets, teemed with people jostling for position along the edges. Angus frowned, forced to step around knots of patrons moving in and out of doorways of dozens of shops. Everyone made to scurry from one side of the street to the other as teams of horses pulling wide-bodied wagons passed by. A waste of time and energy, he muttered beneath his breath, his Scottish upbringing abhorring the inefficient nonsense. Like frogs, he thought, hopping from one place to another without regard for proper spacing.

He came to a sudden stop, several people brushing by, bouncing off his side due to the wide set of his feet and sturdy lower body. He pulled out a piece of paper and compared what Lady Marion had inscribed, with a series of delicate whorls and loops, to the names of several buildings, none of them proving to be a match.

Angus resisted holding the paper up to his nose, wondering if the parchment might have absorbed the scent of Lady Marion's perfume. Then he looked around, peering between the bodies of people passing between him and an open space, spying a vendor standing by a small cart of fresh fruit.

He walked over and showed the man the paper, getting a short nod in return, followed by an avalanche of words, unintelligible due to the rapid pace of the strange language, a gnarled finger pointing to an avenue running at a slight angle on the opposite side of the square. Angus nodded, then turned away, stopped by a hand on his shoulder. He looked up, the vendor's palm held out. Angus shook it, then let go, moving across the crowded street, carefully slipping between two horse-drawn carriages as he headed toward a church spire poking above a row of small shops lining the opposite side of the busy street.

Angus stopped in front of a gray-faced building with dark windows, the letters finally matching up. Men with serious expressions headed inside, avoiding others coming out with relaxed smiles on their faces before ducking their heads, moving away at a quick pace. He stepped up to the entrance, then hesitated, a muttered curse from behind propelling him forward. The interior was poorly lit, with thick wall hangings helping to dampen the noise from the busy street.

The man who'd followed him in shoved his way past, causing Angus to stumble. He reached out, regaining his balance, his eyes slowly adjusting to the dim light, his fingers touching the bared breast of a nymph in a painted scene, one of a half-dozen cavorting in a field of grass, their nude bodies being leered at by what looked to be men with the legs of a goat.

Angus yanked his hand away, feeling a rush of blood in his cheeks, wondering if there had been some mistake made in translating French to English, with Lady Marion given bad information. A flow of unintelligible words washed over his large ears, delivered by a narrow faced young woman standing in a doorway, a desk behind her. She wore a plain colored dress with simple lines, reminding him of Lady Marion's usual attire.

The woman leaned forward, noting his confusion, as well as his drab clothing and mud-splattered boots, changing to heavily accented English. "You are looking for the delivery door—no?" Angus shook his head, thrusting the paper out, watching as the small-framed woman held it up to the light filtering in from a window in the small room. "This is the correct address. You are here to visit with—one of our ladies?"

"*No!*" Angus shook his head, raising his hands. "I'm to meet with the man who lives here. The one who *owns* it!"

"Which one? There are many who are investors—*and* clients."

"The one who served in the war." Angus looked up, uncertain how much to share of what Lady Marion had told him. "Against the English."

"*Which* war?" The small woman smiled. "We have enjoyed *many* disagreements of late—with our friends across the channel."

"The one with the Indians—no, with the *natives* in it. Over in the colonies."

The woman nodded, a smile on her perfect lips, her eyes lighting up. "You are referring to Monsieur Coulombe? Pierre?"

"*Yes!* That was the name given me. Him." Angus hesitated. "Is he here? I need to speak with him."

"He is *here*—but occupied at the moment." She hurried to explain. "In a meeting with investors. In his office—" She turned to one side, pointing to a door on the opposite wall of the small anteroom. "Just there. You are, of course, welcome to wait in here. We have wine if you would care for some."

Angus stepped forward and peered around the side of the door, then made his way inside, holding up one hand waving off the offer of refreshment. "I'm fine. Unless you have some tea—cold *or* hot."

"None is ready at the moment, but I will start a pot." She pointed to some pastries. "Those are for the meeting, once it is over. They will not notice if *one* is missing."

Angus shook his head, his stomach rumbling in hunger as he stared at the food. "I'm here to see the one I came to find." He paused. "But thank you."

The woman nodded, deciding to forgo asking his name, aware the young man was only a messenger, albeit one far from home.

※※※

Pierre Coulombe gave the young Scotsman a wide smile, bidding him sit down across from him at the table where the meeting had just taken place. He reached out, pushing a plate of delicacies toward the youth, careful not to hit a small cup, filled with tea, the vapor rising in the still air of the office. "Please—you must *eat!* Your journey here, no doubt, a long one." Pierre nodded at the cup of tea. "Is the blend of leaves to your satisfaction? They are from my private stock."

Angus ignored the comment. "I am here at the ask of—at the *request* of Lady Marion, wife to the laird of clan Scott." Angus noted the look on the Frenchman's face, seeing he was uncertain as to the name. "Oh —she told me to say she is the daughter of Lady Sinclair Haversham-Knutt." He saw the narrowed gaze of the man sitting opposite him widen into a bright smile.

"A daughter of Lady *Sinclair*—someone whom I greatly admire." Pierre paused, losing his smile. "Widow to a man I was as close to as if my own brother. A great loss—an *untimely* death." He waited, allowing a genuine feeling of pain to settle, then softened his voice. "Lady Sinclair, I am certain, still devastated by it. The two of them *extremely* close. Their relationship noted during a trans-Atlantic voyage I was fortunate to join them on, allowing me to spend time with them until our arrival in Philadelphia." He paused, eyeing the young boy. "Which I understand is now *back* in colonial hands."

"I don't know anything of that. Enough for me, keeping my mind on the work I'm asked to do by Lady Marion, with her mother gone, departed this past year." Angus hesitated, seeing the other man's face fall into a shocked expression. "Heading over to the colonies. To a place somewhere outside Philadelphia." He stopped himself, unsure if he should be sharing the information. "I have a message to deliver, then I'm to be on my way back home."

Pierre watched as the young messenger, his dirt-stained face unmarked by any sign of facial hair, bent one leg, working a soiled boot from his foot. A rank odor of unwashed skin and sweat stained stocking wafted across the table, mingling with the delicate scent of the tea and pastries, wrinkling Pierre's nose.

Angus handed him a thin leather packet, holding it over the tray of baked goods. "It's a bit *damp*, the outside of it. But the paper inside will be dry. I sealed it with whale oil, against the sweat." Angus, unaware of Pierre's discomfort pulled a sweet from the plate, chewing loudly, his hunger gnawing away at his stomach with needled teeth.

Pierre used a slim knife blade to slice away a wax seal holding the flap secured. Then he delicately removed a shingle sheet of paper, a thin layer of wax coating the words, written in French, causing his eyebrows to rise in surprise.

"Second time you've done that." Angus was leaning back in his chair, eyes narrowed in thought.

Pierre looked over at the boy, his sock replaced, another sweet held between the fingers of his overly sized hand. "Excuse me?"

"Your look — one of surprise." Angus chewed a large mouthful of a fruit pastry, then followed it up with a noisy slurp of the tea. He wiped his mouth with the back of his hand, muffling a wet burp. "In hearing me mention Lady Sinclair being off to the colonies. Then again, just now, reading what's in *there*." He pointed with the remnant of the tart, crumbs falling onto an expensive carpet alongside his soiled boot, left lying there, continuing to flavor the air.

"Do you know what she — what Lady Marion has enclosed?" Pierre managed to keep his smile firmly locked in place as he set the packet down on an empty plate. Then he stood up and went over to a large window, cracking it open, taking a moment to inhale the slightly less noxious odors emanating from small piles of horse manure, left scattered in the street.

"No. Of little enough interest to *me*. I do as I'm told. Always have. My parents, not my *first* ones — who died from the bloody flux, when I was a child. My *second* ones, given me by the church, with their own child dead from the same curse."

Pierre turned around, looking at the strange young boy sitting in a room in a gentlemen's establishment, in a city within the borders of a country whose language he couldn't speak, or understand. Having made his way alone, no doubt by ship, speaking as casually as if sitting at home, discussing the day's weather.

"And—?"

Angus narrowed his eyes, licking his fingers clean, the last of the pastry gone. "And *what?*"

"You were speaking of your second set of parents—with my condolences offered for the loss of your first. What of *them?*" Pierre paused, aware he'd started to mirror the boy's strange manner of speaking.

"Oh. *Yes*." The young boy eyed another pastry. "They taught me to get my chores done before opening their room of books for me to pour through. The two of them having taught me to read. Punishing me by closing it off until I '*straightened*' my path."

"Amazing." Pierre came back over and sat down, ignoring the ripe odor of the dirt encrusted boot, surrounded by pastry crumbs scattered on the expensive carpet. He knew the boy was a vital part of the message sent him by the daughter of Sinclair. Along with an invitation for him to visit. One he felt compelled to do, having decided to join the unusual young man on his journey back home.

CHAPTER TWENTY-FIVE
SOUTHERN CAMPAIGN
SUMMER, 1780

A water-logged dugout canoe probed the inner edge of a black, back-water bog. It slipped through the mirrored water without a sound, moving in the thin light of a sliver of moon as if a log in drift, with barely a ripple inscribed on the dark surface.

Chatte, perched in the stern, sat huddled beneath a cloak of gray cloth used to provide concealment and help ward off any mosquitoes. The thin blade of her paddle propelled it toward a small cove where Aaron waited, dressed in brown garb, lantern in hand with the wick turned down. They exchanged a wave of greeting as the narrow nose of the pirogue eased through a slurry of shoreline leaves and twigs. Aaron trapped it between his hands as Chatte stepped along the centerline of the slender vessel, placing a hand on his broad back, then making a leap onto dry ground.

"There was no need for the light. Unnecessary—the risk taken." Her voice was a low purr in his ears, matched by sinuous movements as she unwrapped the cloak from around her lithe body.

Aaron extinguished the lantern, handing it to her. "We do not *all* have the eyes of a *cat*—like you." Then he pulled the small vessel onto a sloped bank and turned it over, letting the accumulated water drain out. The supplies she'd gathered were left tied in place for several of the younger men to come and collect once morning arrived.

He straightened up, gazing at the diminutive voyageur with a welcoming smile. "I was growing concerned, waiting here the past two nights—with the moon in wane. We're encamped a mile up the draw, waiting on the movement of a small British force making its wary approach. We'll move out tomorrow and ambush them again, if they decide to continue their advance, having already suffered several *stings* since leaving their fort, over a week ago."

"And our plans *after* that?" Chatte asked the question then looked away, knowing he would not tell her or anyone else.

Aaron pulled her in, wrapping his arms around her body, inhaling the sweet-sour scent of her sweat dampened hair, unwashed during her recent journey to settlements lying on the outskirts of loyalist towns, trading herbs gathered from swamps and woodland marshes for information on the comings and goings of English forces, sent to hunt down their insurrectionist group.

He leaned back, gazing into her hazel eyes, the crescent moon hanging overhead illuminating them with a silvery glow, her thin face framed by a tangle of uncombed curls. "What is *unknown*—cannot be *told*."

Chatte smiled, then handed him the lantern, a slight wince showing on her flawless face as she did so, noticed without comment by Aaron as he turned away, leading her into the woods.

※※※

The low voices of the men created a subtle murmur in the night, mingling with the sound of crickets in their repetitive symphony of chirping, accompanied by the cooing calls of doves in tree-top roosts. A soft wind gently dragged its fingers through the tops of a stand of hardwood trees, creating a steady rustle, filling the evening air.

Aaron's breathing slowly returned to a relaxed rhythm, a line of sweat beading his brow. He had one arm curled around Chatte's shoulders, their reunion complete, the sounds of their lovemaking overheard and ignored by the hard-edged band of rebels. He sighed, wishing to ask about her most recent wound, a slash from a knife blade made along her upper arm, the edges of her skin pulled together with a row of neat stitches, sewn into her flesh by her slim fingers, now entwined with his.

Chatte opened her eyes, looking into his, reading his thoughts. "It was from the blade of a native—a moment before *mine* found his heart, ending a *minor* disagreement as to who held rightful claim to the pirogue."

"He assumed it to belong to him?" Aaron returned her quiet look.

"It was *me* with first *and* final claim to it." She paused. "As it turned out."

"Will there be any *ripples* left for us to deal with?"

Chatte grinned, a look of pleasure hazing her eyes, seen in the firelight alongside the lean-to they were lying in. "None. I bound his hands to a large bag of stones, then punctured his lungs and bowels, leaving him at the bottom of a deep bog, attended to by the fish." She reached down, finding him, squeezing gently. "Again?"

Aaron rolled onto his side, jaw braced on one hand, elbow angled on the cloak beneath their bodies. He looked deep into her eyes as he considered her request, knowing how easy it would be to lose himself in her body. He remained silent, unable to deny her, leaving the next move up to her.

She withdrew her hand, patting him on his cheek. "I will go and wash. You were—*insistent* with your need, having saved yourself for me."

"I want you *now*. As you *are*." He leaned over, burying his nose in the bed of her thick curls, her light-colored hair reflecting the banked light from a fire-pit glowing just outside their shelter.

"And I want *you*, as well. But not as before. We will need to attend to ourselves with some of the soap I brought back with me. And you will *abide* it—without complaint."

She slipped out from beneath the covering, exposing herself to him, the sight of her naked body drawing his gaze, as too those of the men lying in a circle only a few steps away, all of them quick to avert their eyes. Aaron got up, finding his trousers, stepping into them as Chatte walked away, not the least concerned by the attention shown her by the others.

One of them came over, his sentry duties over for the night. "She is —" The man, given the name Bear based on his squat, thick framed build, stared into the darkness, shaking his head, his eyes with an admiring gaze, matching that of Aaron's. "An *amazing* woman." He paused. "And you, my friend, are a *fortunate* man."

Aaron reached over, clasping him on his wide shoulder, Bear's broad face covered in a thick beard, with a neck that was a match in width to his head, recently shaved, with a ring of dark black hair growing back in along the sides. "She certainly is. Though she straddles the line between what's deemed *acceptable* — in the waging of war."

The man, of a height to Aaron, was one of the hundred unknown men in their group, making their presence felt throughout the South Carolina colony under General Green's directives, sent by Charles on constant forays against increasingly wary British troops.

The redcoats and their loyalist allies had reacted to their deadly intrusion with plodding marches made into the surrounding countryside, led by lancers. Skilled soldiers on horseback, under the command of a British officer known for his own measure of brutality against anyone suspected of helping the rebels, or men captured in battle.

Aaron had managed to stay out of their grasp, destroying bridges ahead and behind the slow-moving columns of men, executing lightning raids, destroying goods critical to the needs of an army in the field. Creating a death of a thousand cuts, meting out handfuls of losses here and there with British soldiers made to pay the price.

Bear looked at Aaron. "Will it be the same as before — our strategy for tomorrow?"

"No. The tide is beginning to turn against us." Aaron gave him a tight grin. "The officer leading them has learned a *painful* lesson — due to our previous tutelage. We need to provide him a more *advanced* course of instruction — with a *new* tactic employed."

The man ignored most of the words used, shaking his head in confusion. "Then it's to be *another* rabbit pulled from a hole in the ground — one of your *own* create?"

Aaron shrugged. "Not mine." He nodded to where Chatte had

slipped into the shadows. "But *hers*." He reached out, touching Bear on his heavily muscled shoulder. "The desire for revenge guiding her to it, especially when it comes to the slaughter of men clad in red and white."

※※※

A seasoned lieutenant, with over a decade of service in the British army, led his advance party toward a small bridge. His eyes were in a constant swivel, searching the edge of thick woods for sign of movement, though his native allies had already swept through them, signaling they were clear. Despite their assurances, he sensed another trap, its jaws spread wide, waiting for the press of a careless toe to trigger it. His instincts, honed by half-a-dozen recent attacks, elicited a tightening in his groin, expecting a shower of arrows and storm of bullets to come tearing through his force of men, the vision haunting his every step.

A miserable country, he thought to himself, with miserable people. Eager to release their anger at dark deeds done by a colonel with a vicious reputation, leading another group of British Lancers, turning their loyalist allies against them. Men, women, and children with sullen looks given him as he passed through their settlements and towns, refusing to acknowledge him or his men with a nod of head, or tip of a cap.

A major with less than five years in service, and only recently arrived in the colonies, came riding up. His left arm hung at his side, wrapped in a blood-stained bandage, sliced through by an arrow during an engagement several days ago. The column of foot soldiers glanced up at the officer, eying the wound, uneasy at the cause of his injury, with no enemy tribes known to be within a hundred miles of their present line of march.

The lieutenant looked up and saluted the young major. "My guts—are in a *ripe* twist, sir."

"Eloquently stated, Lieutenant Jeffers."

The lieutenant ignored the response. "I'll take half the men ahead and check the edge of the woods, sir. Then move on to the second bridge, just beyond. The water no doubt in a fierce rush from the hard rain, two days ago. We'll need both crossings in hand, allowing the rest of the army to continue to move ahead, as planned."

"We are *behind* schedule in distance made this day, Lieutenant. We will continue our approach in column march." The major hesitated, recalling the fiasco of the last engagement. He reached up, touching the edge of the deep slice in his injured arm, the skin swollen, in constant throb. He sighed, then gave a short nod of his head. "Have your master sergeant take *half* the company, moving ahead at a quick pace to secure the second bridge. *You* will take the remainder, checking the first bridge for any sign of sabotage. These rebels will *not* make a fool of me again."

The lieutenant, senior in length of service though limited in financial means to purchase a higher rank, had earned his promotions the hard way, with a host of scars proof of his bravery in battles against enemies of the empire, including these subversive colonists, making a series of intense, though short-lived strikes against their rear and flanks. He hid his frustration from the major, concerned by the constant whittling away of their numbers, affecting the men's morale, along with a lack of food and supplies lost in action, adding to their misery.

"I would suggest you allow *me* to move forward, securing the far bridge, holding it until you and the rest of the company move up to join us." He paused, softening his tone, aware he was close to a charge of insubordination. "Sir."

A sigh from the Major announced a small victory won, a wave of his uninjured arm motioning the older officer ahead. He pressed with one knee, nudging his mount to the side, watching as the lieutenant and one company of regulars moved ahead at the run, the older officer's voice a whip-crack of orders rapidly given. The group of one hundred men crossed the small bridge, half their number disappearing into the woods, while the others stopped and began inspecting both ends of the first crossing. Several men, with ropes tied around their shoulders, climbed beneath it, checking for saw marks in the support timbers, leaving the rest to stand guard with bayonets in leveled point, probing the wood line with wary eyes, searching for any sign of the ghostlike group that kept appearing as if out of thin air, nipping at their flanks with sharp teeth, then running away.

※※※

Bear nudged Aaron in the ribs. "You made the correct call—again. That young officer on horse with the wounded wing—has the makings of a *real* leader, should he manage to survive this day."

Aaron nodded, lying prone on a small rise, watching as the ambush unfolded, his thoughts consumed with concern for his female comrade. Chatte was further ahead, preparing a trap of her own design at the next bridge. Her recent scout downriver, seeking the lay of the land from people willing to aid her efforts to blunt *this* group's advance, had been in support of allowing a large column of colonial soldiers from the local area to slip away, living to fight another day. Their retreat, slowed by bad roads hindering the passage of wagons loaded with supplies and wounded soldiers, had served as a lure to the group of lancers and British regulars, pulling them from their stockades, where they were all but impregnable.

Aaron glanced over. "My arrow would have *done* for him—" He gave Bear a hard stare. "Were it not for a *badly* aimed pistol shot, scoring the neck of his horse."

Bear grinned. "I have already *made* my apologies."

"And I have *accepted* them. Reluctantly." Aaron smiled, shaking his head. "But still—my streak of clean kills came to an end because of it."

Bear grunted, picking a wedged morsel of meat from between his teeth with a dirty fingernail, examining it for a moment before swallowing. "You'll no doubt start *another* today." Then he lifted his hand, finger pointing at a column of thick black smoke rising into the air from the woods surrounding the second bridge. "There's the *signal.*"

※※※

Chatte watched as a thick trail of smoke rose from several crocks of oil, tossed on a bed of glowing coals in the center of the road, just past the end of the second bridge. Topped off with the green branches of fir trees and pitch-pine knots, the smudge of dark, dense smoke spiraled straight up, the current of mid-morning air in temporary pause.

She knew the red-coat devils would come on the run, trying to prevent the second bridge from burning through its supports. Its destruction causing a long delay in their effort to catch up to the General Greene's army, making its painful retreat. Time spent fashioning a new bridge capable of supporting their heavily laden wagons, would take them the better part of two days.

Chatte noted a group of dark clothed colonist insurgents waiting beside a dozen large trees, the trunks cut partway through, wedges in place. A few of the men would hammer them home while others used saws to finish felling them, blockading the narrow road behind the column of British soldiers as they moved forward to put out the fires.

A handful of other men knelt beneath low-hanging branches, prepared to use long poles to shove bales of oil saturated hay into the narrow roadway, dry logs tied on the sides and tops to create a wall of flames, sealing them in. The soldiers, caught between and betwixt, would be unable to retreat due to the trees behind and inferno ahead. Panicked men, left to choose between burning alive or tossing themselves into a thirty-foot gorge where large rocks and a wash of whitewater waited, ready to sweep them under overhanging ledges.

"We wait until they cross to put out the fire, then light the quick burning fuses leading to the kegs of powder tucked beneath the stone foundations at the far end. After we've knocked them back, our men will advance, killing any survivors before making our retreat." She paused. "Their officers, taken alive. Wounded, if need be—but *alive*."

Smoke, whose left hand had been half-gnawed away years earlier by shrapnel from the burst of a French cannon shell, looked over, his face a canvas of waxy skin, burnt as he lay wounded in a field of grass on fire, started from the same shell. He cracked an uneven smile. "We'll burn—then *blast* the *fooking* bastards!"

※※※

The small victory, added to a host of others, left over two dozen men killed, added to a hundred more from the previous ambushes. The insurgents had retreated, gathering in the edges of a large rockfall, with no significant injuries to report. Two British soldiers, left bruised but unwounded, having landed in pools of water between water-smoothed boulders, sat alongside the two redcoat officers. One, a lieutenant with a mortal wound, struggled to breath, his face gray, an arrow from one of the young archers having scored his abdomen, opening a long cut, closed by Chatte with large sutures, hastily placed. The other, a major, sat across from a small firepit, bared to the waist with a severely injured arm, beginning to show signs of corruption.

Chatte watched him as he watched her place the tip of her knife blade in the glowing coals of a small fire, the only one allowed. Their camp was dark, located in a narrow pocket between several fingers of tumbled stones, provided multiple exits, with a watch placed on every path in or out.

"I—" The major swallowed, his youthful eyes swollen with pain from a new wound in his thigh, a musket ball having torn through the muscle, expertly tended to by the woman kneeling in front of him. "I *know* who you are." The officer kept his voice low. "*Chatte Sauvage*—the witch who feasts on the *hearts* of men."

"No. Not their hearts." Chatte leaned forward, gazing into his eyes with a benevolent smile. "Only their *fear*. *That* is what fills my belly. What feeds my *soul*."

"I am—" He swallowed again, trembling as a spasm of pain from his damaged leg raced through him. "I am not *afraid* of death."

"You shouldn't be, having already eluded it—twice. Your destiny to have died several days ago, were it not for a minor wound to your mount—from a misplaced shot." She leaned back. "Your men would have buried you *then*. My man—he does not *miss* with an arrow, once released."

"This man you speak of—is from what tribe?"

"His *own*."

The officer's pinched face held a look of confusion, dampened by the realization his life was near its end, any information shared by this woman dashing any hope of his release. "The two privates. The young men you captured, not yet blooded. Have not fired a *single* shot during their brief service. Only boys, looking for a position where food and clothing would be in ready supply."

"Those are the *best* kind to play with. *Innocents*, like my two brothers were. Like I was—once. A young child, pure of heart, watching as *your* people took my *entire* world from me. My father and brothers, butchered out of hand by British soldiers under the command of an officer. A man like *you*."

The major stiffened his will. "*You* will one day die, the same as *any* of us. And find there will be a special place in *hell* awaiting you."

Chatte nodded, her smile fading to a set of thin, pursed lips. "Yes. Because your kind *delivered* me there, twenty-three years ago. Where I have been living ever since." She leaned in, studying the wounded man's face. "To me, it is a *warm* heat. One I feel deep inside—and desire to keep *fed*. The flames of my hatred ignited when your people forced mine from their generational lands and homes in Nova Scotia. Those of us not left butchered on the sand, doing our best to survive in the cramped holds of transports, suffering from sickness and privation. With red and white clad devils raping the women—beasts wearing the same uniforms *then* as you wear *now*. Innocents killed. Children *and* women. Young *and* old."

Chatte paused, reaching out, pulling her knife blade from the coals, using a piece of leather to shield her hand from the heat of the bone hilt. "I won't be shedding tears of sadness over what comes next. Only those of *joy*."

※※※

Aaron watched as Chatte cleaned the blood from her blade with her slender fingers, using the tip to remove lines of congealed blood from beneath her fingernails. He marveled at the ruthlessness she'd shown, torturing the major without wavering. Without showing him mercy, or any other emotion as she worked with a deliberate calculation of how best to prolong his misery.

As he'd watched her go through the practiced routine of torture, as if a cat playing with a mouse, Aaron wondered about his feelings for her. Able to recall the revulsion felt the first time he'd witnessed her capability to inflict mindless pain on helpless men. The revulsion soon turning into indifference from having seen dozens of farmhouses burnt in the outskirts of Philadelphia, many with their inhabitants still inside. Colonist citizens, their bodies left bleeding in the streets from having dared raise an outcry at their harsh treatment at the hands of a few redcoat officers, fired upon for their impudence.

He and his men had responded in kind, retribution doled out in vicious strikes made from the shadows of moonless nights. From slashing attacks by day, helping bring a measure of balance between the lives lost on one side with the deaths of those on the other. Slain soldiers left stretched across main roads or nailed to trees. Officers, with their faces peeled away, fingers missing, their genitals removed. Payback for the rape of a mother, watched by a teary-eyed daughter. Watching now, a motherless orphan, with tears of satisfaction in her eyes, no longer those of loss.

"We are moving tomorrow?" Chatte knelt before Aaron, looking up, her eyes reflecting the light of a small fire, dying down.

"Yes. Our work here complete, with the colonial forces safely away." He watched as she raised her skirt, slipping the knife back into place, revealing a slim leg to mid-thigh. "We will go ahead, the two of us, so I can make a report to Greene, receiving orders for our next strike."

Chatte noted his gaze as she covered herself up, giving him a questioning look. "What?"

"It's nothing. I was—*reminded* of someone."

She straightened up, hands on her slim hips, eyes boring into his. "Another *woman?*" Chatte narrowed her eyes. "Who?"

Aaron shook his head. "One loved by my *father*. In another time and place. In an earlier war—one fought *here*."

Chatte eased her expression. "Your father—he was an officer for the English, helping the same people *you* are fighting for *now*." She turned her head and spat on the ground. As she reached up and wiped her lips, she noted a smear of red on her hand and rubbed it clean on her skirt.

Aaron nodded, keeping his thoughts to himself as she reached out and touched his cheek, her voice a soft hiss in his ear. "I would gladly *kill* him—your father—if he were with the redcoats *now*."

She glanced at the mutilated body of the major, and those of the three soldiers, two killed by the blade of her knife, drawn across their throats, with the other passing away from his wound. She knew Bear would have his men take their remains to the middle of the road, just beyond the burned-out bridge, where a column of British troops would soon discover it. Their main force arriving in a day or two, in dogged pursuit of the retreating colonials, having trailed the company of men in redcoats sent forward to secure and hold the two bridges. The survivors of the lead platoon forced to retreat, unable to cross due to the raging inferno, withered by deadly fire from muskets and arrows fired from behind cover. Afraid of incurring additional casualties should they have tried an assault across the raging torrent, having to fight their way down and then up steep, moss-covered ledges.

The bodies would drive additional nails of self-doubt into each soldier's nightmares, with new tales added to those told in hushed whispers around campfires and on sentry duty, enhancing the reputation of the woman known to them as the 'wildcat', rumored to devour the hearts of her victims.

Aaron shrugged at Chatte's threat made against his father. "I would watch without flinching—if he *were*." He paused, wanting to share with her what his father had done in striking back against those who were the real enemies of the English empire, its colonies spread across every ocean of the globe. To tell her what he'd done in support of an emergent nation he could only have imagined of, then. One barely formed now, still making its way from out of its cradle, struggling to avoid the loss of its armies. A task Aaron was determined to help General Greene prevent. The officer having earned his respect, a superior strategist of note, serving under Washington's inspired leadership.

Chatte patted him on his cheek, then leaned in, her head pressed against his broad chest. "You will lie with me—this night?"

Aaron took her hand, amazed at how small and fragile it felt in his own. He brought it to his lips, kissing each knuckle, knowing her story, her pain, understanding accepting her thirst for revenge, made into his own. Still unknown to him by her given name. An unnamed woman, dedicated to the death of anyone found wearing English colors. Himself, dedicated to doing as much harm as possible to those he knew were still out there. Still playing both sides against the middle. "Yes, lass. I will."

※※※

Staff Sergeant Collins of the colonial army, attached to headquarters' duty, stepped forward and reached for the bridle of a small mare, holding it as a slim-bodied woman slipped from its back. There was no saddle, just a loose bridle, her moccasin clad heels used to control it. The large man alongside her nodded as he dismounted a large, sorrel-gray stallion with dark mane and tail, wearing the King's brand.

The staff sergeant accepted a hug from the woman, then turned, shaking hands with the tall man. Neither of them were known to him by name, though they'd shared many a meal over the past few months when stopping in to provide reports of actions taken, based on orders given them by General Greene. Their efforts had helped further Greene's plans as to where and when to stand firm, meeting the British forces with deadly resistance, or to slip away, their backs protected by the deadly insurgent force of hard-eyed men, and one small but deadly woman.

More of the latter maneuvers had been happening of late, he thought as he handed the two horses off to a private, with General Greene leading the English on a slow, painful chase throughout the hinterlands of the southern colonies.

"The dry weather settling in will help to lower the rivers that we'll need to cross. Though it will be a *curse*, as well, in allowing the British the same advantage." The staff sergeant, of Scottish blood, glanced at the man known to him as 'Wolf', or *mahdad-alliaidh* in Gaelic, who nodded in reply, then yawned, his eyes red from lack of sleep. "Time enough for all that later—left between you and the General to discuss."

He gave Chatte a quick glance. "I'll take *you* to a shelter where you can wash up and rest. With hot food and drink. I have a bottle of wine in my tent, one I've been holding onto for you, compliments of the

General." The staff sergeant leaned forward, leading them further into the vast encampment.

※※※

General Greene studied the reports handed him, wishing he could read them directly, the unknown man having written them in code. He handed them to his second who put them away until a man of diminutive build would arrive, decoding them, then providing strategic advice of where and when to strike or retreat, based on information provided him by the secretive man standing before him. "I welcome your consistent delivery of information vital to our short and long-term strategies. I commend you and your men for their tireless efforts on our behalf." Greene paused. "And the woman—as well."

Aaron nodded, aware the General had no idea of the amount of blood spilled to produce the coded notes he'd soon pass along to Charles. Only a few verbal details shared between the two of them of what his men had observed, then done, reducing the possibility of British agents within the colonial's camp discovering his plans. Subversive elements much like his own, made up of Tories and native allies alike, nosing around the countryside, each group doing their best to strike the other from ambush with deadly focus, before melting away.

"Thank you, General." Aaron looked at Greene, who gave him a short nod, then reached out, pointing at a map table with a detailed layout of the surrounding area. "Based on your comments, scant in detail as they are, we're no longer in threat of them catching us from behind. The next move is to decide how best to avoid threat of encirclement." Greene shrugged, blinking his eyes, looking worn down by worry and fatigue. "There are three enemy forces trying to pin us down. One to each side—waiting on the one to our rear. Delayed, for a while, thanks to your *excellent* service." He reached over and touched Aaron on his shoulder. "My personal thanks to you, sir."

Aaron studied the markers used to define troop dispositions and size. He reached out, touching a red marker. "Their lead force is seriously depleted. Reduced by a third. The rest left demoralized by a lack of resupply and ghostly spirits, striking from out of shadowy woods.

Leading to sleepless nights, with muskets fired by nervous sentries, seeing phantoms in the mist."

He stifled another yawn, then continued. "We've delayed their advance—enough to prevent tie-in with these fine fellows." He pointed at a semi-circular line of British forces, arrayed to the east and south of where they were currently standing, the colonial troops arrayed in a defensive position, though not yet dug in. "The best path is to the north, drawing them along behind you so we can continue to chew at their flanks, burning their wagons, diverting resupply, weakening them drop by drop until they are forced to snarl in frustration, turning to face us." He gave Greene a cocked smile. "As if a fat bear, trailed by sharp-toothed *mice*."

Greene frowned. "Dangerous—for the mice."

Aaron shrugged, rubbing his forehead, then his eyes. "We have numerous holes available to duck into. Every moment with the British paused, left howling in frustration, helps to lengthen the game. Time is *your* ally, not theirs, with the French bound to enter the fray—at some point." Aaron paused, seeing Greene's expression narrow. "Which you have—*news* of?"

The general looked away; his jaw tensed. "We *all* have secrets to keep." Then he grinned. "It is good to hear from someone who's walked the ground. Seeing this—" He pointed at the display. "As it *really* is, leading us to make an orderly retreat in steady march." Greene hesitated, then squeezed his fingers. "It is why we *need* him. Washington. Not only for his *name*, but for his—*solemn* demeanor. It is what the men respond to. An undefinable quality in detail—but *there*, none-the-less."

Aaron lowered his voice, energy seeping from him due to the long ride and heat of a brazier, glowing in the center of the command tent. "It is due to his *love* for them, in return." He shook his head, remembering the words in his father's journals of his feelings for those who'd followed him into battle. "His love for them—as if they are his own children. And their *return* of it."

Greene nodded his head. "You see it clearly." He stepped away, going over to a side table, removing a cork from a bottle of wine, pouring a small amount into two glasses. "And what of your *own* family?" He handed Aaron a glass, studying his face. "Though you are not known to me by name—I would inquire as to their health. Are they hale?"

Aaron took a sip of the wine, holding onto it for a moment, savoring its flavor before swallowing with his eyes closed. He opened them, staring at Greene. "They *were*—the last time I saw them. No words exchanged between us since then. Or will ever be. The threat the same—in having our identities revealed."

Greene nodded, his glass raised in a silent toast. He finished his drink, then turned toward the map table. "It requires a shift in one's perspective. From the consideration of men made into markers, moved like this—" He touched a red block of wood, sliding it back. "To *that*."

Greene pointed to the leather soled boots Aaron had on, mud-caked along the sides, with a splattering of something darker staining the tops and leather uppers. "How everything changes when one stands at the tip of the spear. The focus not on an army's morale, or national pride, esprit-de-corps, and other such feelings—but only on the personal odds of each man's *survival*. Wondering if they'll manage to live through the next step forward, marching into cannon fire, as waves of musket balls are heading their way."

Aaron shrugged, downing the rest of his wine. "It is a strange game, indeed. One played at when boys, pretending to be men. In falling to the ground, gravely wounded, our last words uttered in faithful mimicry of false words written down by men—scribes—standing far from the spill of entrails and blood. Left to stand up, laughing as we brush the dirt from knees and elbows. Then back to it, over and again, until running home to chores, a hot meal, and comfortable bed."

"I—have not *faced* it. Not as *directly* as have yourself." Greene gave Aaron a considered look, noting the scars on his face and hands. "With decisions made in moments of desperation. Whether or *when* to act, react, maneuver, feint, or to withdraw—going up against an opponent as uncertain of what to do, though eager to engage with you."

Aaron shrugged. "It is a—*delicate* dance, at times. A bare-knuckle brawl—at others. One your army cannot, *must* not engage in—if it is to survive."

Greene nodded, then reached out, his fingers lightly caressing the blue markers. "Like you, I'm not afforded the luxury of a single mistake. Not *one*. As General to these men, this *army*—their fate is in *my* hands, all of them counting on me to make the right decision, every time." He looked at Aaron. "With me trusting you—with your *own* view of the reality of the world outside this enclosure. A man I do not —might *never* get to know the name of, that I can properly thank you."

※※※

Chatte was resting up to her neck in hot water, her knees exposed, steam rising around her face as beads of sweat lined her forehead. She closed her eyes, her fingers grasping the side of a large metal trough, aware of the two soldiers standing outside of a hastily erected shelter surrounding her, keeping watch for men with wandering eyes.

She heard a high-pitched challenge, followed by a low-toned response. A tired smile creased her lips, knowing it was her man coming to find her, like he always did. Their relationship, formed over the past few months, had become familiar, though dangerous to them both if they ever dropped their guard. Any thought of their offering one another a deeper commitment would be a risk to their survival. Unacceptable, for now. Chatte smiled as Aaron came into the shelter, keeping her eyes closed. "I can make room."

Aaron didn't bother with a response, choosing instead to press his lips on hers as he slipped his hand beneath the warm water, sliding it to her waist, then down to her upper thigh, touching the hilt of her bone-handled knife in its leather sheaf, where it always was.

He smiled, remembering how his mother would often reach beneath her skirts, pulling out a blade of comparable size, using it to cut strips of white underskirts for impromptu bandages, or hewing limbs from trees for him and his sister Meghan to use in faux sword play. Never once having thought to question the reason she carried one there. Understanding now that for women everywhere, the threat of violence was never far away. His own woman's lack of size and strength, offset by four inches of honed steel in her practiced hand.

Chatte half-opened her eyes. "Is there something I can—*help* you with?"

"No. We need be going. Soon."

"*How*—soon?" She took his hand, placing it between her legs, sighing as Aaron knelt alongside the tub.

"A—*little* later, perhaps."

Chatte rose from the tub, as if a goddess from the sea. Water streamed from her shoulders, over her small breasts and slim hips, her eyes staring into his. "Undress."

Aaron quickly complied, her hands helping him to remove his shirt, exposing several wounds sewn shut, the boiled horsehair stitches recently removed by the tip of her knife, starting to heal over. He slipped off his boots and a pair of socks, tossed onto a small seat, along with his clothes. As he stepped into the trough and sank down, water splashed over the side, dampening the ground. He leaned back, emitted a sigh of pleasure as it reached his chest, with Chatte settling in between his legs, using a small cloth daubed with lye soap, slipping it across his chest, rubbing gently.

Aaron closed his eyes, enjoying the moment of total relaxation, the tension of the past few weeks allowed to slip away. He lost himself to memories of days spent in highland hills with bow in hand, hunting red stags in mountain valleys, listening to their tremulous bugling as they sought out a mate.

CHAPTER TWENTY-SIX
CROSSROAD STORE
SPRING, 1781

Sinclair glanced at the doorway of the store, seeing her daughter posed there, her extended belly held between her hands with a worried look on her face. She set down an inventory list, having checked off the goods shipped out that morning with Allyn, away to the city, making deliveries to warehouses holding supplies for the colonial army.

"You look troubled, daughter. Is the wee bairn kicking again?"

Meghan nodded, then looked at her mother with a pained expression. "Aye—though my worry is from another direction." She came over and leaned against the counter, resting her elbows on top, belly pressed against its front. "A shadow just crossed my path, when going to feed the hens and water the stock."

"That of a vulture, no doubt. Enough of them around due to the killings this past week. People left lying dead in the woods, along with livestock."

"Allyn said it was a raid by natives in support of the English. The claim made by those who managed to get clear of it." Meghan shook her head. "As if there will ever be peace here." She paused. "Not like home."

Sinclair studied her daughter's face, recognizing the worry of a mother, soon-to-be. "There were deaths *there*, too. In the lowlands and on high. Kept from your ears, but hard deaths just the same. Delivered at the hands of thieves. Young men with too much drink in them. Or soldiers used up, then cast aside, lashing out in pain."

"But the thought of *savages*, no matter their origin—and what they do to the women and children—is a *horrible* thought." Meghan paused, stopping her mother's response with an upraised hand, her face pinched in pain, bending over, elbows helping to support her weight.

Sinclair came around the counter and guided her daughter to a chair, then knelt in front of her, looking in Meghan's eyes as she reached for her wrist, feeling her pulse. It was strong, and steady, painting a smile on her lips as she kissed her eldest daughter on her sweaty forehead.

"You'll soon be on your knees. The child's starting to feel the squeeze."

"But Allyn's not due back 'til *evening!*" Meghan scrunched her face into a constipated look, her eyes tightly closed.

"*Breathe*, daughter. Like I showed you. With me." Sinclair breathed with Meghan, helping her get through the contraction. "Your husband has done *all* he's needed for. The rest is in *our* hands, with mine more than capable enough to help you through this."

A voice called out from the doorway, one of the local women who supplied the store with fresh herbs and vegetables, along with home-spun clothing. "Is it her time—our fair young lady?"

Sinclair looked over, her fingers on Meghan's belly, feeling another contraction tightening her womb. "By evening, I think. Her waters not yet let go."

"Should I fetch my man to help move her to the house?"

"Nae." Sinclair shook her head. "She's of highlander stock and will make the walk herself, with us at her elbows, should you be willing to join in on the wait."

The two women helped Meghan to her feet, leading her across the yard, having to stop while she crouched, urinating through her under-garments, her face red with equal measures of embarrassment and relief.

"You'll be pulling the wagon into the woods." The words came from a man hidden in the shadows at the edge of the road. The sound of a weapon brought to half-cock followed as a tall, thin man stepped into view. His clothing was a mix of loyalist green and black, along with colonial chestnut brown, giving Allyn pause, trying to decide who it might be, attempting robbery in broad daylight.

"I can offer ya food, and a place to bed down for the night. Work, if'n ya in want of earning your stay. For as long as it suits your needs." He chased his words with a smile, giving the man a wave, the ends of the reins dangling from his hand, as he pulled a pistol from behind his back, keeping it low alongside his right leg, already at half-cock. His finger was on the hammer, ready to pull it back and fire. The weapon primed and loaded as Harold had taught him, with a husband needing to be ready to defend his family, hearth, and himself.

"I want what you're *carrying*, along with the wagon *and* team." The man's voice was a quiver of fear, hunger pinching his face, his hand trembling as he stepped hatless into the road, the sun in his eyes, causing him to squint.

"Shade." Allyn nodded. "On the other side of the road. A better place to be standing." He pointed with his chin; the hammer brought back as he coughed. "My offer's genuine—and made in *good* faith. Times are hard for us all, with constant change of one's fortune in the wind."

"You're promise is *false*, now I've shown my pistol. You'll turn me in to the colonials, first chance you have." The man lifted the pistol, trying to steady it, having difficulty, the bright sun causing him to sneeze. The pistol discharged into the side of the road as his finger jerked, no round in evidence, only the priming touched off. An empty threat, made with an empty weapon left dangling from his fingers, dropped as Allyn aimed his pistol at the man, motioning him closer.

"I make the *same* offer again, if'n you're of a mind and *capable* of reaching up and shaking my hand in agree to it." He paused, waiting as the man did so, then motioned with the end of his pistol, pointing at the one lying in the dirt. The would-be thief stepped back and picked it up, holding it by the barrel as he handed it to Allyn. "There's a bag on the seat beside me with food. And spring water in the jug. Climb aboard and help yourself. It'll be coming onto dark by the time we get back to my homestead."

Allyn called out to the team, giving the reins a snap of his wrists, starting them out. The man opened the bag and looked inside, then pulled out a small loaf of bread and thick wedge of cheese, along with slices of dried apple, soaked overnight, wrapped in a damp cloth.

Allyn glanced over. "Eat, friend. It's *all* yours. You can pay for the meal with a story told me of how ya came to be standing alongside the road this day."

≸≸≸

There was no one there to greet Allyn and the failed highwayman as he pulled the team into the yard. The barn door was wide open, and the one to the store, as well. A light glowed in the kitchen window of the farmhouse, with another in the bedroom upstairs.

Allyn handed the reins to the man, who'd given his name as Eldritch. El, for short, as he'd filled him in on every detail of his life and how he'd come to his place in the world, footsore and too weary of mind to make good decisions. "Take the team and wagon into the barn, closing the door behind ya."

He leapt down, starting to run toward the house, knowing of only one reason his wife would have failed to meet him outside on hearing the horses and the wagon as they came up the road. Then Allyn stopped, turning around. "You know anything about horses?"

El waved him on. "I'll *learn!* You go tend to what needs doing. I'll manage things here." Dust flew from Allyn's feet as he dashed away, entering the house, and running up the stairs.

≸≸≸

Harold stood in the edge of a cleared forest in the Ohio Basin, watching as dozens of people moved in and out of a church. Its steeple was under construction, with the bell mounted on a stand outside the door. A small boy with copper-toned skin was making it ring, needing every ounce of his weight to do so, the thick rope in his hands lifting his feet from the ground as the bell swung in the cradle. A young woman, tall, slim of build, with raven dark hair, stood beside him. She looked up when a woman called out to them between chimes.

Harold's breath caught in his throat, seeing A'neewa step through the church door. She stood framed in bright sunlight, with a bonnet on her head, wearing a plain linen dress and black leather shoes. Harold's instincts pulling him back into the shadows of a large elm as she made her way across the lawn, waving at the light-skinned girl, calling out for them both to come inside.

A man appeared in the open doorway, smiling as the three of them approached. He reached out, taking the boy by the shoulder, guiding him inside. The girl followed, with A'neewa close behind. Then she stopped, turning halfway around, a questioning look on her face. The man called out to her, but she didn't respond as she stared across the opening into the edge of woods.

Harold saw her take a deep breath, holding it a moment before letting it out, following the others inside. He waited until the door closed, then slipped away, the information provided by a woman in a nearby settlement having helped him to locate A'neewa, without learning of her personal situation. Only that she was a healer, working in a settlement called Gnadenhutten, located on the easternmost edge of the Ohio Basin. One made up of several people of German ancestry joined by as many people of her tribe as she'd been able to convince to follow her there to assimilate into colonial culture.

Harold had known A'neewa was working with a minister of the Moravian faith, supportive of his efforts to teach them to read, write, and cultivate the earth with colonial tools. The religious leader eager to protect the community of converted natives from becoming linked to outbreaks of violence in remote settlements, sparked by the constant incursion of colonists, pushing further into native lands lying to the west.

He bent his head, remembering the last time he'd spoken with A'neewa while kneeling beside her in front of Meghan's headstone soon after he'd taken Sinclair to where he'd buried her father on top of a hill, close to where he was standing now. Back when George had still been alive. When he'd still been a close and trusted friend.

Harold retraced his path, bending it to the southeast, toward the Carolinas, following the same instinct that had led him to A'neewa, trusting it to lead him to his son.

🌿🌿🌿

Charles read the note, his hands shaking. He closed his eyes as he absorbed the information, then shook his head, a curse on his lips as he placed the paper in the flame from a candle. He held it by one corner, letting it burn down to his fingers before releasing it, watching as the blackened ashes drifted to the floor of the shelter.

A man dressed in dark clothing waited for an answer, his eyes following every movement of the small man who was centering the effort to gather information from leaders on both sides of the conflict between colonies and crown. And from among groups of colonists still loyal to the King. Added in with secrets uncovered by shadowy figures haunting inns, taverns, city docks, and other gathering places, keeping their eyes, ears, and minds open to whatever came their way.

"*Find* him. Give him the note I will prepare and hand you after you've had opportunity to rest. The food in the inn down the road is palatable enough. The ale—slightly better."

"I don't imbibe." The quiet-eyed man smiled, dropping the temperature of the shelter, his eyes holding a chilled expression. "It *interferes* with my work. Though I am liberal enough in buying drinks for *others*." He spun about and slipped away, without a sound.

Charlie sighed, then pulled a small square of parchment from a leather-bound book, the nib of a short quill in hand, small vial of ink balanced on his knee as he wrote out coded instructions of where and when he would meet with Harold, someone he respected more than any other man, wishing to have never heard from him again.

🌿🌿🌿

"The lad is my *son*." Harold crossed his arms, his jaw set, staring at Charles. "I *will* meet with him."

"You will needlessly expose him *and* yourself." Charles shook his head. "Enough that you've caught *my* attention, as if a fly determined to die, slamming yourself repeatedly into a spider's web, causing a disturbance felt—"

"Designed to do *exactly* that. Bring you to *me*. Or rather, myself to *you*." Harold shook his head. "Do you believe me *daft*, that I'd risk bringing attention to—" He stopped, his hands clenched, looked down as he lowered his voice. "Do you think I'd risk your safety, or that of my *son?*"

"Of course not." Charles softened his stance. "And you *do* have the right to see him." He waited for Harold to look up. "On *my* terms. Understood?"

Harold nodded, his body trembling in anticipation of the shadows of familiar pain he'd discover in the eyes of the boy sent off with a wide smile on his face to university in the Scottish Lowlands. A smile exchanged for a dark frown, when last they'd met. "I place myself in your capable hands."

Charles nodded, reaching for another square of parchment, writing out a pass allowing his friend to move along the lines of Greene's army. Another note written with directions to a small settlement where the insistent father would meet dangerous men with hard eyes, left to satisfy them with careful answers to probing questions before seeing his son.

CHAPTER TWENTY-SEVEN
HIGHLAND MANOR
SPRING, 1781

Pierre pulled back on the reins of the small mare he was riding and eyed a rush of water in a narrow pass, pinched between steep ledges to either side. He glanced over at Angus, who'd stopped alongside him, then shook his rain-soaked face, amazed the boy was able to stay aboard the tall, thick-bodied steed he was on, his short legs stuck out at sharp angles.

Angus gave him a nod. "It's nae as deep on the left side, with most of the runoff from the valley above well over ta' the left." He pointed with a thick, stubby finger, indicating a writhing snake of brown and white-faced water, twisting in a sinuous motion, creating a loud, sustained roar that raised the hairs on Pierre's neck. The boy leaned forward, urging his stallion on without use of reins or legs, the animal seeming to pick the unspoken command out of the damp air, moving ahead with a steady stride.

Pierre nudged the mare, who remained in place, shaking her head, forming a cloud of droplets around her thick neck. He leaned forward, forcing it into reluctant movement with a sharp kick to its ribs, receiving a snort of displeasure in return.

The journey by sea from France had met with fair weather, the ship arriving in Glasgow as storm clouds began to gather in the distant hills.

Angus had led Pierre to a small house on the outskirts of the city, retrieving his own mount and securing the mare from an old couple who'd fawned over the boy, wringing their hands in worry, showering him with kisses and hugs, before releasing him to his sworn duties.

They'd made their trek inland, heading into the foothills, progress slowed by frequent stops made along the way while Angus checked in with locals as to the latest gossip, inquiring about any strangers seen to be lurking about. Begged by those he spoke with to stay awhile, accepting their offers of hot food or drink, then moving on with promises left in his wake to return when he could.

Pierre continued to be impressed by the boy's nonchalant attitude, meeting each moment of every day with assurance and a calm demeanor. He'd asked him about his place in the clan community, Angus rubbing his chin with his fingers, giving it a long moment of consideration before answering.

"I meet people as they *are*. Take from them what they *freely* offer. Pay what's *owed*, without hesitation. Keeping my lips *tight* as to what's told me, with the same asked from others in return."

Pierre had stared at him, wondering how, if all Scots were the same as this young man, England had been able to tame them. A second thought followed the first, raising a cold shiver along his spine, knowing that many thousands of Scottish highlanders had fled the high country during the clearances, relocating to the colonies. All of them there now, with righteous anger in their eyes, eager to make certain it would not happen again.

Clearing the watery pass, he followed Angus into the heights, knowing whatever Sinclair and Harold's daughter asked of him, he would do everything possible to see it done. Then he leaned forward, stroking the wet neck of the mare, apologizing to her with a soft voice, using French phrases, telling her how beautiful she was, the animal shaking its head again, picking up its pace.

☙ ☙ ☙

The heat from the kitchen stove, combined with a second bowl of red stag stew eaten around mouthfuls of fresh baked wheat bread, caused

Pierre's eyelids to slide shut. His body had warmed up as he'd listened to the tale told by Angus to the couple sitting across a large wooden table, its surface scarred by generations of knife blades, cleavers, and the rolling out of dough. The mewling of a young infant at suck capped off a moment of pure relaxation. Or exhaustion, he thought, forcing his eyes open, staring at Sinclair's daughter, a familiar vision of similar beauty, returning his gaze, a slight smile on her lips.

"There's a bed waiting on you at the end of the manor hall. Far enough away to keep *this* one's bawling from rousing you." Marion looked down at her daughter, cradled in her arms, the infant's lips loose on her nipple, milk dripping from one side of her small mouth as she slept. Her name was Lorna, due to her thick shock of red hair like her aunt's, with her grandmother's cleft chin and narrow head. The wee one's chubby cheeks were hiding a slim face, one Marion was certain would emerge once she weaned her, a few months on.

Declan stood up and took his daughter into his arms, giving his wife a kiss on her upturned forehead. He went over, placing the infant in a cradle near the stove, then brought a bottle of whiskey back, along with two glasses, knowing Angus would refuse the drink. The misshapen boy had been the victim of a father's drunken abuse when a child, before a flux ended the bitter man's life, along with his browbeaten wife, who'd never dared to interfere.

Pierre raised a hand, starting to turn down the offer, then reconsidered, taking the glass, having never experienced highland spirits before. He forced back his lethargy, watching as the young laird of clan Scot tipped the bottle, stopping him with a nod.

Declan splashed a small amount of the red-brown liquor into his own glass, then set the bottle down. He raised his hand, taking a moment to appreciate the color and rich scent, honoring the demanding work that had gone into bringing it from field to still, to bottle, to glass.

"To a young lad, sent on a perilous journey 'cross dangerous seas. Tasked with bringing back a promise of mutual aid for a just cause. Surpassing *all* expectations, in having delivered not only the message, but the one messaged, as well."

Pierre raised his glass, looking at Angus who sat with crossed arms, his large hands tucked out of sight, face in its usual pose of slight indifference to things said about him, good or bad.

"A lot of words used, to get to ya point." Angus shrugged. "But as laird of the clan, I suppose you've the right to speak as you will."

Pierre spoke up. "I, for one, *second* the toast. To my loquacious and *intrepid* guide—my thanks, for a most interesting and insightful journey, safely made."

Angus stood up, grabbing his bowl, refilling it from the pot of stew simmering on the stove, careful to avoid waking Lorna. He walked by Marion, touching her on her shoulder, her hand reaching up, covering his and squeezing, then letting go. "I'll be in the stable, where they'll be less of a *clamor*." He took a loaf of the bread with him as he left, the wind howling against the eaves as he opened then closed the kitchen door.

Declan downed his drink, nodded to Pierre, then stood up and eased his daughter from her cradle, carrying her past her mother, a kiss on Marion's lips delivered as he went into the salon, where a fire was glowing in the hearth.

Marion studied Pierre, her head angled to one side, one eyebrow cocked, the surface of her face reflecting the light from several sconces on the wall. "You've already *agreed* to my offer, in coming here. And satisfied your curiosity as to *who* sent it to you. The daughter of a woman you know, with yourself no stranger to me. My mother having spoken of you during our trips made to London, and other cities where she has interests in commerce. Mine to manage now, until she returns."

Pierre kept his emotions below the surface of his wind-worn face, looking at Marion, seeing the same strength of will in her as he'd seen in Sinclair. He leaned forward, his hands circled on his glass of whiskey, still untouched. "You've struck the target, dead center." He paused. "Lady Marion, of clan Scot. Wife to its laird, leading your people through turbulent waters in challenging times."

Marion shrugged. "And when are they *not*? Which has led to my reaching out to *you*."

"Able to find me—*how?*"

"Is a woman not allowed her secrets, sir—supposing you to have those of your *own?*" She twisted her head, her hair down, the ends slipping over one shoulder, framing her chest, her dress still unbuttoned, her fingers slipping each tress back in place while she stared at Pierre, knowing him to be a man with connections, according to an article written about him in a Paris publication, delivered to Glasgow, then on to her.

"Of course." Pierre gave her a nod. "And some claim it is a woman's prerogative to *change* her mind—without need of explanation. The same allowed, when it comes to—revealing what she *knows* and how she came to know *of* it."

He was not surprised when the daughter of Sinclair, a woman he held in high esteem, laughed, then slapped her hands on the table. She reached for his glass and took a sip, slipping it back into his hand, closing his fingers around it with her own.

"Drink, Pierre Coulombe. *Friend* to my mother *and* father. In a toast made to the truth told *plainly*, without adornment, or—further riposte. Our guard let down, with a conversation about gold coins, weapons, and the spilling of blood. *English* blood—if my plan's deemed viable, with you choosing to join *my* efforts to *yours*."

※※※

Declan gave his wife a long, searching stare. Marion sat in front of a mirror placed above a bureau in the master bedroom, combing out her hair. Her eyes found his, fixing him with a firm look. "I intend to follow *through* with my plan. The die cast, with the monies on their way to La Havre. With Angus."

Declan broke contact, shaking his head, looking through the nearest window. Bright sunlight streamed into the room, the heavy curtains pulled back. "Am I only a *stag's* rack, mounted in the great hall with a plaque 'neath it, falsely describing my role as laird?"

"You are laird of clan *Scott*, husband. *Not* of me." Marion turned around and leaned forward, reaching toward him. "This is *not* clan business, posing no threat to them by my choice of action. The *threat* is to those wearing red and white colors over in the colonies. *That's* where my arrow's aimed—waiting for its release."

"Put it *plainly*, wife." Declan's voice dropped into a low growl. "As mother to our *child*, you will *abide* my asking of details, concerned as I am with the least possibility of threat to *her*—which I will *not* allow." He stood up and came over, lifting Marion's chin, gazing into her eyes. "No matter what *cause* you propose to support, if the cost paid is not only in gold, but blood. If the English trace the purchase of weapons back *here*, to the highlands."

Marion placed her hand over his wrist. "I would *never* place our daughter, or you, in jeopardy my love. Nor myself. Pierre assures me he will funnel the funds through the same avenues used by others who are supplying arms to the rebels. It is enough to know I have contributed, if only in a small way, to what they—the colonists—have been willing to do these past few years. Spilling their own purses of gold *and* barrels of blood to achieve freedom from tyranny."

"Replacing it with what? *Words* on parchment, proposing a shift in power from the few to the many?" Declan snorted, pulling away, going over to stare through the window, the thick glass distorting the view. He frowned, crossing his arms on his chest, then sighed.

Marion came over and pulled him around, leaning her head against his chest, listening to the steady beat of his heart. She inhaled his scent, wanting his arms around her, frightened for her brother. For her mother, and sister. And for her father. A letter from her mother received a fortnight ago, bringing news of an impending birth. A niece or nephew soon to arrive, separated by hundreds of miles of ocean from its family in Scotland.

"I *miss* them. My mother, determined to remain as near as possible to where Aaron is, without knowing if he's still alive. My sister, now married, with a child on the way. The world spinning out from under me—with no hope of my being able to control it."

Declan relented, unable to deny his wife's fears, circling her shoulders, holding her, his lips to her ear. "It's not a worry to *me*, love. Your brother—is a man who knows what he's about. With reputation gained in running down stags and boars through every hollow and glen, from here to the sea. *He's* the one should be leading the clan, not me."

"*Us*, husband. The *two* of us doing what's needed. My mother's money, carefully managed, enough to make a difference over there, as well as here." She let the tears in her eyes fall onto her cheeks, her milk letting down as Lorna stirred in her crib, crying out in hunger.

Marion went over and gathered up her daughter, soothing her with a low tone as she took her to the window, using the tip of a finger to stroke the copper-red hair on the sides of her head, understanding how her own mother must be feeling, unable to hold her firstborn in her arms, doing the same.

CHAPTER TWENTY-EIGHT
SOUTHERN CAMPAIGN
SUMMER, 1781

The sound of musket fire peppered the air with muted thuds, followed by the buzzing whir of lead balls, spinning men in colonial colors about as if toy soldiers, flicked from their feet as if by a careless finger. They fell to the ground, hands flung to the sides in stiffened pose, or clawing in a desperate search for the severity of the wound, afraid to discover that death was closing in, approaching with every beat of their hearts as their life blood drained away. All their tomorrows, slipping from between their weakening grasp as they gazed into the sky, looking for their mother's face, hearing her voice in their ears, as a warm summer wind swept over them, bearing them away.

"They're led to their deaths by a lack of information, *vital* to our cause. Lost to ill fortune." Charles peered through a glass, Aaron at his side, his own force of leather-clad men scattered in woods to either side. "Greene is reacting as he should, based on what he can *see*. Though it will be the destruction of his army—*if* he fails to pull them back in time."

"I'll take my men and cut across the neck of woods, convincing him to move back to the crossroad and reform the line. While we hit the British from the flank, disrupting their advance."

"You'll sacrifice yourself for *little* gain. The woods will hold cavalry, moving through to cut him off." Charles swore, slamming the glass closed, tucking it away in a pocket of his coat. He looked at Aaron, seeing the determined look in the man's face. "*Go!* You're under your own guidance, not mine."

"Lose your dour mood, Charlie. We'll win through this day." Aaron grinned, his face tight with excitement, blood lust in his eyes.

"A vision?" Charles looked at the young warrior, considering the role he'd played in helping to shape him to his destiny, unable to share with the leader of dangerous men that his father was somewhere in the area, trying to find him.

"No." Aaron turned and pointed at his men. "Based on *them*, when I tell them there are soldiers on horseback in yon woods, waiting to be plucked from their saddles." He clapped Charles on his shoulder, causing him to stumble slightly. Then he was gone, picking up his longbow and musket, with two pistols shoved in his belt, a quiver of arrows in his other hand, used to wave his force forward, following him as he moved away.

Charles watched as the hundred hard-eyed men flowed out of sight, disappearing into the edge of a wood line, looking like wolves' intent on running a herd of fleeing deer to ground.

※※※

A sword flashed toward Aaron's forearm, the bridle of a mount with snapping teeth grasped in his hand. He yanked the head of the animal toward him, the sword missing as the rider, an officer with fear drawing his face into a pinched look of terror, leaned out of his saddle, trying to keep from falling. His journey to the ground aided by a sharp tug from Aarons free hand, his boot finding the man's throat, crushing it.

The horse, its bridle released, slung its body to one side, knocking into another mount, the rider cursing as he turned, looking to see where his officer was, receiving a ball of lead in his chest. He fell away, disappearing into thick brush strung between the trunks of large oaks, the low hanging limbs serving to force the horsemen into small pockets of chaos and sudden death, delivered from close range by men experienced in no quarter given mayhem, winning most of the individual battles.

"Enough!" Aaron raised his voice, the sound of it drawing a few men's attention, their own voices echoing the order, overwhelming the shrieks of men pinned beneath their mounts, or those whose blood lust was driving their emotions, their voices raging as they paced the bloody woods, hammering away with tomahawks, or firing their pistols into the bodies of wounded soldiers, pleading for their lives.

Aaron and his men cleared the forest cauldron of burnt power, blood, and dying men, moving in a scattered group to where Greene was reforming his line, the general having become aware of his exposed flank. The threat reduced by the irregular's deadly advance through thick woods, dispatching the lancers with ruthless efficiency, Aaron's men eager to risk their lives, motivated by memories of the butchery done by the riders on horseback, witnessed in farmsteads scattered throughout the local area.

General Greene looked around, his aide calling out to him, waving one hand, beckoning him to step down from his perch on a stone wall. He saw a group of men in drab clothing standing beside the uniformed man, recognizing Aaron. He leapt down and came over, reaching to shake his hand, then hesitated, seeing a clot of blood covering the back of it, soaking the lower edge of his coat sleeve.

"You're a *welcome* sight! We can use you to bolster our line to the left. One of my officers has noted movement in the woods."

Aaron nodded. "It was us, dispatching cavalry moving to sweep around your flank. No further worries *there*." Aaron paused, cleaning the gore from his hand and lower arm with a thick tuft of grass handed him by Smoke, who wore a wide grin on his lined face, a hat jammed low on his head, shading his eyes. "You'll need to pull back. An enemy force on foot is in a rapid advance, following close behind the lancers. Too many for you to withstand. The hills there—" He swept his arm in the general direction of a height of land a mile distant. "A more defensible location, according to a recent scout of the area. Your position here—*still* precarious."

Greene stared for a moment, his eyes seeing the battleground as if from above, noting the nonchalant attitude of the young man who'd been instrumental in his efforts to pick apart the English forces through attrition. "We will be perilously exposed, while moving back. Our wounded in need of assistance. Cannons limbered, then moved, leaving us at risk of—"

Aaron shook his head. "The order, given *now*, will save many lives *later*. We will remain *here*, meeting the enemy in the woods. Their lead elements believing the way through is clear, with their Lancers, sweeping in from behind your lines." He paused. "A bloodbath for *them* —if done *soon*. With *you* moving back." He paused, giving the senior officer a tight grin. "Sir."

Greene issued the order, his aide sending runners to carry it along the line. Then he gave Aaron a long, searching look. "You are meant to operate *apart* from set-piece battles, striking without warning. This—" He paused, taking in the group of men in front of him, the rest hovering behind the newly formed line, topping a long rise. "Is *beyond* what can be expected of you."

"There's a good chance the British commander will see it the same, helping to balance the scales." Aaron turned away, waving his hand, blood seeping from a shallow cut as he pointed to the rest of his small group of men, waving his arm, then heading back into the woods.

"*Thank you!*" Greene called out, seeing the younger man pause, before breaking into a loping run without looking back.

☸☸☸

Harold eased ahead, staying in the cover of the leaf-heavy branches of a thick grove of oak trees snaking along the heights. He could hear the thud of muskets, mingled with shouts of men as they struggled to find targets in the shadowed woods. He knew the fight would settle into a hit and miss affair of savage, hand to hand engagements, the same he'd been involved in during the previous war. One where men in colored uniforms would be at a distinct disadvantage.

He loosened a tomahawk from his belt loop, carrying it in his left hand, a long-bladed knife in the other. Then he slipped deeper into the shadows, allowing his instincts to guide him where he needed to go.

☙☙☙

Aaron tossed a dying soldier aside, his adrenalin up, each movement of knife and tomahawk made without thought. He'd expended all his arrows, two dozen men left paying with their lives, their red clothing making them easy targets. His pistol, fired into the chest of a soldier coming at him from one side, used to bludgeon a wide-eyed youth standing to the fore, his face paled by the swirl of death surrounding him and his comrades, unprepared for combat at such close range.

Aaron followed up with a thrust of knife, pinioning the youth, driving him to the ground, twisting the blade, puncturing his victim's heart. As he watched the light go out of his eyes, he felt tempted to lie there with him, in an intimate embrace of death, with life. Forcing himself to his feet, he slipped away as shapes in the woods around him resolved into another group of men in red coats, probing ahead with leveled bayonets.

A voice from the side called out in a hoarse shout, Bear making his way toward him, one arm dangling at his side, the shoulder of his leather jacket black, soaked with blood. "Here—to me. We are—pulling back. The others—already clear."

Aaron waved his arm, signaling the large man to go to the ground before the enemy coming on could spot him. The sound of lead sighing past let him know it was too late, Bear left slumping to the ground, his legs still driving him forward as he fell, the toes of his boots plowing twin furrows in a leafy mat of old leaves and loose soil beneath the oaks.

Aaron rolled to one side, several times, clearing the zone of fire, knowing he had seconds to get clear. He knew Bear was beyond help, having paid the ultimate price to assist Greene and his forces to safety. Tears of anger, frustration, and sorrow mixed with a steady stream of sweat, trailing down his cheeks as he darted deeper into the woods. He made a hundred paces before tripping, falling to the ground, his arms outstretched as the tomahawk spun from his hand, falling to one side, his face wedged up against a moss covered stone, his head ringing from the impact.

He twisted to one side, trying to free his lower leg, finding fingers clamped tight around his ankle. Aaron opened his mouth, prepared to shout, hoping to distract his assailant as he readied a thrust with his knife, seeking to end the ambush. His assailant grabbed him by the wrist, forced him to the ground, holding him down, the ringing in his skull still there, with a desperate thirst as adrenalin drained his strength away, along with his will to survive.

"You're a sorry sight for sore eyes. Son." Harold whispered, his lips pressed against Aaron's ear, the sound of men's voices in the woods surrounding their position. "Suggest you lie still and make a count of your remaining lives, seeing if you have one to spare. You'll *need* it."

The voices, of English manufacture, slid by the rocks the two men were lying beneath, the threat of further ambush keeping the cautious soldiers at bay, expecting a rain of fire to fall upon them from every shadow in the woods. With leather-skinned ghosts rising and firing, then running away to lie in wait. English soldiers of the line, out of their natural element, not standing out in the open and squaring off against a foe, standing in plain sight.

The sound of birds slowly returned, Harold releasing Aaron, watching as he sat up. He handed him a canteen, the top open, his son taking some into his mouth, swirling it around, then leaning over and letting it drain onto the ground, careful not to make a sound. He swallowed, enough to slake his thirst, his father reaching out, handing him the stopper.

"Keep it. I have *another*. Worth its weight in powder and shot, on a day as hot as this one's turned out to be." His words were a murmur, trapped by the thick brush covering the pile of loose rocks. "We'll need to lie low until dark. Let the foot soldiers clear the wood, then make our way to—" Harold eyed his son. "To wherever it is *you're* bound."

Aaron reached up, rubbing the side of his head, wincing, his fingers coming away red. "Lucky you didn't cause my head to bust open, in tripping me up."

"The scrape along your forehead is due to my hand on your ankle. The cut—*already* there. No doubt acquired in your wrestling about with that young soldier."

Aaron looked down, staring at his blood-covered hands. Then he reached out, recovering his tomahawk. "As strange as it is—with you showing up like this—" He stared at his father, shaking his head, feeling it to be a dream, the two of them sitting there. "I can't say I'm *surprised*."

"It was Charles, pointing me in the general direction. An old soldier I once fought alongside of did the rest, guiding me to the colonial forces. Once the fighting began, I just followed my nose."

"And they call *me* the wolf." Aaron slipped his knife back into its sheath. "I'll be wanting to find my bow, before we lose the light."

"You've arrows left, tucked away?" Harold looked to all sides.

"Nae. But the bow is—*important* to me. I'll have it back in hand." He paused, wondering if any of what was happening was real, or the product of the blow to his skull. He reached up, touching the gash, wincing, feeling a deep throbbing starting to build now his lust for fighting began to ebb away.

"Four eyes, better than two." Harold leaned back, crossing his arms behind his head. "We've a few hours to wait. You can have first watch. Better if you stay awake, with an injury like yours. No sign of concuss seen in your eyes, but still, wise not to take any undue risk, most of your luck used up this day."

Then Harold closed his eyes and was asleep in minutes, fully at peace in having found his boy, still alive.

CHAPTER TWENTY-NINE
CROSSROAD STORE
SPRING, 1781

The sound of an axe biting into wood echoed from the side of the barn, followed by twin thuds as two pieces of wood landed in the dirt. Eldritch, working his way through the last of a final cord of firewood, placed another length of sawn oak into place. One deemed too gnarled in grain for use as framing or floorboards.

He leaned into the next stroke, enjoying the flex of his shoulders, back, and arms, feeling fully himself again. A shiver raced down his neck, all the way into his toes and fingers as he recalled the long, frigid winter suffered through while serving with the loyalists under the command of the British. He and his group of common soldiers, without a monied officer in charge, reduced to picking their way through leavings tossed aside by the redcoats. Left to make use of cast-off clothing, most of it tattered and torn. All of it with dark bloodstains from friend or foe.

"You have experience, doing work such as this." Allyn stepped into view, a brace of wild turkeys slung by their long necks over his shoulder, making him appear as if a large bird. He held a musket in one hand, and a small leather bag in another. "There's a jug of cider in here, along with what's left of my midday meal. Dinner is a far way off, unless you're of a mind to test the waters, daring to ask for something from the kitchen."

Eldritch grinned, setting the axe into the chopping block with an easy shrug of his shoulder. He came over and took the offering, then slid into a pocket of shade beneath an overhanging ash tree, sitting cross-legged on the ground. Several hens came on the run, seeing him there, followed by a long-legged hound, its nose scenting the air as the slim man opened the bag and pulled out a slab of bread and thick slice of cheese.

"Has there been any more yelling?" Allyn cocked his head, watching the hens scramble for the crumbs El tossed their way, the hound waiting, snatching a pinch of cheese out of the air with a snap of its large jaws.

"The two ladies seem to have settled their difference of how best to swaddle your son. The under and around method being the horse in the lead, last I heard of it." El paused. "A delicate dance, with two such —*willful* women sharing the same abode. Your wife's mother fastened onto the little one with an eagle's grasp."

"They are much alike in makeup, and mood." Allyn slumped forward, lowering his shoulder, letting the two fat birds fall to the ground, dust rising when they hit. The hound came over and sniffed their bloody heads, giving each a tentative lick before lying down beside them, head raised, on guard. "Could use your help preparing these." Allyn stared at the pile of sawn logs. "I'll gladly swap off on the firewood, my legs and back stiff from sitting in the tree, waiting for the birds to feed their way into me."

El glanced at the farmhouse, listening to the sound of voices rising in frustration, working their way toward another argument. He nodded, finishing the bread, cheese, and cider, then got to his feet and grabbed the birds, heading to the refuse pit behind the stable.

※ ※ ※

Meghan removed her hands from the side of her hips, determined not to present an angry stance as she responded to her mother's advice. She kept her voice firm, but low toned as she tried once more to finish a complete sentence, cursing under her breath, not able to understand why her mother was being so stubborn. And pushy. And opinionated.

"I have *agreed* as to the proper swaddling of young Richard. Have heard your *thoughts* as to letting him cry, helping to strengthen his lungs. Have even allowed you to bring him, on occasion, into your bed during the night, to let his father and I sleep."

Sinclair, her arms crossed, leaned against the side of the doorframe leading into the kitchen. She shook her head. "You continue to *reverse* the way I showed you to do the swaddling, soon as I'm not around. And put Richard to your breast the moment he begins to pucker up. And, as to my taking him into bed at night, the two of you are *sound* sleepers, leaving *me* to get up and tend to the lad, his poor heart breaking. In need of comforting."

Meghan muttered something under her breath, turning away, counting all the way to twenty this time, hoping to settle her mood.

"You have something to say, daughter?"

Meghan spun around. Her eyes held a heated glare. "*You're* the one who needs *comforting*, Mother! Needing someone or *something* to take your mind from father. From your worry for him *and* my brother. The reason we *came* here, so you could *find* him. With no news—from either of them these past two months. With yourself *stuck* here, serving the needs of others." She paused, drawing a breath, letting it out slowly. "To what end?"

Sinclair came over, her eyes as bright, needing someone to push back against, her oldest daughter strong enough, willing to meet her, verbal blow for blow. She drew back slightly, seeing the hurt in her child's eyes, then took Meghan into her arms, the two of them clinging to each other, letting go of the tension built up due to the lack of news as to Aaron's situation.

Allyn, having heard the yelling, had come to the front entrance, his son's cries from upstairs signaling need for attention. He started toward the bottom of the stairway, the two women turning their heads as one, telling him to leave. That they had things well in hand.

Allyn fled the scene in haste, making his way back to the barn, attacking the sawn logs with fervent strokes of the axe, wondering where Harold had gone off to, and why. Wondering when he would return, his wayward son in hand, so they could head back home to Scotland where they belonged.

※※※

Eldritch passed the jug of hardened cider back to Allyn, the hound sitting between them, its eyes and nose tracking the movement with a silent stare. "I have people I know, who might be able to help me to find out where he is." He covered a burp with his hand. "Or where he ain't."

"Seems an impossible *ask*, of me to you." Allyn hesitated. "You know you're not beholden to us."

"Meaning I'm not family—is what you're saying."

Allyn shook his head. "Not saying *that*. Just pointing out you don't owe me, or *us*—anything other than what you've already done. In pulling more than your fair share around here. Never once complaining."

"Understood." El gave Allyn a hard stare. "But you see, that *leaves* me beholden to you, in my being included in things. Invited to share meals. Conversations." He hesitated, swallowed, then lowered his voice. "I've even had a hand at swaddling the young'un. Neither one of the women knowing the *right* way to go about it. Like I showed *you*, and you agreed to, seeing the result."

El looked away, his voice softening to a whisper. "We were a close-knit family—the one I grew up in. Seven strong. Two brothers, one to either side of me in age. Two sisters, coming along next. My father, stern-faced and moody, though easy on the strokes when whipping us. My mother, a sad looking woman with turned down lips, seemed to be as satisfied as she *could* be, considering the work it took to keep the house and family in decent shape." He stopped, Allyn handing him the jug while staying quiet, aware there was more to come.

Eldritch stood up, stretching his lower back, cracking his neck with a twist of his head. He sighed, then took a long swallow, covering his mouth as he burped again. "Was out on the edge of the wilderness, where we lived. About as far as you could go, and not be wearing of hides, with feathers twisted in our hair. Trading as we could, with what we had to offer the local tribes. My dad, he had a small forge hauled all the way and gone out there. Used it to fashion things for them. For the Indians. Making them skewers, tongs, and the like. All of us going along, trying our best to get along."

"Sounds like a hard but decent life. With honest labor and good friends made."

"It was. Until some other group of redskins, led by a French war party came through, attacking the ones we were close with, then turning their eyes our way. They—" El paused. He closed his eyes and swallowed, the hound going over, placing its head in his hand, encouraging a rub of its long ears. "They hit us while we were out working in the fields—me and two of my brothers. My father, back in the shed. The girls—" There was a long silence, with Allyn ready to say something to try and change the subject, wondering if he should break the spell.

El looked over, shaking his head. "The girls—they were screaming. The sound of it—making our feet to fly as we ran to see the cause. Thinking a bear was in the coop, or a fire having got loose in the cabin. Never knowing what was happening until we were in the middle of it. My brothers going down from musket fire. My mother, dying under the blade of a knife drawn across her—across her throat. My father coming on the run, firing his musket, loaded for birds, spreading lead pellets in all directions, causing them—the ones doing the killing, to duck for cover, leaving me untouched. Untouched—so able to run."

Allyn lowered his head, his hands clenched, unable to place himself in the same situation. Wishing to have avoided hearing the tale, aware how easy his life had been, by far.

"Which I *did*. Ran, like never before. Without looking back. Without *fighting* back. Without ever *going* back. Just kept on running, walking, falling into a hole 'neath rocks when night came. Waking up, running again. Signed on with the first group who'd have me. Used a false name, making my mark, just looking to duck my head and hide from the shame."

Eldritch came over and stood in front of Allyn. "*That's* the man who waylaid you. That's who I'd became. Facing your pistol, the end of the barrel promising me a quick death." The tall man knelt, then reached out, taking Allyn's hand in his. "You gave me another chance. Gave me back my life. Not the same one as before, but a different one. With opportunity to stick my foot in, becoming part of something larger than myself. And I owe more than I can give you. More than you could ask from me. So, if you want that I should go and try to find your wife's father and brother—then I'm dust in the wind. Starting *right* here. Right *now*."

Allyn squeezed El's hand. "No, brother. You're needed *here*. With us. Harold—he'll be back when he's able to, no doubt with his arm 'cross the shoulder of a man I claim to be as much a brother to me as you."

The wind eased to a stop, the weather beginning to change over to wet. The two men cocked their heads, hearing the voices of the two women, filling the air with the sounds of laughter.

CHAPTER THIRTY
SOUTHERN CAMPAIGN
SUMMER, 1781

The man named Smoke came through the small collection of shelter halves, lugging a satchel picked up from a drop point outside a small settlement. One formed of a group of homes on their way to becoming a town, with a small church and storehouse under construction. People throughout the colonies, busy moving on with their lives, most willing to ignore the conflict between crown and colonies. Those with men or boys in the fight keeping their hearts open and heads down, doing their best to hold dark thoughts at bay.

The thin veteran made his way over to a larger shelter, where Wolf and an unnamed man were sitting, sharing a kettle of tea and plate of hard biscuits. Chatte, leaning over a small fire, was cooking eggs, their scent stirring a rumble in the old soldier's stomach.

"There's dispatches, inside." Smoke tossed the leather bag to Aaron, who caught it, then let go, letting the bag land between his outstretched legs.

"Appreciate it. There's food for ya. Eggs, and biscuits. And a cup of tea to dip 'em in." Aaron attempted a smile, though it didn't reach into the corners of his mouth. "Seeing as you're working with less than a *full* set of teeth."

Smoke returned the weak grin with one of his own. "I've eaten. A sweet little gal we both know having packed me a sack of grub 'fore I left this morning." He gave a warm smile to Chatte, who nodded as she plated the eggs, bringing them over to Aaron and Harold, the two men murmuring their thanks. "There's tales going 'round in the settlement of movement—down in the lower stretches. That bastard colonel making raids among the farmsteads inland. Trying to force our hand, hoping we'll do something about it." Smoke hardened his expression. "Like trimming back his ears or cutting out his black heart." He gave a nod to Chatte, then slipped away without a sound, true to his name.

"He seems a *decent* sort. With a familiar look to him, though I can't place him." Harold slipped a mouthful of the eggs into him, chased with a tea-soaked corner of a biscuit. He swallowed, then took another swig of the dark bodied liquid, filtering stray tea leaves between his teeth, spitting them to one side.

"He knows *you*." Aaron stared at his father, uneasy in seeing him there, wondering what his father saw in return, barely able to recognize himself when looking in a small mirror while Chatte trimmed his beard with the edge of a honed blade. "I can see it in his eyes, though he's too tight lipped to say how or where he might have met you."

Harold shrugged. "I served with a thousand and more men *before*, when first sent over here. Most of them not much older than yourself, and none of them with the experience *you've* gained. Or the same type of mind for—" Harold turned his head, taking in the scattered knots of men, bent to their morning meals, or caring for their weapons, their voices low, a minimal amount of smoke in the air with the fires fed with dead wood. "*All* of this. What you've managed to put together."

"It was built by *them*." Aaron shrugged. "Teaching me what I needed to learn about staying alive, knowing when to duck and run." He fixed his father with a solemn stare. "Or when to lower my head and bull through. If it's the only choice left, exposing men—*good* friends—to their deaths."

"Like the one you were signaling to—before I caught you up." Harold lowered his plate, the eggs finished. "The big man, with a wounded wing."

"Bear. Yes." Aaron looked away, his food cooling off as he lowered his voice, the plate in his hand trembling. "And I wasn't heading his way to try and help him. I was running away, wanting to live to fight another day, like they taught me to do. The older men teaching me how to survive, then trusting me to make the next plan, placing them in danger, with myself standing alongside them."

"Along with an equal say in how *they* chose to die. Your friend sacrificing himself, trying to get you clear."

Aaron nodded. "Just another man, dying due to a senseless cause. Like all of them, on *both* sides of this—nonsense."

Chatte came over and collected their wood slab plates, using her fingers to finish Aaron's meal, then wiping them off with a rub of sand and pine needles. She bent to her work, cleaning the frying pan with a scrub of dirt and quick rinse of water, leaning it in the slanted rays of the morning sun to dry.

The two men had returned from the fight the day before, dehydrated, exhausted, their adrenalin having drained their energy, their feet heavy as they came into the camp, having wiped their trail away behind them like all the others who'd managed to make it back. A half-dozen shelters stood empty, their flaps hanging loose in the evening shadows. The goods stored within shared out between the rest of the group. Their false names, added to others lost during the months of living on the outskirts of civilization's embrace.

Chatte knew the older man with Aaron was his father, the resemblance between them running deep, with a similarity of look and build. Both men, speaking with a common accent revealing a mix of Scottish and English backgrounds, sharing their thoughts across the flame of a small fire during the night. Hesitant questions asked, with silent answers offered at times by a nod or shake of Aaron's head, unable to reply, looking down, a stick in one hand, poking at the glowing coals.

"I will go and make myself ready." Chatte stopped Aaron as he started to stand, ready to provide protection while she went to a nearby brook to clean herself and her underclothing. "I will be *careful*. You will stay here."

Aaron handed her his pistol, a new model provided him by General Greene, one of a matched set offered in lieu of payment for his good service in the woods. "Take this. It's loaded."

Chatte pulled it from his hand, holding onto his fingers, squeezing them for a moment before letting go. Once she'd gathered her personal items and slipped away, Harold cleared his throat.

"She is an *amazing* person. Similar in spirit, if not build, to another I once knew. As wise in the ways of—the harsh lessons life teaches those willing *and* able to learn from them." He looked at his son. "As was yourself, from an early age on."

"That would be A'neewa." Aaron hesitated. "Because of the knife, like the one my mother and two sisters wear, heeding your advice."

"A'neewa—much the same in spirit, though it was Meghan I was speaking of. Not your sister, but the woman—"

"I know who she was, having read your journals. Saw the—the drawing you made of her." Aaron stopped, seeing a wince on his father's face.

"She was a woman of *two* parts. One, caring and sensitive to my every mood and thought. The other—" Harold looked down at the ground, then poured the remnant of the cup of tea onto the ground watching as it soaked into the dirt. "The other side of her—was a different person entirely, chasing a demon who inhabited her nightmares, seeking his death."

Aaron shook his head. "But *not* finding joy in causing pain to others." He stared at his father; his eyes shaded with a questioning look. "You're wondering how I'm able to care for someone so—so far *removed* from her childhood innocence. Capable to—to do the things I've witnessed. Horrible things, beyond my ken."

Harold looked up and nodded. "Pain—enough of it—will cause those suffering from it to forswear joy from ever entering their lives. No matter how much they, or those who've come to love them would have it be otherwise."

"Like *your* Meghan. With *you*."

Harold sighed. "Yes. Which I couldn't accept. Couldn't make myself believe to be true. Thinking—*hoping* I'd find some way to see her through it, coming out the other side. Made whole again."

"Another of those harsh lessons—painfully learned."

Harold looked back down. "Yes. Along with a greater one, made in leaving your dear mother, who'd given me her *all*. Given me three children, left heartbroken when I headed off, tearing apart the bond of love, breaking the back of your mother's faith in me. Going off to follow a vision told me by your great Gran Da. One I felt compelled to follow. Though it proved to be a *fool's* errand—in the end. Coming at a high price paid by myself and dozens of others. Slowing, for a time, what's come to pass. Delaying it enough to have caught *you* in its snare."

Aaron cleared his throat, then swallowed, seeing his father as only a man, no longer cloaked in the raiment of warrior. Of hero. Of someone he'd looked up to, eager to find a mountain tall enough to one day climb, to be able to face him eye to eye. Seeing him now, fully revealed, as a man no different than himself. Nothing more, nor less. With the same fears, and doubts. The same questions asked. With the same hard answers handed him, leaving deep wounds to body and soul. "I made my *own* choice, in coming here. Have made my own choices ever since. Staying here after my—" Aaron looked away. "After Rory, my friend—after he was killed."

He looked over as two men slipped past, heading to the brook. He raised a hand, holding it sideways, moving it side to side in a signal to wait. The men noted Chatte's absence and turned away. "I chose my path, same as you chose yours. With mother made to pay the price each time, sitting on her manor throne, surrounded by my sisters. The two of them married off by now, I imagine."

"Both of them, yes. Your sister Marion taking on your gran uncle's mantle, her husband with the tile, but it's *her* ideas behind every decision made. Meghan, over here, married to Allyn. Your mother's here too, living just outside Philadelphia, twenty miles to the northeast. In a small house with a store. Near a mill and crossroad. Adamant she'd be able to come here and find you. Reason with you, convincing you to return home with her. Waiting for word of you all these months."

Aaron stared, his mouth open in surprise, eyes lighting up at the possibility of seeing them, dashed by the realization he was a marked man, like his father. The English with spies everywhere, seeking him and his men. Seeking the witch who was rumored to eat men's hearts, consuming their very souls. "Why? Why would my mother have left everything behind and come after me?"

"Your absence, sudden as it was, without your disclosure of the reason why, caused her to lose her—." Harold hesitated. "Your gran uncle, the one bringing back news that you'd disappeared, troubling her *deeply*."

"I—I had little choice. My friend, Rory—determined to head over here and join the fight, pulling me along in his wake." Aaron saw his father shaking his head and blushed, knowing the words for the lie they were. "I'd just broken the heart of a *wonderful* girl. My own, broken alongside hers in fulfilling a promise made to her father. My vow—given to him."

Harold shrugged. "You'll offer whatever excuse you need make, when facing her, your mother, in time. But we *both* know the truth. With yourself drawn to the same path I walked, compelled to face the same challenges written about in those *damn* journals. To follow in my footsteps." He stopped, looking at his son, measuring the changes in him with open eyes. "No. Not follow, but to *surpass* my journey along the red path, seeking to make your *own* mark, trying to affect what's to come once the colonies manage to throw off the English yoke. With an opportunity to make a *real* change in the world. One you'll have been part of—should you manage to survive it."

"You really see it as such?" Aaron angled his head, the scar on his forehead oozing blood from around the tiny stitches Chatte had sewn into his skin. "With me becoming something *more* than what I've become? A butcher of *decent* men, led to a senseless war started on the whim of a King. Same as those soldiers you fought with and against over *here*, dying at the feet of vainglorious fools, sitting on their ivory thrones."

"There were and still are *far* worse men standing in the shadows behind the realm, with their hands in the pockets of the power brokers on every side, including all of Europe and other countries, throughout the world. People using nameless men, of similar capability and far less morality than your own, eliminating anyone deemed to be an obstacle to their plans. *Good* and *honorable* men killed, like your own Gran Da, and Grand Uncle Thomas, butchered alongside his wife. Murdered on the whim of those *I* helped bring to their *own* endings. Just outside Philadelphia, including two men as close to me as your friend Rory, or the man with the fire-scarred face, keeping a close watch over you. As close to you as all the rest of these hard-edged men you lead."

"And what of the *woman* I'm bound to?" Aaron's voice was low, his tone sober. "How do you see *that* playing out, in this morality play you describe?"

Harold furrowed his brow, then turned and stared into the fire, smoldering down to ashes, a thin trail of light-colored smoke rising into the still air. "If it's a vision from me you're seeking for, you'll need look elsewhere. Or within. It's not mine to know—or tell you if I did."

"Then I'm to be left to my own instincts in what to do?"

Harold shrugged. "You know of the three women I've met and loved—each in their own way. Any advice I might give would lack an unclouded vision of the lass sharing *your* life." He paused, shaking his head as he looked away. "You'll have to work it out for yourself, son. It's your path. Your destiny."

The sound of Chatte's return from the shadowed wood brought an end to the conversation, both man standing up, going to help her with the two containers of water she was lugging back from the brook.

CHAPTER THIRTY-ONE
LA HAVRE
FALL, 1781

Angus touched the side of a sealed wooden chest with the toe of one boot. "The final payment—is in here."

Pierre, standing a few feet away, refrained from looking over. He stood with crossed arms, watching men pulling on ropes, hoisting dozens of crates to the deck of a transport ship. An agent would meet the ship when it made landfall off the coast of Virginia colony, met by a small armada of small boats, taking delivery of the muskets and other military supplies purchased with the gold provided by the dark-haired woman in the Scottish Highlands. Lady Marion having agreed to support another like purchase, already in the works.

"You'll be wanting to take it to one of them as makes the scents." Angus muttered the words under his breath, bending to undo then retie the knotted laces of his worn footwear. "Due to the stink inside."

Pierre frowned, confused by the unusual message regarding transfer of the funds. "How so, my friend?"

"The *fookin'* coins are in a mix of beaver glands—from the colonies." Angus stood up, then shook his head as he spat over the edge of the dock, muttering something under his breath.

"My *apologies*." Pierre hesitated, a concerned look on his face. "It seems an —*awkward* way of concluding our business. To go to such extremes as to—"

"*Fook*' all to your regard of it. I've the Lady to protect. You've got your payment — and been fair warned as to the opening of it." Angus turned and started away, stopping when Pierre called out.

"I will be making another visit to Glasgow. Two months from now, once I have proof of the delivery, successfully received."

"*Don't*. Ther's nae *need* of it. She — the Lady in question — trusts ya."

Pierre raised one hand, cupping his chin, a thin smile on his lips. "And what of you, my intrepid messenger 'tween highland and La Havre? Do *you* trust me?"

Angus was silent for a count of three heartbeats. "Aye. Same as I would a serpent in a cellar, biding its time, willing to strike if provoked." With a nod of his head, he walked away, his short arms with large hands dangling at his side as he twisted his thick shoulders, slipping into a crowd of people crowding the dock.

Pierre snapped his fingers, pointing at the container, bidding one of his men to gather it up. He stood still, nose angled into the salt-heavy breeze coming in from the ocean, knowing that when the transport returned, it would have a message aboard, coded to his name. With a report enclosed detailing the whereabouts of a woman who would soon become a widow, again. The secretive group he belonged to having spread a small fortune throughout the colonies, seeking a former enemy's location. A man who owed a blood debt, long overdue. An order he'd agree to, reluctantly, proving his loyalty to the cabal.

※ ※ ※

Marion cradled Lorna, sitting in a rocking chair that had borne over a dozen generations of her Scottish relatives. A wash of light fell over her shoulders, one hand shielding her daughter's face who was sleeping as only a child can, with untroubled dreams from having few enough worries in life. Her own sleep had been a restless stir of late, with deep sighs offered to the night air, trying to soothe her nerves. Her husband, snoring away beside her, had drawn cat-eyed glares and angry kicks with sharp-toed feet, momentarily interrupting his steady breathing before sawing away once more. For the third time since her mother and sister had left her, Marion allowed a pang of loneliness to penetrate her firm resolve, prompting a muffled sob, covered up with her free hand. Tears in her eyes, her heart feeling heavy.

A shadow slid across the wall as Declan entered the salon, wiping his hands with a rough-spun towel, his skin red from a good scrubbing with lye soap. "Is she *finally* asleep?" He came over to check on them both, aware his wife was short on rest of late, her unsettled dreams causing her to lash out with her feet, as if chased by spirits, his lower legs left sorely bruised.

"Aye. Her teeth are breaking through, leaving my nipples bleeding. Weaning her to be the next challenge to any hope of getting a solid night of rest."

"The doors to the stables have been rehung, the rollers easing their opening and closing." Declan shook his head. "Another creative idea from Angus, seeing his way through problems, finding innovative solutions." He paused. "Providing the funds for a higher education for him would be a worthy investment, considering his ability to read and write. As well as his skill in other subjects."

Marion nodded, keeping her eyes lowered, knowing if she looked at her husband she'd burst out in childish tears. The midwife Declan sent for had explained that what she was feeling was perfectly normal. Her body's humors soon would be back in balance, with another child the recommendation for a cure. One met by Marion with a silent stare, unsettling the woman who'd crossed herself and scurried from the room.

"You're in tears again, lass. Is it from what the midwife was speaking to you about?"

"No." Marion shook her head, handing Lorna to her father, standing up and going over to the window to stare out at the snow-capped mountains. "It's worry that's eating at my mood. For *all* my family, here and away. For the *risk* I've taken, placing our future on dangerous ground." She turned, giving Declan a tight look. "I accept the risk to me. To you, as well. We've the right of its assign by our own choices made. But to bring the smallest slice of potential harm to our daughter—I *cannae* stand the thought of it."

"There's no trace of a trail leading back to us, with Angus having erased all signs. Clever as a fox in a henhouse, that one—quietly in then back out again, without raising a ruckus."

"Poultry are *not* men. Not like those we're going up against. Men with *dark* reputations." Marion paused. "Or rather, those Pierre is going up against, putting his neck on the block in supporting the colonists looking to shove the British back into the sea." She returned Declan's stare, her husband listening without comment as he gently rocked their daughter in his arms, his face set in a stony stare. She sighed. "I know your *vision* has shown you that Pierre's not to be—"

"*Angus*—the one who saw it, then shared with me."

"But you *agree* with him? With what he told you?"

Declan lowered his voice as Lorna began twisting her head from side to side, seeking her mother's breast, her father's recently scrubbed finger offered as a temporary substitute. "I know he sees a *different* world then others do, including you and me. As if seeing things laid out on a parchment, or a page in one of the books he's always reading, whenever he's got an empty moment in hand."

"I *do* trust him, and *you*. But I trust *Pierre* as well. None of which settles my worry for—something I can't quite grasp, try as I might."

"Perhaps having to do with your family, overseas?" Declan leaned down and kissed his daughter's head, soothing her with a soft lullaby.

Marion watched with tears in her eyes, cursing herself for the tide of emotions experienced since Lorna's birth. She felt as if standing outside herself, her confidence diminished. Frustrated at not being able to see what needed doing next. With a firm shake of her head, she knew it was time to force a return to who'd she always been. A woman of strength and determination, just like the mother she wished was back home in the highlands. A woman who'd always been in complete control.

☙ ☙ ☙

Bath lay ahead, the city seen through a filter of gray smoke and morning mist rising from narrow fields lining the roadway. The carriage made a sweeping turn as it descended a steep hill, with

Marion leaning her head to one side, her lips pursed as she considered the wisdom of having brought Lorna along, her daughter cooing as she tried to tug one of her mother's fingers into her mouth, the ends of several new teeth ready to gnaw whatever came near them.

Marion had scheduled a bi-monthly meeting with the woman responsible for managing the three large homes located within the city limits, arranged for mid-morning at the original structure her mother had purchased, over twenty years ago. She sighed, tightening her arm around her daughter, aware great aunt Millie would be certain to seize the opportunity to abscond with Lorna, tucking her into her ample bosom then scurrying away to show her off to all the women living there. The old woman, while still a love, had grown increasingly dotty as advanced age dragged her along a wandering path.

The driver called out, letting her know the time remaining until their estimated arrival, the horses picking up their pace, the sound of their hooves on the surface of dirt turned to cobblestones matching the rapid beating of Marion's heart.

※※※

The documents were spot on, as expected, matching to within a few pounds' sterling the numbers in Marion's ledger. Well within the difference allowed due to miscellaneous expenses. Marion nodded in approval, knowing the amount unaccounted for would match the cost of the bottles of liquor secreted in great aunt Millies special cupboard. A nightly nightcap used to ward off bad spirits with good. An allowance made the older woman, having dedicated herself to the service of others. A saint in plain clothing, always ready with a welcoming smile and enveloping embrace.

"Excellent record keeping, Mrs. Landry." Marion gave the other woman a nod as she reached for a cup of tea, provided her when she'd entered the large kitchen. She'd steered clear of moving to a small, stuffy office where the middle-aged woman spent most of her time, perched behind a desk, sitting beneath a large painting on the wall of her late husband. A captain of a ship lost at sea, staring at everyone entering the room, his cold eyes the color of a gray, unforgiving sea.

"We are comfortably in the good with the *other* two houses as well. Our investments in businesses started by our former residents continuing to support new ones." The woman, into the latter half of her life, sighed, wrapped her fingers around the side of her own cup of tea, absorbing the warmth. "It seems, at times, as if we are on a ship with a leaky hull. Another hole appearing, just as our efforts in bailing out women in need has begun to make a small gain."

"The need *is* great, Mrs. Landry. The attention *paid* to it by yourself—along with many others, appreciated. Your efforts vital in helping to further my mother's vision of a world where women might find a safe refuge for themselves and their families. One that, while never fully attainable, has proven to be a blessing indeed for those provided shelter. Our financial support of benefit, until they can move ahead into a better life."

"It is *God's* work we are doing, child. Your mother—the instrument through which he provides them his love."

Marion allowed a hint of a smile to find her lips, unwilling to entertain another spirited discussion concerning whether the lion's share of credit was due to divine intervention, or the sweat of one's own brow. "Is there anything *further* we need to discuss?"

"No. Everything is moving along as expected, under the circumstances we find ourselves in, with times as troubling as these. Spain and France, ever at our heels, along with the ungrateful miscreants over in the colonies. A small enough group, looking to throw off the comforting embrace of their loving father, the King."

Marion kept the smile on her face, refusing to enter the political arena, preferring to stay on course, with another city to visit the next day. A weeklong journey ahead before she would see the highlands again. "Then I shall go to the sound of cooing and murmuring of women's voices, doing my best to pry my daughter away from Millie's strong arms."

※ ※ ※

Angus lowered the book he was reading, angling his head as he listened to the sound of hooves approaching at a fast pace. A frown creased the surface of his square cheeked face, knowing it was too early by several days for Lady Marion to be back from her travels. He set the book aside, a treatise on the use of herbs to treat malaise. Many of them located in the edges of woods, fields, and marshes below. Himself, a decent enough healer, with knowledge of such things.

Declan's voice called out, his tone causing Angus to leap up, moving at a quick pace, his short legs taking him outside the stable door, pistol in hand, brought to half-cock, with a short sword in the other.

"There are riders coming, halfway to the Pinch. Not our people, but strangers. Young Dillon riding a mare half to death to reach me, sent back down to watch from the overlook. We'll need gather men and muskets enow, then meet them there."

Angus swung toward the manor, rousing two of the men from out back, working on the mounting of new latches on the storeroom door. They came on the run, weapons handed them along with orders to gather their mounts and hie to the lower fields, just above the narrow approach known to all as the Pinch.

He carried his own weapons slung over his shoulder as he headed to the paddock to do the same, knowing the vision he'd had a fortnight ago might soon be coming true: a screaming of devils in the night, dancing by the flames of a large fire.

※※※

The group of riders, four men strong, pulled up and stared into the mouth of a narrow passage, eying a line of four men on horseback with leveled muskets, plugging the path. The highlanders wore hard gazes on serious faces, their fingers near the triggers of their weapons.

Pierre nudged his horse forward and removed his hat, revealing his face. "Hail to my friend Declan, Laird of clan Scott. And to his man, Angus. You other two—unknown to me."

Declan nudged his mount ahead, waving at the three men to lower their aim, knowing they would remain on guard until told to stand down. "A wild wind indeed, to have blown you here with such speed. Arriving unannounced—with an armed *escort* in hand."

"An acceptable risk, taken upon my shoulders due to news from over the horizon. Of interest to you and your beloved." Pierre turned and glanced at the three men, motioning them back. Then he slid from his saddle and walked up to Declan, the reins of his horse in his hands. "I have information regarding Lady Sinclair, and her daughter."

Declan glanced over his shoulder, watching as Angus slipped from his stallion with a frown on his face as he grounded the stock of his musket, holding the barrel between the fingers of his large hand as he waited on his laird's next move. "And the men *with* you—?"

Pierre shrugged. "Hired for personal protection. My position one that places me at risk of *English* attention. Official—or otherwise, as your own family was known to have experienced some years ago." He paused. "I can send them away. A business associate of mine owns a warehouse in Glasgow, where they'll wait on my return. Though the path 'tween here to there will expose me to—considerable risk."

Declan started to respond, cut off by Angus, who'd come up behind him. "The men are to hie to the port. Yourself, provided an escort on your return there." Pierre looked at Declan, raising his eyebrows, lowering them when the tall Scotsman nodded.

"Seems the proper solution. There being no lack of trust between us."

Pierre nodded. "Then allow me a moment to confer. My men are a *determined* group, sworn to my service. Not easily deterred from their responsibilities."

"If they are *your* men, then *command* them." Angus stepped over, eyeing the three men who stared back, their faces set. He raised his voice, the tone firm. "Clan Scott is responsible for ya man now."

Declan nodded his agreement, a moment of doubt flushing his neck with warmth, caught between not wanting Pierre to question the measure of his sworn friendship, and a growing sense of unease, the faces of the unknown men remaining without expression as the Frenchman ordered them to turn their horses about and head back to the port of Glasgow.

"I have come bearing *two* pieces of information. The first, a hopeful missive. The other—one with a harder edge." Pierre lowered a glass of port, eyeing Declan, who shrugged.

"Not much difference between the two, these days. Events in swing with each delivery of news from afar, brought to our door by Angus each Sunday, returning from his parents' home." He glanced at the main door, the two of them sitting in the salon, the fireplace in a mild roar, trying its best to hold back a cold front painting the grounds of the manor with a white, icy coating.

"Lady Marion's brother has been located." Pierre took a sip from his glass, watching for Declan's reaction, a sigh the younger man's only response. "He is alive, based on the report I received. Though deeply embroiled in the conflict, on behalf of the colonial army."

"His current situation?" Declan studied Pierre's face, still feeling unsettled by his sudden, unanticipated appearance.

"Rumors. Whispers in the wind, difficult to make out. A story told of having spotted him somewhere in the western reaches of Pennsylvania colony. And then again, in one of the southern colonies." Pierre paused, then angled his head. "Have *you* heard anything from him?"

Declan shook his head. "No." Then he stared at Pierre. "The *hard* edge you mentioned?"

Pierre lowered his gaze, turning slightly and looking into the flames, dancing in the hearth. "The news is darker in tone concerning his activities. He's become a sharp thorn in the side of the English efforts, both in the colony of Pennsylvania and the southernmost one in the Carolinas. A *deadly* thorn, with stories told of a witch who travels with him and the men he leads, eating the faces, livers, and hearts of redcoat officers. Taking their *souls*, as well, according to the worst of tales told around campfires in the field."

Declan shook his head. "Aaron is a man of honor. *Deadly*—if forced into conflict. But he would *never* be involved in the occult. Or party to the desecration of soldier's bodies, left lying on the field of battle." He bottomed his cup, wiping his mouth as he looked at the bottle, considering whether to pour another, his wife and child not due back until the next day.

"The stories detailing the activities—indicate that the men were *alive* at the time of their torture. Not deceased."

Declan glared, pointing at Pierre with his empty glass. "They're *lies*. My wife's brother would *never*—would *never* condone such actions as that!"

"Men doling out fatal circumstances often *stray* from the path they've been known to walk. I've *been* there, at the same age and under similar situations, leading men in battle in the wilderness." Pierre stopped, taking a moment to gaze into the flames, his eyes hooded. "I twice stood across from Lady Marion's father, doing everything I could to kill him. Willing in my mind to do so the first time—unable, due to nerves, to press the trigger that might have ended his life." He paused. "My honor all but eroded away by our final engagement, pulling the trigger without a second's thought. A misfire occurring, with Harold stepping in at the end of the engagement, saving my life, and that of my men."

"Changing the course of events leading to you being *here*. Now. In front of a man married to a daughter who might never have been." Declan poured another glassful of port, extending the bottle to Pierre who held out his glass, watching as the dark liquor flowed in. He held it in his hand, staring at the fire again. When he spoke, his voice was a mix of emotions, torn between two sides of another personal dilemma.

"It is a strange consideration—as if time and events within it are nothing more than a stream of water, moving in an eternal loop, from cloud to ground. From mountain top, on down to restless seas. Then back again."

Declan raised his glass. "A *Scottish* view of things, my friend. Spoken by a man with French accent who *kens* a true highlander's soul, sitting near the top of the world, looking to the horizon and beyond."

Pierre nodded, his mood falling as he considered his position within the world, described. "It is good we've had this time to share our thoughts, and the information I've brought with me. Better, having done so before the return of your wife and child. My trust placed in you to help bridge the gap between what we've spoken of openly—and what you'll share with Lady Marion."

Declan shrugged. "She'll have it all. A look at my face enough for her to read every word written there. Like her own mother is known to do. And her father, as well. Bless his eternal soul."

Pierre nodded, raising his glass. "*And* her brother. His reputation growing, with claims he's able to read the minds of men on *both* sides of the conflict, moving to avoid or interdict their plans. Striking when and where least expected."

A gust of wind reached out, slapping the thick panes of the window, the frame creaking slightly as flames in the fireplace danced, stirred by an updraft of air through the chimney. The silence returned, with no more words shared between the two men, each locked in their own thoughts of how future events might play out.

CHAPTER THIRTY-TWO
SOUTHERN CAMPAIGN
FALL, 1781

Aaron reached out, taking his father's hand, clasping it firmly, before letting go. "Give my love to the family—when you see them again." He stepped back. "It pains me to say I don't know when or *if* I shall meet them myself. My plans fractured by circumstances of late. The war here, while nearing an end, still warm outside Charleston." He hesitated. "Greene is bound to need me to intercede in the English efforts to gather supplies from outlying communities."

Harold nodded, his hair freshly shorn, Chatte having performed the deed for him, the two of them exchanging light-hearted bantering, eliciting a slight frown from Aaron, leaving him uncertain as to the cause of his discomfort.

"I will pass along as much of what I have seen and learned as I deem safe to do, making certain to protect your efforts."

"And my mother's *sensibilities*, as well." Aaron lowered his eyes, his face flushed with embarrassment. "How I will ever be able to look her in the eye again, having done things—"

"You've done no worse in this war than *I* did in mine. Committed no greater sins by *your* hand." Harold glanced toward Chatte, standing a dozen paces away engaged in a conversation with the man he knew as Smoke. "Your mother found a place in her heart for me, after I shared my darkest secrets. There's room enough and more there for her son."

Aaron nodded. He started to turn away then stopped, staring at his father. "I've stood in your footprints, facing the same challenges. Closed the eyes of a close friend. And of *new* friends—and enemies, both. And now find myself standing before the man whose words, images, and thoughts I poured through, time and again, unable then to understand what you'd experienced. With journals of my own now in hand, holding nothing of information detrimental to anyone other than myself. Yours to take with you, added to the others." He paused. "If you're willing to do so."

Aaron reached into his coat and removed a leather satchel, handing it to his father. "I want my family to have some record of why I did what I did. In coming here, then staying to fight. At first in revenge for the death of my friend, then later in support of men who placed their trust in me. And now, in talking with you, I realize I've had some part to play in bringing about a portion of the vision *you* proposed. Though my own goal is the *elimination* of British rule, allowing the colonists to forge their own future."

Harold stepped over, taking his son's shoulders in his hands. "My curse, passed on to you. Which I would *not* take back, seeing the results of your journey. The sacrifice of your friend from school, and then of your newfound friends, along with those of the enemy, helping to join the colonies into what promises to be a new nation with a promising beginning. Generations of other patriots to follow in your wake, making the same sacrifices in turn." He hugged his son, then walked away, slipping into the woods, placing the journals in his coat pocket, without looking back.

Chatte came over and placed her hand in Aaron's, squeezing it, then letting go. "You have his *eyes*. And his build." She stepped in front of him, looking up with a questioning look. "And what of *us*? Are we eventually to part with sad eyes—leaving these memories to blur with time? Good memories—*and* bad."

Aaron tried to smile, failing to work up the emotional energy required, his lips settling into a tight line. "There is *still* work to do here. With time enow ahead of us to decide where we will stand and fire our final shot." He hesitated, feeling the pull of her wounded spirit, seeing the pain in her eyes. Always there, due to a lifetime of horrible memories embedded by a woman unable to seek vengeance for herself. A child made surrogate to her hatred, forced to carry the torch. To wield the honed blade.

He leaned forward, placing his forehead against hers, looking deep into her hazel-green eyes. "I pledge myself to *you*, for as long as you're open to me—in return. Until the moment you let me know you're willing to let me go."

⸎⸎⸎

Movement through the tangled wood was difficult. Aaron held Chatte with one arm while moving thick brambles aside. Her calf had been torn open by a musket ball, hobbling her, slowing their escape from a deadly ambush with a large group of men in dark clothing, supported by English soldiers, trailing closely behind.

The sentries, caught off guard and overwhelmed without time to give an alarm, left him and his diminished force facing a wave of lead balls, slicing into their camp. Forced to fall back to secondary positions, they'd tried to regroup to make a stand, hoping to slow the advance of the main element. But the enemy was already there, denying them the opportunity, each man striking out on their own to survive as best they could.

Aaron cursed, a thorn striking the outside corner of his eye, temporarily blinding him. He used his free hand to wipe blood and tears away, looking into the shadows of a nearby stand of trees, trying to spot movement. He could hear the strident yells of men, some begging for mercy, others raging in denial of their fate as bayonets pinned them to the earth, ending their cries.

"Leave me. My blood, leaving a trail—the bandage—coming loose." Chatte's voice was weak, the wound stealing her vitality, her skin growing pale as she struggled to speak.

"There's a place up ahead. An old cabin, burnt long ago in a raid.

With a well." Aaron shifted the small woman onto his back, her arms wrapped around his throat, legs held under his arms, increasing their speed at expense to his face, brambles tearing his skin, releasing a spider's web of blood on his forehead and cheeks. His breathing began to come in short gasps as he forced his way through to a small clearing.

He knelt, easing some of Chatte's weight from his shoulder, clawing a small pile of dry leaves and dead twigs together around a twist of oil-soaked cotton, used to start fires. He forced the hammer of his pistol back, empty, having fired it into the sneering face of a man in dark clothing, one of several dozen who'd led a counterattack against his force. Left unloaded as he and Chatte made their escape. He pulled the trigger, a shower of sparks from the flint coaxing the dry makings to catch, his breath helping it to build, knowing it would soon have the dense brush in flame, helping to cover their trail.

Aaron leaned to one side, using his fingers to tighten the bandage around Chatte's wound, hearing her gasp in pain as he tightened it, stopping the ooze of blood. Then he gathered himself and stood up, her full weight back on his shoulder as he moved at an angle toward the cabin, a few hundred paces ahead, forming a plan in his mind on how they might avoid capture and promise of a long, painful death at the hands of their enemy.

※ ※ ※

Aaron heard men's voices passing by the opening of the well, muted by thick patches of moss on the ground around its opening, carefully avoided when he'd lowered Chatte into the narrow embrace of moss-faced stones. He'd told her to wait there until well after dark, when he'd return and pull her out. His intention to lead the half-dozen men still following them away, having watched as they worked out his tracks in the woods, led by a native with skill at reading sign.

Aaron moved off, kneeling beside one corner of a burnt shell of a cabin, the charred ends of wood collapsed into a small den of dark shadows, placing a piece of Chatte's bloodstained skirt there. Then he reloaded his pistol as he searched the woods for movement, his strung bow slung over his shoulder, along with a half-quiver of arrows.

He knew it would be a fool's end to a game he'd lost due to lack of focus, thinking about his family in Pennsylvania colony, as if the war had ended and finding his way out of it was his only concern. That and his relationship with a woman who would never lose her need, her intense thirst for revenge. Aaron shook his head, forcing away the possibility of failure, his face set in a mask of determination, ready to leap up and lead these men on a twisting path along the base of a rock-faced ridge, lying just beyond.

※※※

The native leading the others hesitated, spying a flutter of cloth in the shadows. He leaned forward, dark eyes probing the interior of an abandoned cabin, looking for movement, ready to leap back and call out to the others, allowing them to finish the work they'd paid him to do. A month spent wandering the dense terrain alone, seeking the whereabouts of the irregular group of men causing dozens of deaths, disrupting the plans of the men in red coats. Finding them, providing vital information used to create a trap, its jaws sprung too late to capture the ones they were most eager to eliminate, known as the Wolf and his woman, Chatte Sauvage.

A whisper of air signaled death in flight, an arrow catching him as he started to turn, driving into his chest, slicing through both lungs and heart as it slipped away, leaving him clutching the ground with his hands as blood flowed from his mouth, unable to breathe as his vision faded to gray, then black.

The other men crouched, their weapons aimed to either side, ready to duck the next arrow when it came. They remained frozen in place, until one spotted a shadow dashing away. He pointed, his pistol offering a flash of sparks, followed by powder igniting, and a wasted lead ball, winging its way into the slope of ground beyond the ruins of the cabin.

※※※

Aaron crouched in the opening of a fall of large rocks, having laid a false trail along the furthest edge of a clearing, studded with the teeth of cast-off stones. He watched as a line of five men made their way from one rock to another, trying to reduce their exposure to arrow or lead ball, having already lost the native guide, and their leader.

Aaron had managed to wound one of the remaining men, whose shirt was dark with blood where a ball had grazed the surface of a boulder, deforming it, left lodged in the man's shoulder after tearing through his flesh, now embedded in bone. He drew the bow back, waiting until the injured man leaned out, then released the string. The arrow pinned the man in place, his body slumping to one side, eyes staring in surprise. The rest of the group dropped out of sight, their heads poking up then dropping down as they searched for him, unable to find his location.

Aaron slid back, working his way through a narrow gap between the stones at his back, seeking another place from which to ambush the men hunting him. Hard-eyed men, unwilling to give up the chase, determined to find, then end him. He focused on every step made as he moved into a new position, keeping thoughts of Chatte's pitiful condition from his mind, knowing he'd soon find out if she still lived once the day had slanted over toward dusk. The time quickly approaching when he'd turn the tables and begin his own hunt, using arrows, pistols, and knife, with death meted out from the shadows. Fear, tightening the legs, arms, necks, and scrotums of his would-be assassins, leaving them as sheep, clamped in the jaws of a wolf.

🌱🌱🌱

A full moon hung overhead, the hour midway between midnight and a new dawn. The opening in the well darkened as a shadow leaned over, then quickly withdrew. A soft voice called out to Chatte, who'd been waiting for the sound of it. She swallowed with difficulty, the bottom of the well holding a slurry of mud and silted water, enough to fill a slight depression formed with the tips of her fingers, with a pool of clear liquid, used to dampen her lips. Her thirst, desperate from loss of blood, left unquenched.

"I am here." She listened for Aaron's reply, then slipped her knife back into the sheath on her upper thigh, always there, ready to fill her hand and lash out.

"Can you manage to hold the end of a rope, with a harness slipped under your arms, made of dead men's clothing?" Aaron stared into the well, barely able to make out Chatte's face as she stared up from the inky depth. "I can tie it off and climb down, if not."

"I will be able to. But not to help climb out. My leg is—is not good."

The end of a rope attached to clothing knotted into a sling slid down the side of the stones. Chatte grabbed it, pulling it around her chest, gasping as she moved, her body in pain, her lips clamped tight against the scream trying to crawl out of her parched throat. When she was ready, she waved a hand, as if trying to catch a moonbeam of light streaming down from above. Aaron pulled her from the ooze, her legs dangling, another wave of pain stealing her vision, the world going dark.

When she came to, a small fire was burning beside her, the flickering light revealing the hideous wound in her calf. Aaron had prepared a mixture of herbs, taken from her pack, soaked in a large piece of a broken clay pot. He glanced over his shoulder, sensing she had returned to consciousness, then handed her a canteen, its shape unfamiliar.

"It's bad. The bone—*fully* exposed. Your tendon, torn. Muscle—" He paused, taking a half-breath, a wet cough sounding from between his compressed lips, using the back of his hand to wipe them dry. "The muscle's shredded. The ball must have deflected from a tree or stone and flattened out, clipping the bone as it passed through."

"No hope of keeping it?" Chatte's voice was that of a child, asking about a loose tooth. The sound brought tears to the corners of Aaron's eyes, though he refused to let them slip down his cheeks.

"No. If left untreated, infection will soon set in. Leaving you to die of a fever. A few days, at best, until—" He turned away. "This is going to hurt. Like hell." He started to lean forward, the mixture cupped in his hand, stopping when Chatte reached out and grabbed his shirt, pulling him around.

"Hand me my pack. I've a potion to help ease the pain. Enough to take it away. Then you can bind it up." Aaron reached for a leather satchel, handing it to Chatte. He watched as she pulled out a small bottle, using her knife to remove a layer of wax, then pry out a cork stopper. She placed it against her full lips, taking a small amount into her mouth, holding it for a moment before swallowing. Then she noticed a dark stain on the front of his shirt, a hole punched through the fabric near his right shoulder, blood oozing from it. His face reflected the light of the small fire as he looked at her with a sad expression, his face pale.

Her eyes widened, no longer focused on herself, but him, wondering how he'd managed to pull her from the shelter of the well. Wondering if doing so had sealed his fate, along with hers. "We are a pair. One body between us, capable of moving on. Me, minus a leg. You, with a damaged shoulder."

"Still ahead of the game played by those who outsmarted me. Left lying on their backs, staring at the sky, wondering how they came to such an end."

"Shut up—and hold me."

Aaron leaned over, pulling Chatte into his embrace, ignoring the tearing inside his chest, having difficulty breathing, putting aside the image of her torn leg. Letting go of everything that had happened that day as he drank in the scent of her hair, her sweat, and blood. Tasting her tears on her lips, along with his own, knowing their entwined destinies had come to a final, bloody end.

"I hear noises." Chatte's voice, muffled by his bloodstained shirt, had taken on a dreamy tone.

"Men. Heading this way. With torches. And English accents."

"Put out the *fire!*"

"They'll not see it. They're further down the rise, moving along an old trail, with the wind in our favor."

"They'll work it out—your path. Finding us by daylight."

Aaron nodded. "Aye, lass. They will."

"We need to keep them from taking us. From what they'll do to me." Chatte tried to swallow her fear, leaving Aaron to take the canteen and tip it into her mouth. She took a drink, then wiped her lips, staring at him. "What they'll do to *you*—because of me."

Aaron nodded again, his pistol in his lap. "I know. And already have half the means to prevent it happening." He pulled out his knife. "And this is the other. A clean death by my hand, offered you. Without the damage of what a lead ball will do to you." He paused, his eyes flowing over with the love he felt for her. Unable to have prevented himself from it, knowing what that love might end up costing him. To both body and soul.

They looked away, seeing the torches flickering through the trees, working their way closer, Aaron aware those hunting them must have hired another skilled tracker. He handed Chatte the pistol, bringing it to half-cock, placing her finger around the trigger. "On three, my love. Together. Give me a moment to release you, then the trigger pulled. My last sight—your beautiful face carried with me until we will meet up again. Whole. Undamaged by what we've seen—and done."

He raised his blade, pressing it against the surface of her thin neck, seeing the pulse of her heartbeat beneath the skin, along with the look of love in her eyes. "One." Chatte swallowed, the sound of the hammer fully drawn back producing a loud click in the night air. Harold closed his eyes, preparing himself for what would happen next. "Two." The hammer struck the frizzen, the flint creating a shower of sparks that burned the side of his cheek and neck, with the pistol failing to fire, purposely left unloaded. "Three." Aaron drew the blade across Chatte's throat as if through paper, the honed edge parting her skin, her jugular, cleaving her windpipe. A spray of blood coating his face, dripping from his cheeks like tears. Chatte's eyes widened in surprise as the light in them slowly faded.

Aaron held her, warmed by her blood on his chest, knowing she had failed him, and herself. Failed to live up to the promise made and sworn to, aware she'd never be able to simply slip away, leaving a single man in red and white alive.

He let her go, then rolled to one side, reloading the pistol, slipping his knife back in its sheath at his side. He carried her to the well, dropping her in, collapsing its top, the mortared joints weakened by years of neglect. Then he picked up his bow and quiver, with a handful of arrows recovered from the bodies of the men he'd killed. Leaving the fire burning, he moved into the shadows, knowing he would need to head west. Deep into the wilderness. Aware that people would be hunting him. Paid to do so by a diminutive man. One playing both sides against the middle.

CHAPTER THIRTY-THREE
CROSSROAD STORE
FALL, 1781

Sinclair looked at the ledger lying on the counter of the store, quill in her hand, ready to inscribe the total of the days sales against value of goods taken in trade. She wanted to settle the account before heading into the house to help Meghan with dinner, left shaking her head, unable to recall the amount as she came to the end of the column, having to start over again.

She dropped the quill and rubbed her eyes, her fingers raw from weeding the garden behind the barn, El able to finish three rows to her one, never letting up in his recitation of humorous stories. He'd been a godsend to the family of four. Now made five, with himself as close to them all as if of the same bloodline.

Her stomach twisted again, causing her to lower her head until the spasm passed, the cramping having increased of late as her monthly flow started to reduce due to age and lack of sexual activity. Then she looked up, startled by a shadow filling the door, knowing Eldritch was at the wellhouse, the creak of the handle used to raise the bucket carrying across the yard. There had been no sound of horses in front, with Allyn not due back from the city until after dark.

Harold stood there, backlit by the setting sun, with Sinclair needing a moment to adjust to what her eyes were showing her. She rose to her feet, hands flat on the counter of the store, unable to speak, balanced between questioning his return after a three-month absence and rushing to hold him, making certain he was real and not another early morning dream, shattered by the crowing of their rooster.

"You're—back."

Harold nodded, his face having aged, with deep lines around the corners of his mouth. His hair, cut short, formed a black, gray tinged blanket of tight curls on his head, along with a thick beard and a pair of glasses resting on his long, aquiline nose. "I am. With news of our son."

Sinclair's knees buckled, her face going white, lips parted in a silent question, wanting to hear what he was waiting to tell her. Afraid of what she might learn. "Tell me."

"He is hale in body, though nicked in a few places. Nothing of consequence. As tall as when you last saw him, though broader in chest and neck. A man in full."

"He is nearby?"

"Nae, lass. He's far away, last I saw of him. Finishing the work started when he first arrived." Harold paused. "*Hard* work." He lowered his eyes, unable to look the mother of their son in hers. "As hard as any *I* was made to do—in service to a different cause."

Sinclair swallowed; her heart unable to decide which way to leap, trapped in her throat, preventing speech. She watched as the man who'd once been her husband came over and took her hands, holding them, looking into her eyes with a firm gaze.

"He's damaged. *Inside*. Same as I was by what war does to a person. Man, woman, or child. But he *is* sound, and still the son you know in flesh, blood, and mind. A leader of men—hard men with experience, bowing to his will. To his methods. Creating a great disturbance to England's efforts to bring the colonies under their heel."

Sinclair pulled away. "He is leading men to their *deaths*! To the deaths of *others*! Because of *you*. Wanting to be like his father. Because of what you put down in your damned *journals*. Your stories. Your—your *vivid* portrayals of war. With him feasting on them, stoking the fire that all young men have inside them, wanting to hold it in their hands, feeling the heat of—"

A voice from behind Harold caused him to spin around, his hand going for the knife at his side. Eldrich stood there, hands rising as he gave the stranger a nod. "You'll be the father, returned. Grandfather to the little one." He glanced at Sinclair; his head tilted slightly. "I heard your voice. Sounded like you were in distress. Didn't mean to interrupt. At least—not until you said the last part." He moved ahead and to one side, slipping past Harold, stopping a few feet away, his arms crossed. "I'm Eldritch. El, as the others call me. A friend of Allyn's, working for my room and board. Living in the stable—not the house."

Harold looked at Sinclair. "*Grandfather?*"

She returned his look with a wry smile. "You thought the world you left to us alone to manage—again—would simply stop until you were ready to return?" She came out from behind the counter, standing alongside Eldritch. "You've a grandchild, here. A boy. And *another* in the highlands. A granddaughter—to Marion. A letter from her and her new husband. *Another* event you've missed, along with Meghan's marriage to Allyn, who will soon be back from the city, pegging you with questions, same as your daughter will be doing when she learns you're back."

Harold nodded, then looked at the tall, thin man standing beside Sinclair. "You were going to say something."

El turned and gave Sinclair a warm smile. "At the risk of disagreeing with you, Lady Sinclair, I take exception to what you were just saying in regard to your son—gone missing." He turned and looked at Harold, getting a nod. "Your boy, or man—he come here with a friend, to try and guide him away. The story, from what Allyn shared during our days spent working side by each—was they had a plan to fight alongside the colonials. The other boy pissed off at—" El looked at Sinclair. "Excuse my language, ma'am." He turned back toward Harold. "*Angered* by the British having sub—" He paused, hunting for the word until Harold offering him one.

"Subjugated?"

Eldritch grinned. "*That's* the very one used." He nodded. "His friend, your son Aaron's, was a Scot. Name of Rory. *He's* the one lit the fuse. All the rest of what's happened—on *your* boy's shoulders." He stepped aside, sitting down on a sack of grain. "I know because I did the same. Without having a father lead me to it. Seeking nothing more at the time than a steady meal, and coins in my pocket. Willing to wear a uniform to secure a place to lay my head, without worry of losing my scalp. Men, taking me in, teaching me hard lessons. Some of them—leaving deep scars. No different for me than your son." He paused, giving Sinclair and Harold short nods of his thin-cheeked face. "Leastways, that's *how* I found it to be. Not saying it's like that for all."

Sinclair came over, taking El's hand in hers. "Allyn told Meghan your sorrowful tale. And she told *me*. Not meant as a violation of your privacy, but only to inform me of your character as a man. Before letting you become part of what we're doing *here*."

"I survived. Others—didn't. Life moving me along the path I was meant to walk, the way I see it. Myself doing the best I could to look as far ahead as possible. Coming up short that day on the road, with Allyn staring me down, then bringing me here. Given a second chance to live a life to be proud of. With people I've come to—" He stopped, then stood up and walked away, unable to continue, heading to his room in the stable.

Harold shook his head. "Lucky. In having found him."

"He found Allyn. The rest just—fell into place." Sinclair came over and took Harold's hands. "I'm sorry, for having said that about Aaron. I realize that what you put in your journals, what you went through—was meant to honor those you served with. To honor the people, you came to love. My words born out of a mother's worries, released without thought."

"There is *more* to tell." Harold's eyes found hers. "But for another time. It would seem I have a *grandchild* to meet."

"A *fine* grandson. Named Richard, after your father. And our son." Sinclair went over and picked up the ledger, tucking it under her arm. She took Harold's hand in hers, leading him toward the farmhouse, the sound of an infant's laughter trickling through the cool air.

☙ ☙ ☙

Meghan came over and touched her father on his shoulder. She leaned down and kissed his forehead, gazing at her son curled up in a doting grandfather's arms, coaxed to sleep by a soft lullaby. She knelt, looking up at her father, seeing past the signs of age on his face, happy to have him back in her life again. In the lives of their reunited family, less her sister back home, and her brother, still missing.

"My son has your eyes. And your chin." She reached out and squeezed her father's forearm. "It's good to have you home."

Harold raised his eyes, looking at his daughter, seeing the woman she'd become. With husband, child, and what had become her home. Along with a flourishing business, self-supporting, with her mother's start-up money fully repaid. "Is *that* how you see it—this place you've settled into?"

Meghan nodded, her eyes on his, the question causing her chest to tighten at the thought of ever leaving, making a return to Scotland. Tied to the soil here by sweat, blood, and tears spent putting in the gardens. By the hugs, helping hands, and broad smiles of the women and their families who'd welcomed her with gifts of advice, and a willingness to include her in their social gatherings.

"I do."

Harold sighed, closing his eyes, then opening them, a warm smile on his weary face. "*Good*. I'm pleased you feel that way. Truly. Our family with a leg on either side of the briny sea, between. A tie binding together our family's heritage, old *and* new."

Allyn came into the small common room, a sack of potatoes in his arms. He nodded, then carried them down into the cellar, his steps on the stairway causing the treads to squeak, the young babe in Harold's arms stirring, his eyes opening, looking for and finding his mother's face, smiling as he reached up.

Harold handed Patrick to Meghan, then got up and followed Allyn downstairs, having to duck his head, the rafters low, with cobwebs aplenty. He watched as his son-in-law emptied the sack into a bin. "A wonderful thing, providing for your needs from the soil you plowed, planted, and weeded with your own two hands."

Allyn turned around, nodding as he set the empty sack on a small bench. "It *is*. And would be hard to leave, when and *if* the two ladies of the place decide what happens next." He angled his head. "*Your* input having sway as to that decision as well."

Harold shook his head. "Not so. I stand to the back of the line. No —not even *in* line, having gone off on my own path. Again."

Allyn gave him a considered look. "To find Aaron. To find your son, then return, providing relief to a mother torn in two, in constant worry for his whereabouts. For his well-being."

Harold nodded, leaning back against the stair post, arms crossed. "She is *still* torn, between the family here and one back in Scotland. A wide bridge to cross, with everyone affected by her decision. Though I ken your wife—my daughter—has her feet firmly planted here with her husband and son." He shrugged. "As it should be, if wanting to know my thoughts on it. A *new* beginning in a *new* place, soon to become a *new* nation. One with limitless possibilities for the building of something—greater, I suppose. Unless men with base ambitions muck it up, taking away the right of people like *you* to speak your piece, with equal say as to which direction it should go—and grow."

"Had heard you were born with a silvered tongue." Allyn raised his hand. "Meant with the greatest respect, sir, for what you've said in Commons, as told me by your daughter and wife, both. Proud as they could be in what you tried to lead other men to."

"Failing. In the end."

"Nae. Not that. You opened men's minds to the *idea* of it. With no knowing which of the seeds you were planting ended up taking root, helping to alter events. Part of the reason we're close to kicking out the old ways, replacing them with something—new. Flawed, as it might be in the beginning, as it is when first building *anything*, starting out with words on paper before the first stone goes into the foundation. Before the final nail goes into the frame. But one I am *eager* to lend my shoulder to, if given a chance."

"You'll no doubt have it. Your *son*, too."

"And *yours*, sir, once finding his way back to us when he's able to. With a family here, waiting to welcome him in."

Harold nodded, then turned to go, Allyn's voice called to him, stopping him on the bottom stair tread, his hand on the railing. "Apart from yourself—with you going off once more, I ken. Your worry for us there in your eyes, weighing down your shoulders."

Harold looked down, silent, letting the words settle in his mind, knowing his daughter had chosen well. "Yes. Breaking the bonds, again. With you and Meghan left having to pick up the pieces." Then he climbed the stairs, his weight causing them to cry out in protest.

※ ※ ※

Eldritch shook his head, staring at Allyn and Meghan, his face red. "It's time I took on a larger share of the load, with the gardens put to bed for the winter. Supplies stored away, with room enough made for goods picked up in Philadelphia. *I* should be the one to go. You, with a strained back." He gave Allyn a hard stare, then looked at Meghan. "Unless it's *you* who don't trust me to go—alone."

"You *can't* believe that of *me!*" Meghan reached out, taking Eldritch by the hand. "It's not an issue of *trust*, El—only of your—" She hesitated.

Allyn looked up from his chair with a pinched expression, his lower back aching, wrapped in a poultice. "It's your inability to *count*, El. That being the *only* worry. The men keeping tally of the loading off and on of the wagon have been known to tip the scales, as it were. A close eye and careful count made for *each* delivery *and* pickup along the way."

El's face reddened further. "I can cross out a mark, as good as yourself. Use a tally sheet, making a slash for each bale, bundle, or bag as they're unloaded. Same when goods go aboard, matching up the marks you've put on the papers, given me." He squared his thin shoulders, unwilling to step down from his offer to go in Allyn's place.

"He makes a good point." Sinclair came into the store, Richard in her arms. "We've had our share of minor *adjustments* having to be made on other runs, with a number jostled out of place during the journey, to and fro." She eyed Allyn, whose face started to turn red, then looked a Meghan. "*Your* decision, daughter."

Meghan nodded, a warm smile easing El's stiff posture. "Of course, you're to go, El. I'll prepare the sheets for delivery and pick up, just as you've described." She headed to the counter, where the ledger and other books were lying, and pulled a stub quill out, dipping it into a vial of ink, covering a parchment with a series of straight lines, in groups of four, adding a word and small picture alongside, indicating the items listed on their bill of lading and order list.

Allyn winced, starting to stand up to help hitch the team. El reached out, stopping him. "I've got this. Let me help. It's the least I can do to earn my winter keep." He gave Sinclair a nod, then spun about on his heel, headed into the stable.

Sinclair watching him go, then looked down at Allyn. "I'll be going too." She saw his eyes widen. "Not *today*. Not with Eldritch. But *soon*. I've a need to return home to see my granddaughter there, along with my daughter and her husband. Too long waiting here like a fretful mother when others require my *refocused* attention."

Meghan looked up from her writing. "This time of year? The crossing would be easier in the spring. The weather, milder then."

"I've developed the stomach for it. A letter already sent, with answer received. There is a ship leaving in a week. One I will be on. My return—sometime in the new year. April, at the latest, unless summoned back earlier by a message letting me know your brother has found his way here to you."

Meghan lowered her head, scratching away, silent as she stared at the papers, marking each with the proper number of lines needed to match the figures written in the ledger. "Do you believe him to still be alive?"

Sinclair started to respond, her voice tight with anger, displeased at her daughter's apparent willingness to consider her brother gone. Allyn's hand touched her wrist, having gained his feet, compelling her to release Patrick to him. He walked away, with a painful gait, a twist in his back and shoulders.

Sinclair softened her tone. "I—realize the pain hidden behind your remark. Mine, though more evident than your own, is no *greater* in depth then what his absence has meant, and *still* means to you. To us both." She walked over to the counter, reaching out and taking her daughter's hand, considering herself blessed to have two such incredible and capable women in her life, helping her to manage the family's vast holdings. "I know your feelings as to Aaron's continued absence, as well your thoughts on ever leaving here."

Meghan lifted her hand, slipping it out of her mother's grasp, wiping tears from her eyes before continuing to fill out the papers. "He's *still* alive. I can feel it—in *here*." She touched her breast. "He *will* return. Aaron will find his way back to us. To me."

"Is the only reason I'm leaving, child. With you able to bear the burden of keeping things going here. A letter sent me with any word heard. One I will answer in kind, or in person. I *promise* you."

The sound of the team neighing with anticipation of a ride ahead came through the still morning air, along with the sound of hens clucking in the yard, filling in the edges of a world in constant movement. A flock of geese passed by, low overhead, calling out as they darkened the sky with their vast numbers, helping to complete the circle of life.

CHAPTER THIRTY-FOUR
WESTERN PENNSYLVANIA HILLS
FALL, 1781

The ache in Aaron's shoulder was a series of pulses, timed with the beating of his heart. The skin on his shoulder was swollen, hot to the touch, his fingers shaking as he pressed the tip of his knife into the hole slashed into his flesh by a lead ball from the musket of one of the final three of his pursuers. Skilled killers, lured into a deadly trap, then attacked from behind. An arrow taking the trailing man in the back. A pistol used to open an extra hole in the head of the second in line. The third, twisting around, managing to get off a shot that skipped off a ledge framing the side of a narrow path, a moment before a knife found a home in his throat, his brown eyes widening in shock at how quickly the tables had turned.

Pus oozed from around the fire-heated tip of steel, causing Aaron to lean back, his senses reeling from fever and fatigue. He'd travelled over a hundred miles by foot through shadowed woods, a poultice in place against his wound, hoping to curb the effects of infection, with minimal results.

He'd used the sun to direct him, heading west, his instinct's nudging him north or south as needed, following the vision in his mind. Of his sister Meghan, tending to his wounds with a soft smile on her face. Turning into the image of the woman in his father's first journal, coming to him as he lay curled up in a ball of pain during the day. Hiding from people, finding food where he could, water as often as seeps from ledges provided it. Two canteens carried, one his own, the other taken, along with vital supplies, from the bodies of the men he'd hunted down before going back to find Chatte.

He shook his head, twisting the blade in his hand, allowing the drainage to continue, tears in his eyes as he recalled having lowered her body into the well, hiding it from any who might follow the others and discover it, preventing the venting of their hatred of her, desecrating her corpse. The image of her face, hovering before him, his free hand reaching out to touch it. To have back the past handful of days. A week having passed since their last moment together. Before her betrayal of their sworn vow.

His hand fell to his side, the knife slipping from his fingers as his head lolled at an angle, the day going over to darkness. When he returned to awareness, he started in alarm, feeling something shift beneath his body, realizing he was lying on a thick bed of straw. An intake of breath brought with it the aroma of food, followed by the looming presence of someone sitting beside him, a spoon held to his lips, a raspy voice encouraging him to open them and drink.

Aaron tried to sit up, a hand on his uninjured shoulder pressing him down, a whisper in his ear telling him to lie still. The spoon was back in place, a cool liquid slipped into his mouth, sweet and sour, swallowed. A thin line of warmth wormed its way into his stomach, his ears filled with the cadence of a familiar song. The voice, cracked with age, luring him to sleep. Not that of his mother. Nor his grandmother. Or Meghan. Without the musical accent of Chatte's sultry notes. A mystery to solve when he next awoke from the dark shadows reaching up and pulling him down.

⁂

The air, filled with motes of dust drifting in lines of sunlight passing through the thin gaps in the side of a small building with rough-hewn siding, was cool. Aaron stirred, reaching up to touch his wound, a poultice in place, secured with a wrap of thin cloth. He sensed his fever had eased, driven back by whoever had tended to him. Some part of him aware it was still there, lying in wait, biding its time, ready to begin feasting on him again, if provoked by sudden movement.

A change in light let him know someone was coming. Faint vibrations, felt through the ground. The sound of leaves pressed beneath soft soled shoes. Aaron reached for his knife, the sheath empty. He turned his head, trying to find it, a bolt of lightning blinding him in a flash of light as a door opened then closed.

"You are still alive. Good." The voice was a cackling of noise, as if a flock of chickens, arguing over spilled meal. "You were standing in the door, hell or heaven waiting on you." The voice came closer, the scent of onions in his nose, causing him to turn his head to the side, though his stomach rumbled in hunger.

"You're a strong 'un. So, *hell* will have to wait. Your scars and recent wound suggesting that to be your destination. But not *this* day."

"Where?" The question was all Aaron could manage, the movement of his head having produced a wave of nausea.

"In the highlands, lad. In western Pennsylvania colony. The exact name of this place, no use to ya. Not unless you've been born here." The sound of a throat clearing, followed by a hawk of spit provided no clue as to the person's identity, or sex. "And less use to ya, if'n you're to die here, neither."

"Water."

"Aye. Boiled with herbs. Cooled, through the night. It'll hurt, my lifting your head enough to swallow." A hand slipped beneath his shoulders caused a wave of heat to rise, overwhelming his ability to breathe, his teeth clenched against the assault until it subsided, a wedge of his bundled pack cradling his head.

The brew, with noxious smell, helped slake his thirst and quell the nausea. He swallowed every drop offered him, trying to grasp the wrist of the person holding the cup, unable to raise his arm, his body too weak to comply.

"Thank you." His attempt to speak, met with another cackle.

"Right proper—your manners. A gentleman, with a skin marked with tales of woe. No saint on bent knees at prayers, are you."

"I am—no saint."

"Soldier?"

Aaron licked his lips, his eyes still closed. "Was."

"Loyalist—or colonial?"

"Does it matter?"

"To me, yes. The risk, if the one, greater than the potential reward if the other."

"Then I'd—" Aaron swallowed, the drink beginning to work, his fatigue lowered just a touch. "Be a fool—to tell you *now*."

"True. And you don't have the look of one. A fool. But your accent is Scottish enow to give the benefit of my doubt to you. For today, at least."

Aaron heard the sigh of wind in the trees outside the thin walls of the shack. The weather was warm, as if had been when he last recalled being able to move. Unusual for the time of season. A day or so, he thought, having passed since he'd lost touch with the world, brought to wherever he was. The weather bound to change soon, returning to its normal pattern. Then he slipped away again, returning to his tortured dreams, left hovering between pain and grief. Between evil and the hope of ever finding good again.

When he awoke, a new voice had joined with the other. One smoother in tone, stronger in spirit, though just as shy with details provided.

"You are a soldier. Fighting with, or against the British."

The voice was female, pulling Aaron's eyes fully open, his shoulder no longer throbbing, his mind clearer. "I am." He hesitated. "I was." He turned his head, expecting pain, pleased to make the movement without wincing, the ache of swollen flesh having subsided.

"You have a look that is familiar. Your name?" The woman wore a cloak, her face hidden in a shadow.

"I would prefer to hold onto it—for now." He waited, seeing her start to pull away. "To *protect* you, and your friend." A cackle of laughter from the shadows followed his remark, the woman in concealing garb frowning, her cheeks tanned brown, visible as she leaned back in.

"Your accent. It *too* is familiar. Not one or the other. Scottish or English." A hand found his wrist, checking his pulse, then gently pinched the flesh of his lower arm. "You're not as dehydrated as I would have thought, with the amount of fever in you. You had sense enough to drink."

"I learned from my father. A survivor of a like wound. Said it was the water brought him by natives that helped to quench the fire, within. That and the care from two women who tended him, night, and day, until his fever broke."

"He is also a soldier, fighting in the colony war?"

Aaron considered for a moment, deciding to trust the inner voice whispering to cast away his concern for secrecy. "He fought *with* the English, hereabouts. Against the French." He took a deep breath, feeling the squeeze in his shoulder, a moment of pain rising, then flowing away as he exhaled.

"My name is Aaron. Aaron Knutt. And I am searching for someone who helped my father, years ago. A woman—a healer. Named A'neewa. A member of a native tribe in the Ohio basin." He turned his head away, staring into the low ceiling overhead, watching as the motes of dust continued to dance between cobwebs gathered there, the taste of his name, sounding sweet in his ears.

A hand reached out, easing his face around, the woman's hood removed, a pair of dark eyes gazing into his. "You have found her, Aaron. Son of Harold. Found the one your vision has led you to."

※※※

A small church bell was ringing, the notes resonating in the air outside a small structure used as both a storeroom and church. A'neewa tilted her head, counting them, a smile on her face as she pictured the young boy holding the rope, his feet coming clear of the floor as the knot he was holding onto rose, pulled by the weight of the heavy metal dome. His weight barely enough to keep it ringing, as he counted out eight strikes of the gong, hitting its curved side.

It was Sunday, with service to begin in an hour, the bell summoning people of the makeshift community located outside an English fort in the upper Sandusky to come together to join in prayer. They were followers of the Moravian religion her husband was minister to. A flock of over one hundred people, made up of natives willing to adhere to a new belief system, guided along the spiritual path by a handful of Europeans.

Tillers of the soil now, with A'neewa stepmother to two children from her husband's marriage to a woman who'd died sixteen years earlier, soon after the birth of their first child. A daughter, grown into a beautiful woman, tall, willowy in build, with dark hair and light-colored eyes. And a native boy of twelve years who she'd adopted, standing outside, eagerly tending to the ringing of the bell.

A'neewa made her way over to a door that opened into a small room, a bed made up inside, holding the son of a man who still appeared to her in her dreams. Another soldier, wounded in body and spirit, his eyes so much like his father's, holding pain beyond the physical damage done to him, compelling her to bring him back to their temporary home to help him heal. Equally compelling to her daughter, sitting alongside him, wiping sweat from his forehead with a cloth dipped in cool water.

It tugged at A'neewa's heart, remembering how Meghan had done the same for Harold, with herself at her side, attending to his wounded shoulder and hand with poultices made of herbs selected to fight his infection. The same type of wound suffered by his son, on the opposite shoulder. Too much like his father, she thought as she came over and placed a hand on her stepdaughter's head, stroking her hair, fine and smooth, freshly washed, soft to the touch.

"He is much better. His color—beginning to return." Eliza, named after her deceased mother, looked up. "The wound is still—terrible to look at, though the edges are not as red."

"The herbs in the poultice will help soothe it, stealing the heat of the infection. Your diligence in attending to him helping him to heal, daughter."

Eliza smiled, reaching up and taking her adopted mother's hand, glad to have her in the lives of her family. Her father's voice stronger since their marriage, his voice more vibrant, eyes clear, leading the others with sermons of praise, filled with the promise of salvation to all who followed in the footsteps of Jesus.

"He has been talking in his sleep. To someone named *Chat*. A strange name for a woman. One he keeps calling out to."

A'neewa hesitated, sensing a shift in her daughter's tone. "Chat seems more a man's name, or rather—a nickname. How do you know to be a woman?"

"By how he—*says* it. Softly. His fingers open, as if reaching for her." Eliza looked down at Aaron's face, seeing the flutter of his eyelids as he drifted in and out of a restless sleep. "She's dead, I think. He keeps saying how sorry he is. As if it were his fault." She looked up at A'neewa. "His wife?"

"Perhaps." A'neewa shrugged. "If he lives, we must wait for him to share what he will. When and *if* he chooses."

"He'll live. His will is *strong*, and God has led him here to us for a reason. For a purpose."

A'neewa felt her chest tighten with concern for her daughter, knowing the bond that could form between a man injured, and the one helping to bring him back to health. "You will need go to prepare for service. People will be arriving soon. And make certain your brother has *clean* clothes on his back."

Eliza nodded, then placed the clay bowl on the floor, leaving the cloth to soak. She stood up, taller than her mother, then leaned down and kissed her cheek, closing the door as she left.

A'neewa sat down and reached out, lifting the poultice, seeing the skin was starting to pale around the deep, penetrating wound, her attempt to remove the fragments of lead successful, though the damage to muscle and bone had been worrisome. The journey from the home of the wise woman living in the hills to the east had been a risk, each untoward movement jostling the young man, stealing what little energy he'd had left, arriving at their makeshift home behind the framework of a new church, barely breathing, his face ashen, unresponsive while she'd used a pair of scissors with bent tips to remove the fragments of bullet and spent wadding, driven deep into his fevered flesh.

"I—*know* you." Aaron's eyes were open, still glassy, his cheeks holding a slight flush of color. His breathing, no longer labored, though still weak. His voice barely more than a whisper. "From before."

A'neewa nodded, reaching for the cloth, wiping the wounded man's forehead. "Yes. Lying in the hut of a friend of mine. A person understanding nature, providing what I needed—to save your life."

"I am—going to live?"

"Yes." A'neewa saw a flash of something dark slip through his blue eyes, along with a wince of pain on his face, the hair of his recently shorn beard showing black against his pale skin. She reached out and touched his forehead, feeling the heat there, still, a frown puckering her full lips as she studied him, wondering if it might have been better to let him slip away, his spirit troubled. Her own beginning to stir, sensing he was battling demons, hidden deep inside.

She sighed, using the cloth to bathe his face, leaving it to God to decide his fate as her free hand slipped down, touching the hilt of the small knife strapped to her upper thigh beneath her linen dress.

※※※

Lukas finished the sermon, spreading his hands to the sides as he gazed at the people gathered in a small shelter, used as a church. The English had forced him and his flock of converted natives from their homes and cultivated lands to the south. To keep them near to hand to prevent any risk of their supporting the colonists. The women, men, and children wore dresses, pants, and shirts, filling the split-log pews, with a handful of the men left standing along the walls, hats in hand.

"Go, my friends—and do God's work *here*, on this piece of earth provided us by the English. And, though the season for planting is already past, we have an abundance of his love and blessings, provided us."

The congregation stood as one, a return chorus of voices washing over Lukas, his eyes filling with tears of emotion, knowing he was where he needed to be, doing what he was meant to do. Once the building was clear, he went over and closed his bible, one passed along to him by his father. Brought with him and his deceased wife to the Ohio Basin a year before their daughter had been born. A year before God chose to lift her up into his sheltering arms, testing his faith, left to deal with an immeasurable loss.

Brought to his knees by the burden, then lifted to his feet by a native woman, arriving at his door, leading a dozen of her people, seeking to join his flock. Returning with more who were willing to make the pilgrimage, expanding the community back in Gnadenhutten. Vast fields placed under cultivation. Solid homes built. New wells dug. A church with attached school erected. Lessons taught by the same native woman, now made his wife. The Lord working in wondrous ways, indeed. Another miracle sent to him, joining him and his daughter, and the addition of an adopted son.

Their lives had been replete with blessings, until another test from God found him and his parishioners. The simmering war between England and its colonies sweeping them up, forced by the British to leave their homes and hundreds of acres of fertile fields behind. Marched miles away, forced onto land lying outside the English fortifications. Faced with a winter of deprivation, unable to plant new crops in time on the lands assigned them. A period of famine, testing everyone's faith, with Lukas determined to lead his people along the path to their salvation. Helped by Anna, the name given to his wife during her conversion.

She'd just returned from a visit into the hills, approaching him with her head down, asking shelter for a man on a litter, pulled behind her, her body bent down with fatigue.

"Of course! We *must* take him in. He is one of *God's* children. Everything done, to bring him back to health."

A'neewa had given him a concerned look. "He is running—from something."

"He is running *toward* the light of God. Guided here by his destiny. Ours not to question the reason for it, or of what it is he *might* be running from."

And now, as he went outside to speak with anyone willing to share their thoughts, needs, or make an offer of their service to the building of more pews, he smiled, seeing his son and several native children pulling the rope of the bell, causing it to ring out to the glory of God.

☙ ☙ ☙

The soup was hot, the spoon cooled by a slip of breath from the young woman holding it, before delivery to Aaron's lips. He swallowed, savoring the warmth as it slid down his throat. Thinned with water, to ease his ability to swallow and digest it, but rich in flavor, filled with nutrients helping him to heal.

"Do you need a drink of water?" Eliza lowered the spoon into the bowl of venison stew, made up of broth, with bones added to the pot, infusing it with strength.

Aaron shook his head, trying not to stare, the face of his angel dressed in a white shift, drawing his eyes. When he'd first awakened from his fevered sleep, still immersed in dark shadows, he'd called out, hands reaching to hold Chatte. The wick of a lantern, turned up, provided light enough for him to see a face. That of his mother, with dark hair and light eyes, reaching to hold him. His voice calling out to her, asking how she'd found him, telling her he'd lost his way. Lost his soul. Lost his will to live. The image of his mother had taken his hands, her words soothing him as she told him it was all right. That she was there to guide him back to the path. To deliver him to God, who would forgive him his sins. Heal his pain. Make him whole, again.

His vision had cleared, long enough to break the surface of the nightmare of him standing in the well, holding Chatte's lifeless body in his arms, wishing to have her back, to take her away from her life of misery. A face in the shadows had leaned in. Familiar, her words fading away as a thick blanket of darkness fell over him, leaving him slipping back into the depths, clinging to the end of a thin rope, a voice offering to pull him up, to help return him to his life.

Returned now, his vision clear as he studied the young woman in the dim light coming through a small window, open, letting in fresh air. Her hair was up, wrapped in a braid, pinned in place, revealing a long, slim neck above thin framed shoulders. Her face fair, not unlike his mother's, similar enough to account for the vision of having seen her in his fevered dream.

Eliza reached out, touching his face. "Are you with fever again? Can you hear me?"

Aaron reached up, taking her hand, feeling the warmth, holding onto it for a moment before letting go. "I'm fine. Hungry. But feeling more myself." He paused, closing then opening his eyes. "I think."

"My mother tells me you will heal. That it will take time, but you will have full use of your shoulder again. Left with a sizable scar, but able to do—whatever it is you do. Or did, before coming here." Eliza hesitated. "I mean, before my mother brought you here."

"A'neewa." Aaron remembered the other dream, one where he'd seen the woman whose image his father had captured in the second of his handful of journals.

"*Anna*. My mother's name, given her by my father."

Aaron tried to nod, his face pulled into a look of pain by the soreness in his right shoulder. "Anna. Your mother." He looked at his nurse. "And you are?"

Eliza flushed with embarrassment. "I have forgotten my manners, in not having introduced myself." She paused, looking down. "I'm named Eliza. My father—is the minister in this community." She hesitated. "His name is Lukas. Coming here from Germany. Or the old country, as he calls it. The community *here* is temporary. Our home is back in Gnadenhutten, where I was born."

Aaron opened his mouth, another spoonful brought to his lips. He swallowed, then started to ask where he was. Eliza anticipated his question. "I have a brother, named Noah. Twelve years of age." She saw his head shake from one side to the other. "Oh. Yes. You're in a place the English call Sandusky. The upper part, with over one hundred souls. All of them our people, once natives, my father having converted them to our faith. Anna, my adopted mother, having convinced many of her tribe to join us here." Eliza hesitated. "Or rather, back there, in Gnadenhutten. Before the English general ordered us to come here."

"I know her. Your mother." Aaron started to tell her that A'neewa, had been a close friend to his father, then stopped, swallowing the words. Aware, painfully so, of the danger surrounding their utterance should they find their way into the wrong ears. That if A'neewa chose to share knowledge of her relationship with his father, then so be it. "I am grateful to your father for allowing me to rest here." He paused. "And for your kind attention to my needs."

Eliza blushed, delivering another spoonful of soup. "I am but a servant of God, doing as he directs me to do."

"Then I give thanks to God, on behalf of his servant's steady hand." Aaron reached out, testing his right arm, unable to lift it, the damaged muscles limiting its movement. "I am as helpless as a child." He paused. "A rather *weak* child."

"My mother—she says you will need many weeks to recover. Months. Until the spring."

"I will owe much to many by then. My ability to repay, limited. Though I do have money in my pack. Or I did. No idea where it might have gone to."

"It is beneath the bed. Untouched by any of us—*here*."

Aaron nodded, another helping of soup delivered. His stomach rumbled in appreciation, wanting more substantial fare. "Is there any *meat* in the pot, from the animal who lent itself to your effort to feed me?"

"I will need to ask my mother. I can do so now if—" Eliza started to rise. Aaron stopped her with a wave of his left hand. "No need. The broth is more than enough. Besides, I'd like to hear more about this place. Gnaden—"

"Gnadenhutten."

Aaron forced another smile, his strength starting to wane. "Gnadenhutten." He paused, trying to recall the meaning in German, one of many languages learned at his father's knee. "A place of graceful houses." Then he leaned back, accepting another spoonful of soup, watching as the light streaming through the small window caressed the side of the young woman's face, able to forget, for a moment, the tortured memories of the past.

CHAPTER THIRTY-FIVE
HIGHLAND MANOR
WINTER, 1781

The screaming of horses in distress pulled Angus from a deep sleep. His dream of being a tall, dashing highwayman shattering, as soon as he sat up, his short legs failing to reach the floor of a small bedroom next to the manor storeroom. He rubbed his eyes, then jumped down and pushed the door open, a strong wind out of the north buffeting him as he leaned into it, making his way toward the stables.

He stopped, pinned beneath a flash of light, followed by the sound of thunder a few seconds later. An image appeared in his mind's eye, bordered in red, his heart leaping into his throat, knowing if for a sign. He spun about, running into the manor, rousing Declan from his bed, averting his eyes as Lady Marion sat up beside her husband, unclothed, her dark hair falling across her shoulders.

"There are men in the stable. Killing all the horses." He turned away, rushing to the arms closet down the hall, pulling out pistols, beginning to load them, Declan joining him, his breeches pulled up, bare chested.

"You've had another vision—or seen it *true?*"

Angus, focused on the job at hand, nodded, glancing up as Marion came over and began loading one of the pistols, priming it, a wad and ball shoved home. "Aye. A vision of blood. More than likely the men we turned away when the Frenchie came a 'calling, a fortnight ago."

The horses had grown silent, a flicker of light approaching the manor, the front door left open. Declan went over and slammed it shut. "They're heading this way."

Marion grabbed a musket from the closet, beginning to load it while Angus took up position by a small hole in the outside wall, removing a wooden plug, peering through with his head angled to one side to avoid thrust from a dirk.

"Pierre—he would *never* countenance such an attack!" Marion shook her head, handing the long rifle to Declan, taking one of the pistols for herself. She glanced back toward the bedrooms, their daughter asleep in her crib, the heavy wooden shutters secured against the storm, with the thick-paned window latched. "Should I go to Lorna?"

Declan glanced over, having taken up a cautious stance along the opposite side of the alcove entry from Angus. "No. Go to the kitchen door and watch the latch. It's bolted tight, but if you see it move, call out. If it starts to open—step to one side and shoot low, aiming to the center."

Marion complied, her hands trembling, holding the pistol with the butt against her waist to avoid dropping it or having it swept aside by an assailant's hand, as her father had taught her and Meghan to do when they'd come of age.

Then they waited, the large clock in the salon counting off the seconds, minutes, and hours until dawn. The sun, when it finally rose from behind a thick layer of clouds, revealed nothing untoward between the manor and stables. No movement seen of man or beast.

⁂

The stable reeked of blood. Three mares, two stallions, and the team of matched geldings used to pull the carriage, lying dead in their stalls, their throats slit. Angus wiped tears from his eyes, not of sorrow but anger, his jaw clenched as he counted each one as a good friend lost to him.

Declan stood back, keeping an eye on the opening, searching the grounds for any sign of a shadow out of place or motion in the grass of the nearby fields. He felt a shiver run through his spine, no tracks found of man or horses anywhere near the barn and stables. Whoever had done the senseless deed, having left along with the storm in the night. He looked around, seeing Angus on his knees, his fingers dragging something from a layer of blood-soaked hay. "What have you found?"

"A coin. With *French* markings." Angus stood up and came over, holding it out so Declan could see it, the taller man taking it from him, turning it over.

"We'll need check the grounds. For sign of where they came in from—then left. *If* they're not lying low, waiting for us to ease our guard."

Angus shook his head. "They've left their message—and are away to the lowlands."

Declan eyed the young boy, acting much older than his youthful age, carrying himself as if a man, full grown. "And what meaning *is* there, in having slaughtered *seven* innocent animals?"

"That we are *isolated*, here. Unable to move without exposure to attack—if *that* had been their plan." Angus wiped his hands, then yawned. "But it wasn't. Only a message sent us—*this* time."

"Because of the purchase of weapons." Declan lowered his musket. "Because we trespassed, having moved against whoever sent these beasts on two legs." He hesitated, then sucked in a breath, his voice rising. "Do ya think it could have been—"

"It was *not* Pierre—much as I don't trust him." Angus shook his head. "He's been paid for his efforts on Lady Marion's behalf." He paused, hearing a cry from the manor, starting to move toward the opening, recognizing it as Lorna wailing in hunger, his focus back on getting down to the nearest croft to purchase new stock. After removal of the dead animals from the stable, getting them into the ground as soon as possible.

Declan watched as Angus walked over to the tack room and began to take down a thick harness. He went over and helped the boy drag it to the first stall, then followed him to a tool shed where they gathered up ropes and two large sets of block and tackle. Then the two of them returned, collecting a large hammer and several metal posts to drive into the ground to secure the pulleys, using the rope to drag the heavy bodies of the slaughtered beasts outside.

※ ※ ※

Marion checked the stew simmering on the stove. She held Lorna in one arm, a large spoon in her free hand, trying not to picture the small mare, her favorite, as she stirred the mix of fresh horsemeat and vegetables. She repressed a shudder as she relived the moment of seeing the death stiffened bodies falling into the shallow ravine behind the barn, hauled there by use of pulleys and ropes. Dirt thrown over them, the work having lasted throughout the day.

The three of them were bone tired, dirty, and despondent, with daybreak seeing Declan afoot, heading below along a secret path, bypassing the Pinch. Once he reached the nearest croft, he'd mount a horse and spread word among the scattered holdings of the clan. A gathering planned, with a decision made on methods of retaliation, once they identified the location of the perpetrators, and had them well in hand.

Angus came into the kitchen, his face lined with fatigue, jaw set in frustration. "I should ha' been the one to go." He paused, staring at Marion, measuring her height. "If not for the length of my legs, given me by my maker."

"Your backbone more than makes up for any difference in stature, Angus." Marion gave him a serious look. "You're a member of *this* family. All who know you—admiring your will. Your intelligence."

He flashed a wry grin. "Along with my *good* looks." Marion smiled, tears in her eyes as she came over and wrapped her arm around his shoulders.

"Better, having you here. Declan trusting you to protect us. To protect the future of our clan." She handed him Lorna, who cooed in pleasure as he took her, reaching out and taking his finger in her hand, moving it toward her belly for a game of tickle.

Angus complied, the sound of her laughter helping clear the fatigue from his spirit and mind.

※※※

As Declan led a group of men through the back alleys of Glasgow he shook his head, wondering if the information given him was accurate. Three men of quiet nature with cold eyes, their names unknown to the man they'd asked and paid to provide a berth aboard a ship outbound to the colony port of Philadelphia, foolish enough to trap themselves in a warehouse lair. The details of the arrangement passed along by the ears and mouths of men loyal to clan Scott, reaching its laird, who was moving with a smoldering fire in his eyes, leading his hand-picked clansmen to the destination. A hide-a-hole, tucked within the shadowy depths of dozens of small warehouses near the docks.

"The other team is in place. Ready to go on your signal." A short man with quiet eyes met them beneath an overhang, water from an ocean born storm pelting down, leaving large puddles on the muck and mire of the narrow passageway. "They've made no move, other than to open the door to accept delivery of their grub, paid for with French coins."

"The one you've selected for the task?"

The man paused, then grinned, his eyes lit up with anger, showing in the gloom of the late-morning sky, angling between the tall walls of a row of warehouses. "My son. Not much bigger than is your *own* lad."

Declan looked down, seeing Angus clench his jaw. "He's my *man*, second to me as laird of clan Scot." He hesitated a moment. "As good at his job as was our former laird, and not a man to be *trifled* with."

The other man nodded, then held out his hand, offering it to Angus. "My apologies. I spoke without knowing who it was I was standing in front of." Angus took the hand, returning as firm a grip then letting go. "You'd be the one known round these parts as a man of vision, with large, capable hands, topped by a cunning mind."

Declan nodded. "And he has the ken of things, *unseen*. The sight of things to come."

The man stepped back, crossing himself, looking over his shoulder as one of his men came up, making a fist, moving it from side to side. He gave Declan and Angus a nod. "You're to get to the front door, with your weapons readied. My lad—or *your* man, if you choose, to offer the sack to the one who answers. A pistol shoved in his gut and fired, while we toss in two small kegs of powder with short fuses, to create a *wee* bit of a fuss. Then we'll stroll in and have ourselves a conversation." He grinned once again. "A long, *pointed* conversation, working the story from them on who it was, sending them into the highlands to kill your livestock."

※※※

Angus watched without flinching as the man who'd answered his knock on the door writhed in pain on the damp soil of the cavernous interior of the warehouse. The reek of burnt powder drifted in thick columns of gray smoke, hanging in the still air. Three lanterns placed in a triangle around one corner of the building's interior framed two men, sitting with their backs to the wall, tied and gagged. The hair on their faces and heads, burnt away in places, their skin pockmarked by bits of wood from the kegs exploding in front of them as they'd stood with pistols leveled, guarding either side of the door opened by the third man, left dying in a pool of blood.

"Who will it be, given the honor of first questioning?" The man who'd met them outside looked at Declan, then down at Angus.

Declan started forward, a hand across his thighs stopping him. "I'll do it." Angus pulled a long-bladed knife from a sheath at his side, using it to end the misery of the one he'd shot with a slash across his throat. "Not a task for a laird to stoop to." Then he walked over and knelt, facing the other two, his face drawn into a serious expression.

"Now—which one of you *bastards* killed my beautiful, big black steed?"

※※※

Declan swallowed the bile rising into his throat, sickened by the unearthly screams coming from one of the captured men. His feet had been stuck between the close-set rails of a pigsty pen, causing him to emit an incoherent stream of information, spittle flying from his mouth. His hands were tied beneath him, head thrashing the ground as a passel of hungry hogs tore at his flesh, their teeth crushing the bones of his feet and ankles, taking him far beyond the border of what his will could endure. He kept screaming a name, over and again, his eyes wide with horror at what the hogs were doing to him. Willing to say anything to stop the torture. Unaware he was not the one they were looking for answers from.

The other man, standing off to one side, looked down at Angus who was staring back, knife in his hand. "I promise you'll die *clean*. I swear it to ya. My solemn vow—if'n ya choose to tell us true what ya know."

The man responded, his voice a low mumble, barely heard above the mingled screams of the pigs, fighting to get in on the feast, and those of the victim, tourniquets tied tight just above his knees, with the swine already halfway up his shins. "How are you to tell the difference—between the truth and a lie?"

"I'll ken it, when heard." Angus leaned forward, looking up into the man's guarded eyes. "My vow to you that you'll be buried in the hills above, with a clear view into the valley below." Angus looked over his shoulder, watching as two men of the clan lifted the shoulders of the man the pigs were eating, shoving him a bit further into the pen. "Unlike your *friend*."

"It was a short man. With dark skin, fine features, and delicate hands. Deep brown eyes. Quiet voice. Sounding like a fop. Him the one giving us the task. Told to only touch the animals, not any of them as were in the manor."

Declan leaned in, his face pale, hands trembling, having had to step away twice to empty his stomach. The others in attendance left to look away each time he returned, avoiding his eyes, respect shown him as their nominal leader. All of them deferring to Angus, following his orders, knowing where the real power lay, for now.

"His accent—it was not *Parisan?*"

"No. Was not one easily placed. His coloration—like fine leather. Curly hair. With the proper sign shown us, along with a bag of French silvers in hand. It was on *his* orders, what we done." The man hesitated, the screams reaching the limit of what a human throat could produce, the sound seeming to incite the heaving beasts, doubling their efforts. "They were only *horses*, not *loved* ones. *Beasts*, not people. No call for such as—" He pointed with his chin, the first sign of weakness showing in his eyes. "Such as *that*."

Angus glanced up at Declan, who nodded. Then he crossed over to the mutilated man, his back arched like an overstrung bow, severing his throat with a careless slash of his blade. He stepped back, pointing at the pen, watching without remorse as the clansmen tugged the body away from the jaws of the ravenous hogs, then tossed it over the railing, letting it fall in amongst them.

The other man stared, his legs shaking as the short boy came up. "You—you *made* your promise. A *vow* sworn for a clean death."

"Aye. And I'll keep it." Angus grabbed the man's belt, pulling him to his knees. "You'll have a splendid view of the valley floor." Then he cut his throat, stepping back as blood spilled out, watching as the light left the man's staring eyes. "Toss him into one of the *other* pens—amongst some other, hungry hogs."

Declan and the man who'd first met them in the alleyway glanced at one another, them at Angus. Declan was the first to speak. "You —*promised*. You *swore* to it."

"I did indeed swear to it, and he'll get his view." Angus turned and looked at the owner of the croft, an old man, with ancient features carved from the granite of the Scottish hills. "Gather up their shite when they're done with him. Bury it in a hole high above—one with a grand valley view, below."

CHAPTER THIRTY-SIX
REMOTE CABIN
MID-WINTER, 1781

Harold rebuilt the fire in the hearth, adding tinder to the ashes, red dots of burning coals enough to bring it back to life, small sticks added until the flames were robust enough to accept a few split pieces of oak, harvested from a grove of trees sheltering the small cabin where he was living. He'd moved further into the hills, over a day's ride away by horse from the crossroad store and farmhouse where his family were living, aware his presence there could place them at risk.

The cabin, abandoned and in need of repair, suited him, familiar enough in size and shape to the wee croft house in the highlands, lying far away to the east. His needs were simple, met with the snaring of fur-bearing animals, their hides traded with supply houses, along with smoked meat from deer and wild turkeys, taken with a longbow.

Harold knew the day would arrive when someone would whisper something into another man's ear, an echo created that would tug the strand of a web, bringing him to the attention of a group of people holding a list of their failures in one hand, quill pen in the other, eager to place a mark through his name. His fate, ordained. The date, unknown, no longer a concern to him, caring only that his loved ones stayed safely out of reach.

Charles had let him know, when providing him the location of his son, that his reentry into the field of action, however limited in scope, might cause ripples felt in London and cities beyond. Including those in the colonies, the cabal with representatives on both sides of the conflict.

"If you had chosen to remain on the outskirts of Pennsylvania with your head down, shorn as it is—as I told you *then*, you might have been allowed to live out a quiet life." Charles shook his head, giving Harold a rueful smile. "Having exposed yourself *needlessly* in coming this far south to find your son, I can make no such promise to you now."

"None is required or *asked* for." Harold paused, giving Charles a hard stare. "I've come to find Aaron. To verify his state of mind, health, and intentions once this war is at an end. To bring that information to a mother, the lack of it gnawing at her soul, worried by his absence, unable to rest." He hesitated. "My risk to self, acceptable—long as I can bring her *something* to hold onto. Something of her son's, to let her believe him to be alive, and able to come to her when he can."

Now, standing in the small cabin, the windows dark behind slabs of wood nailed in place to seal them from chill winter winds, he looked at his meager belongings, accepting his lot in life. His decision, to come here from Scotland and perform a futile attack on those he wished to stop, or at least delay. A challenge tossed into the mix of politics and power, with the result, his own to bear. Then they had threatened his family, all of them made to suffer for his sin, justifiable as it seemed at the time. It would end here, this time. With his death offered up to settle the debt, owed.

The wind picked up, an eerie howl in the cold dry air, the flames flickering in response as Harold leaned down, using a stick to nudge a pot of cold stew over the glowing coals.

⸸⸸⸸

Sinclair glanced up, the front door opening with Eldritch stepping through. His thin cheeks were red, large hands jammed in his coat pockets. She watched as he went over to the fire in the hearth, holding his hands out, trying to warm them back up.

"Had thought you would be staying over in the city." Sinclair got to her feet and brought over a wool blanket, draping it over his thin shoulders, feeling his body trembling from the frigid wind, rattling the panes of glass in the window on the north side of the farmhouse. "You had the money in hand to find a room."

"Wanted to get back tonight. To save—save you the coins." El's voice was tight with cold. "The horses didn't mind the ride, the stable and a helping of oats enough for them." He flexed his hands, wincing as the heat caused them to sting, the cold slipping away from the tips of his fingers. "They're bedded down. The supplies unloaded."

Sinclair had a cup of tea in one hand, a warm towel in the other, having brought them from the kitchen. She handed El the cup, then wrapped the towel around his neck. "Come sit by the kitchen stove. There's soup I can heat up, and biscuits."

El nodded, holding the teacup to his lips, drinking with his eyes closed. He sighed. "That would more than make up for the ride back." He reached into his pocket, pulling out a large purse. "And I've the coins to pay for the fare, ma'am."

Sinclair smiled, nudging him in his back as she followed him into the kitchen. She made him up a meal, astonished at how much food he was able to put away, for such a thin-framed man. The sound of his voice brought a warmth to her mood, enjoying his stories of the men who'd tried to cheat him, not realizing he'd learned his numbers in lessons taught him by her.

The frequent absences of her husband had become normal, his visits in the evening dwindling away to one every month, his eyes in constant rove, eternally cautious in mood, becoming more withdrawn each time. Only smiling when Patrick was in his arms, or when holding onto his tiny fingers, exploring the first floor of his parent's new house. Always leaving before morning, heading back into the hills. As much a ghost as a man to her, their relationship broken on the shoals of what he'd done, years ago. The remnants left scattered along an emotionless shoreline.

"Is there anything wrong, Lady Sinclair?" El was staring at Sinclair, spoon in his empty bowl, his third helping finished. "You look as if about to cry."

She smiled, then stood up, gathering his dishes, heading to the slate sink, a large metal tank suspended from the wall with spigot attached supplying water to rinse them. "I've been—distracted of late. My mood made dour by the winter weather. My departure to Scotland delayed. Again."

El came over and stood beside her, watching as she used a bar of lye soap to wash the bowl, spoon, and ladle. He grabbed a towel and dried them, putting them away. "Worry for your son, still missing, no doubt adding to your burden." He paused, looking at her, noting the look on her face. "I'm sorry. Spoke without thinking. I apologize for-"

Sinclair reached out, touching his forearm. "It's me who should apologize. I've let things slip, unable to focus. Torn between love for my children. And for my grandchildren, one of whom I've not yet been able to see." She pulled her hand back, looking down.

El stepped away, placing his back to the stove, the heat settling into his body, driving away the final vestiges of cold collected during the long wagon ride back from the city. "*And* your husband, I would imagine. Going without saying how close you've always been." He cleared his throat. "I base those words on the tales told me by your daughter, Lady Meghan."

Sinclair forced a tired smile, her eyes drawn, making her face look older than her years. "We're neither of us *ladies*, Eldritch. Not over here. Not anymore. Just Sinclair—and Meghan. All titles set aside, our hands as scoured and worn as are your own." She rose to her feet and came over, taking one of his hands and turning it palm side up, inspecting a deep cut, nearly healed. "Or perhaps a *bit* less."

El started to pull away, his eyes widening slightly as she held on. "Are—are ya feeling a 'right—Sinclair?"

There was a moment of pause, one that stretched between them until broken by a sound from outside the kitchen door. Eldritch walked over and looked out, seeing no one there. He closed the door and turned around, staring at Sinclair, her face angled down, the spell of loneliness broken. With a short nod of his head, he started to leave.

Sinclair's voice called out, stopping him, his hand on the latch. "I appreciate everything you do, Eldritch. Everything you've done since your arrival. You're a fine man, with a good mind." She paused, her voice softening. "Sleep well. It promises to be a frosty night."

El nodded again, then closed the door and walked away. As he did, a thin smile lifted the corners of his lips, his stride loose, aware how close he was to accomplishing the task assigned him months ago. His financial future assured. A single piece of information left for him to gather before wheels would be set in motion, bringing an end to a long and determined search.

※※※

Harold stood in the shadows of the well-house, watching as the slim man crossed the yard and entered the barn. He'd been standing in the shadows, about to head into the house, when the other man had come from the stable, an impulse causing him to remain silent. He'd watched from the sitting room window as the scene played out, feeling the pinch of frigid wind on the back of his neck. Matched by the feeling in his heart, sensing a hint of danger in the air.

Harold went over to the kitchen door and rapped on it with his knuckles. It swung open, Sinclair standing there with a smile on her perfect lips, falling away as she saw who it was. He stepped forward, causing Sinclair to move aside. "We need to talk."

※※※

Charles sat at a small desk in his rented room, reading the report written by the leader of the nameless men assigned to protect him. The information it contained, provided by the tall, thin man hired to keep an eye on Harold's family, contained the latest updates. Provided on a regular basis, the farmhand trusted with the delivery and purchase of products in the city.

Charles had some idea of the whereabouts of Harold's hide-away in the hills, the rough location kept to himself, for now, waiting a final decision by the cabal of when to close the account, long overdue. Their outreach to him providing wealth and position, with promise of a title of nobility, ensuring his future. The issue of morality, let slip away, with advanced age tugging at his coattails, pulling him into the shadows on the other side of the winding road.

The usefulness of the war hero's son had been an unexpected bonus, one he'd not envisioned when meeting with Harold and his uncle on their home ground. The young man's death an inescapable fate, having helped wither the English armies' flanks. The result of the boy's efforts surpassing all his expectations, making him a danger to the plans of the secretive group, now the war was all but ended. Along with renewed interest in the life still owed by the father, stepping out from the shadows, wishing to protect his family.

Charles pursed his lips, touching the tip of a candle-flame to the papers, holding them by one corner until the flames reached his thin fingers. He let go, watching as the ashes fell to the floor of his room, located at an out of the way inn. He'd wished to have been able to avoid ordering the removal of the deadly and determined young man he'd known since his birth. A bow and bloody sheath brought back, his body buried in a rockfall, according to a second group of deadly, unnamed men sent out to uncover the fate of the first group. Though Charles sensed he was still out there, somewhere. A wounded wolf, lurking in the hills. One he would eventually locate and use again, or eliminate, if still alive.

He turned his attention to another element of his latest plan, still waiting to hear from the leader of the men hired to deliver a pointed message into the highlands. His arrival a week overdue, with winter storms causing havoc with shipping schedules all along the colonial coastline. From Philadelphia on north to Boston, and beyond.

CHAPTER THIRTY-SEVEN
UPPER SANDUSKY
MID-WINTER, 1781

The sound of a horse passing by, harnessed to a small wagon, drew A'neewa's attention. She swung her head away from the washing of her adopted son's hair, dark like her own. The boy squirmed, soap in his eyes, his small hands forming into tight fists as he struggled to avoid calling out.

A'neewa smiled, having told Noah how a warrior must learn to bear pain, without making noise. "But I'm a *Moravian*." He'd looked down, his eyes on the ground. "We are not to—to—to—" Then he stopped, taking a deep breath, letting it out slowly like his new mother had taught him to do. "I'm supposed to be a follower. To be at *peace* with others. Turning the other cheek." He'd glanced up at her, his beautiful brown eyes open. "Not to be a—one of *them*. A warrior."

"Then practice being at peace—when troubled by pain, tiredness, or doubt. Trust in yourself, as you strengthen your will."

"And then I'll be one—one of *them*? A *warrior*?"

A'neewa had circled his shoulders with her arm, pulling him in, drinking in the scent of his hair, his skin. A tug in her womb brought tears to her eyes, forbidden to fall. "You'll be the *greatest* one of them all."

She smiled now, as she poured water over his head. "There. All rinsed. You can open your eyes, young warrior."

Noah relaxed his face, eyes blinking as A'neewa handed him a towel. "Thank you, Anna."

A'neewa leaned down, kissing the top of his head, the scent of balsam resin in her nose. "You were *very* brave." She angled her head, giving him a sly smile. "Such an act deserves a reward. A bit of honeycomb, I think—with a piece of bread to put it on." Her eyes narrowed as she considered the wheat remaining in the barrels coerced by her husband from the British fort's warehouse. Every kernel vital, helping see them through until spring, when the ground would warm enough for planting.

"Hard work is its *own* reward." Noah looked around, to see if his sister or father were nearby. "But honey and bread *are* part of God's bounty, provided us. And I *did* get stung, climbing the tree. And then worked so hard, helping to grind the wheat."

A'neewa forced a smile as she led the lean-framed boy toward a lodge, erected behind the storehouse her people used for their church on Sundays. She took his hand, the bond between them as strong as any she'd ever felt before. A song slipped across her full lips, one sung by the native women who'd raised her after the death of her mother and siblings from the pox, the disease devastating her village and hundreds of others. A story of sowing, harvesting, Of hearth and feast. And death, with the threat of starvation hanging over them. Part of the circle of the Great Mother's arms, wrapped around each of her children, in turn.

Later that afternoon A'neewa and Lucas walked arm in arm, making their way back from a visit to a family with a sick child. An illness with the potential to become serious. A mild fever and cough, exacerbated by hunger, seen to with a poultice and herb tea to soothe the throat and sinuses. Each family, suffering from similar symptoms, having arrived too late in the season to plant crops in the poor soil given them by the English to farm. British troops forcing them from their homes in Gnadenhutten, leaving behind acres of fertile fields with abundant crops, left to rot on the vine.

Lukas looked over at his wife, her hair in a braid, coiled atop her head, gleaming in the clear, winter chilled air. She held a haube, a basic form of head covering for women, between her fingers. He started to ask her to put it on, it being their custom for women to cover their heads when in public. Then he decided to swallow his words, aware of how much she'd already given up of her people's heritage and beliefs, having agreed to join the Moravian church, before accepting his offer of betrothal, becoming his wife.

A'neewa, a full foot shorter than her husband, glanced up with a questioning look, gazing into his light-colored eyes, smiling when he tried to hold her gaze, then looked away. "You are wanting to remind me again of the hat." She held it up, the sunlight passing through the light material. "Is it because you are afraid of me getting with—" She paused. "Of getting a cold?"

Lukas smiled, squeezing her hand, another of his people's customs called into question by the honed mind of the woman he could not imagine living without. "No. Your robust health is a truly a gift from God. As well your skill with medicines, with incredible insight into various maladies and the herbs needed to cure them." He paused. "To help save my—*our* people."

A'neewa's face lost its smile, her small hand clasped in his. Lukas stopped, taking a moment to look around the community of shelters built by the efforts of all. Each of them held a family formed from people native to the Ohio region. A hundred and more, mixed in with a handful of people who'd come with him years earlier when God led him to the rich farmland of the basin floor where they'd created a settlement. The English troops coming along a few months ago, with their own view of what God intended, insisting he and his flock migrate further north, closer to their sphere of military influence.

Lukas sighed, wondering how many would survive to partake of the Lord's gifts when mid-summer arrived. "Your beliefs—are not *much* different than my own. Tied more directly to the land. To the natural order, if you will—but consistent in seeking out what God has to offer those who are open to what he provides."

A'neewa nodded, then put on her hat, purposely leaving it off center, drawing another smile from the man she'd come to care for. Seeking him out, offering to bring those of her people willing to make the journey to his settlement. To enter his church with bowed heads, willing to learn new ways of farming, joining them with their own. To become educated in the strange customs and language of his faith. The years between then and now had strengthened their commitment to each other. His daughter, Eliza, no longer motherless, and the arrival of Noah, part of the familial glue binding them together.

"We've *both* made our adjustments, husband. As needed." She warmed him with a wide smile. "I'm fortunate to have found you. My path, straighter now—in walking beside you."

Lukas swallowed, overcome by his emotions, having thought his God to have abandoned him in the loss of his wife, recognizing the miracle of his sending another in her place, bringing along many of her people. No longer lost, wandering in the wilderness, having found their way to the everlasting glory of God's eternal love.

※※※

Aaron swung his right arm in a slow circle, feeling tightness in his shoulder. His wound had healed, though his muscles were still weak, leaving his movements stiff. He scowled, frustrated at being unable to perform many of the chores he was determined to do, wanting to repay A'neewa and her husband for having saved his life.

Eliza reached out, touching his shoulder. "It will not be long until you are back to where you were. Spring will find you alongside us in the fields, planting seeds. Gathering wood from the forest." She lowered her gaze, along with the tone of her voice. "Going to church—with our family." Then she paused, looking up with a shy smile. "With me."

Aaron turned, facing her. His face was still pale, still as thin as when A'neewa had brought him there on a litter, with fevered eyes. They were clear now, reflecting the color of the sky. "I walk you there, before each service. Then escort you home, after." He leaned in. "Would you have me do *more* than I'm capable of?"

"I would have you more capable *of* it." Eliza sighed, shaking her head. "I know it would help you to heal." She touched the side of his head, his hair curled around his ears in waves of black. "In here." She moved her hand onto his chest, over his heart. "And in here." Then she stepped away, her hands clenched at her side. "It pains me, the hurt I see in your face. In the way you look toward the east and stare, without blinking, as if able to see—something." She slowly turned around. "Or *someone*."

"You see a lot—for one of so few years."

"I am to be seventeen. In May."

Aaron leaned back slightly, trying to look away as a flush of blood colored his cheeks, torn between walking away or taking her into his arms. Doing neither, locked in place by another image slipping through his mind. Of another woman as slim in build, with gaping wound in her throat.

The world spun around, his knees trembling as he reached out for the back of a chair, holding onto it as he struggled to breathe.

He felt a hand on his, another on his shoulder, a voice in his ear, telling him to let go of his pain. Joined by another in his other ear, deeper in tone, two pairs of hands helping him to sit, cradling him as he leaned forward, a memory of his mother and sister covering him with their bodies, sheltering him from an icy rain, holding him in a highland valley, the image of two men with their eyes staring into the sky overwhelming him.

A'neewa gave her daughter a look letting her know to be silent. The two of them holding onto the grievously wounded man who was struggling to come to grips with what he'd been through. Holding onto him until he took a deep cleansing breath and began telling them his story.

⚜⚜⚜

Lukas offered Aaron a small glass of wine, poured from a bottle used for communion, refused with a shake of the younger man's head. The minister stared at the narrow neck of the bottle, then sighed, bottoming the glass, his hand trembling as he placed it on the pew between them. The interior of the church was dark. The day overcast, with an icy mist coating the dead grass outside.

Lukas leaned back, considering what Aaron had told him, trying to find a place for it in his role as both spiritual leader and a father. Aware the damaged man's dark aura had drawn Eliza to him, her role as caregiver creating a strong bond between them. He finally broke the silence, his voice low, and carefully measured. "This woman—Chatte. She was a child fed a continuous meal of hatred. Not of her own making, but that of her grandmother's, transferring it onto her shoulders to bear."

Aaron nodded, his head lowered, hands clenched between his legs. His recalling of the events since leaving Glasgow had drained him of his meager reserves of energy, left feeling weighted down with fatigue. His memories, a deep well he was unable to climb out of.

"You *released* her—released her from the demons placed within her by another. Twisted, by events outside her understanding or control." Lukas turned toward Aaron. "Her sins, *absolved*. Her innocence—returned to her. A child of God, again."

"I *wish* to believe that." Aaron sighed. "I *do*." He lifted his head, looking at the man who'd agreed to take him in. Then his eyes slid away in shame. "I *allowed* the actions, taken by her hand. I could have —*should* have stopped them."

"Yes. You *should* have, Aaron. And you *didn't*. A dark and depthless sin to carry with you. One *poisoning* your soul. A miracle—you managing to find your way to a woman who knew your father. Who helped, with the grace of God, to save *his* life, thereby begetting your own." Lukas reached out, laying his hand on the tortured man's upper arm. "A *miracle*—from *God*. Leading you back into the light. Giving you an opportunity to make amends. To *atone*. To bend your knee, your back to *his* service. To become part of a community—one that will not *judge* you. Open to you becoming a member of a family, willing for you to join it."

Aaron shook his head, looking into the shadows. "Wolf." He stiffened his posture, jaw clenched. "That is what my men named me. What they called me. The Wolf." He slowly turned and faced the man who was offering him a chance for redemption, offering the embrace of people dedicating themselves to his beliefs. "And you would have me become a lamb of God. Again."

"*Yes!*" Lukas took Aaron's hand. "A lamb, discarding the pelt of the wolf. Worn to shield you from the death that so many others suffered through. Casting it off, stepping forward into the light of God's love. For *you*." He paused, lowering his voice as he leaned in. "*My* love for you. The love of a woman you know as A'neewa—*her* love for you. And that of my children, Noah, and Eliza. My daughter's love for you evident, along with that of all the others of our community."

"And how am I to do that? To let it fall away—along with all the death dealt out by these?" Aaron held up his hands, staring at them. "All the horror seen. The sight of men—*stripped* of their flesh, *screaming* for God to *save* them. While I watched. Sickened by it—and doing *nothing* to stop—to *stop* the butchery."

"By accepting the love of *one* more person." Lukas paused. "Your own. For the man you once were and can be again."

"Just like that? Forgiving myself, letting it go as if it never happened?" Aaron shook his head, tears in his eyes, hands trembling.

"*I* did." Lukas nodded. "I lost my wife and *cursed* God for having taken her from me. From me and my child. I *disavowed* him in my grief. *Lost* my way. Stepped away from the light, wallowing in the shadows of despair." He stopped, eyes closed, swallowing as he felt a wave of anger rise, then ebb away. "God gave me a sign. A second chance to redeem my soul. Sending me an angel dressed in deerskin. Coming to me from out of the woods, asking for my help to save her people. To guide them to salvation."

"A'neewa."

"Yes. Now known as Anna. Willing to let go of her beliefs. Her way of life. Her people's heritage. Finding her faith, and in doing so, restoring *mine*." Lukas paused, his eyes gleaming, a smile on his face. "*My* miracle, then." He looked at Aaron. "Another, in her having found you in the wilderness, bringing you back from a dark doorway. Healing you. A second chance for you to rediscover the innocent child within. And it starts by forgiving yourself. Forgiving your sins, as God does for those who come to him openly, asking for his love, offering their own in return."

Aaron stared back, balanced on the knife blade of the past and the present, his pain welling up as he pictured Chatte's beautiful face, seeing the child within her, watching her two brothers slain. Her innocence wrenched from her by mindless violence. Wanting to believe her saved, standing in the light of love. Wanting to believe in his own salvation. Understanding, now, the pain hidden behind his own father's eyes, always there, darkening his mood on the brightest of days.

"What do I—how am I to *do* this?"

"Get on your knees and ask God's forgiveness. Allow him into your heart. Into your *new* life." Lukas knelt on the floor; his hands clasped in prayer. Aaron joined him there, repeating the words, feeling the weight of the past two years begin to slip away.

☙ ☙ ☙

A'neewa stood in the back of the church, listening while her husband and the son of the man she had not allowed herself to love murmured in prayer. Then she turned and walked outside into the chill, damp air, a beaded leather bag carried in her hand, containing the finger bones taken from the native men who'd raped her, after killing her first husband and their son. The men she'd tortured years ago, in a previous life, etching their names with the tip of a honed blade onto each bone. When she'd lived and walked in the Great Mother's world, where nature held all the answers to questions asked by a child whose mother, sisters, and brother had died from the pox.

She went into the edge of the trees, kneeling in the leaf-littered soil, her dress pulled up above her knees. Then she reached up, undoing the leather strap holding a leather sheath in place against her upper thigh, holding it up to the dim light of the sun hidden above a layer of gray-faced clouds.

She pulled out the knife and used it to dig a hole, deep enough to hold the bag of bones. Then she placed the knife, beaded bag, and the last of her people's beliefs into the ground, covering them up, giving herself over to the God of her husband. Of her new family, found.

When she rose to her feet, it was as Anna, reborn, releasing the name A'neewa, given her by the women of her tribe.

CHAPTER THIRTY-EIGHT
REMOTE CABIN
EARLY SPRING, 1782

Harold unpacked his things, taking them out of a leather satchel and placing them out on a small bed, fashioned from a sheet stretched over gunny sacks filled with a thick mixture of dry moss. The clothes no longer needed. Used to alter his appearance as he'd made his way into the city of Philadelphia, having followed Eldritch as he'd taken the wagonload of supplies to the markets there.

He'd remained out of sight, staying to the edges of the roadway, tucked into the shadows of buildings as the thin-bodied man finished his circuitous route. The wagon soon emptied of farm produce, handmade clothing, and other goods, then refilled with various trade items brought back to the crossroads store. The man had moved with a loose, confident stride, entering a public house, gone for less than the ringing of a church bell before reappearing, a small purse secured at his belt, a pleased look on his face.

Harold had stayed locked in the shadows of an alleyway, head down, eyes watching the door of the busy meeting place as a steady flow of men passed through it, doing business, or simply enjoying a drink. A familiar face finally showed in the door, glancing to either side before stepping out.

Harold watched as Charles headed toward the docks without looking back as two men, dressed in plain clothing, separated themselves from the crowd and moved in, flanking the short, thin-framed man, their eyes searching every shadow for potential threat to the one they were there to protect.

The realization Charles was behind the infiltration of Sinclair's commercial enterprise didn't come as a surprise to Harold. Too many coincidences over the past two years had taken place, when left to the roll of life's dice. He could feel a familiar tug to his sixth sense, as if an unlit fuse leading to a keg of powder. Eldritch, with match in hand, ready to ignite an explosion of violence. One Harold was determined would not touch his loved ones, having already lost his son to Charles manipulation of events.

He'd waited until dusk, then departed the city limits, head down in a steady pace, knowing he had work left to do. Another message sent to master puppeteers, with strings held in their tentacled fingers. A message sent in blood. After giving his wife a final warning, one he knew she would be deaf to. Determined to make her face, then see the truth, staring her squarely in the face.

⁂

"You have *no* reason to be jealous. No *right!*" Sinclair rounded on Harold, her eyes bright with anger.

"I hold *no* such feeling in his regard, believe me. Your life—your *own* to live. As you will, with *whomever* you choose." Harold returned her stare, looking at her, seeing the same young woman he'd fallen in love with. The same wife who'd given him three incredible children, left standing in a bedroom door, heartbroken when he'd told her he had to leave. Without providing a reason, or when or whether he'd return. Not certain, then, if he would return, his Grand Da's vision ever in his mind. "I am here to warn you, sensing there is *more* to the tale then he's told you. That's all."

"You and your *senses*—can *go* to *hell*, taking you along *with* them. I've no more use for them then I—then I do for *you*." Sinclair stepped closer, looking him directly in the eyes. "I asked for *one* thing, husband.

To find and bring back to me my son. Alive—or in a coffin. That I could return with him to where he belongs. Where his spirit could heal, allowing him to touch the sky once more."

Tears fell down her cheeks, her beautiful lips trembling. "Instead, you brought me his *journals*. Placed in my hands, telling me not to read them. And that, when I *did*, I would not find the boy I once knew *in* them. That I would find a man self-described as a *monster*—with *blood* on his hands. And—if I somehow *did* manage to read them through, that I should try and see *past* the gore. The terrible things described. The horrors revealed. That I would come to know each side of war's leaden coin, revealed. Of love *and* hate. Of the glory of sacrifice to a cause, to one's friends—along with what's required of men to try and *survive* it. Seeing in the words, in the images revealed—the *depths* people must go to within themselves—discovering what they're *capable* of doing. Or of simply standing by, watching it done on behalf of a *cause*. Praying it will be worth the cost to their souls."

Harold stepped forward, his expression hardening. "You'll hear what I have to say, then gone I'll be." He waited while Sinclair worked her way to nodding, her arms crossed on her chest, eyes dark with a mix of anger and hurt.

"I accept *all* your pain, caused by my actions taken. All the damage done to you. To my son. To my father. My uncle and aunt. To my daughter, Meghan." He paused, looking past Sinclair, seeing an army of other's lining up to receive his heartfelt apology. "I tried to climb an impossible mountain, hoping to reach its top and find a world where right would triumph over wrong. Losing my balance, falling, taking you—and everyone else with me."

He took a deep breath, letting it out in a long sigh, looking at Sinclair, seeing her as if for the first time, hand clenched on the locket beneath a black brocade of fabric, silver-gray eyes, framed in curls of ebony-dark hair cupped around her ears. "I have loved you, since seeing you poised in a doorway in Bath. Loved you more than life itself. And let go of you, in believing myself a man of destiny. As if one man could ever change things. Sacrificing your love for me on the altar of my ego. Based on a vision given me. One I made to happen. Bringing death to a valley in the highlands."

Sinclair eased her stance. "You are the man you were *born* to be. No different than our son. Or any others, doing what *they* believe in."

Harold shook his head. "I am a fool, with teacup in hand, trying to hold back the tide." He gave her a soft look that broke the dam of her will, tears flowing from her eyes, lips trembling as her shoulders began to shake. "You need to go. Return to Scotland. Take our daughter and grandson with you. Find Marion, and her family. Leave this place for the months left until this war ends."

"And what then?" Sinclair stared at him.

"Return. Build new houses here, providing women the same opportunities offered there. A fresh start. For them and their children. Making a place here for the generations of our family to come. Each of them building on the foundation *you* will create, making up for the one I blew apart, killing those who would poison the soil with seeds of greed." He stepped forward, taking her hands. "They are *still* there. Will *always* be there, subverting man's inherent belief in the greater good. Of family, and community. Of clan."

"And you? Will you come back to us? Help us to—"

"Nae. I'm to go on a *different* journey. One leading any threat remaining to you, away." Harold smiled. "One final effort made to right as many of the wrongs I've done as I can."

Sinclair leaned forward, kissing him, then placed her hands on his shoulders, turning him toward the door. "Go—and find your ending on your *own*, following your twisted path to *wherever* it takes you. Go and sleep with the ghosts with which you've been living. All those killed in actions taken on behalf of your fruitless cause." She shook her head, then turned away, taking a lantern from the kitchen table, carrying it with her as she climbed the stairs to her cold bedroom on the upper floor of the farmhouse.

Harold nodded, then stepped outside, closing the door behind him. He took a moment to look across the yard, gazing at the store, and the barn lying just beyond. With a heavy sigh he lowered his head and started toward the stable.

Eldritch awoke from a pleasant dream where he was astride a fine steed, the wind of a summer day on his face, riding around the edges of his large estate. Then he opened his eyes, aware the horses in their stalls outside his small room were awake, the sound of their unsettled movements having roused him. He started to sit up, brought to a stop by the feel of a hand on his neck, fingers clamped around his throat, constricting, a knife held in front of his widened eyes, visible in the first blush of dawn's light showing through a fly speckled pane of glass.

"We've a friend in common, you and I." The voice was familiar, causing his eyes to widen further as he tried to reach up and remove the stone-cold hand, desperate to talk his way out of what was about to happen. Harold didn't hesitate, squeezing his fingers, crushing the younger man's windpipe, holding on until his heart ceased to beat, his thrashing of arms and legs to no avail, death finding him the same as any other. Once the duplicitous man was dead, he ran his hand under the mattress, pulling out the purse handed him by Charles. Payment for information gathered, with one strand of a vast web now left untethered.

He slowly counted out thirty silver coins from the bag, placing them on the dead man's chest, cupped between his death stiffened hands. Then, after offering a prayer for his family's safety, he spilled the rest on the floor and slipped outside, walking away, without looking back.

🌿🌿🌿

Harold hung the empty satchel on a wooden peg beside the door of the small cabin. Then he made himself a cup of tea, using the last of the leaves, brewing it strong. Consumed around bites of a dried biscuit. He savored the plain meal, comparing it to the sharing out of bread and wine, smiling at the image of himself sitting alongside the prophets.

It had been a month since he'd made his final goodbye to Sinclair. Enough time for whispers to find the ears of men without names, lurking in the local area, asking questions, willing to pay for information shared. He knew they would come for him this day, eager to balance their books, with a recent debt added to their side of the scale.

Three men, he decided. Or four. Enough to see it done. Enough to bring the needle of the scale back to dead center. He went outside, watching as a flock of crows rose from their nightlong roost, stirred to flight by movement in the woods. A few minutes later a flock of turkeys joined the forced migration, flying away from a path winding its way uphill, ending in the clearing he was standing in.

Harold nodded, then bent to work, preparing himself for the storm of violence heading his way

※※※

Harold didn't bother looking up, having sensed the men as they made their stealthy approach. He dropped his saw, reaching for his bow, a dozen arrows near to hand. Enough he thought, to make them earn their pay. The silver going to those lucky or skilled enough to survive.

The first man appeared to the left of the small opening, a second to the right. A call from a red squirrel from behind let Harold know a third man was there, leaving him time enough to draw and release one arrow before two muskets or pistols would fire, one certain to make a mark on his body. He tossed an imaginary coin, coming up left, the arrow released before the man could finish planting his foot, halfway through a careful step into the open, the shaft catching him mid-step, pinning his coat back against the side of his body, the arrowhead driven deep into his chest.

The hiss of a ball sighed past his head as Harold dropped to his knees, another arrow plucked and nocked, turning to fire at the man coming from behind, the shaft catching him dead center in his upper chest, causing him to tumble forward, a pistol flying from his hand.

A searing thud in his left shoulder spun Harold around, the bow dropped, his hand filled with a pistol drawn from his belt, aiming, and firing at the man on the right, darting toward him, firing a second pistol as he came on. The two shots came as one, both balls finding their mark, ending one man's life immediately, a hole torn in his throat, exiting through the back of his neck. Harold, struck in the upper right chest, falling back onto the ground.

Charles came around the small cabin, nodding at another man who stepped out from the other side. "Do *not* end him. Not yet." The other man lowered his pistol, keeping it pointed toward the dying man, lying prostrate on the ground, staring up at the sun, laboring to breathe, his lung punctured, a foam of red blood on his lips.

Charles came over and knelt beside Harold, gently removing the pistol from his unresisting hand, checking that his other hand was empty. Then he leaned over, looking his friend in the eyes. "You were expecting me."

Harold forced himself to focus, feeling his life draining away, at peace with the results of his efforts, meaningless as they were in the greater scheme of his life to date. "I—was. Having—having seen—you, in—the city. With Judas."

"Dead, I assume. Not having heard from him this past week." Charles watched as Harold nodded. "Your family, all those left to you, are *safe*. My promise made—not one hair on their heads touched by the least of an ill wind. I *swear* it."

"And I am to—" Harold coughed, a small rivulet of bright red blood slipping from one corner of his mouth. "Accept—you believe in God?"

"As a matter of fact—I *do*. though which *one* is still in debate, dependent on what's offered me in return when I meet them. Along with the *requirements* for entry, into their form of paradise."

"I'm sure—you'll know—soon enough." Harold coughed again, his face growing pale. He reached up, touching his coat pocket. "My father's pipe. Already packed. A—final request."

Charles started to reach for it, stopping when the nameless hired man hissed a warning. He ignored him, pulling out the briar pipe, lighting it with a strike from the flint of Harold's dropped pistol. He placed the stem in his mouth and inhaled, bringing the bowl to a steady glow, then folded Harold's fingers around it, helping him place it between his lips. He watched as the man he'd always had the utmost respect for inhaled, a thin column of smoke drifting from his pale lips, his hand falling away to his side, the pipe clasped in his lifeless hand.

Charles looked at his scowling associate, standing a few feet away, staring down at the three slain men lying stretched out on the bloodstained ground. He smiled up at him. "An *amazing* man, this one. To have struck such deadly *blows* to your anonymous group of friends."

"He's *dead*." The man leaned down, his nose twitching. "Or near enough to it." He paused, turning his head to one side, his eyes narrowed. "Do you smell that?"

Charles reached out and gently closed Harold's eyes. "Gunpowder *does* have a unique scent. Though not one to my *liking*."

The unnamed man suddenly straightened up and turned to leap away. The ground erupting beneath all three of them, tossing their bodies into the air, one of them already dead. All of them left pinwheeling in the air as lead balls sliced through them, tearing them to pieces, leaving behind a red mist that gently settled onto the blades of grass, growing in the small glade.

CHAPTER THIRTY-NINE
UPPER SANDUSKY
EARLY SPRING, 1782

Anna leaned back, her knees pressed into a patch of sun-warmed soil, having finished planting several rows of herbs in a circular pattern. She used the back of one hand to wipe the sweat from her forehead, her eyes searching for Noah, who'd gone to get a bucket of water from the community well. Her daughter walked by arm in arm with Aaron, the young man now back to full health. His mood had improved since his conversion, though there were moments when he would stop and stare into the woods, Eliza finding him, slipping her hand into his, tugging him back toward the light.

Anna knew they would need to be married, and soon. Her daughter in full blossom, eager to have a husband at her side, a child in arm, with a home of her own built by the community as a gift to them both. She smiled, feeling a warmth flowing through her from the sun overhead, absorbed from the earth beneath her legs, listening to the sighing of wind in the trees, new leaves opening to the mid-spring day.

A wave of red energy rose from within her, coloring her vision with a blanket of shimmering light. Harold stood before her, a smile on his face as he reached out, before dissolving into a flock of swallows, darting through the sky overhead. Anna blinked away tears, hearing her son shouting something to his sister as he struggled back with a heavy container of water.

Anna leaned down, placing her hands on the ground, bowing her head, allowing her tears to fall on the soil, knowing her vision had come true. That she would see Harold a final time. That he was now gone from this world. Gone from her life, having reached the end of his path.

Lukas came up to her from behind, his steps recognized, moving with a slow thoughtful pace as he hummed a psalm under his breath. He coughed, letting her know he was there, not wanting to surprise her. Anna sat up, turning to look at him without trying to hide her tears.

"I heard your approach, husband. I have not let go of *all* my native wiles."

Lukas gave her a quiet smile. "And I would not want that to happen, wife. We are each of us God's children, whether we have taken him fully into our hearts or not." He paused, glancing over at his daughter and Aaron, the two of them standing beneath an oak tree, having another lengthy conversation. "Those two never seem to run out of things to talk about."

"And neither do you—always with words in your mind, talking to yourself if no one else is around, busy writing your next sermon." Anna took his hand, squeezing it, causing him to wince.

He gave her a searching look, having noted the gleam in her eyes. "Are you troubled, wife—by their relationship?"

Anna shook her head. "*No*, husband. These are tears of celebration, at the thought of new lives to come, filling the void left behind from those who've passed from our grasp."

"Speaking of the filling of voids—I am planning to send our native parishioners to Gnadenhutten, to gather what they might from the fields we were forced to abandon last fall."

"Is that what God has shown you?"

Lukas rubbed his stomach. "It is what *hunger* requires us to do, sickness continuing to spread from lack of food." He paused, seeing their son pick up the unwieldy container and start toward them again. "Along with what God has taught us. That he helps those who help themselves." He turned and looked down at her. "I would ask that you lead them there and back. Taking Aaron with you. To hunt for meat along the way."

"And—Eliza?" Anna eyed Lukas, knowing he was not always attentive when it came to his children's need for parental guidance.

"She will stay here and tend to her brother, encouraging him to his studies. To keep him—"

"Distracted?" Anna shook her head. "He will not abide it long, then be back at your heels, nipping at them with endless questions."

"Then *I* will abide it—as best I can. His health still a concern to me." Lukas fixed Anna with a look suggesting he'd made up his mind, leaving her to return his gaze with a nod of her head, accepting his decision.

"I will let Aaron know. And begin preparing the wagons and supplies needed to get us there and back."

Lukas attempted a smile, failing, his lips pressed in concern. "I would not choose this course of action were it not needed to help see us through until we plant new crops here, waiting for them to come into full growth. My requests for additional aid from the English—having come to naught."

"They see us as a threat, as do the colonials, leaving us caught between them." She eyed her husband, seeing the worry in his eyes. "When people refuse to support one side in a conflict against the other, they are not *trusted* by either."

"God has a *plan*." Lukas reached out, taking her into his arms, feeling the strength of her will, the warmth of her body, aware she still harbored doubts, but was willing to place her trust in him, if not yet fully in God. "And we must walk the path he's placed in front of us."

※※※

Aaron released an arrow, watching as it slipped between two trees, penetrating to the fletching in the ribs of a large bear. It roared in response, turning to bite at what had struck it, jaws popping, saliva flying, its breath a gray fog of anger as it snapped its teeth, looking for something to strike out at. It spun in several circles, its legs finally giving out, falling in a puddle of black fur, mouth agape, eyes wide as it let go of its life force, returning it to nature.

Aaron walked up, using the end of his newly fashioned longbow to tap the huge beast in its jaw, ready to spring back if it showed any reaction. When the animal remained still, he knelt, safely out of range of its claws, offering a prayer for its safe journey along the path. One A'neewa had taught him, explaining how the Great Mother breathes life into the world, then inhales, receiving it back.

Noah came out from under the shadows of a thick-limbed spruce tree, sent up it by Aaron to keep him out of the way while the bear worked its way into the bait pile. His eyes were wide in awe as he came over and stood beside Aaron. "He's *huge!*" Then he turned and looked at Aaron. "It's a *male*, right?"

"A boar. The females—called *sows*." Aaron smiled, the boy's head at a height with his as he knelt beside him, studying the slain beast. Noah's tawny skin, part of his native heritage, seeming to glow in the dim light filtered by a thick canopy of leaves. Eliza had told him how Anna had convinced her father to add the orphaned child to their home a few years ago. Kept busy ever since teaching him a new language, and how to read and write. Aaron reached over and clamped a hand on Noah's shoulder. "And the young ones are called *cubs*."

"Like *me?*" Noah looked at Aaron, who shook his head.

"No. You're no cub. More of a yearling."

"Will you carry it back to the community?" Noah eyed the large body of the dead bear. "Or we could bring a wagon, here." He craned his head, looking around, the woods thick, without room to maneuver a team of horses through them.

"We'll dress it out, letting it cool. Then come back with five men and a thick pole. Carrying it out on our shoulders." Aaron saw the question in the boy's eyes. "You'll come too, shouldering a musket in case there's another bear around. We'll need someone to protect us from attack."

Noah nodded, his eyes lighting up at the prospect of carrying a weapon. Familiar with the process of loading, though not yet having fired a single round. He turned and gave Aaron a firm look. "So—it's a knife needed now to get the first part done." He reached down and touched the hilt of a small knife in a stiff leather sheath, given to him by the woman he called mother.

Aaron nodded, suppressing a smile, knowing the boy would soon be leaning over a puddle of his breakfast, hands pressed in the soil as he emptied his stomach. He also knew Noah would wipe his mouth, returning to the chore, determined to see it through, with another hard lesson learned.

⚘⚘⚘

The first wagon was small, but sturdy. Pulled by a mis-matched pair of horses, it lurched ahead along a weather-beaten trail, a small contingent of native men leading the way. Another wagon, larger, but of less robust construction, followed behind, with a single, thick-bodied horse harnessed in place. A large group of people filled in the space between, made up of women and several handfuls of children old enough to lend a hand in the gathering of winter crops, along with several babes at the breast. The men, split into two groups, moved ahead and behind the column, their voices singing psalms as they made their way back toward their abandoned homes. Their hands carried rough-fashioned spears, denied use of more lethal weapons by the English, who'd allowed them to leave, having come to trust their neutrality in the affairs between King and colonies.

Anna wore a gentle smile on her face, though she felt a shiver slip through her. The weather was clear, the land warming beneath an unblemished sky, the skin on her face and lower arms heated by the sun as she passed through a narrow place in the trail they were following. She kept her hands clasped in front of her, looking down, trying to regain the lightness of her spirit, searching for it in the sound of her people's laughter.

The bear Aaron had killed, along with a handful of deer, had helped provide food enough to keep the wolf of starvation from their door. They had secured the tools and supplies needed to harvest the abandoned crops in Gnadenhutten, in the hopes of returning with whatever they could scrounge from the fields. Seeds collected, used to plant new fields back in what the English troops had named Captive's Town.

"I can hear your thoughts. *Anna.*" Aaron had slipped into place alongside her, unnoticed. "They are a match to mine, though I have never seen the place we're aimed toward." He slowed his pace, matching hers. "Your husband seemed optimistic in the success of this adventure. Sending so many, so far, in the hopes of recovering enough food to make the trip—" He paused. "Worthwhile."

"God has a—"

"*Plan.* Yes. I know, having heard it myself from Eliza whenever I questioned the sense of this—of Lukas's *translation* of what he believes God to have told him."

"You too, are part of his plan. God's plan. In having made your way to where I found you. Where I was able to save you."

"The same way you saved my father." Aaron gave her a solemn look. "Was it God's plan then—or the Great Mother's?"

"I was led by whatever means you care to assign the credit to." Anna shrugged. "I am willing to believe it to have been the work of God." She gave Aaron a warm smile. "Then, *and* now."

Aaron looked away, then spun around, a shout from the back of the column calling his name. He stepped away from the trail, letting the others pass by, watching as Eliza came up, holding the hand of Noah, who was walking beside his sister, shamefaced, looking anywhere but up.

"It seems we have added *another* set of helping hands to our group of harvesters." Aaron leaned forward, giving Eliza a hug, holding onto her for a moment, allowing himself to take in the scent of her hair before letting go. "And he's managed to gather up a beautiful *sister* along the way, further brightening our journey."

Eliza put her hands on her hips, giving Noah a firm look. "He disappeared, the next morning after you left. Taking me all the next day to catch him up. His pace—*determined*." She gave Aaron a questioning look. "When I did manage to find him, there was a decision for me to make. Whether to turn back or press ahead."

"As we're over halfway there, you chose the better path." Aaron grinned. "Not that I, for one—mind the company."

Anna came up, taking Noah by the upper arms, looking straight into his dark eyes. "A warrior walks the path of the tribe *first*. Of his own—*second*." She leaned forward, touching her forehead to his. "You have disobeyed your father. You must make amends for your sin." She stood up, raising her voice. "Our brother, Noah, will walk the end of the column. Shun him as you pass, while he makes his apologies."

Noah looked up, his eyes filling with tears of shame. "Will you stay with me—until I have finish atoning?" Anna nodded, taking his hand. "I will stand with you, Noah, son to my husband and myself." Then she faced the people as they passed, listening as the young boy gave each person a heartfelt and lip-trembling apology.

🌿🌿🌿

The fields, dotted with winter-killed crops in pale yellow and sun-faded green leaves, tugged at the hearts of the people who'd planted them one year earlier. They lowered their eyes as they passed, their voices grown still, the squeaking wheels of the wagons mixing with the clop of horse hooves, mirroring their dour mood.

Aaron, out in front, bow slung over his shoulder, pistol near to his hand, searched the line of houses ahead, looking for smoke from the chimneys, or any movement between them, feeling uneasy as he left the road and angled toward the concealment of the trees.

Once there, he turned and checked on Eliza, seeing her walking beside Noah, listening as he regaled her with a hand-woven tale, bringing a smile to her face. A'neewa, as he still thought of the woman who he felt he'd known before, based on the words written in his father's journals and images placed there by his talented hand, rode in the first wagon, her hip beginning to trouble her during the final day of their approach.

With a heavy sigh, he swept around the small community of homes, heading toward the church, its spire reaching above the backs of the dwellings, like a finger pointing to heaven. A frown crossed his lips, knowing he had not yet closed the gap between the faith expressed in Eliza's heart and mind, and that of his own. Bound by his experience to a more grounded view of the clay used to form men to their earthly roles.

Most men, he added, having watched the light in Lukas's eyes when he spoke to his people. The same energy found when reading the words of the speeches his father had written, trying to create a national effort to accomplish some of what Eliza's father had dedicated himself to doing. Bringing disparate worlds together, forming bonds, helping to strengthen them all.

Aaron shook his head, refocusing on his task at hand, gazing at the ground for sign of game as he moved ahead.

⸙⸙⸙

The nominal leader of the group stood up, looking at Anna for her nod of approval before relaying to those gathered in the church the words Lukas had told him to say. The man, a tall native with close cropped hair, wearing pants and a shirt, held his hat in his hand as he stood in front of the dais, unwilling to stand above the others. When he spoke, his voice was low in tone, but firm, giving out directives for each family to follow. Time was of the essence in gathering up what foodstuffs they could, leaving their other possessions behind, hastening their return to the Lower Sandusky.

As the congregation began to disperse, the speaker came over and took Anna's hand, then let go, following the others as they headed for their former homes. Eliza waited until her mother looked at her, then cleared her throat. "I have a question, having to do with—" She paused, a flush coloring the light complexion of her cheeks. "To do with the joining of a man to a woman. If one ceremony is more relevant in the eyes of—of whichever entity, or higher spirit is—"

"You wish to be bound. To Aaron. Here." Anna hesitated, looking at her daughter. "Today."

Eliza nodded, her hands pressed against her chest, fingers interlocked, as if at prayer. "I do. I mean—if there is a way to do it, with *God's* approval."

"And what of your father's approval—back *there*, at Captive's Town. Would you deny *him* the right to agree to it, before making such a rash decision?" Anna knew the fledgling had left the nest, never to return, no matter the council she might give her daughter. The young woman's mind already made up. As her own had been, countless winters ago.

"I would be married *today*. A simple ceremony, done out of doors. An ancient Scottish tradition. Not recognized by our church, though I would *redo* the vows before God, making them in front of my father, once we return." Eliza looked down. "If he will find it in his heart to do so."

Anna reached out, pulling the young girl into an embrace, shaking her head as she stared through a pane of glass, watching people making their way between their former homes and the wagons, carrying bags of grain, flour, salt, and other necessities, as if babes in their arms. She could scent her daughter's need, having felt it herself. The desire for completeness. A man holding her in his arms, loving her. Taking from her the gift of her innocence. Releasing her to the full flower of what becoming a woman means. To bring new life into the world, trusting in one's faith that the community would welcome it with open arms, treating it fairly, nurturing it with their blessing.

"Your father *will* be angry. And hurt. He will suffer a day or so in silence, avoiding you. Rehearsing speeches to try and turn back the hours, the days, the weeks, to when you were a child in his arms. To when he was your *entire* world. As he remembers it to have been."

Eliza looked up. "He will not forgive me?"

"Of *course*, child. In time. Wanting to see it done in front of his eyes. To witness it himself."

"Will you help me—to tie the cloth around our wrists? To help gather the people to hear our vows?"

"I will do all that and *more*. I will utter a prayer for you both, in my own language, whispering it into your ears alone. One from the Great Mother to all her daughters, standing on the path, ready to share it with another."

"You know about handfasting?" Eliza could tell Anna didn't recognize the term. "It's when you tie your hands together and promise the one you are to wed that you will honor them. And, in doing so, make your promise to honor the rest of the clan—or tribe. Honoring those who've come before, and those who will soon follow." She softened her voice. "Aaron says it is an *old* ritual, from long ago."

Anna kissed her daughter on her cheek, then pulled away, still holding her hands. "Then we shall do our best to *connect* it to the one we follow *now*."

※※※

The ceremony, fully attended by the others, was presided over by Anna, with a few of the older women looked down, frowns on their faces, uncertain if the impromptu marriage met the Moravian definition as taught them by Lukas.

Once they were alone, Aaron took a moment to hold his wife, as if for the first time, feeling her body trembling beneath the press of his arms around her waist. "We can wait. The ceremony—set aside, as too the wedding bed. If you're not ready to—"

Eliza's lips met his, cutting off any further remarks, using the toe of her foot to close the bedroom door. Her parent's room, their house lying untouched over the winter months, other than a scattering of nesting materials from a family of mice, living beneath the floorboards.

"I am ready to be with you. As your wife."

Aaron was the one to tremble now, his hands on her hips, feeling the swelling of her body, his breath shortening as he kissed her, feeling her hands on his belt. Losing himself to the love he could feel overwhelming his senses. The scent of her hair, the sweet flavor of her tongue on his, permeating his soul, driving him further into her willing body as she opened to him, completely, a moment of gasp, wince, then release as she joined him, move for move, their moans echoing one another's until they reached the edge of the abyss, falling over, clinging to one another, promising to never let go.

※※※

Aaron and Noah were deep in the woods, tracking two large deer moving through a swale of brush, using the thick growth to shelter themselves. Aaron knew they would be fat, having helped themselves to the crops abandoned in the fields, filling their bellies each day before moving into their beds.

It had been two days since his and Eliza's unofficial union, witnessed by the one hundred men, women, and children who'd made the pilgrimage with them. Two nights spent plumbing the depths of their physical relationship, with hours of dreamless sleep each night before waking to the miracle of discovering each other lying in the same bed, as if they'd been together their entire lives.

Noah tugged on Aaron's arm, pointing to a horizontal line in the brush. Aaron saw the back of a large buck, antlerless, having lost them during the last few weeks of winter. It was looking away, its long ears twitching as it raised its nose, testing the air. A shaft from Aaron's bow sighed its way across the twenty paces between them, striking the animal behind the shoulder, low enough to cut through both lungs and heart, the gray-tawny hide swallowing the arrow as the animal leapt up, stepping ahead.

The other deer, another large buck, stood up, turning to one side as it leaped away. Then it stopped, uncertain where to go, a second arrow slicing through its chest, higher up. The mortally wounded animal bounded off, its white tail raised in alarm as it disappeared into the woods.

"You were so quick!" Noah stood wide-eyed, staring as the first antlerless deer collapsed to its front knees, then rolled onto its side, blood running from its nose as it kicked its legs, dying by the time the two of them made their way over. Aaron handed Noah an arrow, indicating he should gently touch it to one eye, open, left staring into the approach of a new day.

Once the test for life was over, Aaron recovered the arrow, slipping it back into the quiver tied around his waist. Then he rolled the heavy animal onto its stomach, checking to see if his first arrow had passed all the way through. He found it lying on the ground a few paces away, still intact, the feathers coated in gore.

He handed it to Noah, letting him know to clean it with a rub through the deer's coat, careful not to damage the fletching. Then he pulled out his knife and began dressing out the fat animal, allowing the other deer to find a quiet place to lie down, knowing there would be a blood trail leading to it once they'd finished here.

"You're to return to the settlement, then come back with enough men to gather this one up, using a game pole like we did with the bear. I'll leave a clear trail to the other one, so make sure and bring enough men to handle *both*."

Noah frowned. "I should go with you. To help find it." He gave Aaron a quiet look. "I can help to dress it out, too. I won't get sick again. I promise."

Aaron nodded, giving the offer deliberate consideration. "Alright. You can come along. It'll give ya a chance to try out your tracking skills." They started the process of dressing out the deer, Aaron holding the legs apart, directing Noah where and how deep to cut.

※※※

Anna was the first to notice the approach of men in column, having just entered the woods to look for mushrooms. Their voices stirred waves of birds and a flow of small animals into movement, causing a disturbance in the local environment. She stepped behind a large tree, one hand on its rough bark, watching as a doubled line of soldiers passed by, representing the colonial side of the conflict between the military forces vying for control of the Ohio basin.

A pulse of fear swept through her abdomen, her hand reflexively reaching for the knife strapped to her thigh, coming up empty, having left it buried back at Captive Town. She clutched at the sack in her hands, wondering if there was time to get back to the others, warning them of what her instincts were shouting in her ear. Death was on the march, the scent of blood hovering in the air above the men with serious looks on their faces, their weapons clenched in their hands.

She slipped away, leaving enough distance between herself and the road to stay hidden from view.

※※※

The nominal leader of the converted natives glanced up, using the arm of his shirt to clear the sweat from his eyes. He was satisfied with the progress made, with enough crops collected from the soil to justify the trip there and back. Other goods, stored in sealed casks or gunny sacks gathered from the abandoned homes, were already on the two wagons brought with them, with the baskets of produce stacked on top or placed in sacks, tied alongside.

The sturdiest men among them would carry any game animals taken by Aaron, along with others found along the way. The meat added to the mix, helping ensure the survival of their community until the new crops were ready for harvest in fields set aside for their use by the English.

Movement in the line of trees bordering the large field pulled his head around, his dark eyes staring at a line of men stepping out, muskets leveled, making a steady approach.

The colonel in charge stepped forward, flanked by two dozen men with weapons at the ready. He smiled, nodding at one of the women, a young mother with a child tugging at her hand, fair of face and frame, her eyes shielded with caution, ears shuttered against the pleading cries of her daughter.

"We are here to secure our settlements from threat. To gather you together, to determine whether you've been involved in recent raids made by others. Indians. Some of them members of your former tribe."

The leader of the Moravian converts stepped forward, initiating a series of clicks as several of the soldiers brought the hammers of their muskets to full cock. The colonel waved a hand, beckoning the native ahead. "You are the leader here?" Getting a nod in reply, he smiled. "Please—make your case, *again*, for your innocence in these attacks. Protesting your treatment. Claiming to be God-loving members of a religion *none* of us had heard of, until it showed up one day, as if from out of the air."

"You are *too* late." The native man paused. "The English general has already named us *his* enemy. Forcing us from our lands." He looked to both sides, lifting his arms, causing another stir in the soldiers standing nearby. "From *these* lands. Cleared, planted, and now harvested, to provide food for our people, left starving in the Sandusky. Our minister sending us to collect what we can."

"A reasonable enough story, indeed. And *compelling*—if true." The colonel hardened his voice. "Yet we have just come from a scene of debauchery—" He stopped, swallowing as he recalled the butchery of a dozen families near the Pennsylvania colony border with the Ohio wilderness. "Of *great* depravity. The perpetrators *savages*—with painted faces."

The Moravian leader shook his head, feeling his heart in his throat, recognizing the scent of anger rising from the mass of well over one-hundred men. "We have no paint on *our* faces, having converted, now praying to the *same* God as do you and the English, both. We are farmers, and do not carry weapons of war. Only those used for the taking of game. For hunting."

"Paint washes off. As does blood. You are, by your own admission, *armed*. Your people are known to have committed such raids in the past. A difficult habit to break." The colonel raised an arm, waving his hand in a circle. His men moved forward, surrounding the group of gatherers, moving them toward a spire, poking above the near edge of woods

※※※

Noah was nearing the community, eager to gather the men and let them know Aaron had made two kills. He was excited to lead them back to the first one, then take four more to the second. Aaron had cut the tracks of a wild pig, telling him he would hunt the animal down, kill it, then start dragging it back, hoping to meet up with them at the second kill.

The sound of men yelling in anger caused him to stop, the voices shrill, angry in tone. Noah lowered himself to the ground, sliding ahead until he could see into the village where a large group of men in colonial militia clothing had surrounded the people of the community, standing in the middle of a large field where they'd been gathering the remnants of crops.

The soldiers, recognized by Noah as such, were shouting and

waving their weapons, herding the natives toward the church. Other men were going in and out of the homes, gathering women and children, leading them there. Several dozen men had gathered off to one side, pointing at the others, shaking their heads, refusing to join in. They stayed behind, the men guarding the natives laughing as they headed toward the church.

Noah crept away, torn between going to find Aaron or trying to reach anyone who might still be working in the woods or outermost fields. He chose the latter, hoping to find out what the men he assumed to be soldiers were doing there, before running to find Aaron, letting him know.

※※※

The woods were thick. Sounds swallowed up by leaf-heavy limbs, preventing light from reaching the ground. Aaron knelt, touching a small splotch of blood, lying on a mat of litter from years of fallen debris, showing up dark red against the lighter shade of a pale, mottled leaf.

He stared beneath the lowest layer of the leaf-heavy limbs, able to see for a dozen yards in any direction. There was no sign of the supine body of a wild boar, struck with an arrow after he and Noah had finished tending to the second kill. Its meat, bones, and fat would be a valuable commodity to the group of people under constant threat of starvation.

Aaron shook his head, aware there were worse things known to happen to natives found in the region, accused by British and colonial forces of working as spies for the other. The members of the settlement, careful to maintain a neutral stance, had found themselves trapped between both sides during the protracted war. Colonist officers, seeking fame and fortune in attacks made against the British in the Ohio region, were as eager to earn bounties paid for scalps wrenched from the skulls of any native people encountered, whether kept cropped close to their skulls or not. Men, women, or children, coins in hand when delivered to the proper authorities, with few if any questions asked as to tribal affiliation, sex, or age of the victims.

Rising to his feet, Aaron moved downhill, knowing the wounded boar would be looking for a place to rest, his arrow brushed to one side by a low-hanging branch, striking the tusked beast behind its lungs, leading him on a protracted chase. He checked the angle of the sun, the day more than half over, then sighed, aware it would be a cold camp under a clearing nighttime sky, tomorrow midday at the earliest before he would make it back to the site of the second kill, dragging the carcass behind him.

As he found and followed another drop of dark blood, Aaron was both relieved and slightly concerned with Noah not having caught him up after bringing the pole bearers to the site of the second dressed out animal. The trail he'd left for him to follow clearly marked. Of no real consequence to him either way, other than to make the task of bringing a healthy haul of meat back to the community larder a bit of a slog.

***

The smell of smoke, acrid and sharp-edged, caught Aaron's attention. He stopped, taking several deep breaths, sweat falling into his eyes, his back aching as he stared into the sky. The large boar was a heavy load, tied by its crossed feet to a makeshift travois, leaving drag marks in the ground. Now that he'd reached the top of the small rise, he dropped the end of the crossed poles, strapped around his shoulders with pine tree roots pulled from the ground, his coat used as a pad against the back of his neck.

The body of the second dressed-out deer was still lying on the ground, untouched, bringing a worried expression to Aaron's face, trying to understand why the others hadn't already retrieved the animal. Untying his dark leather coat, he slung it over his shoulder, then strung his bow and started toward the source of the smoke, the day more than half over, his heart in his throat.

***

Noah watched as the soldiers herded his people into the church, the doors closed behind them, with a guard set on all four corners. The remainder of the soldiers formed a circle in a large opening, their leader in the center. The words were hard to make out, an argument breaking out between some of the men in the group.

The young boy slipped back into the shadows, running to another location, hoping to get close enough to hear what the men were saying. As he passed under a low-branched tree a hand found his mouth, cupping it from behind, pulling him to the ground.

Anna spun Noah around, giving him a sharp look, then removed her hand. "You are a *fool*, trying to get closer." She hesitated. "Where is Aaron?"

"He sent me to get men to haul back two large deer. And a large boar he will have in hand by now." Noah pointed into the woods. "That way, a half a day walk from here and back again." He looked over toward the spire of the church, poking above a line of small trees. "Why are they here? The soldiers?"

"To bring misery into our lives." Anna reached out and took his hand. "You will need to find Aaron. Let him know what you have seen. Tell him there is *nothing* he can do. That he can save only one—" She paused. "Perhaps *one* more, including you."

Noah opened his mouth to ask why, stopping as he saw the look in his adopted mother's eyes. He swallowed, then gave her a short nod, darting away as if an arrow shot from a bow, disappearing into the shadows between the trees.

🌲🌲🌲

"Soldiers." Aaron fingered the bow, his hands aching to string it, knowing he would need to wait until closer before using it, if called for, leaving the limbs at full strength. "When?"

"Yesterday. After midday." Noah started to tear up. "I lost the trail, trying to find my way here. It was too dark—so I had to wait until this morning."

Aaron ignored his tears. "How many"

Noah shrugged, wiping his small nose with the back of a dirt-stained hand. "Many." He held up both his hands and concentrated, trying to match his fingers to the line of men, closing and opening them twelve times before Aaron reached out and stopped him, a dark look in his eyes, a soft curse on his lips.

"*Too* many." Aaron took in a deep breath, then slowly let it out. "A'neewa—Anna, she told you I should not make my approach openly?"

"My mother said to not do *anything*—other than to save my sister." Noah lowered his head. "That's what I *think* she was saying."

Aaron nodded, then lifted the boy's head, a finger under his chin. "I will need you to be a warrior, not a man of peace. To be prepared to kill if need be. To take a life." He leaned forward. "Do you understand? To do what we can to save as *many* as we can."

Noah trembled, overwhelming by fear, not of facing death, but of losing his place in heaven, should God not forgive him of any sins committed to try and free his people. "Yes."

Aaron stood up, leaving the boar behind with the other deer, starting toward the community at a steady pace, hoping the boy would be able to keep up.

※※※

Two dozen soldiers moved away from the others, taking up a position inside a large barn. They were angry, disgusted by the attitudes of the other one hundred and thirty men who were determined to find the native group guilty of crimes they couldn't have committed.

The colonel had encouraged his men's false accusations, dangling the lure of coins in hand for each scalp procured that matched that of a native's, in texture, color of hair, or skin. He'd stood with a smile on his face, watching as a young officer, his cheeks red with anger, led his group of faint-hearted men away in a stiff-legged gait, heading toward a barn.

Once inside, the officer rounded on the others. "In a *church*, no less. Under the very eye of God. *Blasphemy!*" He circled the center of the group of men, sword in one hand, as if ready to lash out in anger. "This is *not* the battle *I* signed up to fight. One made against helpless men, women, and *children!*"

"What are we to *do?*" A soldier of the same age shook his head. "We can't *stop* them; only hope they'll falter at the moment of murdering them."

Another man spit, then wiped the tobacco juice from his lips with the back of a gnarled hand. "It's the ones with hard eyes will do the deed. The others made to witness it, binding them all to lies told to others. Too late to stop it once it begins. The first death delivered will lead to the next. Ending with the young'uns. The last to die."

"You believe they will kill the *children?*" The officer stood framed in the doorway of the barn, sword tip touching the dirt, mouth hanging open. "And the young *white* woman, as well?"

The grizzled man gave him a hard look. "She'll die along with the others, though not an easy death. Herself used, a dozen times or more, then tossed hairless in a pile, along with the rest of 'em."

The officer stared, then spun around, sheathing his sword as he strode away.

※ ※ ※

"She is, of course, free to choose her *own* path." The colonel considered the young officer, aware of who his father was, a man of some prominence back in Philadelphia. "You may do with her as you will. She is not *my* concern, only these." He swept a hand, taking in the people sitting in the pews, heads bowed, having been singing psalms throughout the night, aware they would soon die. Committed to vows sworn to God, unwilling to fight back.

The young officer went over to the first pew and knelt, reaching for the hand of the woman, sitting with her hands clasped in her lap, head bowed, her lips moving with no sound coming out of a throat parched with thirst.

"You're to come with me. The other men and I will protect you, seeing that you're returned to your family."

Eliza swallowed, coughed, then looked at him, her eyes a faded blue in the dim light of the church. "These people *are* my family. Every *one* of them."

He sighed, knowing he would remove her by force, if necessary, to save her life. "I understand your position. It is commendable, your dedication to your beliefs. I too wish to save them, as do the men willing to stand alongside me, having voiced our objection to what the others propose." He hesitated, hiding the lie behind a warm smile. "The rest of them, the soldiers standing guard—are not *all* behind this. Many more will come to my side of the line, losing their initial anger at what they saw done—" He nodded to one side. "Back where we came from. Over a dozen killed. Including women and children, their—their hair taken."

"As are *we*. Innocent of the charges levied. And—if there is no intention of following through with the drunken threats made to us during—" Eliza stopped, closing then opening her eyes. "The horrible promises made us during the night—then I am content to stay here, and trust that what you say may come to pass." Eliza paused, looking up at a small cross mounted on the wall. "It will be as God wills."

"Of course. And well said." The officer stood up, bowed, then turned to go. A few minutes later he returned with the grizzled veteran and two soldiers from the barn, overseeing the effort to pick the young woman up. They carried her away from the staring congregation, her screams of outrage and misery filling the church, until her eyes folded back in her head and her body went limp.

After the men departed, the colonel came over. "You have your *pretty* lady. Now do what you will with her, while we finish things here."

The officer nodded, saluted, then spun on his heel, walking away in a measured pace.

⚘⚘⚘

Aaron kept Noah close to his side, wanting to send him to hide in the woods, but not daring to let him out of his sight. The boy gasped, then tried to stand up when a handful of soldiers carried the limp form of his sister from the church, taking her into the barn, the doors left open, revealing a circle of men with sullen faces. As he held Noah down, Aaron squeezed his bow, his knuckles white, relaxing slightly when he heard Eliza's voice, demanding to be set down. The men carrying her hesitated, looking at a man dressed in officers' garb, then complied, keeping hold of her arms, preventing her from running away.

Aaron began to plan how he might save her; aware the day would end in the death of the others. The image of what lay in store for his hand-fasted wife caused him to shudder, his vision going red as rage began to build within him.

Noah, pressed alongside Aaron, looked over at the man who'd always guided him with patience and an even hand. His stomach lurched, seeing the look in his mentor's eyes. Then he clenched the knife Aaron had given him, feeding off his mentor's energy, knowing he'd do whatever what asked of him, when the moment came.

☙❦☙

Anna wore a simple shift, her hair in a single braid. She moved around the corner of the barn, carrying a large metal pot and several wooden bowls. She kicked the bottom of the doors, waiting by the opening until the men inside noticed her. They stood up, confused at her sudden appearance, the officer coming over, looking around for any soldiers in escort, seeing none.

"I bring food. The man in the church, he told me to." She held out the pot, two thick towels shielding her hands from the heat radiating from its metal sides.

The officer nodded, then stepped aside, pointing to an overturned round of wood, used as a seat. Anna placed the pot down, seeing Eliza in one corner of a stable, head down, hands trembling.

"The girl is *not* to eat. The food not for one who is—" Anna struggled with the words, aware of what was happening in the church. She'd been watching from the window of a small house as groups of men led two parishioners at a time into a large building, used as a storehouse. They alternated between bringing men, then women, coming out again after a few minutes, then going back into the church, returning with another set. "Not for one who will soon be with God."

The officer widened his eyes, realizing the colonel had misled him. "She is not—we will *not* allow her to be—"

Anna had already spun around and left, turning the corner of the barn, gone from view by the time the officer followed her out. He shook his head, able to believe it had been a vision, if not for the sound of his men hungrily doling out large helpings of the stew, thick with mushrooms, sharing the bowls between them.

※※※

Aaron, seeing Anna enter the barn, then exit, watched as she went to ground beneath the end of the barn where it overhung a slight decline, pulling an earth-stained sheet over her. He checked the open door of the barn, watching as the young officer came out, hesitated, then returned inside.

Aaron told Noah to climb into the lower limbs of the tree, staying there to signal him if any of the soldiers in the church headed toward the barn. He crouched, staying low, using a line of young spruce trees to close the distance to where Anna was hiding, glancing back toward the oak tree, then scanning the grounds, keeping an eye on a hundred soldiers, or more lining the path between the church and a large house, fixated on whatever was transpiring inside. As he neared Anna's hiding place, he could hear the faint sound of prayers, hanging in the air.

A hiss drew his attention, a hand waving at him from beneath the barn, coming from behind a pile of desiccated manure, left untouched for a half-year or more. He went to the ground, his leather clothing matching a layer of oak leaves covering the thick grass.

"The men in the barn will become sick. Near to death. Soon. Then you can take Eliza away, along with my son." Anna gave Aaron a dark look. "I will stay here—with my people."

Aaron shook his head. "You *cannot* save them. These men—" He swallowed. "I was like them, once. May still be like them now. They are here to slake their thirst for vengeance. And to collect scalps."

"I *know*. And do not intend to *save* my people. God has already *done* that. I am going *with* them, doing what I can to ease their journey." Anna slid out from under the stained cloth. "I knew you were watching. Knew my son had found you. Knew you would want to save your wife—my *daughter*." She smiled, a sad look in her eyes. "And now you have an opportunity to begin *again*. While I have an obligation to my *people*, having brought them to a new way of life, hoping to ensure their safety. Failing, but having led them to their eternal salvation—and my *own*."

Aaron shook his head. "Do you believe it possible? That God *exists*—with what he's allowing to happen *here?*"

Anna smiled, one of bright joy, her eyes gleaming with tears. "Can you not *hear* them? Women and men—praying for the souls of those about to kill them. Praying for *their* own souls, as well."

Aaron closed his eyes, listening to the murmuring of voices inside the building, punctuated with a dull thud. And then another. The voices stilled, the sound of men stumbling through the door, falling to the ground, retching, moaning in sickness at what they'd witnessed, eyes wide in horrified stares.

"I hear *Satan*, and am more inclined to believe in *him*, than God."

Anna rolled to her knees, reaching out, touching his head. "Go, son of Harold, and save my *children*, that they might live and carry on the work of their father. Of our Lord." Then she stood up and walked away, heading toward the large house, parting the crowd of men standing outside, singing her death song in her native tongue, calling out to the Great Mother. Then switching to French, praying to God.

The End of Book Three

ABOUT THE AUTHOR

M. Daniel Smith is a writer of fiction, with interest in producing series covering various genres, including historical and speculative fiction.

His writing encompasses relationships between diverse groups of characters, real to life and gritty at times, helping connect the reader emotionally to people difficult to let go of.

Raised in a blue-collar environment, he spent hours in his mother's extensive library, reading the latest novels, exposed to every genre of literary works, from family sagas on through to sci-fi, military histories, and the like.

Retired, and able to write full time, Daniel fills his days putting down the words sent him by the characters who show up, compelling the telling of their stories, allowing readers an intimate look into their motives, desires, joys—and moments of pain. His own thoughts, beliefs, and experiences, garnered from a life lived full, liberally sprinkled throughout his writing.

You can reach Daniel at mdanielsmith@aol.com, or at PO Box 49, Phippsburg, ME 04562. His website is: www.bayledgespress.com.